...May lay quiet under the touch of her hands, her lips, but not passive. To Magdalena it felt as if she was drinking up the tender caresses. Magdalena paused and raised her head so that she could see May's face. She had never before felt anyone so still under her touch and yet so alive. May's eyes were open but she seemed to gaze without seeing at the ceiling.

Magdalena said softly, "May," and May moved her head so as to look at her from under half-closed eyelids. Magdalena raised herself to kiss her on the lips, a long, slow kiss. Then she sank down beside May, her head on the pillow. May whispered into her ear, "Just be still right here close to me. I must feel you. I must take you into myself." Magdalena obeyed, aware, with wondering surprise, that the hot eagerness that had driven her to take May out of her clothes and bring her into bed had faded into a delicious melting into the warmth of the desire she had awakened in May. She held May's body close to her own, feeling the touch of their skins along their thighs, their stomachs, their breasts, felt the beat of May's blood against her own.

MAGDALENA

MAGDALENA

Sarah Aldridge

The Naiad Press Inc.
1987

Printed in the United States of America
First Edition

Cover design by The Women's Graphic Center
Typesetting by Sandi Stancil

ISBN 0-930044-99-1

WORKS BY SARAH ALDRIDGE

To

TW

MAGDALENA

I

It was a small courtroom and at the end of the day it was rank with the smells of the humanity that had entered, paused and passed on out of it. The lawyers and the court attendants who were in it every day did not notice the heavy staleness but the judge was new to it and felt oppressed and sluggish.

The judge roused herself and looked over the edge of the high desk at the woman seated in the chair alongside. At least, she supposed from the officer's statement that it was a woman. What she saw was a bundle of filthy rags crowned by a head sunk forward, wearing a knitted cap. The fetid smell that came from her added its bit to the odors in the room.

The judge asked, "Do you agree with the officer's statement?"

At first she thought the woman had not heard but presently the head turned slowly upward so that the light at the corner of the desk caught in her eyes and made them glint. She said nothing.

The judge waited, still looking down at her. Languid from fatigue and bad air, she wondered, Is she really stout, or is it just all those layers of dirty clothes? No fixed address, the officer's statement had said. Homeless, of course, living in the street, those dreadful garments her only protection from the weather. Gave no name, so somebody had written Mary Brown on the record. No social security number—or at least she had not responded when questioned. Arrested on a vagrancy charge and brought in here to be held as a material witness to a fatal stabbing in one of those derelict buildings of an abandoned housing project. The magistrate's court was housed in the kind of neighborhood that was convenient to its clients—the judge smiled wryly to herself at the thought.

"Do you deny anything that is contained in that statement?"

The woman continued to stare up at her but gave no sign that she heard the patient voice.

"Do you understand what the officer has said?"

The woman continued to stare at her mutely.

The judge glanced at the policeman. "Is she deaf?"

The policeman shrugged. "I don't know."

The clerk of the court looked alertly at the judge, happy to show his greater experience before this newcomer. "She'll be processed when you dismiss her with instructions." It was more work, he thought, with these new magistrates but it broke the monotony and this one being a woman—

The judge asked, "She has not been evaluated?"

"Not yet. They'll clean her up and find out what they can about her—if you give the word."

The judge nodded and looked back at the woman. It was indecent to discuss another human being to her face as if she was just something to be processed. But familiarity took the edge off sensitivity, she supposed. But why doesn't she respond?

Aloud she asked, "Can you hear what I say? Do you have a statement you want to make to me?"

Very slowly the woman turned her head away and sat as she had before, utterly passive. The judge waited but there was no further movement. Finally the judge sighed and said to the clerk, "Hold her as a material witness until trial of the case. Provide her with legal counsel." She looked again at the woman. "You'll have a social worker assigned to you."

The woman did not move. The policeman, suddenly brisk, took a step towards her. She shrank back into the chair and then obediently got up and shuffled after him out of the courtroom.

* * * * *

The judge sat at her desk, looking at a file she held in front of her. The morning sunlight, streaming in through the tall, uncurtained windows of the office, showed the dust and grime of years of neglect. In the abstract it had seemed to her a good opportunity to renew her contact with the mass of people daily touched by the law in ways more urgent, more personal, than those that affected the petitioners who visited the hushed chambers where she usually sat to consider the rights and wrongs in dealings between individuals representing money and power. A term in a lower court, especially a criminal court, to replace a fellow magistrate on leave—a chance to get out into the world of mortal combat between the city and its guardians and those who defied that authority or fell afoul of it. Her friend had said that it would jolt her out of the routine of court cases in which the excitement lay only in the cleverness some litigants showed in the manipulation of their own and their opponents' wealth.

"You'll know what is meant by the term 'the arena of the law,' " he had said, meaning more than a joke.

There was a quick knock on the door, which opened at once, and a young black woman came in and sat down in the chair opposite, with barely a nod of her head in greeting.

The judge, looking up, said, "Camilla, what can you tell me about Mary Brown?"

The young black woman said, with unconcealed impatience, "There're a thousand of them like her, out there in the street. They're a big nuisance to everybody."

"Well, I don't suppose they choose to be there, wandering the streets all day with nowhere to go," the judge objected.

"I'm not so sure about that."

"Do you mean that you actually believe anybody would choose to be out there in the street, in the dirt, the cold, the wet, without proper food, sick?"

There was a trace of malicious pleasure in the social worker's smile. "You wouldn't, of course, nor me. But when you see as much of them as I do, you get to wondering about some of these people—especially now that they've turned all the loonies out of the mental institutions for us to look after."

They eyed each other across the desk. The judge was aware that she was the focus of curiosity among the people attached to the court. She knew she was a rarity in that setting. In the first place, she was a woman. There were not many women in the magistrates' courts at this level. Secondly, she came from a very different background and though she might accept the differences, she knew the others did not. Now this young black woman in front of her. Paula, the other social worker assigned to her cases, also black but her own age of forty and married to a police captain, had spoken to her about Camilla. She would have a little trouble with Camilla, said Paula. She was a loner, worked all the time, worked herself to death sometimes for all these trashy no-goods. Oh, yes, you had to go on the assumption that the flotsam and jetsam of the big city was worth saving, had to be saved, but experience told you not much could be done for most of them. Camilla knew that, too, but she kept on butting her head against a wall. It was the way she was made, said Paula.

The judge said, "I don't think we need take that personally." She had noticed Camilla's impatience and the smile. There was something called professional burn-out in all jobs. Camilla would be pretty if she took that scowl off her face. Her dark brown skin was flawlessly smooth, her eyes were large and bright, her hair, cut short, a glossy, well-cared-for black. There was something still fresh and youthful in Camilla.

Camilla's impatience broke the surface. "They try to make out it's a great humanitarian gesture—to turn all those poor things out to fend for themselves in the jungle. It's just because they don't want to spend the money to look after them."

The judge studied her for a moment. Camilla stared back at her, annoyed and yet attracted by the palely blonde woman across the desk.

The judge read contempt, defiance, and yet a reserve of another emotion not sufficiently clear to be called compassion in Camilla's glance. "You know, Camilla, in modern times we've gone to the opposite extreme from what was done in the past to the mentally unbalanced. They used to be burned as demons or penned up like dangerous animals—but only the most dangerous and unruly. The rest wandered free—tolerated or driven away, regarded as a manifestation of God's will. We've tended to put anyone under restraint who seems to us out-of-line with conventional behavior. Freedom—control over one's own body—is a precious right. Think what that must mean to some of these poor souls."

Camilla, interested in spite of herself, scoffed. "They're helpless out there. They don't know how to look after themselves. Oh, a lot of these old women are hard to look after. They're obstreperous. They seem to want to get back out there in the street in spite of all you can do for them. They're disoriented. They don't know how to live in a civilized way any more. But you wouldn't set a bunch of children loose to take care of themselves, would you? Most of these old women are scared. They know they can be raped, robbed, killed out there. When they get too scared they try to get arrested so that they get put in jail—have three meals a day and somewhere to sleep—until they can't take that any more and want out."

The judge listened with close attention. "Have you been able to find out anything about this old woman—Mary Brown? Has she been in a mental institution?"

Camilla shook her head. "I don't know anything about her. She hasn't any identification papers—most of them don't. Now and then she'll answer a question. Says she isn't on social security—seems to know what that is. Just shakes her head when you ask her what her name is or if she has any friends."

"Do you think she has lost her memory—doesn't really know who she is?"

"Could be."

"Does she understand your questions? Can she hear?"

Camilla's smile was mocking. "She can hear all right. And I've got an idea that she could give me some answers if she wanted to."

"Are you sure?"

"You want to question her yourself?"

"No, you know I can't do that. She is supposed to have

witnessed the stabbing of that drug pusher over in the housing project. Is she on drugs? Could she have been a customer of his?"

Camilla shrugged. "She's not a user. She's clean.'

"Could she be a pusher herself?"

"Who's to say? Maybe she's pushed a few to get enough to eat. That would have got her into trouble with the suppliers. They keep a finger on the pushers."

"You say she isn't on social security. How can that be? This is 1985, after all."

"Some aren't. Never worked or never claimed their benefits," said Camilla with indifference.

"She has been appointed legal counsel. He will have to get some sort of statement from her."

"She," said Camilla.

"Oh, well, she, then."

"She's just out of law school. No kind of experience. Probably never talked to somebody like this before." Camilla had lapsed into a morose contemplation of a predestined failure.

But even when she's sullen like this, she's attractive, thought the judge. Darker than average but what a satin skin, without a blemish. And her eyes give her away. She hasn't thrown in the towel on the System yet, no matter how scornful she is.

* * * * *

"Well, Ailsa, this is what you're after—looking for the raw material of life, you say. Otherwise, you could have taken your rotation leave and stayed in your own world." Dina put the casserole she was holding with two potholders down on the table. She was a slim woman with short-cut hair smoothed back to fit the fine shape of her head like a tight cap.

"Hm. Perhaps. I didn't envision it in just these terms."

A whimsical smile played around Dina's finely cut lips. "That's contradictory thinking. If you seek adventure in living, you necessarily invite the unexpected."

Ailsa disapproved. "I would not say I'm seeking adventure in living. I'm merely seeking—" She paused.

"What? Nothing so banal as the meaning of life?"

"A clue to the way to a just society."

"There we go. Always bringing moral intentions into the universe. Now *I* know that is a mere aberration. The universe—our universe—does not have a soul. It's laws are merely physical. But so intricate. Never a chance for boredom, if you see it in that light."

" 'The stars in their courses fought against Sisera,' " said Ailsa.

The steam rose from the dish as Dina removed the lid. Good-humoredly she said, "That is the trouble. Anthropomorphism. Attributing our human emotions to physical phenomena. What would the stars care about a warrior leading a battle in the desert?"

"The warrior thought they did care. And aren't we physical phenomena, darling?"

"Of course. You win that one. That is what I say—that we are only physical phenomena. But you say otherwise and so did the recorders of biblical history. You have a long tradition on your side, Ailsa, but I think my notion is more promising."

They were silent as Dina served the dish and they began to eat.

Ailsa said, "That's the easier way to do it. If you stay strictly within the boundaries of physical phenomena, you can ignore the problems of humanity. In fact, you can reduce humanity to a minute speck in the universe— ephemeral, helpless, ultimately worthless. But it is different when you come down to individuals. You can't be so glib about the worthlessness of another human being. Or at least I cannot."

Dina glanced up from her plate. "The old woman has made quite an impression on you, hasn't she? Have you learned anything more about her? She must have quite a personality for it to come through all that squalor and muteness you describe. Or are you in the grip of an idea again?"

Ailsa nodded. "The idea of freedom. What constitutes freedom, for the individual."

"Freedom?"

"Are we free to destroy ourselves by refusing the aid of society? If we want to live on the street, like a stray animal, in danger of death from the weather, disease, the traffic, murderous human beings? Or must we accept the restraints of society for our own good?"

"I don't think I'd like to live in a shelter for the homeless, from what I've heard of them."

"But what sort of freedom is it that places us in such circumstances? If you're on the street, you're the captive of the elements, the need to find food, the fear of bodily harm. You live in a little prison of your own."

"Then you are saying that freedom is a thing of the mind."

"But physical freedom is precious, too."

"Even if it is illusory. Suppose you wanted to take off for the wild blue yonder—kick over the traces—leave me and the State judiciary system high and dry—cast off the shackles of your career—"

Ailsa looked up to see Dina grinning. She laughed. "You always catch me that way. No, I don't want to do that. I am devoted to my shackles—in the order you name. In fact, they give meaning to life." She grew serious. "What sort of meaning does life have for that old woman?"

"Your bag lady?"

Ailsa nodded. "It's Camilla's idea, you know, that she may live that way from choice."

"Hm, Camilla. That girl has her problems."

"I know you think she brings her own frustrations into her job."

"Don't we all! But she's black. That adds another dimension."

"Most of the time I forget that she's black, when we are working on some case—like this one."

"But she keeps reminding you. She can't resist it. Even that time you brought her here and we're having a party and everybody is having fun, she manages to inject that fact, especially with me."

"Not with me."

"Oh, you don't notice it. You have a tolerant nature. You make life too easy for your friends—and your enemies, too, for that matter. So she sharpened her claws on me instead. I suppose if you have serious-minded, industrious parents who protect you and see you through college and then you get out into the world and you meet all kinds of discrimination not only because you are a woman but also black—well, I can see that it would give you a certain attitude—especially if you're young and think things ought to change. Camilla is pretty young, isn't she?"

"Still in her twenties, I should say. Do you think Camilla has given me too personal a view of this old woman?"

"No. I should say that her experience would count for more than yours in this case."

They lapsed into silence for the rest of the meal. Then Dina began to talk about her business day as a theatrical agent. In the evenings when they were together Dina usually rattled on about the ego-tripping, the personality clashes, the maneuvering among the people she dealt with during the day. Ailsa listened with half an ear as they gathered up their dinner dishes and took them to the kitchen. It was not too often that they could share an evening in this way. And it was such a nice place they could afford with their combined incomes. Luxurious, in fact. She looked around the big living room. It was one of the reasons they had chosen this apartment—the living room with the city spread beyond its windows and the ample bedroom with windows that looked across the roofs of lower buildings to a distant glimpse of the river and the bay beyond. That was freedom, too, freedom of the eye to roam further than the cluttered landscape below. And inside there was room for the books they valued, the music they shared, the gatherings of friends when they felt like entertaining or, what was more often the case, when Dina must throw the parties that her job required. She enjoyed all this, even Dina's parties, noisy though they often were. But occasionally she felt a twinge of guilt at being thus singled out among women. Once she had spoken of this to Dina and Dina had scoffed. It was just that super-seriousness of hers. They worked for what they enjoyed. They were not parasites on society. But, said Ailsa, virtue was not inevitably its own reward. There were other women who strove as hard as they did, without the rewards, other women who—Dina broke in, had not found each other as they had. And she had stopped Ailsa's objections by seizing her and kissing her till they were both breathless.

But the feeling of something unresolved went with Ailsa even into bed. In the warmth and darkness, lying close to Dina, this feeling persisted. Finally she acknowledged its origin: the old woman in court. Why was she on the street? She found she remembered with great clarity the long stare the woman had given her, a blank, unfathomable stare.

Dina, as if affected by the tension in her body, stirred and turned over to take her in her arms, mumbling endearments into her ear.

* * * * *

At least once a day, seated at her magistrate's desk, surveying the courtroom and the people who came and went in it, Ailsa thought of the old street woman. In the intervening week she had seen little of Camilla and never for long enough to talk to her about the case. She was aware that she was watched by the men attached to the court, by the clerk, by the sergeant-at-arms, by the lawyers, watched with a certain intentness, as if they were eager to see how she resolved the situations with which she was confronted throughout the court day. Sometimes they offered a little advice, never, she noticed, complete and never, she guessed, in openhearted friendship. The murder of the drug pusher, she was told, was a routine matter. The police had a pretty good idea who had done the stabbing. Usually, in such a case, even if they made an arrest on suspicion, they got no conviction, for want of firm evidence. In this particular case perhaps they had an exception to the rule. If the material witness would admit to seeing the stabbing and could identify the knife-wielder, they could get a conviction. Not that that would make much difference to the drug traffic on the street. It was a drop in the bucket. The detective in charge said that it was not likely they would get anything out of that old woman. Ailsa saw the contemptuous impatience on the face of the lawyer who was prosecuting the case when he confronted the young woman with no previous experience who had been unable to make her client talk. No, the doctor said the old woman was not deaf and he did not think that she was feebleminded. She was not a drug user. She was not alcoholic. She just would not talk. What did that mean? Well, she might be scared to death, scared of the possible consequences of talking, afraid of vengeance from the drug suppliers.

So what happens to her now? Ailsa asked. After a

while, said the detective, when the case would be closed on the books as unsolved, she would be turned loose.

"Where will she go? Back on the street?"

The detective looked at her in surprise. Why, he supposed so. That was beyond the scope of his responsibility. The police would no longer be concerned with her, unless she got into further trouble, was taken up for vagrancy, or perhaps was found dead in a corner somewhere. He obviously thought she was stupid. A little cooperation would make all the difference for her.

Ailsa, when he had left her office, turned in her chair to look out at the grimy street, littered with rubbish blown about by the wind. The only people in sight were of the sort such a neighborhood usually held—poorly dressed, huddling against the cold wind in inadequate clothes, wrapped up in their own affairs except for resentful, sullen glances they sometimes cast at those who passed them by. What would it be like, thought Ailsa, to be alone, unprotected, out in the endless, hostile streets. She tried to imagine the old woman—Mary Brown, according to the charge—sheltering among the rats in the condemned apartment building, watching the stabbing. The police said the dead man had evidently been living in one of the abandoned apartments, or perhaps hiding out there from his enemies. Or perhaps he had used the place as somewhere to meet the people who supplied him with drugs. No doubt he had tried to keep some of the proceeds for himself and the suppliers had found out. Or a customer had quarreled with him, frantically demanding a fix for which he could not pay. And Mary Brown, crouched in a corner to get out of the cold rain, had seen the encounter, had heard the quarrel, had seen the knife flash in a stray beam of light from the street. Why had she stayed there afterwards—stayed while the police squad car's revolving light picked out the body left on the steps, stayed until the police, searching the premises, found her hidden behind a heap of broken radiators and bathroom fixtures, the work of vandals? It had been bad weather—sleety rain, bone-chilling wind off the river. Perhaps the hopelessness of finding other shelter had held her there—perhaps even a jailhouse cell would look preferable under the circumstances.

How strange that in this modern world, with all its means of cataloguing, classifying, numbering people, there should be someone who had escaped it all—someone whose real name and identity was known only to herself. Where had she come from? What had brought her to the street?

* * * * *

A few days later she dismissed the case against the two men held on suspicion of the drug pusher's murder. The police said one of them confessed to the knifing, under promise of release under probation. Plea bargaining, the detective explained to her.

"He says he can put the finger on the big guys—the suppliers, if we let him off this one. He'll take his chance in the street. He's afraid of going to prison. He's an old offender and he's got enemies inside. So I guess we'd better let him go. We can always bring him in again."

Ailsa, studying the detective's impassive face, wondered at the matter-of-factness with which he accepted the hopelessness of the situation. "What happens to Mary Brown?"

The detective looked at her startled for a moment. "Oh, the material witness! We don't need her any more. We can turn her loose.

"And what happens to her? Where is she now?"

"You'll have to ask the social worker."

She sent for Camilla, who took two days to answer her summons.

"Yes, she's sprung," Camilla said, having knocked lightly on the office door and put her head around it before stepping into the room.

Ailsa, looking up from the papers on her desk, heard the words through the fog of details of a case of alleged rape. "She? Oh, Mary Brown."

"Isn't that what you wanted to know?" said Camilla, with the touch of aggressiveness with which she always confronted authority. She came into the room and sat down in the chair next to the desk.

"I know she's been released. What I want to know is what has happened to her. Where is she?"

"She's in Bellevue. She's sick. They finally admitted that. She's got pneumonia—from malnutrition and exposure, I guess. The doctors there say she is not on drugs and she doesn't seem to be a real alcoholic."

"What do you mean, a real alcoholic?"

"The officers say she smelt of liquor when they picked her up and there was an empty bottle there. Even if she wanted to drink she probably couldn't get hold of much. It's harder for a woman to get hold of alcohol on the street than a man. There's a prejudice about buying a woman beggar a drink."

Ailsa said ironically, "The usual ratio of disadvantage for a woman as in everything else."

Camilla looked at her blankly for a moment and then said, "I guess that's so. Anyway, she didn't get any liquor in jail and she didn't ask for it. I was surprised when I told her she was going to the hospital. I thought she'd fight it—she seemed such a diehard. Give me liberty or give me death. She was just as docile as could be."

"Then perhaps you were wrong about her living on the street as a matter of preference."

Hearing the hint of irony in Ailsa's voice, Camilla retorted, "No, she doesn't want to be on the street. She's scared of it." Camilla paused, as if turning something over in her mind. "I just don't figure her out. She doesn't act just like the other old women I've been dealing with. She's got to me somehow. I keep thinking about what will happen to her when she gets out of the hospital—if she recovers, that is."

In the silence that followed this statement Ailsa said, "Don't you get discouraged sometimes by all this?"

Camilla's belligerence returned. "What do you think? I wasn't brought up in this sort of environment any more than you were. But all this goes with my job. There's something wrong with this system."

Ailsa nodded. After another silence she said, "If you'll tell me where to find her, I think I'll go and see her."

There was a gleam in Camilla's eye. "I wondered if you'd want to do that—check her out yourself. I can give you the number of the ward and the room."

* * * * *

The big glass doors of the hospital swung open and shut on the flow of people. Inside the lobby there was restless but subdued movement. People sat on chairs arranged in ranks. A group was gathered together talking like people who were not usually drawn into each other's company. Behind the reception desk were two middle-aged women. One of them looked up at Ailsa and listened to her question.

"Mary Brown? She's a public charge? Then she's in the old wing. Take the elevator and ask the receptionist there."

Ailsa was aware that for a brief moment the woman speculated at her appearance but immediately turned to another inquiry. As she stood waiting for the elevator door to open, she watched the people in the wide corridor beyond—the white-coated figures that moved about, charts in hand, or pushing carts loaded with bottles and strangely shaped vessels, appearing to someone like herself stepping into their world to be beings of a different race, visible but unapproachable.

Mary Brown, she was told by one of these remote figures passing by as she stepped out of the elevator, a white-coated figure with a stethoscope dangling around its neck, was in the room at the end of the hall. When she looked in there she saw six beds. One was curtained off, two were empty and neatly made up, one was rumpled but vacant as if its inhabitant had gone elsewhere temporarily, and the inmate of the fifth sat on its edge hunched over in an attitude of boredom or despair.

In the sixth bed, over against the inner wall, a woman was lying on her back, her still body under the covers neatly in place, her hands resting outside them, her eyes closed. An intravenous feeding bottle hung on its pole beside her. Was this Mary Brown? Ailsa wondered. It was a gaunt face she was looking at, surrounded by straggling grey-white hair spread on the pillow. Was she asleep? She was clean now. The hands that lay on the coverlet were wrinkled, bony, the nails still ragged. Freed from the disguise of layers of filthy rags she looked to be like any old woman, ill and neglected. She could be any old woman, shabby, resigned, tired, that you would see seated on a park bench minding a grandchild, in a queue carrying a string bag of groceries, sitting in the subway train gazing blankly at the advertisements on the opposite wall.

Perhaps because she became aware of being scrutinized the woman in the bed opened her eyes and stared at Ailsa. There was no particular expression in them and the woman seemed indifferent at finding someone standing by her bed.

Ailsa said, "Hello. How are you feeling?"

The woman did not answer and after several minutes, Ailsa said, "I know you are glad to be out of that jail cell."

What did one say to someone like this? The impulse that had brought her to find the woman had not supplied her imagination with suitable topics of conversation. Yet she felt impelled to build some bridge between them. "Do you remember me? You were arraigned in my court."

The blankness in the woman's eyes slowly changed to awareness. "You are the judge." There was a rusty quality to her voice.

"Yes. I came to see you because I am concerned about you."

The woman half closed her eyes and her hands moved, her fingers plucking at the edge of the sheet. She did not reply.

Ailsa sat down in the chair close to the bed. "You understand, don't you, that the case is closed and that you are no longer under arrest? Did they tell you that you are discharged? You do understand that you are no longer in custody?"

The woman moved her head slightly, as if to shake off her questions. "That girl said I was on my own again. But they brought me here."

"That's because you are ill. You had nowhere else to go, had you?"

The woman did not answer. It was like stalking something in the wild, thought Ailsa, who had once tried photographing birds. Deciding to be bolder, she asked, "Is your name really Mary Brown?"

She was startled by the sudden flash in the woman's eyes. "They said my name was Mary Brown, so it's Mary Brown."

In this brief flash of clarity, in spite of its hoarseness, the woman's voice had a quality that surprised her—a full tone, with the echo of certainty, command, assurance. It was the shadow of the voice of a woman who had once known security, authority. Encouraged, Ailsa said, "Well,

Mary Brown, what are you going to do, when you've recovered and leave this hospital? I am ready to help you."

Mary's answer was mumbled, as if she retreated from the ground she had momentarily claimed. Ailsa heard only, "Where I'm going is my business."

"You don't have relatives? You haven't an income—not even social security, I'm told. Is that so?"

"Yes."

"Then what will you do?"

But Mary closed her eyes and did not answer. Ailsa sat for a while longer, gazing at the woman's face on the pillow—sleeping, now, perhaps, or in any case withdrawn from her immediate surroundings.

The nurse's voice startled her. She had not heard her rubber-soled approach. "Well, how are we now?"

The nurse moved past Ailsa to take Mary's pulse and thrust the thermometer into her mouth. In the few moments of enforced silence the nurse's eyes took in the details of Ailsa's appearance, the pale smooth short hair, her expensive suit of fine cloth, her obvious professional status. The nurse's manner said plainly, "What are you doing here, with this old bundle of decay?"

The nurse withdrew the thermometer, read it and began writing down the medical data. "Are you a relative?"

The studied disbelief in her voice was not lost on Ailsa. "No. I'm an acquaintance. I heard she was in the hospital."

"Well, I'm afraid she isn't supposed to have visitors right now. They should have told you at the desk. You'd better not stay. If you want to leave your name and phone number, someone can let you know how she's doing."

Recognizing the fact that the nurse suspected something official in her visit, Ailsa nodded and got up from her chair. With another long look at Mary's unconscious face, she went out of the room. She lingered outside in the corridor, waiting for the nurse to finish, idly examining the hospital cart standing near the door to the room, ranged with bottles of medicine labelled for each patient. When the nurse came out she stepped closer.

"I was told she has pneumonia. Is she ill with something else?"

The nurse looked at her again, weighing what answer she should give. "Her heart is affected. That's all I can tell you. She's getting heart medicine. Are you somebody from Welfare? She's homeless, you know, on the street. There isn't anybody who claims responsibility for her."

"No, I'm not from Welfare. But I have a reason for being concerned about her." Noticing that the nurse's distrust lingered, Ailsa added, "I'd like to help her. I'd like to see that she has care when she is discharged from here."

"Well, in the first place, that's likely to be a while, even if it is costing the hospital something to keep her here. We can't turn her out till she can walk out." In a sudden burst of anger she added, "These old women they bring in here off the street! It's worse than with the men. You can't help feeling they shouldn't be there. She'll go out of here when she can walk and then before you know it she'll be back. The next time they bring this one in she'll probably not make it through the night—that's when they usually bring them in, at night, or early in the morning, when the cops find them unconscious in the gutter."

"That's what I'd like to prevent," said Ailsa.

The nurse's hostility returned. "I don't know anything about that. I don't know what your motive is, unless you represent some charitable organization."

Ailsa almost said, "I've no motive except the impulse to help her," but instead she said, "Can you tell me whom I should get in touch with?"

"There's a social worker comes to see her. You'd better contact her. They'll give you information at the reception desk." The nurse turned resolutely away and began to push her cart down the corridor.

Camilla, thought Ailsa.

* * * * *

When she opened the door of the apartment she heard Dina finishing a telephone conversation.

"Oh, that's you, Ailsa?" Dina said, putting down the receiver and coming across the room to kiss her. "Aren't you late? I'm early. I've just been talking to Neil Clark, the film producer. It's this business about—"

Ailsa listened with half an ear to what she was saying, rattling on about the complications of a film production. The apartment was brightly lit by a variety of lamps set here and there around the big room. The darkness of the early winter evening beyond the windows sparkled with points of light and in the distance the brilliance of advertising signs. Here was shelter, warmth, comfort, taken for granted. What would it be like not to have this secure, welcoming haven, the blessing of Dina's presence?

Dina stopped talking in midsentence. "You're in a dream, Ailsa. What is it?"

"I was just wondering—" the mood she was in prompted her to speak without forethought—"what it would be like to have no home—no spot where you belong, where you can be comfortable and safe, with something to eat when you want it."

Dina looked at her. There was Ailsa again, wandering in some psychic forest. You'd think that law school, law practice, a few years on the bench, would have cured her of this dreaminess, these flights of imagination. "What's the matter now, darling?"

"I've just been to the hospital, to see Mary Brown."

"Mary Brown?"

"The old woman who was being held as a material witness in the stabbing of the drug pusher."

"Oh, your bag lady. Here, take off your coat and hat." Dina passed her hand through Ailsa's pale hair as she took away the coat and hat. "She's in the hospital, is she?"

"I told you I dismissed that case. She was discharged but she was ill so they took her to the hospital."

"Why did you go to see her?"

Ailsa hesitated. "She has the most extraordinary effect on me. I can't even decide what she is—whether she is what she looks like, a worn-out old washerwoman who hasn't any family left or somebody who has gone out of her mind and is wandering the streets. What worries me is what will happen to her when she leaves the hospital—if she does."

"Is she that ill? Or is it malnutrition and they can feed her up?"

"No, there's something wrong with her heart. The nurse said she will probably survive this bout but will probably be back in soon, perhaps already dead."

"I don't suppose they'd put her out on the street if she can't take care of herself. Or would they? I haven't much confidence in our system of social care. If you're unproductive, you're superfluous. If you're superfluous, you must be disposed of—flushed down the drain—"

"No!" Ailsa protested. "There must be some organization that will provide for her. I must talk to Camilla. She must know. It was Camilla who told me that she is in the hospital. She goes to see her."

"Then she's got a friend."

"Yes, but I can't leave this to Camilla."

Ailsa walked over to the long sofa that formed one side of a grouping in front of the window. Dina stood near her, lighting a cigarette.

Ailsa said, "She has made a strong impression on me

and on Camilla. Camilla has told me so. I can't say why. What's behind that outside appearance?"

Dina said, seeking to be comforting, "Perhaps nothing. Perhaps she is just what she seems—a wornout old woman, defeated by life. There are a lot of us like that, Ailsa, though we don't all take to the streets in despair. We cling to a few of the outward trappings of an ordinary life, though it's all dust and ashes in our mouths. And most of us, if we can hang on, will compromise with all our romantic dreams just to be sure of a clean bed to sleep in, some shelter from the weather, and three regular meals."

Ailsa turned her head to look at her. "You sound a little bitter tonight, darling. Something has gone wrong?"

"Nothing I can't set right tomorrow," said Dina, impatiently. "Well, I suppose all these old wrecks out on the street were somebody once, before their luck ran out. I'm glad, after all, that I'm in the theatrical business. It may be frustrating, it may be unreal, but you can keep some illusions. It's a terrible world you work in, Ailsa."

* * * * *

For some reason which she found difficult to explain even to Dina, Ailsa found herself caught between two feelings about keeping in touch with Mary Brown—an unquenchable desire to know more about her and a reluctance to satisfy it. Why, she thought, I am actually shy about going to see her! I felt that I may be intruding on her privacy. But what sort of privacy would a woman who lives on the street have? Was it—she thought about this carefully—the greatest privacy of all that she wanted to protect, the refusal to give access to oneself to any other person, for any reason, even if physical survival was at stake? In the past, in ancient times, such people were recluses, anchorites—or witches. What do you do with someone who defies the power and authority of a modern city and refuses to live by its laws and regulations? What did you do with the Mary Browns, who retreated so far into themselves as to be unapproachable?

Because of this reluctance, Ailsa visited the hospital only twice more. Mary Brown seemed to sleep most of her visit and she wondered whether this was Mary's way of closing the door on her intrusion. A week or so more passed. She was very busy in court. The break-up of the drug ring gave her plenty to do. Then in a momentary lull she thought of Mary Brown and on impulse went again to the hospital.

Peering into the room where Mary had been she found someone else in the bed where Mary had lain. She glanced around. All the beds were occupied this time, with women either sleeping or unconscious of their surroundings, with one exception. The woman by the window was sitting up. Two visitors, a man and a woman sat nervously by her. They looked at Ailsa as if glad of the interruption. She went back out into the corridor. It was empty. She walked down to the reception desk. Where, she asked, was Mary Brown?

The young woman behind the desk, one eye still on the papers she was studying, looked blank for a moment. Then she said, "Mary Brown? Oh, one of the Welfare cases. She was discharged yesterday. No, I don't have any idea where she went. Well, the aide took her downstairs in a wheelchair. She might know, but this isn't her shift. She is not here now."

"Do you mean that you would take someone as feeble as that downstairs to the front door and say goodbye to them?"

The young woman gave her a resentful glance. "She had no personal belongings. I assume someone must have been meeting her."

"But you don't know."

"I can't know what goes on off this floor," the young woman snapped, and then in a more conciliatory tone, under Ailsa's indignant gaze, added, "Since she was a Welfare case, I suppose the Welfare people might be able to help you."

Ailsa turned away. Camilla must be able to tell her.

It took her a while to find Camilla. She was rarely available to the phone in the office out of which she worked. Camilla disliked offices, paperwork. Her time was filled with visiting, checking, tracking down the clients for whom she was responsible. Her appetite for dealing with human misery, humans struggling against odds, was insatiable, thought Ailsa. She seemed to have an obsessive drive to seek out the people who lived on the margin of life, on the fringes of civilization, out in the jungle of tenements, the slums, the streets. Once or twice Ailsa had asked Camilla questions about this unusual dedication of hers. Camilla's answers had been evasive. She was just doing her job. She was paid to look after the people who needed government assistance, paid to supervise their lives. But, said Ailsa, you're so intense about it. Camilla, sullen, replied that if others did not do their jobs as thoroughly as she did hers, they were shirking. Did she believe all that stuff about social workers who welshed on the job, who were crooked and conspired with the deadbeats among their clients to cheat Welfare?

At last she found Camilla, when Camilla answered one of the many phone messages she had left for her. She appeared in Ailsa's office.

"You want me?"

"I want Mary Brown," said Ailsa, looking up from her desk. "I went to see her in the hospital the other day and they told me she had been discharged. Where did she go? She could not have been in very good shape."

"You can say that again. They don't care what happens to you when they discharge you and that's usually when they need your bed. You don't exist any more for them when you leave. That's why I took her away."

"You took her away?"

"She wouldn't go to a halfway house—even if I could have found her a place that could look after her. So I took her home."

"To your own apartment?"

"Yes. I'm lucky. I have a place with two bedrooms."

Ailsa was silent for a moment. Then she asked, "Where do you live, Camilla?"

Camilla told her.

"Do you mind if I go to see her?"

Camilla said firmly, "It's not if I mind. It's if she does."

"Do you think she'd object?"

"No, she isn't going to object. But you might frighten her."

Ailsa stared at her in surprise. "Why should I frighten her? I went to see her in the hospital."

"She couldn't help herself there."

"But why should she be afraid of me?"

"She was under arrest when she first saw you, wasn't she? She might be afraid, if you show up at my place, that other people could be after her."

"You mean the police?"

"Well, maybe. But you remember she saw that guy knifed."

"Yes, but that case is closed. She hasn't anything to be afraid of about that."

"As far as you are concerned. There may be some other people with ideas. She might be right in thinking that somebody might want to eliminate her because she saw the stabbing. She's been on the street quite a while. Maybe she's right to be scared."

"Then you don't want me to go and see her?"

There was a long pause before Camilla said, with a troubled note in her voice, "It's not up to me to say yes or no."

"All right, then. I'll go and see her."

Camilla shrugged, washing her hands of the situation.

"Shall I go and see her tomorrow?"

"I guess so. She isn't going to run away, even if I tell her you're coming."

Camilla's apartment was in a neighborhood that had once been solidly middleclass and had now slid down the economic scale. The street was a neutral zone between a somewhat prosperous enclave and an area that was frankly a slum. The building had been built as a walk-up apartment house of five stories. The glass double doors into the vestibule were unlocked. Above the mailboxes on the walls of the vestibule were buttons to be pushed for the tenant to trigger the inner door for a visitor. Ailsa found Camilla's name and pressed the button. The inner door gave a chirrup and she opened it. As she climbed the flight of stairs, she wondered why Camilla lived here. Even this modest dwelling must be expensive in this crowded city but there would be no relief in such narrow surroundings from the dreariness of her working day. She wondered what Camilla's salary was and whether she could afford better living quarters, whether she lived alone or shared.

As she climbed the second flight she heard the sound of an opening door and steps on the flight above her. A young woman appeared on the upper landing. It was not Camilla but a girl wearing a full skirt colored red and yellow with blue and green patches and a white, puff-sleeved blouse with a wide, low-cut neck. Even in the subdued light of the stairs Ailsa could see she was very pretty, with a mass of glossy chestnut-colored hair caught up in a ribbon on top of her head. A cloud of perfume wafted down to Ailsa.

The girl cried, "Meu Deus! A magistrada!" and burst into a peal of laughter.

Ailsa, taken aback, hesitated and then asked with extra dignity, "Does Camilla Bowden live here?"

The girl stifled her laughter and said, "Yes. But she is not here now. She is in the street—she is not home. You are the judge, aren't you? She said you would come." Her English was careful, with an accent.

"I am Ailsa Cameron. What is your name?"

The girl laughed again. "Oh, I'm Serafina. I am the friend of Camilla. She said you would come to see the old lady."

They had reached the landing and she gestured for Ailsa to enter the open door. Inside they stepped into a living room. There was good furniture, a bookcase full of books, and a television set with a program still on but the volume turned off. Serafina closed the door. "I see how she is."

She crossed the room and softly opened a door at the other end and put her head around it. "Titia? Are you awake? You have a visitor."

Ailsa heard no answering voice and Serafina disappeared into the room. In a moment or so she came back. "I think it is all right. She does not talk much."

Ailsa entered the small bedroom. It was only a little box of a room, with space for a bed and chair. But the chair was set by the window, which looked out on the street below. Mary was sitting in the chair. She wore a dressinggown—Camilla must have bought it for her, thought Ailsa—and her hair had been cut shorter so that it did not straggle over her shoulders. Against the brightness of the window Ailsa could not see the detail of her face.

She stepped closer and said, "Mary, how are you?"

The woman in the chair did not respond.

"You do remember me, don't you? I'm sorry I did not know when you left the hospital. I should have liked to help you."

Mary raised one hand in a gesture meant to acknowledge what she said. Ailsa looked at her hands. They were bony, with mottled skin, an old woman's hands, but now they were cared for. Camilla must have trimmed her nails. They must have been shapely capable hands at one time, not hands that had been roughly used.

"Mary, will you tell me something about yourself?"

She had sat down on the end of the bed in order to be able to face Mary on a level. She could now see Mary's face. It was pale and impassive, with the lips firmly closed.

She scarcely expected to get an answer but Mary unexpectedly said, "There is nothing to say."

The timbre of her voice caught Ailsa's ear. The hoarseness was gone. It was a deep voice for a woman. She was looking at Ailsa. Her eyes were dark grey and for the moment were clear and focussed. She sees me now, thought Ailsa. She must know who I am. Mary turned her head and dropped her eyes.

"You seem comfortable here," said Ailsa.

Mary said, "Yes," and there was another silence.

"If we knew more about you, Mary, we could arrange for somewhere for you to live."

Mary's eyes wandered back to her briefly. "Camilla is very good to me."

"Oh, yes, I know that. But she can't look after you forever."

Mary's eyes wandered away again and she did not answer.

"Why were you living in the street, Mary? What happened to cause you to do that?"

The question seemed to frighten Mary. She started and

drew herself together in fear. "It isn't that! It isn't what you think! I just—" Her own distress seemed to defeat her and she dropped her head and sat in an attitude of despair.

Chagrined, Ailsa impulsively put out her hand to touch one of Mary's. But the old woman snatched her hand away as if terrified of the contact.

Oh dear, thought Ailsa. I've driven her away now. "Mary, don't be frightened of me. I do not mean you any harm."

Mary's eyes came back to her, but this time they were glazed, as if she did not really see her. "I am not crazy. They were wrong. I am not crazy."

Surprised, Ailsa protested, "I don't think you are crazy, Mary! Why should you think that? Have you been in an institution?"

"They said at that shelter that I was crazy. I am not crazy." Her agitation had made her speech thick and clumsy.

"Yes, all right," Ailsa agreed hastily. Well, she remembers some things. Perhaps it is just a matter of giving her time to recover normal health.

Mary was wringing her hands in silent misery. Instinctively Ailsa refrained from saying anything more. Gradually Mary quieted and her hands grew still. How expressive they are! thought Ailsa. Mary sat as she had when she had first entered the room.

Growing bolder, Ailsa asked, "Why would you want to live in the street, without shelter and proper food? I don't think you really chose to do that, did you? You must have known that you were courting death from starvation and illness—"

Mary's eyes suddenly were raised to look into hers. There was anger in them. "What do you mean by saying that? Who told you?"

"Told me what?"

"That I was courting death. What do you mean by

that?"

"Nobody has told me anything, Mary. I don't know anyone who knows you. I wish I did."

Mary had dropped her eyes again. She said in a peevish voice, "Camilla never asks me all these questions. I don't want to talk to you. I want to be left alone."

Reluctantly Ailsa got up. Mary had spoken in a louder voice than before. Serafina put her head in the door and said softly, "Que tem, Titia? What is the matter?" She looked at Ailsa.

"I'm afraid she has got upset," said Ailsa.

Serafina stepped back from the door to let her come through and then gently closed it behind her. She said sympathetically, "She gets upset very easily, even with Camilla."

"That is too bad. It makes it hard for us to help her."

"She is a poor old lady. She doesn't trust anybody. She must be very unhappy. I cannot make her laugh."

"But you try," said Ailsa, smiling at her.

Serafina's face lit up. "Oh, yes. It is sad to see someone so unhappy. Camilla is so serious. I have to provide alegria for both of us."

"Alegria?"

Serafina's eyes danced. "Happiness. That is Portuguese. I am from Brazil, from Rio. Have you been in Rio?"

"No, I'm sorry I haven't. You're staying here with Camilla?" Such a pretty girl, Ailsa thought again, with the fresh, smooth skin of healthy youth, faint pink flushing the peach of her cheeks.

"Yes, Camilla is so kind. I have nowhere else to stay." The sparkle in her eyes seemed to disguise another meaning as she looked at Ailsa. "Do you want her to telephone to you?"

"Yes, I want to talk to her about Mary."

Serafina followed her down the stairs. "It is so nice of you to come and see Auntie. She does not have any friends except Camilla and me. It is so sad not to have friends."

"I'm sure that is something you don't suffer from, Serafina," said Ailsa over her shoulder.

Serafina burst into another peal of laughter. "Oh, no, not now. But when I first came here I did not have any. I was unhappy. But then I met Camilla. Now it is all right."

They had reached the vestibule. Serafina clasped her around the shoulders. "I must give you an abraco. Ate logo. You don't know what that means. I will tell you. It means, till we meet—soon."

"Yes, of course," Ailsa agreed, smiling in spite of herself. She watched while the girl skipped back up the stairs, humming to herself and marking time to the the tune with her hands in the air.

Camilla did not phone the next day but the day after she came to Ailsa's office after court hours. She walked in and sat down in the chair opposite.

"Hi," she said and sat looking at Ailsa.

Ailsa put aside the papers she had been reading. "Serafina told you I went to see Mary."

Camilla nodded.

"We are going to have to do something about her."

Camilla said crisply, "We?"

Ailsa looked at her. "Yes, we. You can't go on looking after her indefinitely. It's not your responsibility."

Camilla flared up. "Is that all you think about—whose responsibility she is?"

Ailsa was intrigued by the sudden defensiveness in Camilla's voice but she went on, "At the moment that is what I am thinking about—whose responsibility it is to look after her. It's certainly not yours. Why have you taken her in?"

"That's obvious, isn't it? There isn't anywhere else she can go."

"You don't do this with all the old women you rescue, do you? There must be somewhere—some shelter—some halfway house—that will take her. We can have her certified as incompetent."

"She wouldn't last a week anywhere like that! She can't run away anymore. She hasn't the strength. But she would give up."

"It looks to me as if that's what she has done already."

Camilla said, conciliatory, "I can still coax her to eat. She'll do it for me."

"I see. You mean, you think she'd go on a hunger-strike. Camilla, what do you mean, she can't run away any more? Do you think that is what she has been doing—running away?"

"I guess that's what I think."

"Running away from what?"

"If I knew that, there wouldn't be any problem, would there?"

"But what makes you think that?"

"She's so jumpy. Most of the time she doesn't pay any attention to what you say or do, but something you say sometimes seems to scare her to death."

"Of course she's jumpy. She must have had some pretty bad experiences—like the one she was arrested for, as a witness to a stabbing. Wouldn't that account for her nervousness? Haven't you told me that she may be afraid of reprisals from the men involved in that?"

"Oh, sure. Most of these old women, if they've been on the street any length of time, their nerves are wrecked. They're always afraid they'll be raped or murdered or tortured somehow."

"Then I should think that would account for Mary's nervousness. What I am trying to get at is the cause of her being in this situation so that we can find a solution."

Camilla took a deep breath and sat back in her chair. "You'll probably never find that out. Maybe I'm imagining things about her. She seems to me different. I've seen a lot of these old women. Most of them, they've just been somebody's mamma, somebody's grandma, or they've never had a family, but somewhere along the way something goes wrong and they wind up with nobody to look after them and no money and nowhere to live. The landlords turn them out. And some of them get a taste for that sort of life—freedom, you know, from what other people think. They don't fit in anywhere anymore and they get so they don't trust anybody. Even when you try to help them, they won't accept it. Sometimes it's because they're ashamed, as if it was their fault, and sometimes they're angry, defiant. But, I tell you, I've never met one just like Mary. Every so often, when I'm talking to her, it's as if the corner of a curtain lifts up and you think you're going to see something that will explain things. But you never do."

"I admit there's something strange about her. Why do you suppose she won't tell us anything about herself?"

"She likes her privacy."

"How private is your life if you live in the street?"

"A lot more private than if you let people put you in an institution and pry into your affairs."

"What would she have to hide that would be that important?"

A sly look came into Camilla's face. "Suppose she's one of these misers who have piles and piles of money stashed away somewhere?"

Ailsa frowned at her. "You're joking, Camilla."

Camilla gave a short laugh. "I don't know where she'd keep it. It certainly wasn't in that bag of rubbish she was carrying around."

"What are you going to do about her, Camilla?"

"Just keep her at my place for now. That's where she seems to want to be." Camilla paused for a moment and then asked, "What did you say to her? Fina says she got upset about something you said to her."

"Something I said? Oh, yes." Ailsa hesitated, remembering in a vivid flash Mary's sudden alarm at the phrase she had used. "I asked her why she was living in the street, why she courted death like that, from violence, disease. She suddenly waked up. She wanted to know what I meant, who had told me—what, I don't know. It seemed to be the phrase I used, courting death."

A triumphant gleam appeared in Camilla's eyes. "You see what I mean? She's running away from something—something inside herself."

Ailsa did not answer. After a few moments she said, "I'd like to help you look after her, Camilla. You can't afford to do this sort of thing on your own."

Camilla stood up. She said offhandedly as she began to go out of the room. "All right. I'll let you know when I need help."

* * * * *

The memory came back, especially in the dark—because it was a creature of the dark. She was there in the condemned building, an apartment house once, that had finally become so dilapidated and vermin-ridden that the city had condemned it. She disliked taking shelter there. The stench of human waste, of dead rats, clung to it, and she had to be careful not to fall afoul of some other derelict already there in the dark. She had preferred the warehouses down by the wharves, great cavernous places where ship-bound cargoes had been stored. They were too vast for human habitation, offering shelter only in their corners and crannies to rats and homeless creatures like herself. You could hear and smell the river, black and oily, lapping at the walls. It was that, she supposed, and the very vastness that frightened a lot of men away—women seldom or never came there. But then the police took to coming every night with big dazzling lights, searching out the few strays sheltered there, looking for drugs. She had avoided being dragged off to a night in the police station but she was afraid then to go back there. This den, this crumbling building with gaping doors and windows, gave some shelter from the cold sleety rain. Only the first floor was safe. The stairs and the flooring of the upper storeys were perilous. She avoided the apartment that lay close to what had been the front entrance of the building. Its walls were blackened, the smell of charring still hung in the air. A whole family of children had died there in the fire on a night so cold the water froze in the firemen's hoses. It had taken that sacrifice and the outcry in the newspapers to force the city to condemn the building. She sought instead some rooms at the back, down what had been a hallway, now half-blocked by debris, where it was less likely that a stray cruising police car would shine its lights in.

She was uncertain what time of night it was. Her memory always began with the sounds of voices—loud, harsh men's voices, suddenly erupting in a quarrel. The place had been empty when she had crept in and settled herself behind a mass of overturned bathroom fixtures, vandalized or looted by those seeking usable objects. It gave her a hiding place in case other derelicts sought shelter there from the piercing wind. There was never complete silence in such a place. Rats, ever restless in search of food, swarmed in the mass of rubbish. She had not got used to the rats. They still frightened and disgusted her. But the fatigue that had fastened itself upon her more cruelly every day was greater than her fear. Sleep or at least a sort of semi-consciousness engulfed her. The men's voices roused her.

Whoever they were, they did not seem to fear or expect police interference. There was a light shining in the burnt-out apartment, a big flashlight of some sort, and it cast shadows onto the wall of the hallway, the shadows of men fighting. She could not tell how many there were. But then she heard the sickening sound of a man gargling his own blood as it gathered in his throat and after that footsteps running out of the building and into the street. The apartment had been built as public housing, in four-storey blocks clustered around a central open space, so there were no inhabited buildings close by. When the footsteps died away the silence was again complete.

The disturbance had roused her not only from sleep but from the lethargy that had taken hold of her during the last days or weeks—lately the passage of time had begun to grow vague to her. In the mental clarity that returned to her now she knew that this must have been a quarrel over drugs. Dope peddling was a common source of money for the people she saw on the streets. When she had been more alert she had observed the pushing of drugs—the passing from hand to hand of small packets and money. She knew that in the combination of insatiable desire and greed involved in this traffic was the fuel for violence. She had seen the sudden fights in the street, the frantic attempt at escape as the less able fled from their pursuers. So her mind automatically interpreted the sounds she heard now.

In the stillness she waited, reluctant to go near the body that must now be lying in the rubbish of the burnt-out room—dead perhaps and therefore daunting, or stirring to life and therefore dangerous. Here where she was, hidden behind the barrier of broken sinks and fittings, she might be safe. When the first daylight came she could pick her way out into the street, avoiding the hazards that lay in the way.

She did not sleep again, waiting for the first gleam of dawn. But the lethargy returned and she was held powerless by it when the sounds of cars coming to a stop in the empty street behind the building reached her. The light from electric torches flickered through the broken windows. Stupidly she was aware of the sounds and the lights but could not rouse herself to action. A brilliant beam of light searched the wreckage inside the apartment. She heard the voices of several policemen as they found what they were looking for. Someone must have alerted them to the hideout of the drug peddlers. "He's dead, all right," one of them said. "He's been slashed from ear to ear." Another one said, "Better have a look to see if there's anybody else here."

The brilliant light played along the wall of the passage, reaching to the barricade behind which she crouched. It blinded her as it shone into her eyes. The voices exclaimed. A powerful hand took hold of her arm and dragged her from her shelter. She did not resist, only half-aware of being urged along the passage and down the walk to the street and then being thrust into a police car.

In self-defense she closed her conscious mind to the questions, the probings, the menacing faces thrust close to hers, the indignities taken with her body as hands searched among the rags that covered it. It had all happened before, when she was better able to defend herself. Now she could do nothing but take her conscious self away into limbo.

She was briefly aware of subsequent events—when she was questioned by a plainclothesman who demanded to know her name, why she was there in that place, did she know the men who fought? She had no answers for him. She was again briefly aware that she was in a courtroom and that a woman with a cloud of pale blonde hair had asked her questions and again she had no answers. After that her memory dissolved into a fog. Vaguely she recalled being in a hospital bed and the same woman had come to see her, rousing her from the white, featureless, antiseptic cocoon in which she seemed to be. When the woman had left she found it difficult to keep her out of her consciousness. She seemed to get in under the cloud of nothingness beneath which she willingly sank. She remembered that the woman had made her angry by probing, she had forgotten about what.

Not like that girl who had come to see her when she was in the jail cell, who had seemed to coax her to answer questions, to allow these strangers to remove her clothes. She had been glad to follow her out of the hospital. For the hospital had now become a dangerous place, open, unguarded, unprotected, where anyone might walk in and accost her, try to stir the past, bring her from the protecting darkness into the menacing light. She was in a little room now, with no one near her. Any sounds she might hear were far away, not in any way connected with her. It was safe here, warm and sometimes, if the girl coaxed her, she could eat.

She did not mind that other girl, who laughed and sang and called her a name in a foreign language. There was a certain feeling of security in the foreign girl's flood of talk. It was protective like the silence she preferred, into which she sank gratefully when all sounds ceased in her room, in the place beyond the door that the girl kept open. But that woman had come again, with all that light blonde hair. Why did that disturb her? What memory tried to stir in the murkiness at the back of her head? The woman had found her again and had asked questions, thrusting into her consciousness as if with groping fingers touching her nerves. She had driven her away but the effort had exhausted her.

When she had rested and everything about her was quiet, a thin thread of meaning seemed to try to weave itself in the depths of her mind. She found difficulty in following it. She looked about the room. It was as if she saw it from a great distance—as if her body sitting there in it was something outside of herself. That was what the thread of meaning resolved into: Who was she?

* * * * *

The weekend had come and for the first time that year they had come to the shore, to the cottage in the dunes, a few hours' drive from the city. The March air was still cold with the chill of the wind off the North Atlantic. The cottage was still largely boarded up. They had merely freed a few windows so that the sun could come in and dispel the damp. The mustiness of winter pervaded the house, the bed, the furniture. They would camp out, bringing their food in a cooler and not expecting indoor plumbing. But, thought Ailsa, remembering the summer holidays of childhood, there was a homelike feeling to that mustiness. It spoke of sea, sand, sea creatures. She sniffed.

Noticing, Dina said, "We never can really get rid of the smell. It's in the fabric, I suppose."

"I don't want to," Ailsa replied.

Dina smiled at her fondly. "No, you wouldn't, would you, my dear romantic. It's the scent of happiness, of innocence, of childhood's heaven, isn't it?"

Ailsa, standing on the sundeck looking toward the glitter of the sea across the sand with its ragged fringe of winter-brown sedge, turned to her. "It's amazing to me still, dearest, that you can put your finger so exactly on me like that, even to your choice of words. How do you know that this is what it means to me?"

"You're as transparent as crystal."

"To you."

"To me," Dina agreed, smiling. "You remember, that is how I snared you. You did not expect anyone to see into you like that, did you? I can remember the astonishment on your face the first time we talked—what were we talking about?"

It was at a cocktail party, Ailsa remembered, a very mixed affair with all sorts of people, serious and frivolous, and they had found themselves sitting on a love-seat in the corner of the crowded room, surrounded by the backs of noisy people, drinking and arguing. She did not like cocktail parties and she had sought out this quiet spot to last out a few moments alone, before she could take leave. Dina had come and sat down beside her.

Dina said, "I said to you, You're not married, are you? You were annoyed at being accosted by a stranger and when you said No, I couldn't refrain from saying, "And you aren't divorced. Do you live with somebody? And that time you said, Really, it's none of your business! Then I asked you, You've never lived with anybody, you must be a virgin. I remember how indignant you looked. You just weren't used to being asked such intimate questions by somebody you never saw before, whereas I was used to much more outrageous topics of conversation with people I had only just met. It was obvious you weren't used to that sort of destruction of your personal dignity. I lived in a world where personal dignity wasn't considered important—didn't exist, in fact. I was guessing, of course, when I asked you all those questions—"

"You're exaggerating them a little bit," said Ailsa.

"For dramatic effect. The last one was just the most impertinent one I could think of on the spur of the moment, trying to make you open up to me. I had been around the loud kind so long that I'd forgotten that your sort might cut me out of your life forever instead."

"You didn't stop at that," said Ailsa.

Dina laughed. "No, I didn't. The way I saw you, you were a princess in a tower, behind a moat. So I asked you if you were a lesbian and you looked at me as if I had a head full of snakes. But you didn't run away. We got down to business. You said, Yes, you preferred women to men, and I said then, are you bi? You gave me a withering look and said you didn't deal in those terms. You had a career to think of. That's when I found out you were a judge—just been appointed one. That stopped me for a while, I asked you whether you were still in the closet. You said, not with the door locked and barred. You weren't paranoid but you had to consider the requirements of your profession. There were things you must refuse to do in order not to compromise the impartiality you must preserve on the bench. That meant disengaging yourself from active participation in a lot of institutional and civic causes. You could no longer be a crusader even for causes you felt strongly about, like women's rights—all women's rights. If you were part of the system, you had to work within it or lose the right to make judgments between advocates. You were committed to achieving justice within the law. You admitted the need for a lot of reform in the system, especially from the point of view of women. You hoped to be able to make some difference there, in time. And then you said, You're in the entertainment world, aren't you? That makes a difference, doesn't it? And I had to admit that it did. Now, wasn't that the way it happened?"

"You've telescoped a few meetings into one, but, yes, that is more or less the way it happened."

Dina came to her and put both arms around her. "Aren't you glad it happened?"

"That's a silly question. Why are we here, otherwise? This isn't the time of year most people come to the shore."

"We're here to get away from it all. Trying to decide whether we belong together. Sometimes I wonder when I see you across a room, surrounded by men. You just stand there and they try every wile, and I begin to think, you really don't like them, just as you say."

"I've been dropped a number of times."

"I can imagine. I expect some of them feel rather sold. You've got such come-hither looks. They couldn't possibly believe you're that innocent or that impervious to their own charms. In any case, I was a surprise to you and that made you pay attention to me."

"Oh, there wasn't any question about my paying attention to you. You say I acted as if I could only be a spectator at life's feast—isn't that the phrase? You said that at the time and I suppose it was true. I was troubled by it. When I was younger it was easier to relate to other girls, but when I got older and into a career, it wasn't so easy. I did not know how to go about being less passive without running the risk of getting into something messy. The law teaches you caution."

"Whereas I was always trying to extricate myself from relationships that had no meaning beyond the novelty of exploring a new person. That gets tiresome after you get older. It doesn't matter if it's a man or a woman. A sated appetite. God! All the old warnings of our Victorian ancestors—too much of any luxury soon palls. Self-indulgence leads only to moral ruin. All that. The trouble is that you can't get away from the essential truth of those old cautions, even if you reject the moral judgments. It's the way we're made, isn't it, darling? But you don't pall. That's the amazing thing."

Ailsa was smiling at her with a trace of irony. "Are you looking for it to happen?"

"Of course not!" In annoyance Dina walked away to the railing of the sundeck and stood leaning on her elbows looking out to the sea. Ailsa watched her. Dina's black hair gleamed in the sunlight. There was a flamboyance about

Dina's way of dressing, about her gestures. You could not treat Dina casually no matter what your dealings with her were. Her mere presence prevented it. She had countless times watched Dina with total strangers, casually met acquaintances, people she confronted in public places. Dina sailed into any encounter and dominated it without effort. This often left you disconcerted, regretful later that you had not resisted her. And yet the combination of surprise and the strength of Dina's self-assertion made resistance seem pointless, except for stupid people in whom it created a sense of rancor. She remembered very well the emotional turmoil she suffered after the first real encounter with Dina, how she had gone home in a state of angry confusion, as annoyed with herself as she was angry at Dina. If you showed that you did not care for personal questions, anyone of any breeding should recognize the fact and desist. Dina hadn't. It was very fortunate that Dina hadn't.

Dina turned around and leaned her back against the railing. "Do you want a walk along the beach before lunch?"

They walked along the sand, hard-packed by the winter storms, occasionally meeting other people who had responded to the lure of the first hint of spring. They were chiefly silent. Ailsa recognized the sudden drop in spirits that Dina often suffered after they had talked about themselves. Her own more equable nature was not so disturbed by a consideration of the fact that they were still at the stage of exploring their feelings towards one another. She had no doubt about herself. It was Dina or no one. It was a decision that she had not made with her reason but one which had been made for her—by what? She could not say. Whatever its consequences she would have to accept them. One could not change the stars in their courses nor the rising and the setting of the sun and the moon.

With Dina it was different. She did not know whether

Dina was in doubt about the choice she had made—whether she doubted her choice or was dissatisfied with the results or uncertain about her own ability to stick to such a decision—or even whether Dina doubted the validity of deciding to live with someone else excluding others. She really knew little about Dina's former affairs. It was certain that she had had them, but Dina did not like to talk about them. Had the affairs themselves left bad feelings? Or was she regretting that she had had them? Dina seemed to make herself angry in recalling any details about them, angry and then short-tempered with Ailsa, which she regretted immediately in remorseful apologies.

It had been Dina that had suggested this weekend. A certain restlessness had taken possession of her, which she mockingly attributed to the rising of sap in the spring. Ailsa, eager to escape for a while from the grimy squalor of life as it flowed through her courtroom, welcomed the suggestion. She thought she understood what had prompted Dina. There was a crowded, hurried character to their life together, compounded by the great diversity between her work and Dina's. Her hours were more regular, though they were filled with unrelieved reality in its most sordid aspect. Even with the extra professional activities she took on, she spent more evenings at home, more time in calm reflection. Dina, partly because she was involved with temperamental clients, night-time activities, and partly because she had long since acquired the habit of late nights, spontaneous engagements, unforeseen commitments, spent a far more hectic life. They had accommodated to this difference, with its difficult moments, since it was a necessary element in their joint lives. Now, after so many months, Dina seemed to be under a growing strain. Dina at first revelled in the harum-scarum quality of her life. Now she seemed on the verge of rebelling against it, as if she wanted something quieter, more predictable. Perhaps this was only the first hint of the passing of youth. They were both forty years old. But Dina did not care for introspection. When it overtook her she plunged into melancholy.

By the time they got back to the cottage and began to arrange their lunch on a table by a seaward-facing window, Dina's spirits had begun to rise again. She was never downhearted for long. They ate their lunch without talking much but now the silence between them was filled with a feeling of tenderness. They did not talk, Ailsa realized, because neither of them wanted to bring into this intimate moment the conflicts and irritations of their daily lives nor the disturbing memories of their lives before they had met. The present was enough and this seemed so to both of them.

Afterwards, lying on the bed in the bedroom cluttered with objects which had been stored there for the winter, with a large beach towel spread beneath them as a sheet, this feeling grew stronger. When they had first encountered one another and had reached the point when they acknowledged the strength of the pull of each other's presence, it was the lack of privacy they had felt most. There was a hurried quality about hours or nights spent in the apartment of one or the other. Ailsa had shared a house with several other women. Dina had a noisy flat often intruded upon by actors and artists. That had brought them to their first joint decision, to live together in their own apartment, to have their own bedroom, secure against intrusion. This had been a bigger step for Dina than for herself, Ailsa realized. Dina had always sought the anonymity of a crowd, where the finest edge of feeling could be blunted by the presence of other people. She had been surprised by the apparent contentment with which Dina had made the change.

Ailsa stretched herself out closer to Dina's body, so that they touched. Dina lay quiet, making no move. This was unusual. Dina was characteristically full of restless energy. Even in sleep, unless she had sunk into a sound and dreamless state, she was seldom still. Dina must always have been that way, going out to meet life as it came toward her, never waiting to see what it might bring to her. Thus, everything that came to her she dominated, taking it by surprise. Not like me, thought Ailsa. Here I am, lying here waiting for Dina, because, for me, there is a transcendent delight in waiting for her approach, for her hands to steal gently over my skin, radiating out from wherever she first touches. And then those soft, leisurely kisses that follow. In this Dina was never hasty, never impatient. At times like this nothing counted except the featherlight touches, on her breasts, on her stomach, along the inside of her thighs, in the soft warmth of her cleft, when suddenly they became strong, powerful, dominating, enveloping her in the hot wave of her climax.

Lying back, regaining calm, she welcomed the pressure and urgency of Dina's body covering hers. Dina's lips demanded hers, Dina's desire fueled her own. The pulse of Dina's quickening blood awoke the beat of her heart. Her own response was always slower than Dina's at the beginning of their love-making. But then Dina's hair-trigger surge of energy roused in her a fury that carried them both beyond any clear awareness of anything except the other's body, the other's crying out for love, for completeness. The first few times they had gone to bed together they had both felt a certain shyness after they had made love, as if not quite believing the thoroughness of their joining. But now there was only an unalloyed acceptance of the fact of their mutual fulfillment.

Dina rolled away from their embrace onto her back, quiet again. Ailsa lay on her stomach, her hand gently stroking Dina's white skin, invading the silky mass of hair at her pubis, as black and soft as the hair on her head. The bedroom was on the ocean side of the cottage. From the bed they could see the sky over the sea, the delicately tinted, mauvish light from the sun setting on the other side of the cottage reaching the light clouds gathering at the horizon.

Ailsa said, "When I was in my teens I heard Myra Hess play Brahms' second concerto. I was carried away into a sky like that."

Dina snatched her hand and kissed the palm. "That's what's the matter. Here you have me by the short hairs"—she brought Ailsa's hand back to her pubis—"and the first thing I know you are flying away into the sky. You're always a little out of reach."

"Really?" Ailsa's tone was skeptical. She put her head down on Dina's stomach where it lay in the hollow between her hip-bones. "But how wrong you are. I'm very much here, with you. It is you I want to take with me." She paused to kiss Dina's skin at the edge of hair. "Sometimes I am here when you seem only half with me, thinking of something else, really something else, something outside the two of us, not music or something of that sort, that opens my senses to the seduction of your body. Let me see if I can tell you what it is. We're here alone, you and I, as ourselves, not as the women we are back in the city. When I heard Brahms I was carefree. I could follow after the seduction of the music without a thought of myself as anything but the self I was then. I did not have you. I did not know that there could be something more. It is very hard to capture that freedom now and only music brings it back. And now you are here, in a way that you are not—always."

Dina reached down and with her strong arms drew her up in the bed until they lay breast to breast. "Give me time, darling. I am learning my way."

* * * * *

The door of the apartment opened. Serafina entered first, followed by Camilla. The silence that greeted them in the dark living room made them both pause, stilling for the moment Serafina's chatter.

Camilla made an exasperated sound in her throat. "Why doesn't she turn the damn TV on? I've told her she can come out here and watch it. Gives me the creeps—her sitting there staring into space, in the silence of the tomb."

Serafina's laugh peeled forth. "Maybe she is practicing."

Camilla whirled around to her. "Practicing—? Shut up!"

Serafina came close to her and put her arms around her, giving her little nibbling kisses on her cheek and neck. "Oh, minha negrinha, how angry you get with me! It's only a comedy. You're always so serious."

Glowering still, Camilla retorted, "I don't appreciate that kind of humor."

With a final loving pat Serafina turned away. "I am going to talk to her—cheer her up. Coitada da velhinha! She is here all day by herself. That is wrong. She needs people around her. Everybody needs people around them. It is not good to be solitary. It is bad for the soul."

Always serious, thought Camilla, her nerves still quivering. But it was experience that did that. She had never had much chance to be anything else. If you want to succeed against odds, you don't have time for frivolity. With her parents' help she had worked her way through college, at the most menial jobs, cleaning motel rooms, as kitchen help. And her present job—there wasn't much cheerfulness in looking after people who were so defeated by life that they could not look after themselves even if they had a helping hand. Serious. Yes, she was serious. She had a burden of care that sat on her shoulders twenty-four hours a day. Not like Serafina. Serafina could not worry over the direst of threats—what would happen when she had used up the money her parents had given her, what she would do if the immigration authorities found out she was no longer in college though she was in the country on a student visa. Serafina never worried. The happiness of the moment was sufficient. It never occurred to her to fear the future. Not only would the future take care of itself, it would bring new excitement, new joys, new adventures, a new beginning. The past would fall away and with it any disappointments, frustrations, failure of happiness.

Camilla hung up her own coat in the closet and picked up Serafina's. Her ear was cocked for sounds from Mary's room. She could hear the wheedling, coaxing tones of Serafina's voice. She hung up the coat and went into the small kitchen, carrying the bag of groceries she had brought home. Automatically she placed the cans on the shelf, the milk and vegetables in the refrigerator, her mind still preoccupied with the contrast between herself and Serafina. She rejected the idea that she was a masochist—Paula, at work, had said she was—that she sought the burdens she always found herself bearing. She had been accused of seeking that sort of emotional enslavement by someone she thought loved her, someone who would not put up with the encroachment on their private lives of Camilla's constant and all-pervading responsibilities. But if you took up a career in social service, if your work was involved with the personal lives of people who needed help, you couldn't confine yourself to a nine-to-five workday. She thought again of Paula. Paula had a husband and children, a husband with as demanding a job as her own, and even Paula did not escape from out-of-hours commitments. Even the judge, who kept telling her she should organize her day so that she kept some of it for herself—even the judge carried her own responsibilities beyond the close of the business day. Look how she was always worrying about Mary.

Serafina's voice came from Mary's room in a half-shriek. Camilla tensed. She was still not used to the extravagance of Serafina's manner. But the shriek seemed to be of excitement, delight. She walked across the living room to Mary's door and looked in. Serafina stood in the middle of the little room, babbling chiefly in Portuguese, as was usually the case when she reached a certain level of excitement.

"Hello, Mary," said Camilla, looking curiously at the old woman in the armchair. "How are you doing?"

She was used to the lacklustre look that Mary usually gave her when she came in this way to check on her. She did not really expect Mary to respond. It was as if she really doesn't want to see me or anybody else. "What were you whooping about, Fina?"

Serafina began in Portuguese and switched at once into English. "This lady knows Rio! She has been there!"

Camilla glanced quickly back at Mary, half-expecting that Mary would realize that she was revealing something about herself and would take fright and pull down the iron curtain of silence again. But Mary looked at her with clear eyes and said in a hesitating voice, "I believe I was there. Years ago. It must have been years ago, mustn't it?"

Camilla stared at her. It was almost as if another woman spoke, not mumbling, fumbling Mary. But Mary dropped her eyes and seemed abashed.

Serafina cried, "But you know Rio so well! You recognized places I talked about! You mentioned the Opera House!"

Mary looked up at her, puzzled. "Yes, I did speak of it."

"You see! You know its beauties—its mountains—that marvelous Guanabara Bay! You have not forgotten them, have you? No one forgets them who has seen them. It is magnificent—uma maravilha—"

Camilla cut in, "You're homesick, Fina. Mary hasn't said anything about all that."

"Oh, but she did! Before you came in."

"You really do remember?" Camilla asked Mary. "You really were there?"

Mary nodded. "I sang there in 1960."

Camilla stared at her in astonishment. Mary was looking down at the floor, smiling to herself.

I've never seen her smile before, thought Camilla. "You sang?"

The disbelieving note in her voice made Serafina laugh. "Que coisa! Why shouldn't she sing? I like to sing. You know that I sing, don't you, Titia? You've heard me sing here. I've told you I want to be a singer, a famous singer. I like that better than dancing. I only dance because it is easier that way to make my name. But I wish to be serious. I will be frivolous and vulgar now so that I can be serious later. I can make money being frivolous and I will be popular dancing. But when I am famous I shall stop doing that. I shall be serious. I shall sing in concert halls—in Carnegie Hall, and perhaps in opera. You remember the Opera House in Rio. Did you sing in the Opera House?"

Camilla cut in again. "Stop that nonsense, Fina. Why should she sing in the Opera House there? Why did you go to Rio, Mary? Are you sure you did or is Fina just putting ideas in your head?"

"I went there to sing," said Mary simply.

Camilla gazed at her for a long time, wondering. Mary's brief clarity seemed to be evaporating. She sank back into her chair and did not respond to any more questions. Camilla put a hand on Serafina's arm and gestured towards the door.

In the living room Camilla said, "You had better be careful, Fina. I don't know how successful you are getting into nightclub acts and stage skits. You haven't been telling me lately. But if you make a show of yourself like that, your parents are going to find you. Then where'll you be?"

Serafina looked at her unhappily. "You're being bad, meu bem. You are angry because Mary talks to me and tells me things. It is because she is like me. She is a singer. We like to soar up into the sky and you always want to bring me back down to the earth. If I become famous, my parents will forgive me, they will be proud of me."

"All that's in the future. Right now you'll get yourself into a pickle if you're not careful."

But Serafina had gone away across the room, humming to herself. She wandered about, touching the bright band of red silk that held her glossy hair in place, looking critically in the mirror over the mantel to see if a pimple that threatened to mar the smooth beauty of her forehead had grown any worse.

"I'm not cross with you, Fina," said Camilla humbly. "I'm just worried. I don't want you to have to go away."

Serafina looked around at her and then came over and put her arms around her. "She is such a poor old lady. She falls asleep and when she wakes up she remembers little things and she gets sad. I try to cheer her up."

"Yes, yes," Camilla agreed anxiously. "You're wonderful with her, Fina. I mean it. She comes out of her fog when you talk to her."

They went into the kitchen and Camilla began to take pots and pans and bowls out of the drawers and set them on the table. Serafina often offered to help her get a meal but she had learned that Serafina's way of preparing food turned the kitchen into a shambles. Obviously she was used to maids whose business it was to clean up after her.

Serafina's thoughts had left Mary and were running now on interviews she had had with people she wanted to impress with her talents. Camilla listened with half an ear.

Camilla's mind dwelt on the strange phenomenon of Mary's brief emergence from behind the curtain that closed her off from the world. She broke into what Serafina was saying. "What did she say to you before I came into the room?"

Serafina stared at her for a moment blankly. "Oh, Titia! I was telling her about my family and the house we live in in Petropolis—in the mountains above Rio. She said Oh, she had been in Rio. She had been in Petropolis. It was astonishing. She said she remembered how it looked, seeing it from the mountain and the sea."

"She told you she was a singer?"

"No. She told you that."

Camilla lapsed into silence. What did this mean and was it true, was it important? It was important if it really threw light on Mary's past. This was what the judge was trying to find out. Who Mary was. I suppose, thought Camilla, I had better let her know what has happened.

Serafina's voice penetrated her preoccupation. "These old women—sometimes they are very deep—they have powers—"

"What are you talking about?"

"This old lady. Perhaps she is a santa. Perhaps she is a mae d'agua. That is very dangerous."

"What's a santa? What's a mae d'agua?"

For a moment Serafina looked a little puzzled as to how to explain. "A santa is a—what do you say?—a holy woman who speaks for a god or a goddess. A mae d'agua is a—a water mother. She is very deceptive. She can take all kinds of forms. In Brazil there are many people who believe in macumba—in the spirits that govern the earth."

"Do you?" Camilla demanded.

Serafina looked uncertain. "I have been to many meet- ings—many gatherings where rites are held. Oh, yes, I am a good Catholic but there are a lot of these beliefs—some of them came from Africa with the slaves, some are from the

Indians in the forests. My parents do not approve of this. But I have seen things that make me shiver."

Camilla was looking at her with a disapproving frown. "What are you trying to tell me—that Mary is some sort of a witch?"

"Oh, no, not what you'd call a witch. She may be much more powerful, especially if she is a mae d'agua. She can make herself appear to be anything—a beautiful woman, someone who tempts you, makes you follow her, you know not where."

"Sounds like a Lorelei," said Camilla.

"A Lorelei?"

"That siren that sits on a rock in the middle of the Rhine, in Germany, luring people—men, that is."

"Oh. Well, the mae d'agua is a little different. She can make you do anything she wants, brings you all sorts of happiness and then she takes it all away. Even if you please her in everything and she likes you, she will get bored perhaps, and destroys everything and goes away and leaves you all alone and unhappy."

"I know some human beings that will do that sort of thing," said Camilla drily.

"So you see," said Serafina, "you must be careful about the old lady. You don't know what she might be."

"I'm careful with her all right, for her own sake. I don't believe all that kind of nonsense. You'd better listen to your parents."

She felt herself suddenly caught from behind as Serafina's surprisingly strong arms held her immobile. Serafina was laughing in her ear. "If I listened to my mamae and papai, I wouldn't be here with you, minha nega."

Camilla felt the warmth of Serafina's body pressed against her back, felt the beating of Serafina's heart, felt Serafina's mouth against the back of her neck, heard

Serafina's voice gurgling in her ear endearments she could not understand except with her heart. She stood still, her eyes shut, trying to believe that this was really happening to her, that it was not one of the fantasies she sometimes indulged in. She murmured, "How do I know you aren't one of those come-hithers you've been talking about?"

Serafina released her in a sudden burst of laughter. "Meu bem! What an idea! You mustn't say things like that!"

* * * * *

The apartment was brilliantly lit by tall standing lamps, small bougies in wall sockets, clusters of lights in the middle of tables—the way Dina liked it when they were entertaining in the wintertime. Beyond the big windows the city was a great blackness punctured by myriads of glittering points of brightness. Dina, in a long clinging robe that set off her slim figure, went about the room giving little touches here and there to the decorations, the trays of glasses and cups. Dina was in her element in such a situation, thought Ailsa, mistress of the art of creating a fantasy.

Dina said over her shoulder to Ailsa sitting in an armchair watching her, "Ha! Serafina. A pretty girl from Brazil. So Camilla has a private life after all."

"I always supposed she must have, in spite of what Paula says."

"She doesn't open up about herself much, does she—from what you tell me? I've only seen her once."

"I don't feel as awkward with her as I used to. I think she has grown to distrust me less than she did at first."

Dina glanced at the ornate little clock that chimed. "God! It's eight already. And there's the door."

The signal from the reception desk downstairs sounded.

Within minutes the room was full of arriving guests, women dangling wraps over their arms, men standing about surveying the gathering. Many of these people, Ailsa knew, were Dina's clients, successful people in the entertainment world. They gathered around her like bees after the source of honey. The small maid Dina had hired circulated with trays of canapes and pates. The tables where the drinks were set out were ringed with people. The hubbub of voices rose.

Ailsa, going to the door in answer to a ring, found Camilla and Serafina standing outside. She drew them in, taking their wraps. Camilla lingered in the small vestibule, peering anxiously into the crowded living room. She is not exactly frightened, thought Ailsa, but she obviously feels threatened by a failure of nerve. Serafina, on the other hand, fairly danced with impatience to join the crowd of talking, laughing people. The thought crossed Ailsa's mind that without Serafina Camilla would not have come.

Serafina's face was alive with anticipation. She gave Camilla a little shove and followed her into the room. Dina came to greet them, her hands held out in the gesture with which she usually greeted her guests, drawing Camilla towards her and planting a kiss on her cheek. Ailsa could see that Camilla was nonplussed by the exuberance of this style of greeting, unused to the easy extravagance of show people. Serafina responded enthusiastically with an impulsive hug.

"You're Serafina," said Dina. "You must come and meet people."

Before the party was over Serafina had become the main attraction. She had the uninhibited zest of a born entertainer. She sang, in a seductive, throaty voice, songs that had been popular in the Carnival a month before, and demonstrated the proper way to dance the numerous variations of the samba.

The party lasted much longer than they had expected.

Dina, gathering up ashtrays and empty glasses abandoned in odd corners, yawned and said, "Is she a professional dancer? She has a professional finish."

Ailsa, opening the French doors onto the terrace to let the cold night air in to clear the smokiness, replied, "I don't think so. I think she wants to be."

"What an exotic bird to be caught in Camilla's cage! Poor Camilla. Did you see her eyes when Serafina was performing? So intent on her—the burning glance, if I ever saw one. *Her* prize, *her* darling!"

"Yes. I'm afraid Camilla is far gone."

"You say she's here in the country as a student and is staying with Camilla because she does not have anywhere else to live? She doesn't strike me as being poor."

"It's more than that. She is a runaway. She's come to the big city to make a name for herself as a singer and dancer. I don't know how Camilla found her."

"She certainly is not just a boarder. Didn't you tell me that Camilla doesn't like men?"

"Yes, I did tell you that. She thinks most women's troubles come from being victimized by men. What she sees every day in her work would certainly reinforce that idea. She especially despises white girls who go with black men. They're just asking for trouble."

"But what about white girls who go with black girls?"

"Ah, that's something else." Ailsa was thoughtful for a moment. "You know, it's strange. I've just realized that I've felt all along that Camilla is like me—she prefers women. When Paula talks about her there is an undertone to her voice, as if she doesn't quite want to come out and say that Camilla is a lesbian. You remember who Paula is. When she talks about Camilla she always stresses the fact that she is solitary, unsociable—"

"The cat that walks by itself."

"Of course, Paula can't know for sure. Camilla would be very careful not to jeopardize her career. It means too much to her. That in itself tells you how powerful her feeling for Serafina is, for her to take such a risk in having her live with her. You may be sure Paula has noticed this."

"She is a busybody, isn't she?"

"I wonder what she thinks about me. Her curiosity is insatiable."

"And what does Camilla think about us?"

"I think Camilla has reached the right conclusion. She is no fool. I think that is why she is more friendly with me."

* * * * *

At first glance Ailsa scarcely recognized Camilla. She was standing on the street corner where Ailsa went each afternoon after court hours to look for a cab. This was a fact that Camilla must have observed. She was dressed in jeans with turned up cuffs and a man's shirt with a turtleneck sweater over it. At work Camilla always wore a skirt. This must be a day off work for her.

Camilla stood in front of her on the sidewalk, silent as if uncertain what to say.

"Hello, Camilla," said Ailsa. "You do take a day off sometimes, then."

Camilla looked down at herself in response to Ailsa's glance. She seemed surprised that Ailsa should notice. "Oh, that. Sure. But I wanted to see you. I didn't want to go to your office. Everybody seems so interested when I do that. They're just too curious for words."

"They're probably bored," said Ailsa. "They're still not used to me."

"They never will be," Camilla said flatly. "You're a rare bird around here. What I wanted to talk to you about was Mary."

"Mary? How is she?"

Camilla shrugged. "Same as always. It is something that happened last week, before your party. I thought maybe I could say something to you then but there was too much going on."

Ailsa said nothing, waiting.

Camilla went on, "You know, Fina talks to her a lot, especially when I'm not there. I didn't think Mary paid any attention to her, any more than she does to anybody else. Well, I was wrong. She pays attention to Fina, at least sometimes. We came home together that day and Fina went in to talk to her. I heard Fina getting excited, so I went to see what was going on. Fina said Mary said she remembered being in Rio. I asked Mary whether that was true. Why was she in Rio? And Mary said Yes, she went there to sing in 1960."

Ailsa gazed at her, incredulous. "What an extraordinary thing for her to say! 1960. That was twenty-five years ago. Does she mean she was a singer then?"

Camilla shrugged again. "It sounds like it. I thought maybe she was just imagining something, that Fina's chattering put an idea into her head. And maybe that's what it is. She wouldn't tell me anything else—just went back into that fog she's always in. She has not answered me since when I've asked her questions. Fina has been too busy the last few days to talk to her much. Did you know that Fina met some people at your party who want to audition her?"

"No. But Dina probably does. About Mary. Can it possibly be that she was a professional singer?"

Camilla said tentatively, "Maybe Dina could find out something about her, if she was a singer. Dina knows a lot of people like that, doesn't she? Artists and newspaper people? There seemed to be a lot at your party."

"Yes, that is true. If we only knew what Mary's real name is. It would be difficult to trace her without that."

They stood together silent for a moment. Then Camilla said, "Well, I thought I'd let you know—for whatever it's worth."

"I'm glad you told me. I'll tell Dina."

That evening, while they were having a drink together before Dina left for an evening out, Ailsa told Dina what Camilla had said.

"She's in doubt, you understand, about whether Mary is talking about something that really happened or whether she is imagining things, under the influence of Serafina's chatter."

Dina took a sip of her drink. "It sounds rather specific—Rio in 1960. That would be before Serafina was born. She is not yet twenty-one, she told me. If Mary is fantasizing, why would she pick a specific date?"

"It must be a date that has some significance to her, even if it wasn't Rio and singing. Do you suppose there is any way you could find out who she is from that bit of information?"

Dina gave her a derisive smile. "Now, how on earth could I do that? There must be hundreds of singers who have gone to Rio to sing. And where would I find traces of them? I suppose there would be notices in local newspapers, but I don't read Portuguese and I don't know any Brazilian newspaper people. That's twenty-five years ago. It sounds impossible, darling."

"Suppose she was an opera singer."

"Mary? An opera singer? Ailsa, I've never met Mary, but from what you've told me about her, it seems highly unlikely—well, unlikely that she is a singer at all."

"I suppose so. She is such a beaten down, defeated old thing."

"Opera singers are not shy, retiring types. They can't be. I'd guess that if she had been such a thing, now she would be less docile, that she would be giving you and Camilla and everybody else a lot more trouble—just as helpless, but crazier."

"Who can tell?" Ailsa sighed. "It is tantalizing to have this bit of information and no way to make use of it."

"Perhaps she will come through with a little more about herself," said Dina, comfortingly. "Perhaps she is getting stronger physically and her mind is awakening."

"I wish you could be right."

"How old do you suppose she is?"

Ailsa thought for a few moments. "It's impossible to tell from her appearance. Her experiences have made her look older probably than she is. She could be seventy—perhaps older."

"Then she would have been singing professionally in Rio when she was forty-five—"

"Or fifty or fifty-five."

"Singers don't usually last that long. Their voices wear out."

"So that would mean she hasn't sung professionally for the last twenty years or so."

"And therefore would not be remembered much now unless she was very well known earlier."

They left it at that. Lighting a fresh cigarette Dina said, "I have something to tell you. I had lunch with Serafina today."

Ailsa looked at her in surprise.

"Yes. I invited her because she intrigues me. She's such a sparkling little character. I asked her at the party. I set a date, a place. I was curious to see if she would come. We had lunch at that little French place that tries to pretend it is perpetually spring in Paris—you know, the splashing fountain—think of the number of tables they sacrifice—and flowers fresh from the florist's. We were embowered in a corner. She was only fifteen minutes late. I had just given her up but there she came, in a dress of real silk and a fur coat—the real thing. A poor student, I thought. How remarkable!"

Ailsa laughed. "Really, darling! She's only penniless at the moment."

"Well, in any case, she noticed my glance, I'm sure, and so was prepared for my probing. We went through the usual catechism—how long had she been here, how long did she expect to stay. I knew already that she had enrolled in Hunter last year. Why did she choose to go there? Oh, because she wanted to be in New York, in the midst of everything—theater, art shows, the ballet—anywhere where the young people are—the young people who want to do something new, something different, who do not like tradition. The rebellious young, I said. Oh, yes, she said. So of course I asked her how her parents felt about all this. Did they approve? Oh, no, they didn't approve at all. She looked at me with that very bright smile. She speaks English very well but she talks so fast that she lapses into Portuguese constantly and then catches herself up and gives a translation of a sort. So perhaps I do not have an altogether accurate idea of what she is up to. But I believe that she persuaded them to send her here to go to college and gave her money for a year's expenses."

"They're well off?"

"I gather so. And she assured me that she had been very well brought up—that her family is entirely traditional in its outlook—that they only agreed to her wish to go abroad to college because she convinced them that she is a serious young lady."

"How could she have convinced them of that? I've

never met a girl less so."

"Well, it's obvious they dote on her and that she can wrap them around her little finger. In any case, they wanted to send an older woman along as chaperone but she got out of that in some way. Now she is AWOL and shortly she says they will discover she is not staying where they think she is and they will become frantic and begin to search for her—if not already. She told me in detail about all the red herrings she has drawn across her own trail to delay their success in finding her. She seems to be enjoying it all, like a child playing hide and seek. They'll never find her with Camilla, she says. Her father is an influential businessman with contacts with executives in large American corporations. I don't suppose she will escape his wrath for long."

"I suppose Camilla must know all this."

"I suppose so. I don't think Serafina would be very good at keeping her own business to herself."

"I wonder if Camilla is fully aware of the trouble she may get into."

"Oh, you and your legal mind, Ailsa! It punctures all the romance. For that matter, how do I know that Serafina is telling me the truth? It could be a tissue of lies. I'm sure she has a very fertile imagination. It may have been all invented for my entertainment as a luncheon conversation." Dina was silent while she blew a cloud of smoke into the air. "Though I do hope that Camilla has enough sense to protect herself."

"How easy is it to protect yourself when you are in love?" Ailsa finished her drink. "Besides, Camilla spends her days and a good part of her nights with people who flout the law, who are trying to escape it. She hasn't the monumental respect for it that you think I have. She knows firsthand that there are sometimes good reasons for someone to evade the letter of the law."

"Ailsa, you sound downright subversive! So Camilla is in love."

"She is sick with love for Serafina. You have only to watch her as she follows Serafina's every move. I have never seen anyone more desperately in love."

"Poor thing."

"Really?"

Dina looked into her eyes, and said softly, "Oh, I don't mean being in love. It's the danger involved. I think Serafina's feelings are a lot more volatile. Oh, yes, right now she is Camilla's darling and she likes that very much. Will it last? I would not like seeing Camilla devastated."

"Nor I."

They were silent for a while. Then Ailsa said, as if she had remembered something, "Did Serafina say anything about Mary?"

"Yes, she did."

"Did she tell you what Camilla told me?"

"No. I don't think she thought it important. But she did talk about Mary. You know, Serafina's style of conversation is to rattle along about everything and everyone. Following her thought is like riding a rollercoaster. You never know where you'll be next. She was talking about how nice it was to be living with Camilla—she's so comfortable there and also she is so free. Not like being with her parents, who are always watching her, she says. At the same time Camilla is always there if she needs love and protection from evil things. That is when she mentioned Mary. She likes Mary, she likes to talk to her. She can tell her all about Rio and her family when she gets homesick. She calls Mary Titia, which I understand means Auntie in Portuguese. Then she added, You have to be careful with old ladies like that. They may be very deep. Let me see if I can remember the Portuguese words she used and not mix them up with what little Spanish I know. She said she is sure Mary is a 'boa alma'—a good soul—cheio de bondade—full of goodness. But nevertheless she probably has powers that she can use for good or evil."

Dina paused to stub out her cigarette.

"Is she calling Mary a witch?" Ailsa demanded with rising indignation. "The poor old thing doesn't need that."

"You forget, my dear, that witches are very well thought of by feminists these days. We're feminists, aren't we?"

"Don't tease, Dina! You know what I mean. Witches haven't lost their reputation for evil with most people, whatever we may think of them. What does Serafina mean?"

"I told her I didn't understand what she meant. Was she saying Mary dealt in evil spirits? She got quite excited and her eyes got big and she said, Oh, no. She tried to explain to me that there are many spiritual beings—I don't know whether you'd call them gods and goddesses—the Brazilians call them orishas—who must be propitiated. They can be called upon to help you in difficult situations or they can do you harm if you are careless in dealing with them or ignore them. There are certain individuals—men and women—who can speak for them, communicate with them, for the benefit of humans. These are called santos or santas. I've heard something about this."

"Are you talking about voodooism?"

"Well, it is something similar, probably. In Brazil they call it macumba. It is a mixture of African and Indian religious beliefs and practices, with borrowings from a primitive sort of Catholicism. Serafina says her own parents were very severe with her for going to gatherings where those rites are carried on but that a great many Brazilians of all sorts go to them. Serafina thinks Mary may be a santa who can exercise certain powers over the people she comes in contact with."

"Good God!" Ailsa exclaimed.

"Or Goddess, remember," said Dina, laughing at her consternation. "I found it a very entertaining lunch. What do you suppose Camilla makes of all this?"

"Camilla thinks she is just a poor old woman who hasn't got any friends or kin left and no means of support, so she sleeps in the street. Dina, can you imagine what it must be like to live in the street when it's freezing or storming, what it is like not to have a place where you can sit down without a policeman telling you to move on, not to have a toilet when you need one, not to have anything to eat without stealing it, not even to be able to go into a store or an eating place because you won't be let in?"

"Yes, yes, Ailsa. Don't get so upset, darling. Yes, of course, Mary is a poor old unfortunate and she isn't the only one. I know you think it is terrible that Serafina should be imagining all this. But, really, I'm sure she doesn't mean to mock Mary. She's just a silly girl who likes to add excitement to her life. It might get boring otherwise." Dina lapsed into silence, watching Ailsa. How strange that the calm, cool blonde woman she had first seen in repose amidst a boistrous crowd should have turned out to have such depths of feeling. It was one of the things she had had to learn about Ailsa. There were fires that burned very hotly under that impeccable exterior. But that sort of banked furnace took a toll and sometimes she had begun to worry about its effect on Ailsa. This tour of duty in a police magistrate's court—a gallant and no doubt worthwhile thing for someone as deeply committed to social reform as Ailsa. But in personal terms she regretted it.

After a long moment of concentrated thought Ailsa

said, "Could you possibly make some effort to find out whether Mary was in fact once a professional singer?"

"Of course, darling," said Dina, anxious to soothe. "I'll try to think of something."

* * * * *

Yes, but what could that something be? Dina sat in her office, a nondescript room cluttered with files, the walls lined with the signed photographs of actors and actresses, stage directors, play producers. She was seldom in it, since most of her activities took her elsewhere. But it was a place where she could discuss business deals and contract requirements and, more importantly, where she had a haven in which to sit and think out problems without much interruption. Her phone calls came in on an answering device. When she needed secretarial services, she knew where to get them.

Who did she know who could remember a singer who toured South America—Rio would be one stop on a tour of the Latin countries—in 1960? She herself had no business dealings with singers and musicians. She had met plenty of them but none that she could call to mind that were old enough to be useful. Those she knew were chiefly young popular singers, members of combos, entertainers in nightclubs and on television. It was not likely that any of them would be of help.

But there must be someone. Her mind slowly found its way to a name: Ed Holder. He was also a theatrical agent but he was one of the oldest and he had an extraordinary acquaintance among people in the entertainment world. Nowadays she seldom saw him, but in the past, when she had been a newcomer, he had been a sympathetic and encouraging friend. Surely he could name someone as a connection, a bridge into the more exalted world of concert musicians and opera singers.

She reached for the phone and was gratified when he remembered at once who she was. She knew his style of carrying on his business was quite different from her own. He seldom met clients for lunch or attended cocktail parties for celebrities. That was doubtless why she had seen so little of him lately. But now he was as affable as ever.

Dina said, "I'm trying to trace a singer who was last heard of in 1960." That was a bald statement, she thought, which might well not be true. But at least she had not heard of her since.

His surprise was obvious in his voice. "Gosh! That goes pretty far back. What do you know about him?"

"Her. She sang in Rio, in Brazil, in 1960. I suppose she must have been on a tour of South America."

"Yes. Rio and Buenos Aires, at any rate. What's her name?"

"I don't know."

"You don't know? Now, look, Dina, how do you know she sang in Rio in 1960 if you don't know her name?"

"That's just it. I know the fact that she sang in Rio in 1960 but I don't know who she was. How many singers would go on a tour of South America in 1960?"

"Search me. Probably quite a few. A lot of well-known musicians and singers tour like that. They've always been very popular down there—people like Toscanini and most of the big opera stars."

"Well, how do I go about finding out who might have been on the tour in that year?"

There was silence for a while on the other end of the wire. Then Holder said, "You'll have to give me a few days to find somebody who might know. I sure don't. Do you know anything else about this woman?"

"She was probably about fifty years old in 1960. That's old for a professional singer, isn't it? I think she was an American."

"And you want to know where she is now?"

"Yes. Ed, you are a real friend."

"Oh, yes, yes. I've heard that before. Right, I'll call you when I have something."

A week passed and the subject of Mary ceased to dominate her thoughts. Ailsa made no further mention of her. She did not see Serafina again. But the problem hung in the back of her mind, behind the events of her day-to-day business. It was a puzzle and puzzles attracted her. When it came to the surface, in a quiet moment, she thought of it in the context of her life with Ailsa. She had never supposed, before they had met, that she would ever place anyone in such control of her emotions, to the extent of setting aside things of importance to herself at that someone's behest. She was generous enough of herself when what someone else wanted fitted easily into her own program. More than that she consciously refused to allow. It was the modern way, the way of enlightenment, to put one's own requirements ahead of any commitment to someone else. To do otherwise was to perpetuate the psychological slavery of women which society had required through the ages. But now she was astonished how all that had gone out of the window when she met Ailsa. What Ailsa wanted took precedence. She knew Ailsa was unaware of this change in her priorities. Ailsa seemed untroubled by these pronouncements about what women should do. Ailsa did things by instinct, by some basic principle of her own nature.

It wasn't that she was not sympathetic to Mary. She sincerely regretted that an old woman should reach the nadir at the end of her life. She saw plenty of these old derelicts on the streets. They were a commonplace of life in the city. They were a problem that should be resolved. But their plight did not touch her with immediacy. It was beyond the scope of her power to solve it.

Holder called her at the end of the week. He said, "Say, Dina, what have you got up your sleeve about this singer you want to know about?"

"Nothing. Why?" She was intrigued by the tone of interest in his voice.

"I've got hold of a musicologist I know, an old fellow who can remember back when Yehudi Menuhin was a child prodigy. He says there is only one singer he knows of who could fit your description who to his knowledge sang in Rio in 1960. That was Magdalena Gibbon. Does that ring a bell with you?"

"Yes, I've heard of her but that's all. Is he sure that she sang in Rio in 1960?"

"Yes. He says he remembers that she did. You remember, she was an opera singer—one of the greatest in this century. Well, her voice began to go and then she had pneumonia and gave up opera. It was one of the great events of the fifties here in the States. She decided finally to go on the concert stage and the tour to South America was her debut as a concert artist. That is why he remembers it."

Dina said cautiously, "I suppose I can find out something about her?"

"Oh, yes. She's in everybody's memoirs. She was a very magnificent sort of character—put everybody else around in the shade. All you have to do is look in old files of musical journals and that sort of thing. Opera has never been my bag but I remember hearing a lot about her at one time. Everything she did got into the papers. She's a legend in opera history."

Stunned, Dina said, "Where is she now?"

"My friend wouldn't say. He was very cagey, asking me who you were, why did you want to know about her and so on. He said that for the time being her friends aren't giving out information about her. It's got me really curious. What are you up to, Dina?"

"I'm not up to anything. I really doubt that the woman I'm trying to find is Magdalena Gibbon. I'll have to think this over. Can I come back to you, Ed, if I turn up anything else I need to ask you questions about?"

"Oh, sure! It won't be too hard for you to find some old publicity pictures of her."

Dina listened while he told her how to find them. When she hung up the phone she sat for a while sorting out her thoughts. This must surely be a wild goose chase. But in any case she would follow up his leads before she told Ailsa.

The first evening they were alone together getting dinner in the kitchen she broached the subject. She explained who Ed Holder was and why she had called him. Ailsa listened with the careful attention she gave things she considered of the first importance.

"He consulted an old friend of his, a musicologist, who came up with the idea that the only American singer who was in Rio in 1960 was Magdalena Gibbon, the opera star. You remember her, Ailsa. I know you went to the opera when you were in your teens. I know I did. I was taken there in the interests of culture. I'm sure we must both of us heard her sing. It looks as if we have a red herring."

"Is she the only singer this man could suggest?"

"Apparently when he thought of her he looked no further."

Ailsa stirred the tomato sauce. "Yes, I went to the opera with my parents. They thought of it as a part of my education and I was not always in a receptive mood. You shut out things when you do them unwillingly. So I don't remember Magdalena Gibbon, though her name is familiar enough. Have you found out anything about her?"

"She was born in 1910, which makes her seventy-five now. She gave up opera in 1960 because her voice could not cope with it any more. That is when she began a career on the concert stage. She sang in concert and on the recital platform for another ten years. After that she retired completely. That was fifteen years ago. She has not been in the public eye since." Dina broke off with an exclamation. "Isn't it disgusting to get old?"

Ailsa smiled at her. "Never mind, darling. You don't have to worry about falling apart for a while longer. What else did you learn about her?"

"She was a vivid personality, one of the great divas of all time. She was called a mezzo soprano, but her voice had an extraordinary range, so that, though she sang soprano roles, she also sang some that were usually sung by contraltos, like Orpheus in Gluck's opera. The music critics raved about her in those days."

"What about her private life?"

"She was entangled in a number of affairs when she was younger. Some of them must have been female, from what I read between the lines."

"Oh, really? Did she marry?"

"No. It seems she lived for opera. She not only had a magnificent voice, she also had an extraordinary sense of the theater—of drama, of costuming, of staging. She re-created some of the roles she sang, re-interpreting roles that had been sung many times before by other singers. She was a force in the development of modern opera, after she ceased to sing herself. Her heyday was in the years just before the second world war—the thirties and forties. The war interrupted her career abroad. But she sang in New York, at the Metropolitan. She also sang a lot in England during the war, as a contribution to the war effort, morale building and all that, with the bombs falling on London." Dina paused and smirked at Ailsa. "As you can see, I took

Ed's advice and went to the Public Library and did a little research." She pointed through the kitchen door to a pile of manila folders lying on a chair in the living room. "You didn't know that was one of the things I learned at Sarah Lawrence, did you—how to do research."

"You're very versatile, darling. I've always known it. Well, there must be plenty of recordings of Magdalena's voice."

"Yes, there must be. That will be the next job, to find them."

"Where is she now?"

"Ah, there's the rub." Dina sought among the things on the kitchen counter for her ashtray. "Ed's informant would not say. He told Ed that her friends are not giving out any information about her these days."

"What's the reason for that?"

"Ed has no idea. Of course, she has always been the focus for a lot of publicity. She was often in the news back during the fifties and sixties. The gossip columnists liked to speculate about her private life. Perhaps she doesn't want any of that now."

Dina got up and went into the living room. "I found several photographs of her, publicity photos, dressed in the costumes of the roles she sang. I have one here."

She looked through the manila folders and came back to the kitchen with a large photograph in her hand. She laid it on the counter under Ailsa's eyes.

Ailsa stopped tearing up the lettuce and exclaimed, "What a glorious woman!" She looked up at Dina. "How long ago was that taken?"

"It must have been taken in the fifties. She would have been in her forties."

"Thirty years ago. There could be a lot of change in that length of time."

"Ah, but look at this one." Dina put a small photograph

on top of the other. It was the reproduction of a magazine illustration and showed a woman walking along a city street. "That was taken in 1980, by a photographer with a candid camera. She must have been seventy."

"She does not look it!" Ailsa exclaimed, examining the photograph. "Who is it with her?"

Dina looked at the photograph. Behind the figure of the singer was another woman, slighter and shorter, not clearly seen. "I've no idea and the caption does not say. But, you know—" She paused.

"What?"

Dina smiled at her shyly. "Magdalena had a devoted friend and lifelong companion—yes, one of those. I learned this from reading about her. I did not ask Ed for confirmation."

"Who was she?"

"She was someone called May Skillings. She always accompanied Magdalena wherever she went and looked after her personal affairs, took care of her social engagements, that sort of thing. There's very little comment about her otherwise. She obviously wasn't as flamboyant a personality as Magdalena. And perhaps she purposely stayed out of the limelight."

"Is she alive now?"

"I don't know."

Ailsa looked back at the picture and then turned away in disappointment. "As you say, we must have a red herring. Mary could not possibly be Magdalena Gibbon. Perhaps the poor old thing was just confused, as Camilla says. Serafina must have put an idea into her head."

Dina's gaze lingered on the photograph. "But, you know, I come back to this. Why did Mary give such a definite date? That's not something she would pick up from Serafina."

In a burst of vexation Ailsa tossed down the spoon she

was holding. "No, it's impossible! No woman could go down from such a height to the depths Mary is in. Besides, what would lead to this? What could possibly happen to her to bring it about?"

"I think you are right. I think Magdalena is probably living in retirement somewhere with her friend. You would think that a woman who had had such a brilliant career would appear occasionally in public. Like that photo in the fashion magazine. You know, 'Among the guests at so-and-so's wedding,' or 'at the gala for such-and-such a charity was Magdalena Gibbon, the former opera star.' Yes, you'd think so. But on the other hand she may just want to avoid publicity—she and her friend. Having reached a good old age, they don't want any more attention from the world. You know very well, Ailsa darling, it isn't easy to escape unfriendly comment, two women like that."

"That's more likely. The idea that Mary could be Magdalena Gibbon seems preposterous, the more I think of it, when I remember what Mary is like, poor old thing." Ailsa suddenly put her arm around Dina. "Are you prepared to put up with me when I've lost my wits and slobber my food?"

"Ailsa!" Dina clasped her tightly to her.

After a moment of silent love-making Ailsa broke away. "I suppose I could ask Mary pointblank if her name is really Magdalena Gibbon."

"Do you think she is capable of telling us? Would she remember her own name?"

"I think I had better talk to Camilla about this," said Ailsa.

* * * * *

Camilla pushed the cart down the aisle of the super-market, her hand reaching out automatically for the brand of breakfast food she wanted, the right soap powder, the canned soup. She stopped at the shelf where the coffee was displayed, hesitating. Serafina said she could not drink any of the varieties of coffee for drip pots or percolators. Camilla had always drunk whatever brew was readily available, wherever it could be obtained, and for her own house bought a popular brand of instant. She rarely had the time and attention to give to the niceties of flavor or mode of preparation. Serafina went to a small grocery nearby their apartment favored by neighborhood Puerto Ricans and brought home whole coffee beans that she ground by hand in a small mill and dripped through a bag. Camilla found it difficult to drink the strong dark brew that resulted.

The trouble was that Serafina loved the supermarket and to bring her here was like going to a fair. Impulse buying must be a phrase that was invented to describe Serafina's way of doing, thought Camilla. She had trouble restraining her from filling the cart with a hundred and one things which, Camilla learned, she would sample once and discard. She was enthralled by the sheer abundance. Oh, yes, said Serafina, they had supermarkets in Brazil and in Rio you could find a great variety of things. But then, she never went shopping for groceries in Rio. The family cook did that. Nobody expected a girl like her, a student with an active social life, to concern herself with the grocery shopping. But here it was different. She and Camilla had their own little casa, their own little kitchen. They must provide for themselves.

"That's fine," Camilla said under her breath, "if you don't bankrupt me doing it." But her protest was half-hearted. There was a sweet joy in giving in to Serafina, a kind of joy Camilla had never savored before. She compromised by picking the moments to go to the supermarket when she knew Serafina was taken up with her own affairs.

Camilla boarded the bus with her armload of groceries. It was an off-hour of the day and she had no trouble finding a seat. She wondered just where Serafina was. She seemed to have an endless number of engagements. She picked up new acquaintances every day, with a reckless, cheerful disregard for the circumstances under which she met them. It was vain for Camilla to protest, to warn her that the big city was full of queer characters, of people ready to take advantage of her innocence, her obvious foreignness. But Serafina brushed aside her cautions. After all, she knew Rio, she said. She was not a country bumpkin. She could recognize bad people, those who wanted to take advantage of her. And another thing, said Camilla, if you go around with all those theatrical people, these people you say may want to put up money for a show for you, aren't you in danger of meeting up with somebody who may get curious and find out that you've run away from your parents and let them know? Serafina laughed and told her not to worry. Her parents would never find her here with Camilla. They would look for her in all the wrong places.

Camilla, getting off the bus, thought, I'm not so sure, my friend. At the door of her apartment house she put down her bundles and got out her key, first taking a quick look around to see that there was no suspicious person close to her in the street. There were often people who were mugged while opening the doors of their dwellings—especially old people, the natural victims of the strong and agile. In the vestibule she looked in the mailbox. A white envelope was the only item. She turned it over to read the sender's name. The judge. Now why, she asked herself, was the judge writing her letters?

She entered her apartment and carried the groceries to the small kitchen and deposited her bundles on the table. She looked again at the envelope in her hand and laid it down beside the groceries. First she must check on Mary. She had not seen her since early in the morning.

Mary's door stood open, as it always did except at night. Camilla walked toward it quietly. She did not want to startle the old woman, though she wondered whether Mary was ever alert enough to be startled by sudden noises. Now she sat in the chair by the window, her head drooping forward as if she might be asleep. Camilla walked across the room and stood silently for a moment by her chair. After a while Mary raised her head enough to see that she was there but did not look up at her.

"Hello," said Camilla. "Had a good day?"

At first Mary did not respond but then she slowly nodded. She'd tell me Yes anyway, if she answered, thought Camilla, aware that Mary's acquiescence to such a question was a means of keeping her at a distance.

"When did Fina leave?" There was not a hope that she would know, thought Camilla, but I've got to treat her as if she's on the ball. I hate to see helpless people treated as if they were idiots. It makes them stupid sure enough.

Mary gazed vaguely around the room and, surprisingly, said, "I haven't heard her for quite a while. But perhaps I have been asleep."

"Oh, you'd hear her all right, if she was in the apartment. She likes to sing, doesn't she?"

Again there was a pause before Mary spoke and then she said, "She has a nice voice. I like to hear it. She says she wants to go on the stage with it."

Astonished, Camilla stared down at her. This was the longest conversation she had ever had with Mary. And what was she saying? Talking about Fina as if she had had a normal conversation with her. Fina had told her that she talked to Mary about singing. Fina seemed to be able to draw from her bits and pieces of sensible information, which she relayed to Camilla interwoven in her headlong chatter. But to Camilla Mary had remained the almost silent, helpless creature she had been at the beginning.

Eagerly Camilla said, "You've talked to her about that? Maybe she will listen to you. I've tried to tell her she must be careful about the people she gets to know."

As she talked Mary seemed to listen at first but presently Camilla was aware that her attention had once more faded. To Camilla it seemed as if a door had been closed softly but firmly against her and her indignation was roused. What business did Mary have shutting her out in this way? She knew she should not let this happen, should not let herself become angry. It was a basic premise of her work that she should never lose patience with the people she was supposed to help. But she also knew that the temptations were great and that few of her associates succeeded in reining in their own frustrations and anger when confronted with the endless provocation of willful, contrary, unresponsive clients. She had long ago rejected the idea that hate should be an element in dealing with people, hatred and contempt and a thirst for revenge, which she had seen manifested by some of her black associates. She realized why they did so, anxious to be accounted real champions of their race in its confrontation with white injustice, that they were unwilling to be thought in any way instruments of a white society. Her own sturdy self-reliance allowed her to defy this concept. She knew that Paula called her a loner and that this was one reason why. Sometimes in herself Camilla detected the germs of the same feelings, and she strove to deny them. She tried not to feel contempt for those who had apparently started out in life with every advantage and had wound up in the gutter through their own perverseness or lack of character. Her own experience of life had been hard and she had achieved what she had through perseverance and a robust self-respect that nothing could shatter. And, she told herself, there was so much luck involved in whether you won or lost in the struggle of life. It was the system that was chiefly to blame, a system that denied the fundamental right of everyone to decent housing, adequate food and medical care—the right, she insisted, that should not be converted into a charitable handout from the well-off to the destitute.

But she was aware that sometimes her rational self was for a moment defeated and the underlying frustrations of her work boiled to the surface. Why was it that Mary seemed to be triggering such a moment now? What was it about Mary that had led her to bring her here into her own house, an impulse she could not refuse? She stared down at Mary now, noting the ragged grey hair that had been left too long untended to respond well to grooming now, the gaunt thinness of her body, crouched over in the chair like someone expecting more blows to her already shattered self-esteem.

She suddenly shouted at her, "Why don't you own up to me who you are, Mary! Why don't you give me straight answers when I ask you questions? You stubborn old white woman! No wonder you don't have any friends. They've all lost patience with you. You'll wear me out one of these days!"

Her tirade brought no response from Mary and she was at once guilt-stricken by her own outburst. How could she yell at her like that, as if it was her fault? She walked out of the room quickly, trying to excuse herself. It was the end of the day, a difficult day as they all seemed to be. And perhaps she was a little bit jealous that Mary talked to Fina and not to her, while depending on her like a child on its mother. Why did Mary affect her this way? Why? The answer came quietly into her mind: because she did not like to be shut out of Mary's attention. Mary had something of extraordinary value, a sort of jewel that she had placed trustingly in Camilla's hand.

In the kitchen she wiped her brow and drank a glass of water to quiet the turmoil of her feelings. After a while her eye lit on the letter she had brought in with her. She picked it up and tore open the envelope. It was only a few lines. The judge said, "I've been trying to get you on the phone for days. I want to see you about Mary. Will you call me?"

* * * * *

They agreed to meet in a fast food place that had booths and was not crowded in the middle of the afternoon. There was a tacit understanding between them that they should not meet in Camilla's apartment or in the judge's office. Camilla, whose meal times were erratic, ordered a hamburger. Ailsa sat with a cup of coffee in front of her.

Ailsa said, "You remember what you told me the last time we met—that Mary had talked about being a singer in Rio in 1960?"

Camilla, biting into her hamburger, nodded.

"Well, I asked Dina if she could possibly trace her from that bit of information. You know that Dina is a theatrical agent?"

Again Camilla nodded.

"Dina has gone to a good deal of trouble looking up singers who were well-known at that time. There is one particular one who fits, as far as age is concerned."

Camilla looked up at her from under her brows but went on chewing.

"However, it doesn't seem at all likely that she could be Mary."

"Why not?"

"Well, look at these photographs." Ailsa opened the

zipper in the slim briefcase she carried and drew out the prints Dina had given her and laid them on the table.

Camilla turned her head on one side to look at them. In the larger one she saw a full-bosomed woman in a long glittering gown and elaborate headdress, a beautiful woman who looked out at the world with a confident, regal gaze. "Who was she?" Camilla asked.

"She was Magdalena Gibbon. Thirty years ago she was the most famous opera diva. That was when this photograph was taken. And this one was taken five years ago."

Camilla, without taking her eyes away from the photographs, said, "You think she's Mary?"

"It is not believable, is it?"

Camilla turned her attention back to her hamburger. "Just a little time on the street can do a lot of damage to you."

"You think it is possible?"

Camilla glanced back at the photographs and shrugged. "What made you think of this woman?"

"Her age, for one thing. She'd be seventy-five now. Dina has found a musicologist who remembers that she went on a concert tour of South America in 1960."

"I don't get this. Isn't this woman living somewhere now where you can find her? Or maybe she is dead."

"I don't think she is dead. But it is true that we don't know where she is."

"Doesn't she have friends who would know where she is?"

"We haven't found any so far. Camilla, what I came here to ask you was whether we could show Mary these photographs and see if they would jog her memory or bring her to some sort of recognition of herself. Don't you think—What's the matter?"

The dam of Camilla's indignation broke. "What's the matter! I'm surprised at you. I thought you had some real sensitive feelings. That poor old woman, trying to hide herself from something that's hurting her, something she can't get far enough away from, and you want to flash these pictures in front of her and say, Is this you?" Camilla choked and snatched up the paper napkin to wipe her mouth. "I can't believe you'd think of doing anything like that. Just because she's reached the bottom and can't help herself doesn't mean she hasn't got feelings—"

Ailsa, surprised by this sudden outburst, was at first angry. Then she noticed that there were tears in Camilla's eyes. "Camilla, what is the matter with you? I certainly don't mean to harm Mary. If you think it isn't a good idea, we won't do it. It would certainly be a kindness to her for us to establish her identity and find out what can be done to rehabilitate her. You agree with that, don't you?"

But Camilla's anger was not yet spent. "It's not her fault she's down and out. What's happened to her could happen to anybody—you or me. You'd be surprised what little it takes to destroy your self-respect, to make you a nobody, a nothing. I've seen it happen, I see it every day. You think you're invulnerable, you think that nothing like that can happen to you. That's not so. That's what a lot of people think, that God Almighty has picked them out for a special place on earth, especially if they've got white skins and money. They're on the way to heaven. That gives them the right to control other people, to say who gets enough to eat, a decent place to live, an education, and who is scum, to be thrown away in the street—"

Ailsa held up her hand. "You don't have to lecture me, Camilla. I don't think I'm one of the Lord's elect. Now calm down. What's made you so unhappy? I've never seen you so upset."

Camilla pushed away the paper plate with the remains of the hamburger, but she did not answer.

Ailsa said, "Let's get back to Mary. Why did you say

you think Mary is trying to hide from something? What do you mean?"

It was a while before Camilla answered in a sulky voice. "I can't tell you. I've just got a feeling she is very unhappy about some particular thing. She's like somebody who wants to commit suicide but hasn't got the nerve to or isn't crazy enough."

The thought flashed through Ailsa's mind, She did get angry when I said she was courting death. Aloud Ailsa said, "A while back you thought she was afraid of the men who were arrested for drug pushing."

"Oh, I guess she still is. She certainly doesn't want to go back on the street. I think she feels safe in my place. That's not the kind of thing I'm talking about. This is something that goes back a bit, that has something to do with why she was in the street in the first place."

"Has she said anything about that to you?"

"She doesn't talk to me," Camilla's tone was angry. "She talks to Fina."

"So you are guessing."

"If you'd call it guessing. It's a real feeling I have. She shuts herself up in herself, shuts you out, because she doesn't want to face something, doesn't want you to know what it is."

Ailsa gazed at her, speculating. Finally she said, "I'm not prepared to dispute you, Camilla. I think you have a real feeling for her, some sort of basic sympathy. That is why you took her out of the hospital. I don't want to interfere with that."

Camilla said brusquely, "I just don't want her thrown into a nervous crisis by being shown some pictures and asked a lot of questions about somebody she never heard of. It wouldn't be right."

"All right. I'll take your word for it. But I'm not letting it go at that. I'm going to ask Dina if she can find out anything more about Magdalena Gibbon. If we come up with something conclusive, I'll get in touch with you again."

Camilla nodded.

* * * * *

It was Ed Holder who called Dina. His voice over the wire said, "Are you still interested in Magdalena Gibbon? Well, in case you are, I thought I'd call and tell you that Rodney Winger is in New York. He's based on the West Coast these days and only comes East for a day or two at a time, when the notion takes him."

"I know who he is," said Dina. "But what has he to do with Magdalena Gibbon?"

"He had an affair with Magdalena back in the 1950s. Now he's an elder statesman in the movie business but back then he was a young go-getter on the way up. He was fifteen years younger than Magdalena and that added a lot of spice to the gossip. They said she agreed to marry him and then jilted him at the last moment."

"Well, well, So what do you think I should do?"

"Call him up and see if you can interview him. I saw him yesterday and mentioned your name and that you're doing a book on Magdalena Gibbon. That's a downright lie, isn't it?" Ed chuckled. "Anyway, it's all I could come up with on the spur of the moment. I wasn't at all sure he would want to meet you. Maybe that's a dark passage in his life he wants to forget. At first he wasn't eager but then he seemed to get enthusiastic. He loves publicity. He loves being in other people's books. He'll do quite a lot for that."

God, thought Dina. A narcissist. But she took Ed's advice and found herself with an engagement for lunch the next day at a fashionable restaurant.

It was a place with bowing, supercilious waiters, palms and other tropical plants, and reproductions of abstract paintings on the walls. Dina, anticipating what it would be like, had dressed in an outfit of the latest avant garde fashion. She had been surprised that Winger had invited her to be his guest. Perhaps this was part of his play for attention. He was actually waiting for her in the foyer of the restaurant and seemed unhesitating in his identification of her as the woman he awaited. It was a brilliantly sunny day with a cloudless blue sky above the city's towers, so Dina had worn dark glasses, which she did not need but which she often used as a costume accessory—lenses set in extravagantly designed, bejeweled frames. She took them off now, as if to signal the fact that she was indeed Dina Raimondi. She knew that suddenly removing the dark glasses had a dramatic effect, since then her large dark brown eyes were revealed, framed by her naturally long, curling eyelashes and silky, thin, arched, unplucked eyebrows. Winger, who had candidly looked her up and down, smiled his approval.

He was a slim, dapper man an inch or two taller than she, with short-cut silvery hair. He obviously had always felt confident in the knowledge that he was a handsome man and that now (he must be nearly sixty, thought Dina) he still projected a youthful image to the world.

"Miss Raimondi?" he said.

"Mr. Winger?" said Dina.

"Surely we can be Dina and Rodney," he said.

Dina, used to this instant familiarity among the people she worked with, shrugged. They walked to the table he had selected, following the waiter. Dina, with canny patience, waited for him to lead the conversation. He was in no hurry to talk about the reason for their meeting. First, they engaged in a discussion of the relative merits of the dishes offered for lunch, Winger providing detailed information on the strength or weakness of the chef. Then, when they had finally chosen—or, rather, he had chosen for both of them—he entered into a long consultation with the wine waiter concerning the best choices to accompany their meal. He can't go through this every time he orders a meal, thought Dina. He must be stimulated to show off before a new audience. While they waited to be served he talked volubly about the reasons for his coming to New York at this time—he was interested in the script for a biography of a major movie star who had recently died under scandalous circumstances. Dina watched him covertly, noticing the brief, sidelong glances he sent in her direction and the lordly gestures with which he accompanied his own remarks. He is practicing on me, she thought. For a woman really to interest him she would have to be twenty years younger. But he obviously appreciated the chic with which she was dressed, the general elegance of her appearance and manner. If there was a candid camera anywhere about to record this moment, he would not be ashamed of being seen in the company of such a sophisticated and up-to-the-minute woman.

He interrupted the satirical comments she was making to herself by saying, "Ed Holder says you are writing a biography of Magdalena Gibbon. May I ask why you have chosen her for your subject?"

"I'm not really at the stage where I can say that I am writing her biography," Dina replied. "I'm really just gathering material, seeing whether it is a feasible project."

"Oh. Well, what led you to her?"

"Why, she was such a spectacular personality and there does not seem to be any book about her. I have found just brief accounts in reviews and in concert notes. It seems a serious lack, since she was really a major part of opera history during the forties and fifties."

"Ah, yes, she was indeed." There was a certain wariness in his tone.

"I have been trying to find people who knew her during her heyday. I had no success until Ed Holder put me in touch with you. She seems to have dropped from sight altogether. Can you tell me where she lives now?"

"Now that's extraordinary! You don't know?"

Dina looked at him, feigning alarm. "You don't mean she is dead?"

He was returning her direct gaze but suddenly switched his eyes away. Instead of answering her, he said, "I'm prepared to give you my version of my relationship with Magdalena, but I must have an understanding with you that I am to see the manuscript of your book before it is published. Otherwise, I'm prepared to go to court to protect myself from any statements you may make to which I take exception." His voice had a hard edge to it. This is his bargaining voice, thought Dina. That's the purpose of this expensive lunch. He wants the publicity but he wants to get his word in first before I have some other version.

She said, "I think I can give you that assurance." After all, I'm not writing this book, she thought. I can promise him anything. "Of course, you realize that the project has developed so little at this time that I've got no idea what I can do with it."

"Do you have a publisher?"

"No, I don't. I need to develop the material a bit more before I can make a presentation to a publisher."

He seemed to accept this statement as diminishing the importance of the subject. "Well, if you ever get that far, let me know. I'll probably be able to help you find a publisher."

"That's kind of you. But, first, won't you help me

gather some of the facts I need? I only know the bare minimum about her life—when and where she was born, that she trained as a singer for a while in Paris. Of course, there is all the publicity that appeared during her active career—her triumphs as an opera diva, a good deal about her personal life—that is, gossip about her relationships with various people." She threw this last in to goad him a little.

The waiter brought the appetizers that Winger had ordered and for a few moments his attention was on the dish before him as he exclaimed at its excellence and insisted that she sample hers and savor its special quality. Finally he said, "You realize, of course, that someone like Magdalena would attract a good deal of gossip, much of it highly inaccurate. I'm afraid I can't tell you much about her life as a young woman. You see, I did not meet her till she was in her forties. I, of course, was quite callow at that time."

"What I should like more than anything else," said Dina, "is to meet her. Can you put me in touch with her?"

He suddenly laughed derisively. "If you succeed in doing that it will be more than anybody else I know has been able to do."

"What do you mean?"

"I mean that no one I know seems to know where Magdalena is at this time. When she finally retired from the concert stage—that was sometime around 1970—she began withdrawing from the usual kind of social life she had maintained before that. It became hard for even her closer friends to see much of her."

"You mean she became a recluse?"

"No, no. I don't mean to imply that. I mean that she seemed to lose interest in her former associations. She kept an apartment here in New York and when she was here she saw a lot of people but in a strictly private way. You understand, this is hearsay information I am giving you. I think it has been thirty years since I last saw Magdalena."

"She has disappeared?"

"That may be too strong a statement. What I can say is that no one I know who is a friend of hers can say where she is. Of course, that may mean that she has voluntarily vanished—just cut connections with everyone she used to know."

"That would be a strange thing to do."

His only answer to that was a shrug. They went on through their meal, talking in a desultory way about the food, about other things. When they reached the dessert he said, "Well, now, at least I can give you my personal reminiscences of Magdalena. I first met her in 1952. I was on my way up in the motion picture business. I had a marvelous idea—I thought it was a marvelous idea, then—that was partly ignorance, I'm frank to say—of making a motion picture of a well-known opera. I don't mean taking an opera and making a movie script of it. I mean transferring the opera stage to film, so that people who never went to the opera or who lived where operas never were staged could enjoy an idea of opera. That has been done since then, of course. There is a wonderful Der Rosencavalier done at Salzburg, for instance. But at that time people still were uncertain about the capabilities of motion pictures— about what you could put on film."

He stopped and took the last spoonful of his dessert. His voice had changed as he spoke. He sounds much more sensible, thought Dina, now that he is talking about something he understands. "I thought I had the vision and the technical experience to attempt such a thing. What I needed was financial support and professional singers. You can't have an opera without real singers. That's obvious, isn't it?"

Dina nodded.

"Well, I talked to a lot of people, my friends, various

musicians and other people in the musical world. It was my first introduction to music critics, really the most extraordinary race of people. I've never encountered elsewhere the varieties of arrogance, extravagant praise, esoteric nonsense, personal venom that I found among them, even among people who set themselves up as connoisseurs of painting. However, they were unanimous in pointing out to me that the sine qua non for what I wanted to do was the interest and support of someone who commanded great respect in operatic circles. Somebody—I can't remember who it was—quite by accident introduced me to Magdalena. It was in the lobby of a hotel and she was coming away from a benefit for a charity of some sort. She was magnificent, as magnificent as she ever was on the operatic stage. She swept in, paused graciously when the person I was with spoke to her, and smiled at me when he told her who I was."

Winger paused, gazing off across the restaurant, obviously now unaware of his present surroundings. "You can have no idea what an impression she made on me. I was used to lovely women—they are an essential element of my profession—beautiful girls, intelligent women, dynamic women. Magdalena was quite beyond my experience. She was truly regal and at the same time most friendly, as if she focussed on you as a personal friend, when you knew perfectly well that you were a speck on the horizon as far as she was concerned. In fact, though I made every effort after that to be around her, she paid very little attention to me. After all, why should she? And that only fired my determination that she should really see who I was and pay attention to what I wanted to do. She was quite amiable and listened to all my wild plans with a very sweet patience. As a matter of fact, as a professional singer with great and triumphant experience in opera at the Metropolitan, at Covent Garden, in Paris, she actually had grave misgivings about lending herself to this new scheme, this new medium. She had a personal manager—I suppose you could call him an impresario—in fact, he had been one in Vienna—who was dead set against it. He was one of these polyglot Europeans, with an Italian name and Viennese musical background, Jewish in origin. You could hardly expect him to see the possibilities of what I was after. I can say this much for him: he was absolutely devoted to Magdalena. The gossip was that he was or had been her lover. In any case, I overlooked his influence with Magdalena, which was a mistake."

Can I possibly remember all this? Dina wondered. I couldn't very well bring a notepad and pen. What I really need is a tape recorder, but he would not like that either, not here in a place like this. She said aloud, "He scotched your plans?"

"At first I was not aware of this. I was mesmerized by Magdalena and though she wasn't enthusiastic, she did not throw cold water on the project. We got as far as setting up a production schedule, lining up a cast—or at least approaching people who might be willing to join it. Naturally she would be the diva. Oh, by the way, it was a Mozart opera we were going to do. It was one of her most famous roles. I was living in a world of fantasy, really. I thought this great scheme of mine was becoming reality and at the same time I was in a fever of adoration of Magdalena." He stopped and looked at Dina with a sneering expression on his face. "I was considerably younger then and I did not realize the special hazards of a relationship with a woman so much older than I—and so much more experienced, in every way. I was so drunk with all this splendor that I actually blurted out one day that I wanted to go to bed with her. I was absolutely amazed when she agreed. I should have been terrified. I didn't know enough to be."

He looked at Dina again and smiled savagely. Dina prudently kept silent. He obviously had been carried away by his own recollected emotions and was being more candid perhaps than he had intended. She waited for him to go on.

"We had an idyll—I think that's what they call such things—for a few weeks. At least I thought it was an idyll, though Magdalena was always reserved about our lovemaking. Again I did not allow for the difference in our ages." He paused to cast a contemptuous glance at Dina, as if to say that he would like to pursue the matter but restrained himself. "But things began to go wrong." A peevish note had come into his voice.

"You never made the film?"

"Oh, no! And that was a very good thing, as I realized in later years. It would have been an unmitigated disaster. There was constant bickering between the people on the opera side and the people with motion picture experience. They simply could not understand each other. Of course, so long as my honeymoon with Magdalena lasted, I was oblivious to these warning signals. But then, as I said, things got completely out of whack."

"Your honeymoon?" Dina asked, pretending that she did not understand him. "Do you mean that you and Magdalena married?"

"Oh, no! We never actually married. I could never get her pinned down to say Yes. Looking back on the whole business I'm forced to the conclusion that she never had any intention of engaging in anything more than a dalliance."

Watching him covertly Dina thought, He's stretching the truth. He is telling me what he wishes had happened—that he actually had an affair with Magdalena, that he went to bed with her. She never let him go that far. He is telling me this so that I will put it in my book for the world to read.

Winger went on. "I think she became disillusioned with the realities of production and she wanted to withdraw from that, too. She was vain of course, like all prima donnas. Perhaps she was not so unquestionably the focus of everyone's attention, everyone's deference, as she was used to being in the opera world."

There was a malicious pleasure in his voice. Ah, yes, thought Dina. I am to put that in, too. It is a clever way of tearing her down.

He was not finished. "I suppose I should have been more aware of what was really happening, but I wasn't until it was all too obvious that she had tired of me and of the whole idea." His hands clenched and unclenched. He was by now sitting sideways at the table, and he moved further away to lean on the back of his chair and gaze angrily out over the restaurant. "As a matter of fact, she never had any real interest in me or in my ideas. That was a bitter thing for me to realize. But it was all too plain when the production plans broke down and the money ran out." He paused and gave Dina a dark look. "There was something further I learned, after I was back out on the West Coast. I heard stories about a little friend of hers who came from abroad and took over the management of her personal engagements and that sort of thing. She could have had something to do with Magdalena's fickleness."

Dina looked at him with raised eyebrows. He leered at her. "Yes—she."

"Who was that?" Dina asked, in a neutral voice.

Winger shrugged. "I never really knew who she was, except that her name was May Skillings. She and the impresario—his name was Francusi, by the way—took over Magdalena's affairs. Magdalena paid no attention to anybody else, I was told. This caused a lot of resentment among her other friends."

There was a world of malice in his voice. Dina hurried to ask, before his mood should change, "But you really know nothing about Magdalena now?"

"No, I do not. When we parted company we ceased to have any further communication."

"Did she—?" Dina began, hesitating.

"Have any other men in her life? I don't know. There was gossip, of course. She lived abroad a good deal after she finally retired from the concert stage. All this is hearsay, as far as I am concerned."

"There's one thing, please, before we part—I realize you find some of this distasteful—"

He switched around to glare at her. "More than distasteful. I have been quite candid with you—but after all, if I'm going to give an account of my relationship with Magdalena, it should be truthful. But I warn you again. I must see whatever you choose to include in your book about this episode. If there is anything I take exception to, I expect you to delete it or amend it. If not, you and your publisher will be in trouble."

Annoyed, Dina said, "You've made that absolutely clear." She saw that he was preparing to get up and leave. "But before we part, there are some practical questions I'd like to ask."

He paused, with the air of giving a moment more of his time.

"She must have property, royalties and so forth. Can't she be traced through that sort of thing? You say no one knows where she is. She must have an income from some source."

He seemed a little surprised, as if the thought had not occurred to him. "Why, yes, I suppose so. There is a lawyer—he was giving her legal advice when I knew her. Let me think. He is a well-known man. Ah, that's it! His name is John Ruddle.."

"Really!" Dina exclaimed. "He is very well-known."

"You've heard of him?"

"I have a friend who is in the legal profession. I've heard him spoken of."

"Then you'll have no further trouble. Well, let's conclude this occasion on a happier note. I have enjoyed our luncheon. If you come to the West Coast, look me up."

In the evening, when she told Ailsa about her lunch with Winger, Ailsa said, "Do you really think he had an affair with Magdalena?"

"I don't know. He was pretty savage in his tone about that part of his recollections. The final rejection still rankles. Perhaps he has convinced himself that there was more to it than there was."

"Hm-m. Well, I know one of the partners in Ruddle's firm. He is Thomas Barnhorst. Why don't you call him and say you know me? It will make it easier for you to get an interview. Otherwise you'll probably be passed around from secretary to secretary until you get down to the newest associate."

Dina followed her advice the next morning. The male voice that finally answered said, "Barnhorst here. Is this Miss Raimondi? How is Judge Cameron? I haven't seen her for some time."

"Oh, she's fine. She gave me your name. I have an inquiry I want to make of Mr. Ruddle."

There was a momentary silence on the other end of the line, before Barnhorst said, "Mr. Ruddle does not see clients these days. He's in his eighties, you know."

"I don't want legal advice. I want to ask him about Magdalena Gibbon, the opera star. I understand she is a client of his. I have been talking to Rodney Winger, the film producer." Dina paused for his reaction.

"Oh, yes, I recognize the name. He has won several film awards lately, hasn't he?"

"Yes, that's so. I'm a theatrical agent. I consulted

Rodney because he knew Magdalena Gibbon at one time. She is your client?"

"Yes, she is a client of this firm," Barnhorst said cautiously. "What do you wish to know concerning her?"

"I want to get in touch with her."

There was another pause on the line before he said, "I'm afraid that will be impossible."

"Well, then, can you give me a current address where I can write her? Or perhaps if I address her in care of Mr. Ruddle, he will see that she gets my letter?"

He was irritated, as if he was being pressed to do something he would like to avoid. "All I can do, Miss Raimondi, is to report your call and our conversation to Mr. Ruddle. I will give you a ring in a day or two and let you know what he decides. I'm sorry I can't undertake anything more."

Alone with Ailsa that evening Dina said, "Do you suppose the old man is senile and his associates cover up for him?"

"I don't think that," said Ailsa. "I've been introduced to Ruddle at a bar association dinner. He has the reputation of being very autocratic, very unyielding in his opinions. He made his name and money forty years ago. He is at the top of the profession now. He did not seem to me vague. In fact, it struck me that he is unusually alert for a man his age. Wait a couple of days and see what you hear from Barnhorst. Magdalena Gibbon must have been an important client at one time. Her name may unlock a door."

She was right, thought Dina, when she received a phone call from a secretary saying that Mr. Barnhorst would like her to come to an appointment the following day. There must be some magic in Magdalena Gibbon's name.

Dina arrived on the fortieth floor of the chillingly elegant new building in midtown at ten o'clock the next morning. There was a hushed magnificence to the reception room into which she stepped from the elevator. The woman behind the big desk greeted her with a voice muted by the thick carpet, the richly panelled walls. Mr. Barnhorst would come to meet her very shortly. Dina sank into the enormous armchair indicated and waited, observing the flitting past of several young women and young men, who came and went like actors on a stage.

A young woman came up to her presently and, bending over her to speak in a low voice, asked her to follow her. You'd think, thought Dina, I was being led to a holy of holies. And perhaps I am. She was used to a certain degree of lavish luxury in offices and furnishings. Some of her clients, now extremely prosperous, liked to indulge their fantasies of great wealth dreamed of in their humbler days. But this cathedral calm was daunting. She was led down a corridor whose thick carpeting made footfalls silent, to a very large room dark with panelling and massive furniture but lit by a glass wall from ceiling to floor that gave her a limitless view of the city away to the distant glint of water and bridges.

Barnhorst came forward to greet her and lead her across the room to the tall old man who rose from behind the big desk. He took her hand in his own dry, cool one and drew her gently to a chair. He said, "I am John Ruddle."

He wore no glasses and his dark eyes were hooded by a fold of skin at the outer corners. She was conscious of a sense of power that seemed to emanate from him. She murmured an acknowledgement and waited for what he would say next.

He said, "My associate, Mr. Barnhorst, says you are inquiring about Magdalena Gibbon. May I ask why?"

"I want to know her present whereabouts."

"For what purpose?"

No beating about the bush here, thought Dina. She had debated with herself what she should say when she was asked this question. To Winger she had talked about a biography she was going to write. Here that premise did not seem feasible. After the interview with Winger and now lapped in this ambience of luxury and professional power, she felt keenly the incongruity of imagining a connection between Magdalena Gibbon and a derelict old woman rescued from the street. She took a deep breath and said, "I really want to establish the fact that she is living and that her whereabouts are known."

She was not prepared for the sudden fire that appeared in Ruddle's eyes. He half rose from his chair. He glared at her with a mixture of anger and alarm. "Are you implying that there is any doubt about that? What evidence do you have that she is not living?"

Dina stood her ground. "I just want to know if she is alive."

"Why do you want to know?"

"Because I have talked to Rodney Winger. You must know him. He spoke of you. He says she has disappeared and none of her friends know where she is."

Ruddle sat back again in his chair. "Mr. Winger has not been in touch with her for thirty years."

Barnhorst, who had been hovering in the background, withdrew once more. Dina said, "That is what he told me. He also said that you are in charge of her affairs. That is why I have come to you. You are also a friend of hers, aren't you?"

"Yes, yes. A dear friend."

"Then you know where I can reach her."

He was slow to respond. "Miss Raimondi, I cannot possibly divulge information about a client to a stranger unless I am satisfied that there is a good reason. What is your purpose in trying to get in touch with Miss Gibbon?"

Well, here it is, thought Dina. "There are friends of mine who believe that a woman they are assisting is

Magdalena Gibbon. They want to find out if this is true so as to provide her with a means of support."

There was outrage on Ruddle's face. When he could speak, he said, "Who is this woman and where did you find her?"

"I did not find her. The police did. She was a derelict in the streets."

His eyes burned as he stared at her and his tone was scathing. "And you believe that a destitute old woman wandering the streets of this city could be Magdalena Gibbon, the most magnificent diva this country has ever produced, that incomparable singer, one of the most beautiful women—" He broke off as if aware that he was being carried away by his own feelings. "It is preposterous that such a person should claim to be Magdalena Gibbon."

Sensing her advantage as his indignation cooled, Dina said, "She does not claim to be Magdalena Gibbon. She refuses—or she is unable—to identify herself. She does say she is a singer."

"Where is she now?"

"At the moment she is being looked after by a social worker."

Ruddle began to mutter to himself. Dina could hear only fragments of what he was saying—outrageous—a scheme of some kind. Presently he stopped and the room was silent. After a while he said, "You do realize, Miss Raimondi, that what you tell me is incredible. Such a woman could not be Magdalena Gibbon. I must warn you that any scheme to extract money from Miss Gibbon's estate on such a pretext will result in criminal charges."

Miss Gibbon's estate! The phrase registered in Dina's mind as she retorted indignantly. "Mr. Ruddle, our only interest is in establishing this woman's identity. If she is Magdalena Gibbon, she should have whatever income she is entitled to. If she isn't, that's that. You're the one who can tell us if Magdalena Gibbon is alive and residing somewhere. If so, that would settle the matter right there. Is she? and where is she?"

She thought he was going to refuse outright to talk to her any further. But some consideration seemed to weigh with him. Was it that she had mentioned the police? Or was there something within his own knowledge?

He said, with great reluctance, "Magdalena Gibbon has not been seen or heard from for about three years. We assume that she is dead. Her property is being held in trust. I am the court-appointed trustee."

"Why do you assume that she is dead?"

He seemed even more reluctant to speak. "She vanished from her apartment, leaving no message of any kind. No trace of her has been found. She was in a very despondent frame of mind. It has been assumed that she committed suicide, though her body has never been found. In accordance with the requirements of the law in such cases, we must wait for seven years before any distribution of her estate can be made."

The room was again filled with silence for a long moment. Finally Dina asked, "You say she was despondent. What was the reason?"

"That is a difficult question to answer. Perhaps it had something to do with her advancing age. She was always a very vital person. She was no longer able to sing professionally. A close friend of hers had died shortly before and perhaps that precipitated a fit of depression." Ruddle's voice was now bland, as if he had come to terms with the surprise of this visit and was now once more completely in command of himself. "One thing I can assure you and that is that anyone claiming to be Magdalena Gibbon will be given short shrift."

"You mean to say that you will not accept any proof that might be available, no matter how conclusive?"

"In my opinion there can be no conclusive proof. This woman you speak of. She claims to be a singer. The world is full of singers."

"She says she sang in Rio in 1960. Magdalena Gibbon sang in Rio in 1960."

"And how many others? On the basis of what you have told me, your claim that this woman could be Magdalena Gibbon is a wild guess not worthy of serious consideration. Or else it is a conspiracy to obtain benefits from Miss Gibbon's estate."

Infuriated but realizing that he was about to end the interview, Dina asked hurriedly, "Are there any friends of hers who might have more information about her?"

"There is no one who would know more about Magdalena Gibbon than I. I cannot discuss this matter with you any further, Miss Raimondi. Mr. Barnhorst will see you out."

He rose to his feet and stood, tall and rigid, looking down at his desk while Barnhorst came forward and with a fixed smile escorted her out of the room. In the corridor Dina stopped and said, "Mr. Barnhorst, I am not a lawyer, but I know that if some proof of this woman's identity is established, it must be accepted by a court of law."

He smiled apologetically, trying to be both sympathetic and noncommital. "In a case like this, the facts may be difficult to establish. Please remember that Mr. Ruddle is very much distressed by Miss Gibbon's disappearance— presumed death, I should say."

"Of course I realize that it would not be easy to prove that some unknown woman is Magdalena Gibbon. But if she simply disappeared, there is always the possibility that she could be found. What were the circumstances of her disappearance?"

"She left her apartment here in the city one morning. She was seen to leave. But after that she has never been seen. She seems to have vanished."

"For somebody who is well-known, at least to a number of people, that can't be easy to do."

"There have been some famous cases."

They walked slowly towards the elevator.

"I suppose you made an investigation," said Dina.

"Unfortunately, two or three days passed before anyone began to look for her. In her latter years Miss Gibbon avoided publicity. She kept her apartment here in the city and she came here for long visits. She did not entertain much and she saw only a few friends regularly. It was when no one could get an answer from her, by letter or phone, that suspicions were aroused. Her apartment was maintained by the management of the building—the cleaning and so forth. She had a maid, who reported that she had left that day and had not returned thereafter. That is all anybody has been able to determine. Her disappearance was reported to the police. They made the usual checks, hospitals, etc. Mr. Ruddle was able to keep the matter out of the newspapers. There has been some speculation from time to time in popular magazines. Some of her friends, you know, believe that she may just have become a recluse somewhere. But if so she has never sent to us for money or help of any kind."

"So it is possible that she is still alive."

As the elevator arrived he replied, "I can't say that isn't so." He waved amiably as the elevator door closed.

* * * * *

Ailsa listened thoughtfully. Dina, still angry, paced around the living room.

"He made me boiling mad. You'd think he was God Almighty."

Ailsa said mildly, "He has had a good many years to

build up authority and power. The law is a conservative profession, especially among men of his generation and training."

"Well, anyway, we know a few more things. Nobody knows whether Magdalena Gibbon is dead or alive."

"The weight of the evidence is that she is dead. Ruddle thinks she is dead. She hasn't been drawing an income from the property he holds in trust for her."

"Do you suppose he is an old lover of hers?"

"Your friend Winger would be better able to guess at that than I am."

"But Ailsa, she could simply have gone away, forgotten who she was. She may be Mary."

"It is a very slender thread that links Magdalena to Mary. This all began because Mary said she was a singer. She may not be. That may be a fantasy of hers. As for other evidence—they are two women of generally the same physical type. They seem to be about the same age. The photographs we've seen of Magdalena show a woman with a magnificent presence, a regal bearing. Mary is a shrunken and stooped old woman, cringing from the world. By the way, I looked up the police record on her. It seems they could not get good fingerprints because the tips of her fingers are so badly worn."

"Ruddle talked about suicide—that her friends think Magdalena left her apartment that day and went somewhere to commit suicide. Her body was never found or at least it was never identified. She could just as well have been murdered. All this happened three years ago. How long can somebody last living in the street?"

"I've no idea. Probably it depends on the individual. Some people have the physical endowment to survive great hardship and some don't."

"But a woman like that, who is used to every luxury. You'd hardly think that she would last long."

"And why should she do it? Why would a woman like that abandon her normal life, no matter how despairing she was, to live like a homeless derelict?" Ailsa thought for a moment, while Dina lit a fresh cigarette. "You know, I've been looking into this question of homeless women. Like you, I've been aware of it. How can one avoid it, living in a large city? But though I have speculated sometimes when I see a woman like that, trudging along the street with no destination, no aim, I haven't thought too much about what could have brought her to that pass. The important reason, I've discovered, is simply lack of money to pay for proper lodging. Women like that are dispossessed because they can't pay the going rent. Once they're out on the street they give up trying to cope with society. They become disoriented and unable to benefit from efforts made in their behalf. The first part of this reasoning certainly doesn't apply to Magdalena. But the second part might. In other words, once out in the street, distraught, cut off from her friends and usual associations, she might have reached the point where she could not sort herself out, couldn't find her way back to familiar territory."

"But wouldn't you say that someone like Magdalena, if she had a serious psychological problem, would have gone to a therapist, sought professional advice of some sort? That's the modern way and she seems to have been an independent sort of woman."

"She could have been so distraught that she didn't think another person was going to be of any help. She was beyond seeking such help. It must have been a very deeply felt, devastating catastrophe."

"That is what Ruddle indicated. He said she was unhappy about getting old. He said she became depressed, especially after the death of a close friend."

"So then she rushed out to commit suicide."

Dina came to sit beside Ailsa on the sofa. She put out

her cigarette and reached for Ailsa's hand. "Hold me tight, darling. I've got a real case of jitters over this business. It doesn't make sense. I've never met Mary but there is something that is getting to me about her."

Ailsa took her in her arms. "You're like a cat, Dina. Your fur gets full of electricity when you're on edge."

* * * * *

All day long, underlying the demands on her attention, Camilla was aware of a nagging sense of not doing something she should be doing. By the middle of the afternoon, when she came to a break in her case-load, she sat down in the cafeteria of the hospital where her work had brought her and drank a cup of coffee. The pause in the day's burdens allowed her to clear her mind for a moment. It was Mary, of course, Mary and her mystery that weighed on her. This was not like anything she had experienced before. She had learned in the course of her experience as a social worker to insulate herself from the emotional impact of the human tragedies she dealt with day by day—from the harrowing feelings that might be aroused by the frightened women with children for whom they could not provide, by the battered women whose self-respect was so badly eroded that they could not do the simple things that would alleviate their own plight, by the defeated old women wandering aimlessly in the streets. At first Mary had been merely one of these, but there had been a change in Camilla's feelings during the time when she was seeking to find out the details of her particular history. There seemed to be no details. That was the first fact that made an impact on her. Mary seemed not to have a history. She had nothing to distinguish her as an individual, so that she had seemed to be only the epitome of the forlorn old woman. She had made no more response than an automaton. Then by imperceptible degrees Camilla had become aware that, without words, without gestures, Mary had become a person. She was like a neglected plant beginning to revive under watering and cultivating, thought Camilla, whose childhood had included a few years of country upbringing. It was impossible for Camilla to put a finger on just how Mary manifested this increasing openness to her. She rarely spoke and then only to answer questions. She was altogether passive, obediently passive, when Camilla woke her in the morning and told her to get up and bathe and dress or to go to bed at night.

It was more than ordinary dependence, more than the dependence on her that her charges so quickly developed. That dependence was something she fought constantly, aware not only of the burden it placed on herself but also of the fact that it was not good for the people who thus attached themselves to her. It was hopeless with most of them. Dependence was the one habit they could learn and the one they were the least likely to unlearn.

No, with Mary there was something else. Camilla often thought that if she were to abandon Mary, turn her over to some agency or other, Mary would make no protest. She would allow herself to be placed anywhere and there await whatever might befall her. When she thought of this, Camilla felt a conflict of emotions—resentment and disappointment that Mary would show no gratitude, no recognition of the efforts she had made on her behalf, on the one hand, and, on the other, an anxious concern at what would happen to Mary. Thinking along this line she realized she could not abandon Mary. There was something she had to find out about Mary, something that one day Mary might tell her. She could not explain to herself why this feeling had such an overriding importance.

Trustfulness. That was what it was. That was what made this link between them. Mary had long since lost any trust in other people. Now, through some strange compatibility between them, she had grown more and more trusting in Camilla. It was as if she had come to assume that there was a special understanding between them, that Camilla had some quality that made it possible for her to trust her.

Ever since her last meeting with the judge, Camilla had been thinking this out. The judge was right. She had been upset with Mary, upset because of her frustration in the face of this wall of noncommunication. The judge was quite right also in saying that eventually some solution must be found for looking after Mary. Mary could not indefinitely live with her. Camilla stopped herself here and drained the last drop from her cup of coffee. That wasn't quite true. As long as she had nowhere else to go, except to an institution, Mary could stay with her. That was not the reason why some other solution must be found for Mary. The reason lay in Mary herself. There was no use continuing to think of Mary as just another hopeless, shelterless old woman. She owed it to Mary to find this key to Mary's memory of herself.

And yet—Camilla found it hard to put this feeling into words even for herself—did Mary want to be found? Did she want to be released from this prison of anonymity in which she now was? Was this strange homelessness, of spirit as well as body, in itself a shelter she had created from the world she did not want to acknowledge?

"And how am I going to find that out?" Camilla muttered to herself and became aware as she spoke that a couple of nurses' aides seated nearby were eyeing her with misgiving. She got up and threw her paper cup into a nearby trash container. If I'm going to start talking to myself in public, I'd better watch out, she thought.

When she arrived home that evening these thoughts were still dominating her. The apartment was quiet as she entered. That meant that Fina was out. She looked in on Mary. The old woman sat motionless in the chair by the window, perhaps dozing, not aware of Camilla, who made no effort to rouse her.

Camilla sat down at the kitchen table. Perhaps there was one way she could try to reach Mary. Fina. Lately she had restrained Fina from talking so much to Mary. Perhaps that had been a mistake. But Fina had gone off on this tangent about good and evil spirits and she had feared that, if some of the sense of what she said had penetrated to Mary, it might have frightened her. She looked at the kitchen clock and wondered if Fina would be home early.

As if in answer, she heard a key rattled in the front door and Fina's fine contralto voice singing out, "Querida! 'Sta aqui? Como va?"

"Yes, I'm here," Camilla called out, having learned what Fina meant by these phrases.

Serafina whirled into the kitchen, dancing samba steps around the room before she came to where Camilla sat and leaned down to smother her face in kisses. Camilla, who had always believed she did not like perfume, found herself enveloped in a cloud of Serafina's. She had grown used to having the apartment and everything in it permeated by the scent.

"I see you had a good time this afternoon," she said.

Serafina laughed and kissed her again. She began to chatter, giving Camilla a rapid-fire account of the people she had been with and what they had been doing. It did not matter to Camilla what she said. It was the sound of her voice, the fact of her presence, the feel of her body, that, like her perfume, invaded Camilla's senses, subverted her sobersides nature. She luxuriated in this orgy of lively feeling, awash in this richness of response Serafina brought out of her, something she had never felt at any other time, with anyone else. Serafina, merely by existing there near her, awoke the most vivid sense of life, of desire. At such a moment there seemed to be no limit to the world, nowhere in the sky she could not soar.

With an effort she brought herself down to earth. When Serafina came to a brief pause, taking the bandeau off her hair and shaking her glossy hair free in a gesture of freedom, Camilla said, "Fina, have you been talking to Mary about being a singer—about her being a singer?"

Serafina opened her eyes wide. "But you told me not to. You said she would be upset. You said I would frighten her."

"Yes, I know I said that. But have you been talking to her?"

Serafina was pouting at her tone of disbelief. "Of course, querida, I have said a few things to her. How could I not? Why should she be frightened if I tell her that I know that she was a famous opera star? She would want to tell me about that—"

"She may not be a famous opera star. That may all be a mistake."

"But she said she was a singer—"

"There're lots of singers. Has she said anything to you when you talked like that?"

Serafina put her head on one side and raised her eyebrows. "You know she does not talk—just a little sentence sometimes. She has forgotten how to talk. I tell her that. She must learn how all over again. Look, Titia, I say, tell me, where did you sing? What did you sing? She doesn't answer me. I know she understands me because sometimes she smiles, just a little bit."

"She's probably thinking what a character you are," said Camilla, tartly.

Serafina looked at her for a moment soberly. "What was the name of that opera star?"

"Magdalena Gibbon."

Serafina made a face. "What an ugly name! Why should she call herself that?"

"Ask her parents," Camilla snapped. "Maybe she didn't think it was ugly."

Serafina repeated, "Magdalena Gibbon," giving the vowels extra emphasis. "I must tell some people I know. They have asked me who she is."

"You will not!" Camilla exclaimed, in sudden anger. "Who've you been talking to about this?"

Serafina opened her eyes wider at her. "Just people I know. They are actors, singers. Naturally they would be interested."

"Fina, you must keep your mouth shut about some things. It's nobody's business who Mary is. You shouldn't be talking about her, about her staying here with me. She isn't somebody for you to make up stories about to entertain people."

Serafina pouted and said peevishly, "Minha nega, you get so cross with me sometimes about nothing. It does not hurt Mary."

Realizing the futility of her protests, Camilla got up and walked away from her. She did not hear Serafina follow her but she was not surprised when she felt herself encircled by Serafina's arms. She knew that Serafina understood very well how to placate her. Serafina held her close and murmured Portuguese endearments into her ear. In spite of herself Camilla felt her body relaxing, her spirit softening, under the touch of Serafina's long-fingered hands. Serafina, aware of this effect of her embrace, kissed her behind her ear and let go of her.

Serafina said, "What do you think would happen if I asked her if she was Magdalena?" She gave the name its romance language pronunciation.

Uneasy, Camilla answered cautiously, "I don't know. Perhaps she will not recognize it because she is not her."

Serafina said impatiently, "That is the way to find out. I shall say to her, I know who you are. You are the great opera star, Magdalena—Gibbon." She stumbled over the name. "How much better if it was something easier, nicer to say."

Still cautious, Camilla said, "Wait till you are just talking to her about a lot of things—the way you do—and then ask her. That way she'll just think it is some of your nonsense. It won't seem so important that way."

Serafina's smile had a trace of mockery. "There, you see! You should always let me talk to her the way I do. You're so serious, meu bem. You always look for the disasters."

After their evening meal, while Camilla cleared up the kitchen, Serafina went in to see Mary, carrying a tray of food that Camilla had prepared. She set the tray down on a little stand near Mary's chair. Mary, who had raised her head at the sound of her entrance, turned away at the sight of the food.

Serafina exclaimed, "Que coisa esta, Titia! You must eat this good food that Camilla prepares for us!"

But Mary kept her head turned away. Serafina sat down on the footrest and dipping a spoon into the stew, lifted it to Mary's mouth. At first Mary simply looked at it but under Serafina's coaxing she at last took it into her mouth. For the next ten minutes Serafina spooned up the stew and coaxed her to eat it. When the dish was half-consumed Mary leaned back in her chair and shook her head.

"Bom!" said Serafina. "That is very good, Titia. You must eat. You will get strong and then you will remember about the time when you were a famous opera star. I want to hear all about that." She glanced obliquely at Mary, wanting to judge how this statement affected the old woman. Mary did not move but her eyes shifted to look at her. Perhaps she does not understand me, thought Serafina.

"I myself can never be an opera star. I don't have the temperament. It takes a lot of discipline, doesn't it? Much hard work. And you have to memorize a lot of words and music. I do not mind hard work but I wish to be spontaneous, to improvise. When you were my age, did you want to sing in opera?"

She was looking directly at Mary now and Mary returned her gaze. She could not tell what was in Mary's eyes. They seemed clear and intelligent, not cloudy and vague as was usually the case.

Serafina, with an air of putting the matter to the test, went on. "Somebody has told me that your name when you were an opera star was not Mary. It was Magdalena. Is that true?"

Mary continued to gaze at her but there was no look of recognition or shock in her eyes. They remained clear and untroubled, as if Mary had not heard what she said.

"Because, if I knew that was your name, I can ask people who know more about such things and they can tell me about you. When you were in Rio, did you sing in opera? My parents may remember you if that was so. I was not born then so of course I can't remember." Serafina found this idea amusing and laughed. But a glance at Mary showed her that Mary's manner, Mary's steady gaze had not changed. With a sudden sense of chill, Serafina shivered and jumped up from her seat. "I will take this away," she said, wanting to get away. She picked up the tray of food and hurried out of the room.

In the kitchen, Camilla, stowing dishes away in the cupboard, turned as she came into the room, surprised at her silence. "What's the matter, Fina? Has something happened?"

Serafina set the tray down, still silent. Camilla asked, impatiently, "Did you say something to her about being Magdalena Gibbon?"

"Yes, yes! I asked her if her name was Magdalena. She

did not answer me, querida. She just stared at me. And her eyes, querida! Such a look! Querida, I have told you about the mae d'agua. How she can come into your home, into your heart, and then go away, stealing everything and leaving you with nothing."

Camilla made a sound in her throat to express her disgust. "That's a lot of nonsense, Fina! I've told you you shouldn't believe in that stuff. Do you think Mary understood what you were saying? Maybe she was just looking at you because she was baffled. You say she looked at you, looked right at you?"

Serafina moved her shoulders as if she felt a draught of cold air. "Oh, querida, she understands very well. She is deep, very deep. I tell you, querida, she is dangerous."

* * * * *

Camilla faced the judge across her desk.

Ailsa said, "I couldn't take the time to see you somewhere else, Camilla. I have something to tell you about Mary." She glanced at Camilla to see how she received this statement.

Camilla made a slight gesture with her hand that said, "Go on."

"Dina has talked to two men who knew Magdalena Gibbon well. One of them was her lawyer—is, perhaps I should say. He has control of her property now. He says that Magdalena disappeared three years ago—simply walked out of her apartment and vanished. That is negative evidence of a sort, isn't it, that Mary might be Magdalena. In other words, Magdalena is not known to be alive and living in retirement somewhere."

"What did he say?"

"He does not accept the idea that Magdalena is alive. He thinks she committed suicide. Her body was never found. Camilla, could a woman like her survive on the street for three years?"

Camilla shrugged. "It's hard to say. I'm surprised sometimes at what some of these old women can take."

"Yes, but Mary is pretty fragile."

"She is now. She wouldn't last a week on the street the way she is now. But why should she do something like that? She must have had plenty of money."

"Money wasn't the problem. She was very unhappy—very despondent—"

"She was trying to run away from herself."

"Ah, now I think you've put your finger on it!"

Camilla pondered for a moment. "That's what I've always thought Mary was doing."

"I see. So what do you think we should do now?"

Camilla did not answer her question. "I've got something to tell you, too. Fina has been talking to Mary some more. She asked about her being an opera star. Mary didn't deny it."

"Did she use the name of Magdalena Gibbon?"

"I think she asked her if she was Magdalena. Fina has trouble with Gibbon."

"And she got no response?"

"Mary didn't bat an eye."

"Do you think she took in what Serafina said?"

"Yes, I do, because Fina got upset—she said she was staring at her in a funny way. Fina has this crazy idea that Mary is some sort of a ghost."

"A ghost!"

"That's not the right word. She thinks she's a spirit of some sort, with good and evil powers. It's got something to do with a religion they have in Brazil." Camilla paused and then said indignantly, "I was raised a Christian and I don't hold with all that kind of stuff! But Fina gets real scared."

"She's afraid of Mary?"

"It doesn't sound reasonable but it's true."

A quick remembrance of Dina went through Ailsa's mind. "Mary seems to have the power to affect people profoundly, even if she is so helpless and remote. It's something in her nature. Well, what shall we do, Camilla?"

"I guess you'd better see her."

Ailsa looked down at the calendar on her desk. "Tomorrow morning, before court hours. Will that be possible?"

Camilla nodded.

It was a mild morning, damp, with a haze lying over the city so that the sunlight was diffused. Spring was finally arriving, thought Ailsa. The neighborhood of Camilla's apartment was quiet, the streets largely empty, since it was beyond the rush hour and children were already in school. Camilla had said that Serafina would be there, though she herself would not. But she would probably be asleep, having got home in the early hours. "You'll have to ring a couple of times to wake her up."

Eventually Serafina responded to her ringing and she heard the click that released the door. Going up the stairs she looked for Serafina but there was no sign of her. When she reached the apartment door it was open a crack through which Serafina was sleepily peering.

Ailsa said, "Good morning, Serafina. Camilla said she would tell you that I was coming."

Serafina opened the door wide for her to come in. She was very sleepy, wearing a filmy dressing gown, her glossy brown hair hanging over her shoulders. What a very pretty girl she is, thought Ailsa. Serafina's greeting was mumbled and once Ailsa was inside the apartment she closed the door and stood uncertain and silent.

Ailsa said, "I can just step into her room. You had better go back and catch up on your sleep."

Serafina gave her a quick smile and went away back to Camilla's bedroom.

The door to Mary's room stood half-open. Ailsa looked in and saw that the old woman sat in the chair by the window with her head thrown back. Is she asleep? Ailsa wondered as she stepped into the room. She decided to find out.

"Good morning, Mary. How are you?"

Slowly Mary brought her head down to look at her.

"Did Camilla tell you I was coming to see you?"

Mary started to shake her head but stopped and said, "Perhaps she did. I do not remember."

"Do you know who I am?"

Mary gazed at her steadily. Her eyes are much clearer, thought Ailsa. They're not so unfocussed.

Mary finally answered, "I think you have been to see me before."

"Why, that's right! You have seen me several times. Do you remember that you were in court, when the police found you? I am the judge you were brought before." I wonder if I should be saying these things to her, thought Ailsa, fearful of the response she might get yet driven irresistibly to tear the veil covering Mary's mind. "I saw you in the hospital after that and, you're right, I have been here to see you before."

Mary raised her hand to her forehead but she did not answer.

Ailsa went on, "I know you are comfortable here, Mary. Camilla takes very good care of you. You are not alone any more, out on the street, surrounded by danger."

Mary's hand moved as if to ward off what she was saying.

"We don't need to talk about that. I just want to assure you that you don't need to be afraid any longer. You have friends now who will take care of you. You know that, don't you, Mary? It must be a great relief to you."

Mary put her hand back down on the arm of the chair. Her eyes, which had looked down while Ailsa was speaking, were raised now to gaze at her again. She said, "Camilla is kind. She looks after me. I don't know why. I am not afraid here."

Ailsa listened to her closely. Her voice was low-pitched and somewhat hoarse but it had a certain resonance. Was it the same voice she had heard on the records that Dina had finally found, records of Magdalena's? Magdalena's voice had been magnificent, with an extraordinary range and quality, remarkable enough in recording; in life it must have been spellbinding, compelling. Mary's phrases were mechanical, as if she was rehearsing words that had no great meaning for her. Yet no one had taught her to say them. And they were spoken as by a woman with a cultivated background, like Magdalena's.

Ailsa brought her attention back. "I am glad of that."

Mary looked away again, as if the effort to converse and be attentive tired her. For a while the room was still, the quiet broken only by the shouts of a gang of boys going by in the street below her window. What can I say, Ailsa wondered, that will lead her to tell me something about herself? Everything she remembers must be painful to her.

In a mood of desperation she asked, "Mary, can you tell me anything about what happened to you before the police picked you up? What happened to you? Why were you living in the street? Can you remember anything at all? I don't want to distress you, but we are your friends and we must know what we can do to help you. You understand that, don't you?"

Mary seemed to listen to her plea with a detached air. She said in the same low voice, "That is all over. There is nothing now."

"What is all over, Mary?"

But Mary seemed to retreat behind a wall of noncommunication. They sat together in silence for a while. Then Ailsa tried again.

"What is your real name, Mary? We call you Mary because you told us your name is Mary Brown. What was your name in the past? You told Serafina that you were once a singer. What was your name then? Who are you, Mary?"

Mary raised her eyes to look directly at her. There was an anxious look on her face, something like fright in her eyes. She did not speak.

Instinctively Ailsa put out her hand and laid it on Mary's arm, noticing its boniness. "Don't be afraid, Mary. You said you were not afraid here. What was it you were running away from? Tell me."

She is frightened, Ailsa thought, but she is far more comprehending. She waited for Mary to reply.

She was aware that Mary was looking at her with much more seeing eyes than heretofore. When she spoke her voice had dropped almost to a whisper. "I cannot tell you. It is too difficult."

Ailsa was aware that the arm she held was growing rigid under her hand. She wanted to say something to soothe, to console, yet could think of nothing. Finally she demanded, more peremptorily than she expected, "Mary, are you Magdalena Gibbon? Are you the opera singer?"

Mary's arm suddenly went limp under her grasp. Startled, for a moment Ailsa did not realize what had happened, until Mary's body sank down into her chair, her head dropping forward.

Why, she has fainted! Ailsa sat staring at her, not knowing what to do.

II

It came back to her as a dream—a dream, not one of the terrifying nightmares that snatched her up into a vortex of fear.

The scene that came back to her was the garden in the south of England. June. The day was so perfect that its perfection was unobtrusive. The sunlight lay on the patch of grass with a feather lightness. Now, in the middle of the afternoon, the birdsong was stilled. There was no one about or at least she could hear and see no one. The tree-lined street beyond the low wall and thick hedge was quiet. There was never much traffic on it and at this time of day none at all, no cars seeking the cul-de-sac at the end, no passersby.

The scene had a charm much enhanced by its rarity—the rarity, for her, of being entirely alone, even if fleetingly. This was an interlude, of course, a curious interlude in her life. What was really unusual, for her, was this reflective mood. She was not prone to reflection and did not seek, as a rule, moments of reflection. All her life she had equated reflection with moodiness. Some trick of conditioning in childhood, she supposed, since one's undirected feelings arose from unconscious memories of the child one once was. In her adult life she had shunned reflection for that reason—she detested moodiness and avoided moody people. Thinking too much about feelings, motives, wishes, one's own and those of others, led only to uncertainty, shook one's confidence in one's ability to act, in the rightness, the importance, the justice of what one had chosen to think or do. Hamlet had put his finger on it: the pale cast of thought that sicklied over resolution. This prejudice came, probably, from her having been born to elderly parents, in a community in which values, habits, the proper attitudes towards life had long been fixed. It was to her claustrophobic.

But this was a reflective moment and she felt inclined to indulge it. There was no escaping the cause of her being here, in this enclosed garden, solitary in this placid town. She could disperse it by going back into the house, busying herself with the letters delivered in the morning mail, thinking about the future, the return to her normal life of music. But she felt disinclined to do those things. Especially to look into the future, with its great question mark. She allowed herself to be seduced by the mild, fresh air, the quietness, the scent of the roses, pink and yellow and red, in the beds that took up the greater part of the garden. She felt an odd pleasure in seeing herself as from the outside in this charming setting—Magdalena Gibbon on an unscheduled holiday, far from the crowded, busy life she usually enjoyed. This idea of contrast added a piquant touch to the moment, made her smile at this fancy of herself seen in surroundings so strange in her personal history.

She was there, of course, because she had been ill. The

fact that this interlude was only that, a temporary absence from her usual surroundings, added to its pleasure. She could enjoy it now because she could look beyond it to a return to activity. She had never been really ill before. It was a new experience, not to be in control of one's daily life. Her career had been built on her splendid health. She had come through the war years unscathed—singing opera during the season in New York, crossing the Atlantic several times when her ship had to go in convoy, to war-beleagured England, to sing in draughty halls, spending exhausting days in trains with no fixed schedule, suffering extreme cold in unheated quarters, extreme heat without the comfort of proper bathrooms and toilets. Disease had not fastened itself on her until now, when all that was past. Now, when she had finished the most successful season of her career, she had been laid low by bronchitis that had turned into pneumonia. The doctor had hemmed and hawed. He had not wanted to say that it might have left her with a permanently damaged throat and a cough. She had turned resolutely away from that verdict. It could not be. It was unthinkable—so unthinkable that she had banished it from her mind. He was aware that behind her denial of the possibility that she might not be able to sing again had been panic. The doctor, hesitating, said it was not inexorably so. Perhaps if she went to some quiet place, made no effort to try her voice, distanced herself from the city and all the friends who strove to comfort her, to cheer her up, by drawing her once more into the round of dinner parties, theater parties, cocktail parties, she would be able to recover her strength and with it her voice.

It was the doctor who had recommended this particular spot, a convalescent home in a small town in the south of England, within a few hours of London. She had accepted the idea, intrigued in an indolent sort of way by the thought of prolonging convalescence in the leisureliness of a country setting. She had rejected at once the idea of going back home to the States. That she would not do until this question was settled. She shuddered at the very thought of such a retreat, as she saw it, a giving up before a fair trial could be made. Here, in a town, really a village, several hundred years old, that had never been stirred from the sleep of ages even by war, was the place to try to recover the self-confidence she knew had been shattered, though she tried to deny that even to herself. The doctor had explained. The house had once been the dwelling of a prosperous merchant, whose remaining daughter, an elderly spinster, had preserved it for her own home by turning it into a home for elderly and convalescent people.

She was finding the experience amusing, pleasant, not yet boring. The fine weather had the effect of turning this into a fairy tale, so much in contrast was it to the more vital, clanging, striving episodes of her real life. How remote from all this, she thought, has my way been. She knew that eventually, as she grew stronger, she would tire of this caught-in-aspic tranquility. She would know when she was really well when the moment came. She would get suddenly impatient, eager to go back to that more familiar world. She turned to look back at the house, a big house of red brick now mellowed by time and the ivy that grew over one wall. The window of her room was the one in the corner. Once, her hostess had told her, it had been the master bedroom where her parents had slept. It was the choice room, for, though nothing had been said by the doctor or anyone else, it was tacitly understood that this guest was someone out of the ordinary. An element in this cure was anonymity. She was to be cut off from all the associations that created stress. She was amused now by these precautions. She turned back to stroll a little further along the garden path.

At first she mistook the splash of color for another

flowerbed of tall roses, perhaps. Then she realized that it was a woman seated on a bench separated from her by a massed planting of rugosa roses. The woman, whose back was towards her, wore a brightly colored summer dress and a straw hat. She must be a visitor, someone come to console an ailing relative. Magdalena walked around the roses and along the pebbled path towards her.

The sound of her footsteps on the pebbles caused the woman to look up in her direction. A young woman, fair and wearing no lipstick or make-up. That was the first thing she noticed—the fresh, unmade-up face.

"Hello," said Magdalena, coming close.

"Why, hello," said the young woman, moving slightly, so that there was more room on the bench.

Magdalena accepted the tacit invitation and sat down. "Are you staying here?"

"Only for tonight. I must go back tomorrow."

"You've come to visit someone? I hope it is not a distressing occasion." Someone—mother, father, aunt—not husband, no, not husband—dying, perhaps of cancer. That was so common a reason for a young and healthy person to come to a nursing home.

The young woman seemed a little startled. "Well, yes—no. That is, I am not here because of anyone related to me or a friend. That is what you meant, wasn't it? But it is distressing to see any old person alone and very ill, even if you're only sent on an errand concerning practical matters."

Magdalena looked at her keenly, not really interested in why she was there, but entranced by her. A very pretty girl. Perhaps not quite a girl, but younger than herself. She could not resist the attraction she felt to her—a ridiculously strong pull, a wish to touch her, as if to see if she was real. "What is your name?"

"May Skillings," said the young woman, looking away

with a little frown, as if embarrassed by the intentness of her scrutiny.

Magdalena was seated half-turned toward her, her hand on the back of the bench. The young woman seemed to draw back from the intangible pressure of her nearness, her gaze. Half aware of this, Magdalena nevertheless did not relax her attention. Instead she gazed around the garden and said, "When I was a child I spent holidays with my grandparents in an old house like this—oh, not nearly as old as this, of course! There is nothing in my country so old. But old nevertheless and lived in for more than one generation, so that you had the same feeling of ancestral ghosts. Rather odd to think of such a place as a nursing home."

"Perhaps that makes you unhappy, then."

Magdalena, surprised at the anxious solicitude in her voice, turned back to look at her. "Oh, no! I never felt any great attachment to my grandparents' house. I was very eager in those days to get away from anything old and mouldy—that is how I thought of it, of my parents' and my grandparents' lives. I wanted to get out into something new and exciting. I have never felt any nostalgia for a return to the past."

"Why are you here?"

"Because my doctor recommended this as a means of recovering my strength. He pointed out that not only would there be absolute tranquility, it would be easier to get butter and eggs and milk and so forth outside the rationing."

"You've been ill?" The large blue eyes were fixed on her.

"Yes. Silly, isn't it?"

"I wouldn't have thought of you as having been ill."

"That's comforting," said Magdalena, smiling at her, and her heart suddenly soared out of the low spot it had inhabited for some time, in spite of the surface cheerfulness she tried to maintain.

"It certainly doesn't show."

"How happy I am to hear you say so. I do not care for invalidism." The blue eyes were still fixed on her. Magdalena reached out her hand—a large white hand with rings—to cover the smaller hands that were clasped together. She felt a tremor in them, as if May intended to withdraw them from her grasp but decided not to.

May said in a doubting voice, "Are you really here to recover from illness?"

"Oh, yes. I have had a bad siege of pneumonia."

"Then I'm sure you must be well on the way to recovery."

"Oh, I am sure I am!" Magdalena felt a twinge of anxiety as she said this. Of course she was getting her strength and energy back. She had no serious doubt of that. But her voice—. She banished the thought and said, "You say you are staying here tonight?"

"Yes."

"You have come on business for someone?"

May nodded. "Do you know Mrs. Harcourt?"

"No. Is she a patient here?"

"Yes. She is quite old and now has cancer. She does not have any close relatives left. It is a question of arranging for the disposal of her property. She owns some valuable paintings. I am an assistant in a firm of appraisers of objets d'art. I have been sent here to tell her what her paintings have been priced at. She wishes them sold so that the proceeds can be donated to charities she supports. This is not my first visit to her."

"Is she able to understand?"

"Yes, but it is a matter of waiting for those moments when she is able and willing to receive me. We don't want any disputes with her lawyers after she dies. I cannot talk to her for long at a time. She tires quickly."

"And you find it distressing."

May's gaze, which had wandered away over the garden, returned to Magdalena's face. "Yes. Dealing with someone like that—sometimes she seems to be coming back to me, to our conversation, from quite a long way away. After all, these material concerns—so important to us when we are well—must seem trivial to someone so ready to take leave of them. Why are you troubling me with all this, she may really be thinking. Don't you think someone so close to dying might well find questions such as mine impertinent?"

Magdalena, surprised at the turn her thought seemed to have taken, pondered for a moment. "I expect it is a matter of temperament. Some people don't let loose of their grasp on this world till their last breath. Perhaps it is because they can't really believe they are dying, that this world could possibly go on without them. I wonder if I am one of them." She laughed as she said this.

The seriousness in May's face did not lighten. "Still, I am uncomfortable trying to explain to Mrs. Harcourt all the factors involved in appraising her paintings—all this talk about money and the best strategy to be used in marketing them." She seemed about to go on elaborating this subject but stopped, looking off into the distance.

Magdalena looked in the direction of her gaze. From where they sat on the bench the side door of the house was visible. A woman in a white uniform stood there beckoning. May got up hurriedly. "There is the nurse. That means I shall be able to see Mrs. Harcourt. They take so long, these sessions. There is nothing I can do except sit there beside her chair, while she wakes and dozes and sometimes is able to hear what I say and perhaps answer me. I must seize every opportunity."

Impulsively Magdalena caught her arm as she stood up. "I'm delighted to have found you. Since you're staying tonight, do you suppose we could have dinner together? In fact, could we have a sherry first together?"

May looked down at her in surprise. "Why, yes, certainly. Where shall I find you?"

"In the lounge."

May walked away up the path to the door where the nurse stood. They disappeared into the house together. Sitting alone on the bench Magdalena found that some of the magic appeal of the garden had fled. She felt alone as she had not felt before she spied May. Abruptly she got up and walked towards the gate to the street. She would walk down to the center of town where the shops were. It was not far but halfway there she found herself breathless and then realized that without thought she had moved with the brisk pace that had been characteristically hers before her illness. For weeks now she had moved slowly, lackadaisically, without the impulse to expend herself. Illness, she supposed, did create a consciousness of one's bodily weakness,—and yes, timidity. But now, at this moment, for the first time, she had forgotten her invalidism. She had expected her body to respond to the demand her will placed on it. The sudden check was a shock. Her mind went on at once to the question, Why had she reverted so wholeheartedly to her usual vigorous way of acting? She knew the answer at once. It had something to do with meeting May.

By then she had reached the gate and she wondered, her burst of energy waning, whether she should think better of the impulse to walk down to the street where the shops were. She shook off the caution and strolled on slowly as far as the small shop where newspapers and magazines and paperback books were sold. She needed something to while away the time till evening.

When she got back she sat in the garden, in a patch of sunlight, reading in a desultory way the mystery story she had bought, till teatime. She was more aware of the passage of time than of the plot of the novel. Should she go in where the tea things would be laid out? She had done so every day as a way of marking the waning of the afternoon, otherwise so empty. But now she was disinclined and picked up her book again, her mind still fastened on the prospect of the evening's rendezvous with May. Finally an attendant sought her out, rolling the tea trolley down the path to her bench. She took the cup offered and said, no, she did not want a scone. Five o'clock. Presently she would go in and get ready for May.

When, after dallying in her room for a while, she reached the lounge, the evening light flowing through the long windows and searching with golden fingers into every corner of the big room showed that it was empty. There were not many of the residents able or perhaps eager to spend the hour or so before dinner in the subdued companionship of other convalescent strangers. The constraint of illness, thought Magdalena, illness in progress or illness only half conquered, gave a certain melancholy to these efforts to provide the normal amenities of life.

She sat down near the windows and gazed out at the garden, where the sun, still bright, lit up the colors of the flowerbeds. The walk had tired her. She could not deny that, but it was a start on the road back to normalcy. It stood to reason that she must first regain her natural vigor before her voice would recover. The worry, lying always at the back of her mind, came forward, as it seemed to do in the evenings, so that she dreaded the approach of darkness and the quiet of her bedroom when the lights were turned low and the sounds of the house, muted though they were, ceased. Perhaps if she could begin to walk every day, the outdoor exercise would induce a readiness for sleep that would—

She turned her head at the sound. May had come into the room.

"Oh, there you are!" May said and came over to sit down on the settee in front of the windows. The evening light gave a glow to her fair hair and pale skin.

Magdalena sat forward in her chair. "Was it a successful session?"

There was a frown on May's face. "I suppose one could say it was. She made no objection to all the things I was told to explain to her. But how does one know, in a case like this, how much she takes in? And if she says Yes, whether that is a real decision or merely acquiescence?—that she doesn't want to be troubled any more by being required to think of such things and says Yes so as to escape from the need to listen?"

She looked directly at Magdalena, her eyes full of worry.

"Does it make much difference? Isn't it true that she has hired your firm because she needs expert advice and even if she were perfectly well, she might have to rely very largely on your recommendations?"

"Oh, yes, that is true. I have spent the last hour or so arguing the matter out with myself."

When you could have been down there in the garden talking to me, thought Magdalena. "I hope you have settled it now in your own mind so we can enjoy our sherry. Do you stick to sherry or would you like some scotch? I have some." She knew that, with the postwar shortages still current, it was as if she spoke of a pocket full of gold.

May looked at her in astonishment. "Really? Well, then, yes, I should like some." As Magdalena got up she added hastily, "I did not mean to burden you with my problem."

"You haven't. But I do think you take upon yourself too much concern. What troubles you is not the financial aspect, is it? It is Mrs. Harcourt herself. Have you known her for a while—before her illness?"

"Oh, no! She is really just a client of the firm's."

"So you see, I am right. What is it the Victorians used to say—you have too much heart." Magdalena smiled mischievously as she said this.

May's fair skin turned a rosy red with a blush. "Oh, dear me! What a fool I must seem to you!"

"Why, of course not! Real sympathy isn't something to make fun of." Magdalena opened the door of the sideboard where she had been provided with a shelf for her own bottles of wine and spirits and took out a bottle of scotch and served two glasses. May said nothing, watching her seriously.

Magdalena looked up and smiled again at her. "You needn't be concerned about me. The doctor agrees that a little scotch before dinner is good for me. It keeps the demons away."

"The demons?"

"Of discouragement, of despair."

May, looking at her smiling face, was plainly puzzled. "Are you really unhappy? Or perhaps it is because you are not quite well yet."

"That logical mind of yours. You seek reasonable explanations for things, don't you? Why should I be unhappy, if I can come and stay in luxury like this, am obviously no longer ill, can obtain scotch—"

That made May laugh. "You're pulling my leg. No, that's not what puzzles me. It's you. You don't seem to me to be someone who would be unhappy without a cause. Is there something in particular that makes you unhappy?"

Magdalena looked away from May's frank gaze. No, she would never confess to anyone the eroding fear that possessed her in solitary moments, the fear that her voice was ruined beyond repair—that the purpose of her life was gone. Yet she felt the strongest pull to tell May about it. "There is something that worries me very much. But it is not something that I can talk about. It is purely a personal matter, something I must solve for myself."

"Oh," said May, as if she felt the rebuff. "That is unfortunate."

"Unfortunate? Unfortunate that it exists or that I can't talk about it?" Magdalena demanded.

"Well, both," said May and lapsed into silence.

After a while she asked, "Will you be here very much longer?"

"I think not. When you left me in the garden this afternoon, I walked down to the news agent's. It was a long way, for me, since I have not walked at all for weeks. It made me tired but I believe it was a first step. I shall try to walk every day till I regain my usual energy."

May nodded. "One comes to these turning points when one is recovering from illness. So, when you return to town and your usual ocupation you will cease to be depressed."

Magdalena smiled at her. "You're very reassuring. However, it will be some time before I can return to my usual occupation."

May's glance was a question.

Magdalena took a swallow from her glass. "I am a singer," she said, in as casual a manner as she could muster. "It will be a while before I recover my voice."

"Ah, I see! That is your worry. Your voice."

May was looking at her intently. Magdalena, disconcerted, said nothing. May asked, "What is your name? You know mine, but you have not told me yours."

Magdalena looked up at her from under her brows. "I wonder if you will recognize it. I am Magdalena Gibbon." As she spoke she raised her head to look directly at May.

May opened her eyes wide and an expression of delight appeared on her face. "Are you really? I thought it surely could not be!"

Magdalena looked at her uncertainly. May gazed at her for a long moment. "I've not heard you sing in opera, only in concert. During the war you sang in a benefit for displaced artists, did you not? Someone gave me a ticket. At that time I could not have afforded it otherwise. Ah, now I understand fully."

"You understand what?"

"Why I knew you as someone unusual at first glance. Then I thought I recognized you and yet I could not believe it—that you would be here."

Magdalena laughed, delighted. May was obviously not an intentional flatterer. "And why not?"

"To find you here—like this. Oh, no, it seemed impossible. You must be magnificent in opera. You have not sung in this last season at Covent Garden, have you?"

"No." The momentary happiness left Magdalena. "I fell ill at the very beginning of the season."

"And now you are worried because your voice may be affected."

"I am told that in order not to risk ruining it altogether I must be very slow about returning to singing. Opera especially is a great strain. It demands much of a singer besides singing."

A soft chime sounded somewhere in the house. May looked at her for an explanation.

"That was the first warning bell for dinner. We have time for a little sweetener."

She was pleased that May allowed her to add a few drops to her glass. May asked, "Does that mean that you will not be singing next season?"

"I don't know."

"How tiresome that must be, not to know. Are you staying on this side of the Atlantic?"

"I am undecided. It depends on how this question of

my voice comes out. There is nothing to take me back to America if I do not have professional commitments."

"No family?"

"Well, yes, if you mean by that my parents. But I cannot conceive of paying them more than a brief visit— especially in my present frame of mind. They would drive me mad and I'm sure I would be a disruptive presence in their lives."

"Really? They are not sympathetic?"

"Oh, I suppose they would be sympathetic enough about my illness. They would regret that my career might be finished, for my sake. They would certainly not understand what this would mean to me, however."

"They are not proud of you? You are a very great artist."

Magdalena gave her a brooding look. "Why, I suppose that, now, they are, in their own way. They don't value the same things I do."

"Not music, not opera?" There was genuine puzzlement in May's voice.

"Yes, of course. They are cultivated people. They appreciate music, opera. But, you see, opera singers are not members of one's own family. My parents are not people who like public notice of any sort. They think of it as notoriety."

"Like being a movie star?"

"Exactly. Or perhaps not quite as bad. In any case, I have been away from them for so long that I do not fit into their lives any more. Brief visits, yes. I have lived in a different world from theirs for a long time, one they don't really approve of."

May was looking at her speculatively. "Did you leave home in order to become a professional singer?"

"How did you guess?" Magdalena asked, mockingly.

"Did it make you unhappy, when you were younger, to leave your parents?"

Magdalena was aware of the deliberate probing of her questions. She smiled at May with a mischievous light in her eyes. "What would you say if I said No? I'll be quite truthful. I was not unhappy. In fact, I was very happy. I felt free! I felt I had achieved a goal—the first on my way to the sort of life I wanted. I had tried all through my adolescence to provoke my parents into seeing me as myself, not just as their child. They thought that no matter how naughty I was, how rebellious, eventually I would be like them, living a muted kind of life, not really doing anything that would give rise to deep feeling, upheavals in the emotions, which they greatly distrusted. I was not like that at all. I wanted to take life with both hands. I wanted excitement, I wanted really to know other people, to find out what they were really like, what they really thought, not what they pretended to think. I could not get them to understand that."

"You were an upsetting child to your parents, weren't you?"

"Oh, yes. I enjoyed upsetting them—and my grandparents, my aunts, my cousins. So when I got old enough and had the chance, I left home."

"How?"

"I had an uncle who had been out in the world. He knew I could sing—I had had music lessons for years because it was obvious I had a gift for music and being musical was an acceptable thing for a girl like me. He introduced me to a friend of his—she was a well-known voice coach. She discovered that I was gifted with natural voice placement: I knew without training how to project my voice, how to breathe. I did not have to learn these two essentials as many singers do. Years before she had been an opera singer herself and she realized that I had an unusual range in my voice—that I could sing as a soprano and also as an alto. She taught me carefully, in order not to spoil these natural gifts. It was only later that I realized how very fortunate I was that she was my first voice teacher. She saw also that I had a natural dramatic ability and an aptitude for memorizing the music and words of songs. Opera, she said, should be my goal, but to get there I must learn to work very hard. If I worked hard not only in memorizing the music and the words, but in trying to understand the emotions the composer had tried to convey, then I could learn to project my own musical image of a role. In that way I could dominate my audience, require my listeners to feel the emotional impact of my singing. Oh, she was a wonderful woman! And she was quite convinced that I had the natural endowment to reach the goal she foresaw."

"She must have been. But how did you manage to study with her? Did your parents approve?"

"Oh, they knew nothing about it! My uncle paid for my lessons. He was very impressed with what his friend said about me. My parents knew I was taking singing lessons. They never understood anything beyond that. When my voice teacher arranged for me to sing in a musical show—it was a small affair but a professional one—I went ahead and did it without telling them. When they found out they had me on the carpet. I defied them. I said I had an offer for a contract to sing with a musical company—it was the result of my being in the musical play. It was a summer company that toured resorts in the mountains where people wanted entertainment in the evenings after a day of fishing, climbing woodland trails, that sort of thing. They would have none of it. I was to stop immediately and get ready to go to a private school in the autumn."

"Did they disinherit you?"

"I pointed out that I could support myself. No, they

didn't cut me off with a shilling." Magdalena laughed, the hearty, full-throated laugh that went through May like a wave of warmth and then made her shiver, as Magdalena could see. "No. What do you suppose they did? They said that since I was determined on this madness, they would give me an allowance and would pay for me to go to Peabody Institute in Baltimore. It was all done more in sorrow than in anger. Oh, how I enjoyed that confrontation! This was something real and it was such sweet triumph!"

"It was very generous of them," said May, faintly rebuking. "They really did not need you, did they?"

"Need me?" Magdalena looked at her in surprise. "That thought did not occur to me. In fact, it hasn't occurred to me till now. No, I suppose they didn't and that was at the bottom of my feeling about them, about wanting to escape from them."

"And what happened after that?"

Magdalena got up from her chair and came to sit beside her on the settee. "You know, by the time I left school I was financially independent. I went to Paris, with letters of recommendation from my teachers to teachers there. I had no difficulty in finding the right coach to take me—a famous one who was not easily available to young singers. Everything went like a charm. I knew no sort of check in what I wanted to do. The world was my oyster."

"You were in Paris alone?"

Magdalena nodded. "My uncle came and went. He traveled a lot and he soothed my parents. They had no idea what sort of life I led."

"Were you very wild?"

Magdalena's eyes sparkled as she looked down at her. "Oh, it was not as bad as I pretended! I lived with a family of musicians. It is true that their outlook on life was very different from my parents'." She took May's chin in her fingers. Their lips hovered close together, May's inviting and yet retreating. Finally Magdalena straightened up again and May settled back where she sat.

The soft chime sounded again. Without a further word May got up and walked towards the door.

In the dining room they were no longer alone. Several people came in and sat at the long table. Some of them were entirely silent. One or two murmured an almost inaudible greeting as they sat down and then lapsed into silence. Magdalena, used to them, paid no attention. May, with an anxious glance around, accepted the muted atmosphere.

Watching her, Magdalena said, "You've not spent the night here before?"

"No," said May.

The maid, coming in to place dishes on the sideboard and then to hand around plates, created a slight bustle. Otherwise the meal passed in silence.

When it was over Magdalena got up, saying to May, "There will be coffee and tea in the lounge. Would you prefer to come to my room?"

May murmured Yes and followed her across the vestibule and up the stairs. They entered the big corner room. The long daylight of the midsummer evening lingered in the corners, the last glow of the sun shining softly on the ceiling. Magdalena raised her hand to switch on the lamp, glancing at May as she did so. May, as if not fully conscious of what she was doing, barely shook her head.

Magdalena stepped over to her and took her hand. "Come and sit over here." She led her to a love-seat placed before the window. As they sat down the fading light caught the bright strands of their hair and tinted their faces with a youthful blush.

Magdalena raised her hand and touched May's hair. "How old are you?"

"Thirty."

"I'm forty."

May looked at her for a long moment. "You don't seem that old. Oh, no! That is not it. You're not any age. You've always been like this. You'll never be different."

"Are you so sure? Are you a witch? Yes, you must be, you have bewitched me."

May was no longer looking at her. She was gazing out into the darkening garden, where the roses glowed dimly like specters. She seemed to struggle to express some feeling that filled her heart but was unsuccessful. Hesitantly she raised her hand to touch Magdalena's face. Magdalena seized it and kissed the palm. They sat for a while longer in silence.

Then May asked, "What did you do after you were in Paris?"

"I went back to New York. I had a chance to try for the Metropolitan Opera. My luck held. I was offered a role. I went on from there, singing in New York, a few times here at Covent Garden, several times in Paris. I was ready to try Italy but the war came along and I went back to New York. During the war I came back here to give concerts, like the one you heard. I don't need to tell you that life in wartime was very trying—draughty dressing-rooms, poor protection from bad weather when one traveled—irregular eating, not much real rest. I stood it all very well at the time—I've always been able to rely on my body. I've never worried about my health. But in the end, after the strain was over, I became ill, and now you see—"

May nodded, hearing the thread of anxiety in her voice.

Aware that it was there and that she was allowing May into that closely guarded chamber where she kept vigil for her voice, Magdalena went on, "I never meant to admit to anyone that I am frightened, that I have nightmares—"

May cut in, as if she had not heard, "Is your name really Magdalena?"

Surprised, Magdalena said, "Of course not—that is, if you mean, is it the name my parents gave me. Can you imagine such people as they giving their child such a name—such a foreign, such an outlandish name? But of course you don't know them. You can't appreciate the incongruity."

"You gave it to yourself?"

"Yes." Magdalena's eyes were dancing with mischief. "I wanted something shocking—shocking in my world. It is a perfectly good name for an Italian or a Spanish woman. But exotic to my people and somehow suggesting something scandalous—the Bible, no doubt. They would not see her as the penitent, only the whore."

"What was your name, then?"

"Well, the first Magdalene was a Mary, wasn't she?"

"Then you are Mary? The same as I, really, since May is Mary."

"So it is."

"I cannot call you Magdalena," said May with great decision. "Mary is more natural."

"But don't you think that Magdalena is a good name for an opera singer?" Magdalena asked, teasing.

May looked at her gravely. "It makes you sound like a character in an opera."

"And that is why you can't call me that."

"Well, yes. You are very real to me."

Magdalena sat turned sideways on the love-seat, her elbow resting on its back, her hands clasped. She suddenly unclasped them and put her arms around May. "How dear you are!"

In the almost-dark May turned her face to her, not moving in her embrace. Their lips sought each other's. Magdalena, at once overwhelmed with desire, caught her closer and thrust her tongue between May's lips, searching confidently within her mouth. May, receptive, did not stir but seemed to drink as at a spring.

When Magdalena drew slowly back, May said, with a little sigh, "I've never had a kiss like that before."

In the darkness Magdalena saw her face only as a palely luminous tone of color. She leaned forward again to kiss her cheek, her ear, her throat. Still May sat passive, as if absorbing her eagerness, the warmth of her desire. When Magdalena paused, she said, "I like that very much."

Magdalena, unable to sit still any longer, let go of her and reached to turn on the lamp by the love-seat. In its sudden glow she scrutinized May. There was no change in May's composure but her stillness was betrayed by the blush that made her skin pink, even down her throat into the neckline of her blouse.

"Come, May. Let's take our clothes off. I want to be in bed with you."

May looked at her with surprise. But she did not protest when Magdalena began unbuttoning her blouse. She seemed to watch with wondering detachment while Magdalena took off her clothes, stripped off her stockings, pulled her up from the love-seat and passed her eager, searching hands over May's white body, fresh and cool in the air that came in the window. She let herself be led over to the bed, where the maid had earlier turned down the covers, and sat there, watching with candid interest as Magdalena undressed quickly and came to get into the bed beside her. Magdalena lay down beside her and for a moment they neither of them moved until Magdalena once more put her arms around her and began to kiss her, first her face and neck, and then, pulling her down beside her on the bed, her breasts, her stomach. May lay quiet under the touch of her hands, her lips, but not passive. To Magdalena it felt as if she was drinking up the tender caresses. Magdalena paused and raised her head so that she could see May's face. She had never before felt anyone so still under her touch and yet so alive. May's eyes were open but she seemed to gaze without seeing at the ceiling.

Magdalena said softly, "May," and May moved her head so as to look at her from under half-closed eyelids. Magdalena raised herself to kiss her on the lips, a long, slow kiss. Then she sank down beside May, her head on the pillow. May whispered into her ear, "Just be still right here close to me. I must feel you. I must take you into myself." Magdalena obeyed, aware, with wondering surprise, that the hot eagerness that had driven her to take May out of her clothes and bring her into bed had faded into a delicious melting into the warmth of the desire she had awakened in May. She held May's body close to her own, feeling the touch of their skins along their thighs, their stomachs, their breasts, felt the beat of May's blood against her own.

All this seemed to merge, without conscious direction from either of them, into the moist intimate touching, seeking, exploring, as her fingers first sought May's secret treasure, moist, welcoming, and eventually May's fingers found her own hot, anxious cave of pleasure. Beyond the lamplight, beyond the open window, the summer night lay quiet, moonlit, its soft breath reaching them in the ecstasy of their embrace.

They lost the sense of time and were not really aware when sleep overtook them. It was only when the early daylight began to pale the glow of the lamp that they roused from this deeply dreaming state. They lay still, slowly realizing that the night had fled and with it the profound sense that they were one, not two.

May said, "It's morning."

Magdalena said, "Yes, it's daylight," and heard the regretful note in her own voice.

May lay on her back, gazing at the ceiling. "My love, you've gone to my very marrow." She raised herself on her elbow. "It is you. It could not be anyone but you."

Magdalena, under the gaze of her grave eyes, stilled the words that rose first to her lips, "How do you know, since you have never been loved by anyone else?" But even as the words rose and died she knew that they were false.

May, with her uncanny insight into her innermost thoughts, said, "I know what you're thinking: How can I know since I've never loved anyone else? But it is not a comparative matter. How I love you is absolute, incomparable."

The certainty with which May spoke made Magdalena silent. After a few moments she reached over to touch May, whose head had sunk back into the pillow. May's fingers touched her cheek, and May said, "Dearest," and they were silent again.

After a while, by common consent they got up and began to bathe and dress.

May said, "I expect I had better go to my room before the maids are about."

Magdalena said, turning out the pale lamp, "It's quite a while till breakfast. Shall we meet out in the garden presently?"

"Why, yes, and then we can talk."

Talk? Magdalena did not question what she meant. Half an hour later she walked up and down the garden path near the seat where she had first seen May. Talk about what? She was puzzled by her own feelings, somewhat apprehensive of what May might say about their night together. In the clear light of the bright summer day the mysterious quality of the night became vivid but remote, like a clearly remembered dream. If May had never spent such a night before, she might well have a number of emotions—chagrin, perhaps, embarrassment, misgiving. But none of these things seemed to apply to May. Why? Because—her answer seemed to come of itself—May did not fit into any category of experience she herself had ever had. May was no companion in a pleasurable game, played with one eye to outward effect, embellished with passionate words vowed with tongue in cheek—a game she herself had played numerous times before with partners as uncommitted as herself. She had never wanted such a commitment but she was committed to May now.

Her thoughts broke off as she saw May coming down the path toward her. Yes, she was a pretty young woman, but as Magdalena thought this she also thought, But that has nothing really to do with it. She is May, uniquely May.

May said as she reached her, "Do you know when you are going back to town?"

Taken aback by the abruptness of the question, Magdalena hesitated. "Why, I have no definite date. I am staying here by the week. Before long I must go up to town to check with the doctor. I suppose what he says will determine how much longer I stay."

"You're dreading that visit. You're afraid that he will not give you good news about your voice."

Under May's direct gaze she said meekly, "Yes."

They sat down on the bench. May seemed lost in thought and Magdalena waited uneasily for her to speak. Finally May said, "I wish you knew more definitely." She glanced at her wrist watch. "It is seven o'clock. I must take the half-past eight train to town at the latest."

"Then you must have some breakfast early. Or do you eat breakfast?" How little I know about her, thought Magdalena, and yet how much.

"Oh, yes. I inquired. They place breakfast on the sideboard in the dining room at half-past seven. The maid brought me tea right after I got back to my room. I was lucky I was not ten minutes later getting back there."

Magdalena laughed at her seriousness. "As far as the maid is concerned, you could always have come out here for a breath of air."

"I hadn't thought of that."

No, you wouldn't, thought Magdalena. You're not used to subterfuges.

"Besides, it didn't seem important," May added.

"It would have been a joke if the maid had come to my room half an hour earlier," said Magdalena, mischievously.

May looked at her gravely. "You wouldn't really have minded."

"I would have minded somebody interrupting us."

May did not say anything further and they sat together without thought of the time until Magdalena remembered and said, "I expect we had better go in so that you can have some breakfast."

May got up without a word and went with her into the house.

The dining room was empty and they sat at a small table by the window, having served themselves at the sideboard. After a few bites May suddenly asked, "Are you married?" Her eyes were on Magdalena's hand, which this morning was bare of rings.

"No."

"But have you been? Are you a widow?"

The idea was so strange to her that Magdalena laughed. "Oh, no! No, I have not been—married."

Her tone was purposely ambiguous. May seemed to pick up the nuance in her voice and dropped the subject. Instead, she said, "I shall always be able to follow you in newspaper accounts. I have ever since I heard you sing that one time."

Abashed, Magdalena said, "Oh, I shall give you an address! But, come to think of it, I haven't a clue as to how to find you once you leave here. I know your name, of course, but I shall need a little more than that."

May lifted her purse onto her lap and began to

rummage among its contents. She found a business card
and handed it across the table to Magdalena. "That is the
firm of appraisers I work for. I'm there from nine or so
until five or later."

Magdalena, holding the card in her fingers, looked at
her ironically. "What earthly use is this to me? I haven't
anything I want appraised. Where do you live?"

May said patiently, "If you are in London, that is
where you can reach me. It would be better if you got in
touch with me there."

"I see." Magdalena put the card away in her own purse
and then took out an old envelope and wrote on it. "I stay
at this hotel," she said, putting the envelope down by
May's plate. "You may call me day or night, when I reach
there."

"And how will I know when you reach there?"

Magdalena laughed. "Don't worry! You will know as
soon as I leave here. In fact, I shall hang onto you as long
as I can."

She suddenly reached across the table and took May's
hand in her own. May, startled, glanced about to see if
they were alone.

"There's no one about," Magdalena reassured her. "Besides, no one would wonder if they saw me holding your
hand. I can't let you go so coldbloodedly. Come up to my
room."

"No," said May decidedly, "Come to mine. I shall go
up first. You come up in a few minutes."

Magdalena obeyed, watching her get up from the table
and leave the room. She sat for a moment longer, idly
nibbling on a piece of toast. She was nonplussed. For years
now she had been used to controlling whatever she did
without consideration of anyone's demands. Overnight this
had changed. The hours with May had brought into her life
an entirely new quality—an awareness of the fact that

May's wishes had as great weight with her as her own. How odd to find so suddenly another dimension to her life, an extension into the life of another. Before this, when she had had affairs, the intrusion of someone else into her intimate life or hers into the other's had had definite and easily reached limits. With May there seemed to be no limit.

After a few minutes, when someone else came into the dining room, she rose and went up the broad staircase. When she reached the landing she paused. She really did not know which was May's room. She went slowly down the corridor, wondering what she should do to identify it. But May had remembered that she would not know and had left her door ajar. Magdalena stopped before it and tapped on the panel, relieved when May's voice said, "Come in. Close it behind you, please."

Magdalena did as she said. May stood beside a small traveling bag she had just closed and locked. They stood and looked at one another.

Presently May said, "A cab is coming to take me to the station. He'll be here directly."

"Shall I come with you?"

"Oh, no! I need time to collect myself. I cannot do that if you're with me."

Magdalena said nothing, waiting.

May came over to her and put her arms around her neck, looking up earnestly into her face. "I wish I knew what to think."

Magdalena, putting her arms around her, asked, puzzled, "About what?"

"About you—about myself—"

"About us? About last night?"

May was still gazing at her seriously. "Do you love me?"

Magdalena caught her tightly against herself. "I've never

loved anybody like this. May, this is as strange to me as it is to you. It has not happened before."

May gave a little sigh, breathing against Magdalena's neck. "If you did not do it because you loved me, it would be dreadful."

Magdalena loosened her grasp so as to look down at her directly. "Yes, I've been to bed with people who attracted me. But I know now I never loved any of them."

"It would be humiliating, degrading to me, if you felt that way about me. I love you very much. I haven't known till now what loving someone meant. I have heard of it. I have never wanted to marry. The idea of a man possessing me was horrible. It is twice so now."

Magdalena, treading carefully in unknown territory, said quietly, "May, I'm not just talking. My life has been changed since I first saw you yesterday."

The slight resistance in May's body ceased. She leaned against Magdalena and pressed her face against her throat. "It's so extraordinary. It is as if I had been waiting for you and did not know it until you appeared."

"Perhaps that's what has happened."

Then as if by tacit agreement they let go of each other and May picked up her hat and put it on. There was a knock on the door and the maid's voice came through the panel, "The cab is here, madam."

"I'm coming at once," May responded and suddenly caught Magdalena in her arms for a last kiss. Magdalena held her fiercely, so long that May pushed her gently away. "You'll let me know when you come to town, of course. Goodbye for now, my darling."

* * * * *

She could not remember just how many more days she spent in the convalescent home. She remembered impatience with her physical weakness. She remembered urging herself to be prudent—walking too far one day meant another day's delay in recovering her strength. Rome, said the nurse who checked her each afternoon, was not built in a day.

But she also remembered a certain state of bemused indolence, when she enjoyed the unheeded hours, thinking of May. May wrote her each day, odd, short, cryptic letters that seemed to say more than the words would have meant to anyone else reading them. They seemed to Magdalena intensely personal, intensely intimate, yet in substance they were chiefly about May's day to day activities. She never mentioned her life outside of her working day. Where did she live, she wondered, and with whom? And was there a real, a practical reason, why she did not speak of this? Or was it that May did not want any contact between herself and whoever it was who shared May's life otherwise? May was not devious or secretive. She was sure of that, so that this mysteriousness did not have its origin in a wish to deceive or tantalize. Did it arise from fear or from some other reluctance?

By the time she was able to take the train up to town she was in a fever of impatience. First she must visit the doctor—her impatience to see May warring with her anxiety over what the doctor would say about the state of her health and the question of her returning to singing. She told no one about her trip to town. She wanted no one to know. She did not want to be besieged, surrounded by the people who made up her normal world. She had been out of touch with them, both from the doctor's recommendation and her own inclination, since she had gone to stay at the convalescent home. She had not wanted to listen to a superficial sympathy, curious inquiries, speculation about her future as a singer. Her nerves were too tender to support any of that.

There was still this visceral, quaking fear that her voice

was gone for good. Unless she braced herself sternly she would be reduced to a jelly of despair at the thought. Her voice, after all, was herself. This had been the case ever since she had first realized that she held a peculiar treasure that could unlock the door to personal freedom, to her life's fulfillment.

And now there was May. Every relationship she had ever had—amorous, platonic, artistic—paled into nothing beside what she felt about May. She shrank from the very thought of mingling her feelings about May with the superficialities of other contacts. When she had seen the doctor, she would see May. Whatever the future was to hold for her, May was her anchor.

The ordeal of waiting in the doctor's office seemed endless. In the end, when she saw him, there was no clear-cut prognosis. Her general health was very much better. He praised the steadiness with which she had been able to achieve a sound recovery. But it was still early days. No experiments yet, he said firmly, no testing of her voice. Perhaps in a month or so—

She hurried away from his office. One thing at least had been accomplished. She need not return to the convalescent home. She could stay in town, in the hotel suite in which she made her home. May's office was not far away. She went there at once.

It was the noon hour and in the thronged street she sought the name of May's company. It was on a brightly polished brass plate beside the doorway of a refurbished town house. Obviously the appraisers shared quarters with a firm of lawyers. Inside in a large room furnished with a few antique chairs and paintings on the walls she was greeted by a woman who sat behind a polished desk. "Miss Skillings? She is expecting you?"

"Oh, yes," said Magdalena without hesitation, aware that the woman assumed from her appearance that she was a prospective client. Miss Skillings' office was down the corridor, the first door on the right.

The door was partly open and she saw in the somewhat dim light that May sat at a desk poring over prints onto which she had trained a brilliant lamp. She was dressed in a soft light blouse with long full sleeves and a dark skirt. The lamplight caught the strands of her fair hair and made it glisten. Magdalena tapped lightly on the door panel. Her heart leaped at the sight of the sudden joy that appeared on May's face as she recognized her.

"My darling!" May cried. As she got up from her chair Magdalena caught her in her arms. But before allowing herself to be embraced May reached behind her to close the door.

"No one will come in if it is closed. I leave it open when I don't mind being interrupted."

Magdalena laughed. "Ever discreet, my little May! I'm sure your receptionist thinks I am or will be a client."

"This is hardly how I greet clients! But what did the doctor say? In your letter you said you would be seeing him."

"I'm very well. I'm no longer an invalid."

"And how about your voice? Can you sing?"

The bright cheerfulness went out of Magdalena's manner. "Not yet. He still promises nothing."

Matter-of-factly May stepped back to her desk and turned out the lamp. "Let us go where we can talk."

"Let us go to my hotel. I can have some lunch brought to my room."

Magdalena's suite was a large one looking out on a square with a railed garden in the center. May looked around her with curiosity while Magdalena ordered a meal over the phone. They were in a large sitting room, luxuriously furnished. A door stood open to a little hallway and a bedroom beyond. When Magdalena put down the phone and came over to her she was gazing out of the window.

Magdalena put her arm around her from the back and said into her ear, "You've no idea how I've looked forward to this moment."

"Oh, but so have I! But I had not thought of you as wealthy."

"Am I?"

May made a gesture to take in the room. "This must cost quite a lot of money."

"Well, of course it does. I've never suffered financially." Then more thoughtfully she added, "I wonder what the future will bring. I've never worried about the future before."

May moved closer to her and put a hand on her shoulder. "Dear, don't worry so. I'm sure everything will come out all right."

Responding to the softness of her reaching out, Magdalena said harshly, "May, of all the things that might have happened to me—death, illness, loss of my possessions—the loss of my voice is not something I ever imagined. I suppose it was naive of me. Or perhaps my mind has always been shut against that eventuality. After all, I have heard enough tales of singers who found they could not sing professionally after an accident or an illness. I've even known some personally who have lost the quality or strength of their voices and have had to abandon their careers. One of my early voice coaches was one such. And age puts a stop to all of us sooner or later. But I never thought of all this in connection with myself. Silly, isn't it?"

"No. It's not silly. It is you. But you need not worry about money, need you?"

"Not now. Not any time soon. But I have acquired extravagant tastes. That is something I must consider, perhaps. When I was young I did not have much, but then I had the spur of the future. I was extravagant even then."

There was a knock at the door and the waiter pushed a

serving cart into the room and arranged their meal on a table. May watched him with half-abstracted gaze and when he had left, moved to the table and rearranged some of the dishes with automatic gestures, as if the original settings did not please her. Magdalena, watching her, smiled. May's fastidiousness was very characteristic.

Expressing the thought that had come into her mind she crossed the room to catch May around the waist. "You darling! I've only known you a few hours—letters hardly count—but it is as if I had never been without you."

May nodded, lifting her face for a kiss.

Magdalena looked down into her eyes. "You're not really thinking about me—about us. Your mind is on something else."

"On the contrary. I am very much concerned with you, with me. I find it difficult to concentrate on my work. Come. Let us have some lunch. My first appointment is at two."

Magdalena glanced at her in annoyance. "Must we be bound by time?"

"I am afraid so. This can only be a small foretaste of what will come later. I cannot be away for more than an hour or so. I do really have clients who will be coming to see me."

"I object to that—to your even having to think of such things when we're together for the first time in so long."

May patted her cheek. "Suppose, my dear, you were rehearsing for an opera?"

A flash of anger showed in Magdalena's eyes. "Don't joke about that!"

May said softly, "Of course, I am not joking. Now, come, let us have lunch."

Obediently Magdalena followed her and they sat down to the meal. After a few mouthfuls, Magdalena asked, "When can I come for you this afternoon?"

"It would be hardly worthwhile for you to come to my office this afternoon. I do not live in town. I take a train from Victoria at six o'clock, if I am fortunate in being able to leave at a reasonable hour."

Magdalena looked at her in consternation. "Does that mean that we shan't be together tonight?"

"No, we shan't be. I could not arrange it. But this weekend I can come up to spend Saturday and Saturday night in town."

Magdalena flung down her fork. "This is outrageous!"

May contemplated her calmly. "My darling, you have to go back to the nursing home to gather your belongings and conclude your arrangements, don't you? Besides, when you wrote and told me that you were coming to town to see the doctor it was very short notice and even so you were not certain of the day. Saturday is the earliest I can manage."

"And this is only Wednesday," said Magdalena in anguish.

"I did not think you should change your appointment. After all, that was paramount."

"You might have let me know that this would be the case."

"Would it have made a difference? You would not have wanted to delay in any case. You would have fretted and fumed if you had."

Magdalena sighed. "How right you are! But, May dear, can't you possibly make a change in your arrangements?"

"Of course I would if I could." May laid aside her plate and reached over to cover Magdalena's hand with her own. "Darling, I am trying to arrange things so that we can be together as often as possible, without arousing any objections."

"Objections? Whose objections? Nobody has anything

to say about what I choose to do."

"Ah, but you're a free agent."

"And you are not? You are old enough to be independent."

May was silent for a moment. "My dearest darling, I live with my parents. You don't know how difficult it has been to arrange this weekend. Fortunately the work I do does require that I go away from time to time to view collections of paintings or antique objects, wherever they are housed. Or sometimes I must go to see people like old Mrs. Harcourt. But these are not spur of the moment occasions. I need to prepare the way for them. If I am going to be away on most weekends—and I intend to spend them with you—I must let my parents get used to that."

"God! Your life is completely governed by them? But you are a grown woman. You ought to be able to arrange your life to suit yourself."

"It is not as simple as that. My father was an air raid warden during the bombing of London. He was badly hurt. He is an invalid now. My mother depends on me. She is used to being dependent on someone. It was a big step for me to take this job and come to work in town every day. It took considerable persuasion to get them to agree and not be unhappy about it."

"Are you an only child?"

"No, I had an older brother. He was killed in the fighting in North Africa. You see how it is. My parents cling to me."

"You should have simply moved to town and got your own flat."

May said thoughtfully, "Most girls would have done that, I think. But, you see, I didn't have a real reason for doing so. There was nothing I particularly wanted to do away from home except carry on my work. That interests me very much. It is the door to a world of great riches. I live among paintings, historical treasures, art of all sorts—the products of the hearts and minds of people with visions they were compelled to make into material things. They were far more interesting people than the sort I would know if I lived in town and spent my time in the ordinary pursuits."

Magdalena gave her a long look, which May returned frankly. "My poor little May, you've never had a chance to find out what there may be in the world for you."

"I suppose that might be the case. But now I have found you, haven't I? I have lost nothing, really."

Magdalena looked away from her. Then brusquely she said, "It does not look as if we shall have a free hand in doing what we want to do. Your parents call the tune, don't they?"

May said in a meek voice, "Is it worth it, for you?"

In exasperation Magdalena snapped, "And what if I said it wasn't?"

May looked down at the table and did not answer. Shocked at her own harshness Magdalena came over to her and dropped on her knees beside her chair. May was passive as she put her arms around her. "May dear, I'll take you at any price."

May raised her head to look at her. "But it is a price, isn't it? You have always been free to do just what you wanted to." She sighed. "Things will get better as time goes on. I've always been patient and let things take their course."

Because, thought Magdalena, you've never seized the moment, you've always built for permanency, you don't want transient joy, you distrust anything that comes suddenly without preparation. She said gently, "You can be too patient, too cautious, May. You can lose the moment. It can go by you and never return."

May was silent, apparently considering what she said.

Magdalena sat back on her heels. "Well, in any case, you say this weekend, this Saturday. You can't simply stay in town on Friday—not go home that evening?"

"No. That would be too big a surprise for my mother. I will say that I am coming up to town to spend Saturday and Sunday at a special exhibition at the National Gallery, with others engaged in the art business—there really is a special exhibition of paintings that have been recovered from the Nazis. This is important for my work."

"And where will you stay Saturday night?"

"I usually stay in a small hotel in Bloomsbury—not always the same one. My mother never pays any attention to that. But this time I shall stay with you."

Magdalena's face lit up. "You little fox. You'll come early?"

"As early as I can. And now you will have to let me go back to work."

"What if I come to get you for lunch tomorrow and the next day?"

May shook her head. "No. I have engagements with clients. You see, I often have to go to people's houses or meet with visitors for lunch. You have no idea how many art objects are being sought and found nowadays, things lost or stolen during the war. I am often called upon to identify things. Besides—surely you must realize, darling, that you are far from inconspicuous. If people don't recognize you at once, they certainly will know that you are no ordinary person."

"Really!" said Magdalena, not disguising her exasperation.

Left alone when May had gone, she fell back into the perplexity that absorbed her. May was right. She was not used to accepting any check or hindrance. Even when it came to her professional career she had seldom had to compromise. She pondered over her own response to May. Quiet and undemanding though May might be, she nevertheless set the rhythm of their interaction. What surprised her most was the fact that she had no real wish to change that state of things. She was a willing subject of May's dominion. The novelty of this in itself captured her.

But she was also not used to being at a loose end. And now there stretched before her a solitary two days. It would not take her more than one morning to conclude her arrangements with the nursing home. All the time she had been there she had been held passive by her anxiety about her voice. She was frightened and she knew this, unable to imagine what her world would be if she could not sing. Her annoyance at May's inaccessibility rose to the surface. She picked up the phone and called several of her friends, people she had shunned during her convalescence. A wave of restlessness swept her, causing her to push to the back of her mind the doctor's caution about too hectic a social life, too many late nights, too little rest. If Francusi was there in London, she would have called only him. For several years now, since the war, he had been the manager of her professional engagements. She realized that she needed a stabilizing influence and he would have provided it. But he was in New York. She visualized him, a short, stout man with a bald head fringed with bushy, grizzled hair, outwardly unruffled by any of the contretemps that often erupted in her professional life but always sympathetic. He was firmly her friend, never her lover, as the gossips insisted. She had not told him, in her last letter, that she was coming to London to see the doctor. A superstitious fear had withheld her hand.

The voices on the other end of the telephone were surprised, curious, teasing. "Well, welcome back from the dead, Magdalena! The sun returns to the heavens! The winter of our discontent is made glorious by your return."

"Are you in town to stay, Magdalena, or just to see the doctor? What will you do now?"

"You're free now? How about dinner tonight?"

"I suppose it is not comme il faut to ask if you're ready to come back to opera?" This voice was sly, malicious, taking revenge for a fancied slight in the past.

Several large bouquets of flowers arrived at her hotel suite. The phone rang constantly. By the time Saturday morning came she was exhausted, chagrined and somewhat worried by the demonstrated proof of the soundness of the doctor's caution. She had dined, lunched, spent the afternoons and evenings in the midst of a noisy, talkative, contentious crowd of people. Once she had thrived on this constant social whirl, had been stimulated by the contradictions, friendly rivalry, malicious intrigues that composed it. But now her energy was depleted, even though she had cut short her own participation before it could reach the stage of intimacy she had once welcomed. She knew that this was observed by some. She caught sidelong glances, overheard snatches of cryptic conversations. There was more curiosity than friendship in many of these gatherings, she knew.

She had gone to bed too late and slept fitfully, disturbed by commonplace noises from the street that she would in the past have ignored. When the early daylight came and she opened her eyes to see it filtering into the room through the small gaps in the heavy curtains, she had a sudden sharp memory of the morning at the nursing home when she had awakened to the realization of May's presence. All at once the feverish exhilaration in which she had been immersed in the last two days, the atmosphere of heightened stresses that had made up her familiar world hitherto, was erased by the quieter emotional state she had felt when she was with May. Was it quieter or was it really more highly charged—more highly charged because it was more intimate, went deeper into her feeling of self? She was familiar enough with the emotional absorption of the early stages of an affair. She had had enough of them to know the stages through which they passed—the first exhilaration, the carelessness engendered in her dealings with others, the release of inhibition. But she knew that in these remembered affairs she had never really lost complete control of what was happening to her. Some portion of her stood off and observed, mocking the extravagance of her own behavior and that of her current lover, prudently withholding the ultimate capitulation. She knew now she was not in complete control with May.

May arrived before she was fully up and dressed. The breakfast tray still lay on the small table by the window. She had nothing on under the voluptuous folds of a satin dressing gown she wore. Her hair, naturally wavy, was caught up from her face by a large jeweled clasp.

May, coming into the sitting room and then standing aside to allow the waiter who had followed her into the room to take the tray away, stood for a while silently looking at her.

When the door closed behind the waiter, she said, "Do you look like that on the opera stage?"

Magdalena, her fearfulness swept away, burst into a laugh. "When I'm on stage I have more on." She crossed the room to take May into her arms again. "Darling May, it has been such a long time."

"Only two days," said May, practically. "But time isn't measured by the clock. I have found that out."

Her voice was somewhat muffled because her face was pressed against Magdalena's throat. Magdalena, having learned that May did not like perfume, wore none, but from her robe and her body there rose a characteristic scent, compounded of herself and the soap and cosmetics she used.

This scent filled May's nostrils as a delicious reminder. She murmured, "I sometimes wondered if you really did exist, but now I know because I can smell you."

Magdalena's arms tightened around her. "Can you possibly realize how I've longed for you, little May?"

May drew back to look up at her. "I know how I have longed for you."

Magdalena's hands were seeking over her clothes. "Take them off and let's get in bed." There was more urgency than command in her voice. She drew May into the bedroom and closed the door. The bed invited them, open and tumbled as Magdalena had left it an hour before. May shed her clothes with methodical fingers and folded them neatly on a chair. Magdalena, returning from the bathroom, lay down on the bed and watched her. With a sigh they came together naked.

When they rolled apart, May said, "I never really imagined it, you know."

Still a little foggy from the effects of desire released, Magdalena asked, "Imagined what?"

"What it would be like to be fondled, caressed, aroused by someone else's hands. I never thought it would ever happen to me—in fact, the idea was repugnant. There was nobody I knew or had ever met that I would have wanted to touch me intimately—caress my body, search in my private places."

'Did you think of a woman, or only a man?"

"I detested the idea of a man. I scarcely allowed myself to think of a woman."

"And why not? You must have known that women can love women—that women do love women. There are many examples in history, in literature."

"Oh, yes. But I thought of that sort of thing as only emotional—all the outside feelings—jealousy and spitefulness and a longing for someone's love and company. I did not think of something you did naked, not a desire to feel and caress somebody else's body. Of course I knew what the sexual act was, between men and women. But I did not like to think of it."

"You hid your eyes."

"Yes, I suppose I did. As nuns are supposed to do. I was not really tempted to think of it, until I saw you the first time." She gazed up at Magdalena, hovering over her as she lay on her back. "There cannot be anyone just like you, with a body just like yours." She reached up her arms to encircle Magdalena's waist. "You're full of fire. You've got so much life that you invade me with yourself. I never even thought that something like that could happen."

Magdalena, confused by her own emotions—exultation, amazement, sudden shyness—did not answer but sank down slowly on top of her.

When they got up the day outside invited them. It was warm, sunny. They both felt the same impulse—to recapture some of the country freshness, the country bloom of their first encounter. They walked in the big park, surrounded by people making the best of a fine Saturday in the city. Magdalena was still held by the contrast, for herself, in this tranquil, cheerful atmosphere and the sophisticated social turmoil in which she normally lived. They sat on a bench close to a pond where ducks swam.

They had not talked much as they strolled along. Now Magdalena said, "You're very quiet, May. Are you troubled?"

"What would I be troubled by?"

"Do you wish we had not met?"

May looked at her in surprise. "No, no. Why should I? Do you?"

"What we are doing is not acceptable to most people, especially the sort you live among."

"You mean, that I love you and I go to bed with you?"

164

"Yes. It occurs to me that you might be having second thoughts."

"Oh, no! That would never bother me."

"Yet you are careful, even anxious about our being seen together by others. You seek to disguise our meetings."

"That is only common sense. Does that bother you?"

"Not really. I've never been concerned by what other people think of me. But it does bother me that you are concerned."

"But you don't have responsibilities to others. You don't have to worry about earning your living, being accepted by the people you are in daily contact with."

"That's not quite true, but I realize that there are differences in our situations. But you don't feel any inner doubts—any religious questions?"

"No. Not with you."

"We're unique and the world cannot hold us accountable by its ordinary standards?" Magdalena saw her mockery register on May's face. "Oh, I don't mean that, really! May, I'm out of my depth with you."

May, sitting so that she could contemplate her, said nothing for a while.

Magdalena went on, "I find it amazing that you're so self-assured and I am very thankful that is the case. I would be chagrined if I thought I had come into your life to disrupt it. I've never worried before about any havoc I might cause in having an affair—havoc, that is, for the other person. It has always seemed to me to be a natural risk—and besides, most people enjoy the upheaval—it's the excitement that breaks up the monotony of life."

May said quietly, "I am not having an affair with you."

Magdalena was thunderstruck. It was a moment or so before she realized what May meant. Impulsively she put out her hand to take May's. May withdrew her hand firmly but without haste. Her response reminded Magdalena that they were surrounded by people—a man and woman sitting on a nearby bench, others walking by on the path in front of them.

"Forgive me, May. I don't have a blueprint to go by. I've never met anyone like you before."

May nodded, matter-of-factly.

* * * * *

As the weeks went by, Magdalena realized that May was right. Things did improve. May must gradually have accustomed her parents to a new routine for herself, to the idea that she would be away more often in town.

For Magdalena it was a strange interlude, a double life, half of it spent among her usual associates, half of it in this odd new world of herself and May. Though she dissimulated, saying that on weekends she accepted no social engagements, that she needed the time to recoup her strength from her week's activities, she thought she noticed that some of her friends were aware of a difference in her manner and curious to know what caused it. She warded off questions. She welcomed the gossip that said she was having an affair.

The day came, when May, sensitive to any nuance in her feelings, after watching her pace restlessly around the hotel suite, asked what was the matter.

"I see the doctor again tomorrow," said Magdalena.

"Ah, I might have known!"

"He must surely say that I may try to sing again. I can't go on like this, holding back, frightened to death. I'll burst out in some ridiculous way."

"You mustn't do anything rash." There was worry in May's voice.

"You've no idea what it's like. I feel it is all pent up in me. Why, May, I have been singing all my life! It is not life to me if I cannot sing!"

"When do you see him?"

"Tomorrow, at ten. But there is more than that to it. If he says I may try singing—and he must! he must!—then I must have a real tryout. My friend Francusi has arranged it. He is just back from New York. He came back when I wrote and told him that this might happen. I am to go to a theater and try out on the stage—to an empty house, of course. I cannot risk failure before a crowd of people."

May, watching the play of emotion on her face—the fierce desire to burst through the bonds of silence, the uncertainty, the anticipatory defiance, the fear of failure— moved closer to her and put her arms around her. "Dear, don't allow yourself to get so upset. Yes, I know how you must feel. But you must be calm to be at your best." She reached up to kiss her.

Magdalena seized her in a violent embrace. May said, hesitantly, "Do you want me to go with you tomorrow? It will not be easy but perhaps I can manage it."

"No. I can face that part of it by myself. But I shall have to call you afterwards. Either way, I shall not be able to contain myself."

"Yes. I'll be waiting to hear."

The next day fortunately was fair, because Magdalena could not sit still and await the time when she would go to the doctor's office. She went for a walk through the city streets, needing the noise and bustle—the people hurrying by on their own concerns, the occasional idler dawdling along looking aimlessly about. A woman came close to her as she stopped to gaze into a shop window, and she heard her furtively asking for money. She looked at her curiously as she handed over some silver and saw a nondescript creature in shabby clothes and wondered why she was reduced to begging and why she had singled her out instead of a man. The woman seemed anxious to get out of sight—probably anxious to escape the notice of the police.

Finally when she entered the doctor's consulting room she found it difficult to restrain her overwhelming need to sweep aside the preliminaries and tell him that the result must be favorable. In fact, it was, and he congratulated her on the completeness of her recovery. At the end he eyed her curiously and asked if she had been able to restrain the wish to try her voice.

"Oh, yes, I have and you don't know what it has cost! But tomorrow I have a try-out to see how things are."

The doctor smiled and said with casual confidence, "Oh, I'm sure it will come out well." It was obvious to her that, amiable though he was, he did not grasp the overwhelming significance of this moment to her.

To May she said, over the phone, "How will it be, really? I haven't sung for so long. I am afraid now to try."

May's voice over the phone was judicious, somewhat stilted by her obvious awareness that she might be overheard. "Well, you must be careful. Don't get too wrought up. That won't help."

The sober quality of May's voice made Magdalena burst out in protest, "But now, can't we possibly spend the night together? Oh, come, May find some excuse! I must have you to myself tonight."

"I don't see how—Besides, aren't there other people anxious to see you this evening? People who will be with you tomorrow?"

"Oh, no! I took care of that. Only Francusi. I shall see him this afternoon. Of course, he must know at once. He has made all the arrangements for tomorrow—a place where I can practice, the musicians, all that. But he is a true friend. He understands what this means. May, you must, you must arrange to be with me tonight!"

May did, though she did not tell her the details, simply saying, when she arrived at the hotel suite, that her mother must really believe this was a matter of life and death. Freeing herself from Magdalena's arms she looked at her radiant face.

Magdalena said, "I sang for Francusi this afternoon. Oh, May, how can I tell you? It is marvelous! I have my voice back! It is as if I have tapped an eternal spring! It is mine! It is me! There will be no trouble tomorrow!"

May reached up to take her head in her hands. "My darling, how thankful I am! But you must be very careful."

"Yes, Francusi pointed that out, too. I must go on by easy stages, not tire myself. Tomorrow will be a test. But now the future is open. I feel free, May, free and strong."

After the dinner in Magdalena's sitting room, Magdalena pulled May up from her chair and across the room to the seat in front of the window. Outside the sky was filled with sunlight though the square below was in shadow. The vigor and energy in Magdalena's body enveloped May, conquering the reserve in which she was usually wrapped. She lay in Magdalena's arms in happy abandon. They kissed slowly, savoring each other's mouths.

May sighed. "My darling, I never imagined this."

Moving her lips along May's throat Magdalena paused to say, "Why not?"

Dreamily May responded. "I've heard, I've read about great loves, of lovers who dwelt in one another's love, but I think I never quite believed that it could mean so much. People, I thought, cannot quite lose themselves in someone else that way. One's own demands must interfere. I think that is so. But you, my love, break every barrier down. You invade me. I have no defense left against you."

"Do you want a defense against me?" Magdalena spoke softly into her ear.

"That's the greatest surrender of all—you make me

want you to destroy every shred of reserve that might separate us."

"Do you regret that?"

"Perhaps I shall end by not being myself any longer—not being anyone—only an echo of you."

Magdalena loosened her embrace so as to laugh heartily. "What a silly idea! May, that would be impossible. You, of all people, would never be an echo of anyone, except yourself. Why, you lead me around by the nose! Do you suppose anyone else has ever told me what to do and when to do it?"

There was some reproach in May's glance. "That is not true. All I am doing is making it possible for us to be together. If I did not manage things, I should never be able to see you at all."

"Oh, you don't think so? You'd be surprised what you'd force me to do if you didn't manage things like that."

"Ah, I am a little afraid of that!"

"I might even—" Magdalena was looking down at her with mischief in her eyes—"I might even come down to your home and carry you away from under your parents' noses."

May smiled faintly but it was obvious that she thought this fantasy too close to a possible reality.

"Would you struggle very hard if I did?"

"It would be useless at that point. They'd disown me."

Magdalena's gaiety was checked. "Really, May, we're not in the Victorian age and you're not a child. Surely you can find some way to assert your independence."

May took a deep breath. "I have asserted my independence. If I had wanted to do more, I should have done it. That is what you do not understand. I have created this situation because, up till now, I have not wanted anything else badly enough. Now my parents are certain that, since I haven't married, I shall be their dutiful daughter for the rest of their lives. The only way, darling, that I can change that is by very slow steps. You are not very patient, are you?"

"I'm quite sure they would get along quite well without you."

"Yes, but if I were to leave abruptly, for them it would be a terrible blow."

"They would get over it."

"But I could not stand the unhappiness it would cause me to give them so much pain, even if it was temporary. What excuse would I give them?"

Magdalena studied her for a moment. "Suppose you married. You'd surely have to leave them then."

"Ah, yes, but that is something they would consider in the normal way of things. Even then there would be some unspoken reproach."

"Emotional blackmail," Magdalena muttered. "Oh, well, let's not spoil the rest of the evening squabbling about that!"

But the next morning, while May ate her breakfast and Magdalena sat nervously drinking tea, the subject came up again.

May said, watching Magdalena's restless movements, "Darling, I know things will go well this morning. You have told me that you are confident of your voice. What shall you be doing after that?"

Magdalena sat still for a moment. "To tell you the truth, I haven't thought about that. What happened yesterday is too tremendous. I suppose Francusi has some idea. He will arrange for me to sing again. I have a contract that was suspended when I got ill. I don't know whether it is still alive or whether there will have to be new arrangements. He will know."

"Who is he?"

"Francusi? He is—shall we call him my manager? He is a very good friend. He has had an unhappy life. He is Jewish and most of his family—his wife—were lost in the concentration camps. I was able to help a little in rescuing some of them. He has been devoted to me ever since. I rely on him entirely."

"Oh." May was silent for a while, then she said, "You will be singing in opera?"

"Why, of course—if everything goes well today."

"Here, in London?"

"I don't know. I was due to sing here, last season."

"But if you don't sing here? If you have to have a new contract?"

"That would depend on circumstances."

"You would go back to New York?"

It was only after a long pause that Magdalena answered, "I don't know. If I can depend on my voice—yes, I think so."

Wrapped up in her own thoughts, she was not aware that May had pushed away the last of her breakfast and had got up from the table and walked away across the room. When she realized that May had put a physical distance between them, she looked up, half-surprised.

She said, "May?" and stopped, the answer to her unspoken question forming in her mind. She got up and walked across to May, who kept her head turned away. "May, there is nothing else I can do. The only reason I could stay here would be if I could no longer sing. You realize that, don't you?"

For a long moment May did not answer, did not move, and Magdalena waited patiently, thinking, these moments always come in any intimate relationship, this conflict. Finally she put her arm around May's waist. May did not pull away from her as she half-expected. "You do see that, don't you?"

May turned a bleak face towards her and said quietly, "Yes." What she did not say and what Magdalena understood without prompting was, And you did not think at all of that, did you, that we should be separated by an ocean, that this joining of us will vanish, and that it really means so little to you that you think of it only now because I have reminded you.

Magdalena burst out, answering the unspoken reproach, "That's not true! It is simply that in my anxiety about my voice I have not considered what would happen. How could I not think of what it would mean, once I know what the future holds for me? I know I am selfish but I cannot be selfish with you. The two of us—this is something beyond my power—"

May, taking hold of her arms, cut in firmly, "Do calm down. You must be calm for today. We will think about all this afterwards. We should not worry about it now. I should have been more careful. There, do be sensible. Just think of what is ahead of you now."

May's quiet words dissolved the tension between them. In the memory of the fiery episode in the theater that followed, this scene in the hotel room vanished only to be recollected much later.

She had wanted absolute solitude in which to put her voice to the test. She knew that was impossible. Francusi was there, the men who handled the mechanical equipment, the handful of musicians. Beyond the lights on the stage she was aware that in the half-lighted theater, in the shadowy rows of seats beyond the lights were people— friends, acquaintances, journalists, music critics. She knew it was curiosity that drew them, in many cases a ghoulish curiosity whetted by the possibility of a disaster or at least an incomplete success.

The preparations seemed endless, with people coming

and going and Francusi talking softly to her of trivialities, seeking to ease the strain. Finally everything was ready. She stood where Francusi indicated. The musicians—a small group recruited for the occasion from the regular orchestra—readied their instruments and the conductor stood ready to raise his baton.

At that moment she was overwhelmed by the sense of her own mastery. It was a familiar feeling, which had come to her on many occasions in that confident past, when no hint of any possibility of failure had ever reached her. The first notes of the aria told her what she had wanted to know—that her voice was there as it always had been—a bird in flight rising from the power within her chest to dominate the universe, that inexhaustible spring of breath and sound. She could fill the theater as she had always done. She could captivate her listeners, to awake in them an irresistible response to her voice, to overwhelm them. She was even grateful then for the presence of those she knew had come to witness disaster. She knew she gave them no satisfaction. She did not need the enthusiastic clapping, the bravos, the stamping feet to tell her that there was no question of her recovery, of the survival of her career as an opera diva.

"A little practice to smooth the edges, to strengthen your breath control," Francusi said, smiling proudly. "We must celebrate."

In her hotel suite, in the midst of congratulations, conviviality, she withdrew to her bedroom to call May.

May, hearing the exultation in her voice, knew at once. "You can sing? There is no hindrance?"

"None at all. Ah, May dear, if I could just make you feel what I feel! If I just had you here!"

"I think you must have a great many other people there just now. I shall hear you sing some time."

"When shall I see you?"

"On Saturday. No, not before. Besides you will be very busy, won't you? You will have no time for anything besides your own affairs."

"Well, you're one of my affairs," said Magdalena, joy making her frivolous.

"Well, when I see you, you will be a little less tipsy," said May indulgently.

The rest of her stay in London was a whirlwind of activity, blotting out the tranquility of the preceding weeks. She must return at once to New York, said Francusi. There was no opportunity for her to sing at Covent Garden now. That must be postponed to some future date. But in New York, at the Metropolitan, she was wanted, to prepare for the coming season. There was no time to be wasted in resuming her singing career.

The strength of her drive to take up again where she had been forced to leave off muted the feeling of dismay she felt when she thought of the separation from May. She was both chagrined and annoyed by this new situation. She had never before found herself in a relationship that could not automatically be relegated to second place where her career was concerned. When she had met May she was a cripple—there was no other word for it—crippled in the most essential part of herself. Now she was whole again and again independent of any prop, needing no one's love and solace to bolster her self-esteem. But that after all was not what May meant to her. May had certainly given her comfort and strength. But there was May herself. As the time drew nearer for departure the thought of May invaded her mind and spirit.

What she must do was persuade May to come with her. Pacing around the hotel sitting room while May sat silent in a big armchair, she railed.

"Why can't you cut loose—just say that you must make a change? In fact, can't you invent some business reason for a trip to New York? That is plausible enough. Americans are buying European art at a mad rate." She stopped, seeing May shake her head.

"Yes, dear," said May. "That is quite true. In fact, I have been offered the opportunity to go to New York for my firm. But it is impossible. I can't go on telling you the same thing. You must realize it by now. My father is failing. I can't leave my mother now."

Anger filled Magdalena. Irrationally her anger was directed towards May, yet May could not be blamed for her father's physical deterioration. She realized once more that in May she had encountered something she had never met with before, an effective check on the excercise of her own will. The feeling bred another, a resentment against May. But that was outrageous, deplorable. How could she resent May?

"Then you mean to say that there is nothing for it except for me to go to New York and leave you here? May, do you realize what you are doing?"

May did not answer at once. After a moment's silence she said, "I can do nothing else now, my darling. I can only depend upon your love."

Each time they were together after that there was a constraint on the way they acted towards one another. It irritated Magdalena that May preserved such a disciplined manner. She's not cold, she told herself. She's not indifferent. But she could show a little more grief, a little more regret, some weakness, some crack in that stoic reserve. And then, having indulged in this self-pity, she reproached herself for wishing May more unhappy than she was already.

In the end, in the hurry and bustle of Magdalena's departure, they scarcely found opportunity for a proper farewell. The morning after their last night together they stood facing each other in the middle of the hotel sitting room, eyeing each other in an attempt to say what was filling their hearts. The attempt failed, checked by a sense of the barrier that was growing up between them. There was too much to be recalled, too much to be argued, feelings too powerful and yet too nebulous to be spoken. Magdalena, in the end, shocked to see tears in May's eyes, found the words she had at last summoned up, stilled on her lips. May reached up for one more kiss.

When she was gone Magdalena did not move from where she stood. In her anger and frustration of the last few days she had come to think of this as a final farewell. In her heart of hearts she did not believe it, yet angrily she clung to the idea. She reminded herself that she had never wanted dangling ends to affairs. A clean end to any episode was the thing. That was healthier, less wounding in the long run, leaving the way open for an unfettered future.

In some confusion she wondered whether this could really be the case now.

III

Ailsa, opening the door of the apartment, saw the cloud of cigarette smoke hanging in the air over Dina's head where she sat in the middle of the outsize sofa. She crossed the living room to plant a kiss on the dark glossy hair. Dina reached up to catch her arm.

Ailsa said, "You're home early."

"And so are you."

"Yes, I had a bar association meeting and I did not stay for all the arguing."

Dina turned around to watch her take off her hat and coat. "I have the whole story now."

"About Mary-Magdalena?"

"Yes."

"What's the source of your information?"

Dina grinned at her. "You want to know if the evidence is sound, don't you? Yes, it is. Ruddle had second thoughts, after our interview. I suppose he began to worry

177

that I might talk to a journalist and he would get publicity he did not want. I had a call from his office suggesting that I might like to discuss further the Gibbon case. That is the way it was put. That way you exclude all individual responsibility."

Ailsa nodded as if to say, Get on with it.

"I went and I was ushered into a sort of baronial hall where they had a lunch table set up. Ruddle was there and your friend Barnhorst. It was all very civilized. While we were at lunch we did not talk about Magdalena. I figured out that they were holding out till we had finished eating and the waiters had cleared away the table. If we were going to talk about Magdalena, it would be only among the three of us. Ruddle put on his best social manner. I wasn't treated as if I was someone who should have come to the tradesman's entrance. We moved over to some easy chairs by the windows—I've told you that they reach from ceiling to floor. I had to turn my chair around so that I did not look out."

"Poor Dina!" said Ailsa, smiling.

"Yes. Poor Dina. It was forty floors down to the street."

Ailsa came over and sat down beside her. "Then?"

"The old man let Barnhorst start things off. Barnhorst said that they were chiefly concerned that someone might attempt to impersonate Magdalena in order to get hold of her money. As her trustees they had to be very vigilant. In fact, prudence dictated that they go on the theory that this woman I talked about was an imposter.

"I said, Simply because you believe Magdalena to be dead. Barnhorst agreed, saying they thought the evidence of that was pretty strong. He went on to say that they did not necessarily accuse our old Mary of having some criminal intent. She might simply be deranged. People who lose their wits often do think they are someone else. So I said, Why should she think she was Magdalena? Well, he said, she may have admired her back in the days when Magdalena was a famous diva and there was a lot of publicity about her."

"All that is reasonable," said Ailsa.

Dina glanced at her ironically. "Especially if you're arguing the case that Mary is not Magdalena."

The image of Mary came up in Ailsa's mind—the broken creature so vulnerable that she had fainted under the stress of a confrontation with reality.

Dina went on, "I said, Don't you think you should start by seeing her? You knew her personally. When I said this to him, Ruddle looked as if he would explode. He hadn't said a word up till then, but now he let me know in no uncertain terms that he would under no circumstances countenance this woman's claim, even so far as to seeing her, that he thought the whole thing outrageous, that the police should look into the matter in the light of the fact that the file on Magdalena Gibbon was still open, that they had never reached a solution of her disappearance. He really went on and on and Barnhorst was getting fidgety. Finally he ran out of breath and sat back in his chair as if he was washing his hands of me and the subject. I've never seen such a display. And you know what it was? It was fear. He's afraid."

"Afraid of what?"

"Magdalena."

"Why should he be afraid of Magdalena?"

"How should I know? But it was fear that I saw."

Ailsa said thoughtfully, gazing into space, "That is strange. If he really thinks Magdalena is dead, he is surely not afraid of anything she could do. She has no heirs, isn't that right? Or at least no immediate ones. Her property might well go to the State of New York. He can't be afraid of being caught out in some shady dealings with her property—not a man like that. He may be—"

"A bastard."

"In some ways, but he cannot be a thief. Do you suppose there is some scandal that Magdalena was involved in that he thinks may at long last come to light?"

"But he wouldn't want the police digging something like that up, would he?"

"You wouldn't think so. Perhaps his comments about the police weren't really serious."

Dina was pensive, mulling over her own recollections. After a moment, she said, "Do you suppose that it has something to do with his own relationship with Magdalena? Do you suppose he can't bear to think that the woman he remembers has surfaced as an old beggar? That he can't—"

"Face the thought of shattering illusions he has held all this time?" Ailsa finished, picking up her thought.

They looked at each other.

Ailsa said, "I wonder."

"I said to Barnhorst, while the old man was simmering down, that there are ways of establishing a person's identity. Even if they're dead, there are ways. With a living person it could be easier. Doctors, dentists—they have records of their patients. A trained person might be able to awaken something in Mary's mind that would throw light on her past. Her statements—"

"If she can be got to make any," Ailsa cut in.

Dina nodded, "—could be evaluated. Barnhorst was very smooth in his reply. He said the firm would have to pursue every clue to Miss Gibbon's disappearance. So naturally they would have to look into this claim. He looked at the old man when he said this, but Ruddle acted as if he didn't hear him. So I asked him what they proposed to do. He said he saw no reason why he or another one of his associates shouldn't interview the claimant. I pointed out to him that she is not a claimant. She's not making a claim. We, the only friends she's got, are trying to establish her identity. At present she's a public charge. She has no funds and no means of earning a living. The only clue we have to who she might be is our supposition that she might be Magdalena Gibbon. He said that, nevertheless, they would have to treat her as a claimant."

"Didn't Ruddle have anything to say to this?"

"All he did was to say Yes when Barnhorst appealed to him, asking him if this wasn't what they should do. It was then that Barnhorst suggested that I set up a meeting with Mary, evidently thinking I could bring her to their offices."

"Well, that is impossible," said Ailsa emphatically, remembering her last visit to Mary. "Even if you got her there, she'd be too frightened, too upset to speak."

"I said something of the sort—that her health was pretty frail—that I didn't think it would be fair to her to subject her to catechism by total strangers. He just waved his hands and said, in that case I had better work something out and let him know. So then I said that we wanted some more information about Magdalena's disappearance, that we could not find any newspaper accounts at the time. Why was this suppressed? He said it wasn't suppressed. At the time, they—meaning Ruddle and company—did not realize that she had disappeared. It was thought that she had gone away unexpectedly—had gone away to recuperate."

"Recuperate?"

"The moment he said this the old man was alert, and Barnhorst began to pull grass. He said something about her friends believing that the death of a close friend had precipitated a health crisis—she had passed seventy and wasn't as robust as she had used to be. So nothing was done for a while and by the time the police were brought in, there was very little to go on. Some of her friends thought she had committed suicide. The police were noncommital. She hasn't been seen or heard from since. I asked Ruddle pointblank if he thought she was the sort of person to commit suicide. He countered by saying she could have met with foul play. There are plenty of unsolved murders."

Ailsa said thoughtfully, "It is true. It is impossible to say ahead of time that someone will commit suicide. As for murder—from what Camilla tells me, it's a wonder that Mary has survived on the street, rape or murder or both."

"The police thought she might have been wearing jewelry and had been attacked for that reason. Her maid wasn't much help there."

"Her maid? Where is the maid now?"

Dina smiled. "I thought of that, too. Ruddle kept track of her. She was a Barbadian, not young. She went back to Barbados and Magdalena's trustees sent her a monthly pension, which Ruddle believed would be in accordance with Magdalena's wishes. She died a year or so later."

"So that's out. But did she tell the police anything about Magdalena?"

"She told the police that Magdalena was very depressed, that quite often she did not speak to her all day, that she seemed out of touch with things. She tried to persuade Magdalena to see a doctor, but Magdalena would not even answer her, acted as if she did not hear her. Barnhorst, when he was telling me this, reminded me that the maid was from the islands and that she had superstitious ideas about Magdalena having been possessed by evil spirits, that she was bewitched, in other words."

"By whom?"

"I don't know. Perhaps by the spirit of her dead friend."

"In which case, it would not be an evil spirit, would it? Well, I suppose that is one way of explaining depression."

"I did not get much further. It was obvious that Barnhorst was getting more and more nervous about Ruddle's reactions to my questions and his answers. He said the only avenue we can take is to arrange an interview so that she can be questioned. If after that it looks as if there is some substance to what we think, perhaps some further steps can be taken. He was getting more and more tentative, every time he looked at Ruddle. So there we are. What do we do now?"

Ailsa thought for a while. "What can we do? You haven't seen her. You can't realize how—remote she is. Living with Camilla she seems to feel that she has reached a refuge. I hate the thought of breaking into that refuge."

"Yes, but if she is Magdalena Gibbon, she should be living in ease. She should enjoy the sort of life her money can provide. It's no kindness to leave her in destitution—to say nothing of the burden on Camilla."

"Yes, yes. That is all true." Ailsa hesitated and then added, "She is such a pitiful thing. There is such a well of despair in her."

Dina put her arm around her. "It upsets you, doesn't it? Well, we'll have to think of something." Dina lit a cigarette and smoked for a while, as Ailsa picked up her hat and coat and put them in the closet.

When Ailsa came back Dina said, "Do you suppose we could bring her here? That perhaps the lawyers could interview her here?"

Ailsa replied slowly, "I would have to talk to Camilla first."

Dina glanced up at her. "Camilla really is her fortress, isn't she?"

Ailsa nodded. "She seems to feel that Camilla will protect her from the world."

* * * * *

"This lawyer," said Camilla, "you say he has her money?"

"His firm has been appointed by the court as trustee until her case has been resolved—that is, until she's either found alive or declared dead from the passage of time—that's seven years according to the statute."

"Can he identify her? Did he know this woman well enough to say that she's Mary?"

They had met by appointment in the fast food place where Camilla often ate a meal that could be breakfast, lunch or dinner. Ailsa, with a cup of coffee in front of her, watched Camilla automatically shake ketchup on her french fries with the mechanical gesture of long habit.

Ailsa said, "I've not met him but I have an idea, from what Dina tells me, that he knew her very well, that he seems very unwilling to confront Mary for some reason—"

Camilla said flatly, "He had an affair with her and he holds a grudge because she showed him the door."

"That's leaping to conclusions, but I suppose it's a possible explanation."

"That fellow out in California that Dina talked to—he feels the same way, doesn't he?"

Surprised, Ailsa said, "Why, I suppose you could interpret what he said that way."

"That's right. Men don't like women to tell them to leave. They like to think they're the ones to say when it's time to say goodbye. They naturally think they're more important to a woman than a woman is to them."

Ailsa studied Camilla's impassive face as she chewed her hamburger. "I'd say, from all I've heard about her—it's all hearsay evidence, of course—that Magdalena was the kind of woman who did just what she liked with men and women. I expect she left quite a lot of emotional wreckage behind her as she went through life."

Camilla paused in her eating long enough to raise sharp dark eyes to look at her. Returning her attention to her food, she said, "What's this lawyer preparing to do?"

"His firm is going to investigate to see if Mary could be Magdalena Gibbon. Dina got them to agree to that."

"They?"

"One of the younger men, probably. Someone I know. His name is Barnhorst."

"You mean, not the old man who knew her?"

"Apparently not."

"That's not going to work."

"Well, I suppose, he can go through the preliminaries—get a statement from her—clear the ground. Ruddle is going to have to see her sooner or later. He's the one who can say whether he recognizes her or not."

"She says she's Magdalena Gibbon."

Ailsa challenged her. "Does she really?"

"She doesn't deny it. You were the one who asked her."

"It will take more than that, Camilla. It will take more than her assertion, if she makes one. One of the questions raised is whether she is suffering from delusions."

"Why would she want to pretend to be Magdalena Gibbon if she isn't?"

"It's not a matter of her pretending. She may have convinced herself that she is Magdalena. You know as well as I do, Camilla, that some people think they're somebody else, somebody they admire or for some reason become obsessed with. It's a common form of psychosis."

Camilla merely nodded.

"That's the first thing that has to be established. Is she simply deluded?"

Camilla flared up. "Mary is not crazy! How many times do I have to tell you that? She's very unhappy. She is sad, so sad that she wishes she was dead. That doesn't make her crazy."

"I know, I know. You're convinced of that and I'm not ready to say it isn't so. What we have to do—"

"Besides, she shouldn't have to be inspected by some stranger, somebody she probably won't like, somebody who will frighten her. She's not going to say anything under those circumstances. They'll just write her off as feeble-minded."

Ailsa said slowly, "That's very likely what would happen. But we have to do something. We have to start somewhere."

Camilla did not answer. She pushed away the paper plate and sat brooding with her elbows on the table. Ailsa touched the cup of cold coffee in front of her and grimaced.

After a while Camilla said, raising her head, "I don't see any way to go about this."

"Dina had a suggestion."

Camilla looked at her.

"Dina suggested that we take Mary to our apartment and have the interview there. It is a strange place to her but if she was there a few days, she could get used to it. Do you think we could do that?"

Camilla considered the idea. "You know, Judge, she seems to be stronger since you saw her, when she fainted. She was out of it for a day or two. But maybe it was a good thing, shaking her up that way. She doesn't talk any more than she used to, but she seems to take in more when you talk to her."

"Then you think we might try taking her to our place?"

Camilla nodded. "She knows you and I don't think she is afraid of you anymore. But there's another thing. That lawyer—"

"Ruddle?"

"Yes. He's the one who is going to have to talk to her. She's not going to answer any questions from a stranger."

Ailsa frowned. "Perhaps Dina can persuade them of

that fact." She thought for a moment. "There's something else I've thought of. Magdalena had a maid. Her name was Rosa Martin. She came from Barbados and she went back there when Magdalena disappeared, and died there. Do you suppose you could ask Mary if she remembers her?"

"I can try," said Camilla.

The next day Camilla called Ailsa in her office. Mary, she said, had recognized Rosa's name.

"I told her," Camilla reported, "that I'd heard that Rosa Martin had gone back to Barbados, and died there. I said, She was your maid, wasn't she? Mary didn't answer me right away and I left her alone to think it over. Then later on she said to me, out of the blue, Yes, Rosa was my maid. How did I know about her? And I said, that lawyer who is looking after your property told me."

"How did she take that?" Ailsa asked.

"I watched her. She was real calm. All she said was, Poor Rosa. Did she have enough to live on? I said, Yes, the lawyer sent her some money."

"Did she say anything about the lawyer?"

"No. She wouldn't talk any more. Just shook her head, as if she had dredged up all she could."

* * * * *

"So then," said Ailsa that evening to Dina, "we agreed that we should bring Mary here and arrange for Ruddle to come here to see her."

"Hmmm," said Dina, dubiously. She smoked for a while in silence. "He's not going to be very cooperative. Ailsa, I think he *wants* Magdalena Gibbon to be dead. I don't think he can handle the idea that she is alive."

"Well, of course, you're the one who saw him and talked to him. Why do you say that?"

"Ailsa darling, there's an involved situation here—"

Ailsa laughed. "That goes without saying."

"I think this has something to do with Magdalena's friend—May Skillings. He may be afraid of scandal."

"Scandal? Have you turned up anything about her?"

"No. And that's suspicious in itself. There was always a lot of scandalous gossip about Magdalena. You know, the sort of thing that's said in oblique remarks in gossip columns, a sort of obbligato to the stories about Magdalena and her triumphs as diva that appeared on the front pages of newspapers. But nobody ever talked about May Skillings. Of course, apparently, soon after May came into her life she left the opera stage. She sang in concert for a while after that. And then she retired and there's very little about her anywhere after that."

"Sounds as if she became a reformed character."

But Dina did not laugh. Preoccupied with her own speculations she said, "I feel in my bones that it has something to do with Ruddle himself. He acts like a man who feels personally threatened."

"You'll have to see whether you can cajole or bully him into seeing Mary."

"Bully him?" Dina made a face. "I'd say that was impossible. But I do think this. I think he is really anxious to know the truth about Mary. It's something that nags at him. He is an old man and a somewhat embittered one, I'd guess. He's just waiting for the day when Magdalena can be legally declared dead and the books can be closed on her. Mary has thrown a monkey wrench into that. He passionately wants her to be eliminated from the case."

"I wonder how it would be if he does see her. Will he take account of the fact that she is ill and frail?"

"I wouldn't say he was capable of being very compassionate."

"But he must see her."

"I'll talk to Barnhorst tomorrow," Dina promised.

* * * * *

It was decided, after they had consulted Camilla, that they would bring Mary to their apartment for a week or so. Ailsa, going down the corridor to the elevator, saw them approaching her. Camilla stood solicitously by Mary's side as they paused for a moment before walking towards her. What she saw was an elderly woman, somewhat stooped, obviously ill at ease in strange surroundings. It was the first time, Ailsa realized, since that first meeting in the courtroom, that she had seen Mary standing, and she was surprised to see that, even with the stoop, she was taller than Camilla— perhaps as tall as Dina. She wore the sort of dress and hat and shoes that could be bought in any middle-priced department store. She looked, in fact, like a woman you would pass in the street without a second glance. It was nevertheless, she reminded herself, a transformation from the half-wild, raggedly dressed creature she had first seen. Gathering herself together, Ailsa greeted them and led them to the apartment door. They all three walked slowly, at Mary's pace and in silence, Camilla's hand under Mary's elbow.

Once inside Camilla led her to a chair by the window. She seemed to accept this guidance without question. Ailsa brought a coffee tray and set it on a low table. She poured a cup and offered it to Mary, asking, "Do you take cream and sugar?"

Mary surprised her by saying courteously, "I should prefer some tea."

Ailsa glanced up at Camilla standing by Mary's chair.

There was an ironic smile on Camilla's face, as if she recognized Ailsa's bewilderment, created not so much by what Mary said as by the fact of Mary's quietly stated preference.

Camilla said, indulgently, "I'll get it, Judge. Your kitchen is this way, isn't it?"

She walked out of the room and Ailsa, left alone with Mary, found herself tongue-tied. Glancing at Mary, she realized that this silence did not trouble Mary, that she sat withdrawn, incurious about her surroundings. Camilla came back with a steaming cup of tea and gave it to Mary.

Ailsa found the presence of mind to say, "Mary, Camilla has told you that we want you to stay here with us for a few days."

Mary raised her head to look at her but remained silent.

"You won't mind that, will you?"

Mary looked at Camilla, who nodded, but she still said nothing.

"We want you to talk to Mr. Ruddle. You know him, Mary. Can you remember him?"

Mary gazed at her as if trying to take in what she said. Ailsa persisted. "If you can't bring him to mind now, I think you will remember him when you see him. He was someone who was important in your life."

Mary looked away. Ailsa continued. "He wants to establish the fact that you are Magdalena Gibbon. He will be able to recognize you."

Mary raised her free hand to her forehead. Camilla leaned over to take the teacup from her shaking hand.

Camilla said, looking at Ailsa. "I guess that's it, for now."

Anxious, Ailsa said, "She had probably better rest for a while."

Camilla said, helping Mary to her feet, "You take her

to her room. I'll get her things. I left them downstairs with the receptionist."

Ailsa passed her hand through Mary's arm. She was aware again of how thin and bony it was. "Your room is this way, Mary," she said, urging her gently in the right direction. Mary did not resist. They walked slowly, Ailsa noticing that she breathed heavily, as if this slight exertion taxed her. Why, she thought, being close to her like this I can see that once she was a tall woman, taller than Dina. The image of Magdalena Gibbon in the photographs Dina had found came to her mind—a tall, vigorous woman with a commanding presence. They reached the bedroom and she led Mary to an armchair. "Camilla will be back in a few minutes with your things."

She was relieved when Camilla came into the room and she was able to escape back to the living room. When Camilla came out, she asked, "Do you think she will be all right?"

"I guess so." Camilla's manner was matter of fact. "She's a lot better than she used to be. But she's still frightened of strangers and she can't stand crowds. She kept her eyes closed all the way over here in the cab. I'd let her eat her dinner by herself, if I were you. If she'll eat it." She picked up her own handbag. "Well, I'll come by tomorrow and see how she is."

Dina came home early, eager, Ailsa knew, to meet Mary for the first time. She was disappointed when Ailsa told her that Mary had to recover for a while in solitude.

"You mean, she's not having dinner with us?"

Ailsa nodded. "Camilla says she has to get used to things by easy stages. Of course, that's the whole idea of having her here before she sees Ruddle."

Dina lit a cigarette and sat deep in thought for a while. Finally she said, "Why do you suppose she did it?"

"Did what?" Ailsa's thoughts were far away.

"Why did she just leave her apartment and go out on the street to live?"

"We don't know for certain that that is what she did."

"You think something else happened?"

"She could have lost her memory. She could have had an accident that caused her to lose her memory. She could have been mugged, ditto. Perhaps she has not been on the street all this time."

"Well, none of these things explains how she wound up there. And wouldn't she have had some sort of identification on her, if she was picked up by the police, by an ambulance?"

Ailsa sighed and shook her head. "I don't suppose we'll ever know unless she tells us."

* * * * *

She looked around at the strange bedroom. She felt orphaned, bereft of the protection she had learned to feel in the familiar room she had been living in. That room had become a sanctuary. She had grown used to its furnishings, used to Camilla's presence. Her mind, like her body, had sunk into the ease thus created, lulled into quietness by the promise it made that nothing menacing waited within it, that nobody would enter it who would threaten her with bodily harm. A cloud of half-visualized images hovered over her in remembered glimpses of her street life, the jail cell and its clanging metal doors and shouting people, the uneasy quiet of the hospital ward. These stages had all passed, as if they had happened to someone else.

In a sense they had happened to someone else. Yet this someone else was the woman who sat in this chair, the woman who inhabited this body. That woman sought some place into which she could retreat and seek oblivion from self, which alone would provide peace and an absence of pain. That woman struggled against the voices of the women who asked her questions, who demanded of her that she reach behind the curtain that hid the past and drag forth the identity of the woman who dwelt there.

She could not hide behind that someone else any longer. The women who called to her, demanding that she come out to meet them—she could not gainsay them. They did not know that she looked at them across a wide chasm of darkness from which she shrank in terror. At the thought of crossing it her mind balked and turned away.

But there must be a bridge that she could cross, ignoring the blackness below. She sank back into the luxurious chair, exhausted by the physical efforts of the last few hours, the mental struggle against the attempts made to awaken her memory. Yes, she knew she was Magdalena Gibbon. She knew very well who Magdalena Gibbon was. May had returned to her, or rather the image of May. May. It was agony to reach out for May and find her only a wraith of memory. As she sank into a semi-sleep, there arose before her mind's eye the events of the season in New York when she had returned to the operatic stage.

She had crossed the Atlantic in a suppressed rage, the anguish she had felt in the separation from May masked by the anger that had taken possession of her. She had refused to face the fact that she could be thwarted in something so fundamental to her life, and her response had been to deny that this was so, to affirm that this episode in England was only a romantic interlude, a dalliance like those she had had before. The unadmitted realization that it was not fueled her anger. She would drown it in the more violent emotion.

In New York she plunged into the life she knew so well, the life that stimulated her, that brought her the exhilaration of feeling that every nerve, every muscle of her body felt the demand that her spirit made on them. The threat of age, the menace of the loss of her voice, the suggestion that her command of her musical life was threatened—all this was nullified.

She was greeted back with enthusiasm by friends, musical colleagues, even by the critics who so often took pleasure in seeking some flaw in her performances, in her vocal excellence. They never had found anything that was not a passing lack of perfection, but it was an ongoing contest between them and herself that she enjoyed, since it always ended in her victory.

Francusi, who had preceded her across the Atlantic, was there to welcome her with his usual cheerful smile. He was delighted.

"We have all missed you. Who else is so worthy of our greatest attention? Who else challenges us all to find less than perfection in paradise, feet of clay in the goddess?"

Magdalena laughed. "Oh, amico! How much honey you have on your tongue! You're not including my critics, are you? If so, you make them out much more amiable than they are. They are a breed of vipers. Wait till tomorrow morning."

Francusi was not perturbed. They were sitting in the living room of his small apartment, in the corner by the window with a glimpse of the trees in the park at the end of the street. She knew he had worries, financial and personal, that as a refugee in the war he had fearsome memories, that he was often the target of those envious of his success. But he never showed any of this to the singers he cosseted and cajoled, taking for granted their arrogance, their tantrums, their moments of irrational despair. He did not speak of the artistic temperament, but she knew he assumed it to exist as a necessary element in an artist.

Magdalena said, "I feel as if I could sing all day and all night."

"That is wonderful, my child. But please do not succumb to this enthusiasm. As you say, we must await the verdict of the performance."

It was the nearest he would come to reminding her that the tensions of actual performance posed the real test of the recovery of her voice, that she had six months of nonperformance to repair, that days and weeks of rehearsals lay ahead before she would sing to the audience that was to hear her in the role of Alceste, Gluck's opera, requiring her presence on stage almost continuously, taxing her to the limit of her professional capacity. They would be looking, his words implied, for that magic she had always brought to the opera stage.

She, touched on the quick, reproached him, "It's not like you to rattle skeletons."

He raised his eyebrows and put his head on one side. "Of course we must have optimism. There can be no future without optimism, without faith. But we must temper it with a little—what do you say?"

"Caution," she suggested.

He smiled at her. She thought, he has the sweetest smile I've seen on a man. He was a round little man, a head shorter than she and she realized how valuable the sight of his pink, soft face and black lively eyes were to her. He seemed to have no vanity, never to be prompted to impose his own will, his own feelings on her. She knew this soft exterior was deceptive. Once or twice she had glimpsed the flash of steel under his sympathetic manner. She had heard that there were those who did not find it easy to oppose him when he had made up his mind to something.

"Caution. That is it. Enthusiasm, yes. It is expected of you, cara amica. How can you be the greatest diva of our time without it?"

Magdalena laughed again. "You don't tell that to the others, do you?"

"Of course not, my dear." He looked a little offended. "I am entitled to my opinion. I do not flatter for the sake of flattering."

She reached over and patted his cheek gently. "You are a dear friend." He was indeed a true friend, she mused. Regardless of what the gossipers might say, she had never been his mistress. His loyal support through the years had not been based on an amorous relationship. She had never thought of him in those terms. She had never seen in his eyes the speculative, acquisitive look that she had seen in many men's eyes. Few people besides herself knew anything of his personal life. He did not talk about it himself and avoided speculation by others. The pain of it was too great.

"I'm only teasing," said Magdalena.

Still seated he made a little bow and dismissed the subject with a change of voice. "There is someone I should like to present to you. He wanted me to bring him now, but I explained to him that you could not be disturbed, distracted, in this time when you are preparing for the new season. He has heard you sing before."

She looked at him with raised eyebrows. "Why is he important?"

"Important?" His manner was bland.

"Why is he important enough for you to bring him personally to meet me?"

"Ah, well! He is a lawyer, a very important man in his profession. He deals with wealthy people. He has become a great admirer of yours."

So that was it, she thought. Francusi brought his iron-fist-in-the-velvet-glove technique into all his dealings. He knew and used the value of wealthy patrons; they never knew the contempt in which he often held them. She knew this was part of the reason for his great success in the difficult world of opera management and production. If, without trouble to her, he could use her as—well, yes, bait—he would do so. Considering the value he placed on her, this effort to please must mean that the man concerned must be of the first importance to him. Her curiosity was stirred. She saw that he noticed this.

"Who is he and is he married?"

"His name is John Ruddle. His firm is very well-known. He has no wife now and so far as I know, he has no other attachment. I know you would never be interested in being the other woman."

He looked at her slyly as he said this. Laughing, she said, "And why are you so anxious to set me up in a romantic situation?" She grew more serious. "I don't like such contrivances."

He shrugged as if to minimize the significance of what he was doing. "It is not my contrivance. Mr. Ruddle is very importunate."

"So, if you do what he wants, he will get off your back. And he is important financially to you."

He smiled again. "Yes, my dear. You are used to dealing with enthusiastic admirers. He can be very useful to me."

She looked at him gravely. "I don't like this. I am not in the mood for that sort of thing."

Ordinarily, she knew, he would not take such a statement seriously. But now she saw that his sharp black eyes studied her face as if he sought further information. She turned away to escape his gaze. Within herself she knew the reason for her rejection of his overture. Often, in the past, they had laughed together over such a situation. He came nearest to knowing the truth about her private life. It amused her that she was credited with such an undeserved reputation for romantic adventures with men. When she was very young she had experimented with men but had immediately discovered that she much preferred women. Nevertheless it was on supposed affairs with men that her reputation was based. Nobody seemed to notice the discreet alliances she formed with women, or if these were noticed, they were not considered to be what they were. She herself did not take them seriously. She never shied away from the invitation to a new affair, but then she also never tolerated an affair that had lost its pristine quality. She brought any affair to a close before it became tiresome. She never pined for the past. Affairs did not last. It was not in their nature. Very often she kept old lovers as friends. She was chagrined when this did not happen, when the passions she aroused did not subside into the cooler temper of affection.

But there was no slot into which she could fit May.

For days now, in fact for weeks, she had systematically suppressed any thought of May. In the tension, the excitement, the physical demands of the preparation for this resumption of her operatic career, she had largely succeeded. Only occasionally, in an unguarded moment, the thought—it was more than a thought, it was a remembrance deeply seated in her being—of May overtook her and brought to a momentary stop every other thought or feeling she might have.

She pulled herself together and said sharply, "We've got more important things to talk about."

He made no further reference to the subject.

The days went by and she was engrossed in the details of preparation for the opening performance at the Metropolitan. In later moments of recollection the evening of the performance shone in her mind not so much in clearcut scenes but in a luminous cloud of exultation, filled with the tumult and sound of a triumph. When she sang in opera she always experienced this sensation of soaring beyond the confines of the stage, of losing awareness of the audience beyond the sense of a presence of many people absorbing the emotions her voice aroused. But this time the sensation was intensified far beyond the usual. The world outside of the theater building vanished and with it all the anxieties, preoccupations, regrets, aspirations that dominated her normal life.

Francusi, when the performance was over and they were together for a brief moment in her dressing room, was ecstatic. For once his praise, his joy, were pure, untinged by the careful optimism with which he cloaked any flaws, shortcomings, disappointments. She sensed the enormous relief that he felt. It was the measure, she realized, of the anxiety he must have felt before this seal was placed on the demonstration of the survival of her voice.

"You were marvelous, Magdalena! I've never known you better. It was wonderful, magnificent! There can be no doubt left in anyone's mind that you are still indeed the queen."

She clucked at him goodhumoredly, discounting the flamboyance of his praise, but she knew she was flattered. She knew she had triumphed. She had no grounds for doubt in her own recovery, in the renewed strength and quality of her voice and her control over it. She was glad he was there to reinforce her own relief, to fortify her against the inevitable reaction, when the first flush of triumph would begin to recede, undermined by her sense that perfection still evaded her. She knew there had been flaws, little ones, perhaps, but there. This aftermath of any success always overtook her. Sensibly she laid this to fatigue, but it gave her those familiar moments of discouragement, of a sort of black night of the spirit that must be suffered through, the obverse of the medal of success.

Lost in this reverie, she had been sitting perfectly still, unaware of anything outside of herself. Now she roused enough to realize that Francusi was still in the dressing room. When she glanced at him she saw he was gazing at her with anxious eyes, as if there was a further problem in his mind.

"What is it?" she asked sharply.

"There is no doubt that we shall have a very successful season," he said, in an especially conciliatory voice. He still hesitated. She knew he had long since learned, with his special sensitivity to the psychic demands of artists, about her plunge from triumph to melancholy after a successful performance. "You can rest now with confidence in the future."

She continued to look at him, still annoyed but with a dawning curiosity. "You have something particular you want to say to me."

"Yes." His tone now was businesslike. "You will not like what I am going to ask. It is about our friend, Mr. Ruddle—"

"*Our* friend?"

He ignored the interruption. "He is pressing me to introduce him to you. He has arranged a supper party for you with some other prominent people. He has sent me here to ask you to join him."

Anger rushed over her. "You know perfectly well that I do not go to social engagements after a performance. I am exhausted. This is outrageous!"

"Now, now, Magda, don't fly off the handle. Yes, of course I know what your rule is and I know you must be worn out after that triumph. So naturally I do not lend myself to this request without thought."

She did not answer and he waited in silence while she sat sinking once more into unhappiness. She was prepared, from experience, to wait to outlast this reaction induced by fatigue. But this time there was a flatness in her spirit, a taste in her mouth of uselessness, of the feeling that no such great effort was of sufficient value. It was a moment of despair such as she had several times experienced in the convalescent home, when the way ahead had turned into a dreary, hopeless path leading to nothing. Then suddenly there flashed before her mind's eye the image of May, May sitting on the bench in the sunshine of the garden, surrounded by the scent and color of the roses. The discipline of the last weeks was shattered. She had used the stress and demands of preparation for this night for a means of burying in oblivion the memory of that episode in London. But the remembrance had been there always, lying in wait for her. She was suddenly afraid of going back to her hotel suite, to be a prey to the agonizing sense of deprivation she had tried all these days to escape.

She looked around again at Francusi. He was looking at her anxiously, aware that some sort of storm was taking place in her emotions. He hurried to say, apologetically, "You see, Magdalena, he is a new trustee of the Opera. It would be only sensible to respond to his great admiration for you."

He seemed half-ashamed to bring into the open this ulterior motive. Her annoyance faded. After all, Francusi had his own problems, which he seldom brought forward. His life had been so tragic and yet he had the courage, the resilience to face what lay ahead.

She said, in a softer voice, "All right. On your account, I'll come," knowing, as she spoke, that this decision was made also on her own account.

He looked at her in frank surprise. He got up from his chair and came over to kiss her lightly on the cheek. "In a few minutes, then, diva," he murmured and went quickly out of the room.

Her recollection of that evening was dominated by Ruddle. He was a forceful man, tall and slender, who had learned to cover his aggressiveness at will with a smoother manner. After the theater party, when she refused to break her rule against social engagements after a performance, he had invited her to lunches, to dinner on nights when she was not singing, affairs at which there were other influential people in the public eye. Whenever she was in his company his bold eyes, set in a long, narrow face, were fixed on her. He was a number of years older than she, but there was no question of his virility. She supposed she should be flattered by the concentrated attention he paid her. But she did not like him. He was a man, she realized, who must possess whatever he wanted. He made it plain, especially when he took her to tete-a-tete lunches, that he wanted her. She pulled away from these encounters. I'm no one's possession, she told herself.

Part of the time she agreed to go out with him from a certain sense of perversity. It amused her to see that she had the power to deny him something he demanded. She never invited him to her hotel suite. She refused to go to his apartment, no matter how subtly he suggested the possibility, unless he was giving a dinner party there, catered and elaborate, with other guests. She thought about her own motivation in all this. Partly it was for the exhilaration of a test of wills. Partly—and she only looked at this obliquely—it was a driving urge to leave herself as few spare moments as possible for musing on her own inner state. On those occasions when she found herself thinking of May, in spite of herself—May seemed to creep into her consciousness in any unguarded moment—she worked hard to convince herself that May was no longer in the place of first importance to her. The trouble was that she could not put the memory of May in a safe place of storage.

For a while after she arrived in New York she did not hear from May. May's first letter came the morning of the first rehearsal. It was brief and said that her father had been so ill she had had no chance to write. He had improved and her mother was now less demanding. She had been very frightened, said May, so that any time I have free must be spent reassuring her.

Magdalena threw down the letter at this point. She had really not expected that she would hear from May. Or so she had told herself. Remembering the bitterness of her own words to May, she had taken for granted that their breach was final, that May could not see it as anything else. Nevertheless, she was aware that, having now received a letter, underneath her denial to herself that May would write she had yearned for one, a yearning she had refused to acknowledge.

She picked the letter up again and studied it, the phrases, the formation of the words, with an avid hunger. For the moment she felt humbled—that May, with that matter-of-fact steadfastness, could write to her in loving terms, without recriminations, with no demand for a revival of their relationship. After several more minutes of brooding she folded the letter up and put it in a drawer.

When a few days later she sat down to reply to it she purposely did not reread it but was dismayed to find that she had it by heart. It was inevitable, she supposed, that this was so, since there was an overpowering simplicity in May's thought, an inescapable honesty, which she had learned to recognize and respect when they were together.

After that first one May's letters arrived more or less regularly. They were short, matter-of-fact accounts of her life at work, her life at home, a commonplace round of activities. Occasionally, when she became involved in some unusual case of art-discovery, she gave a lively description of the circumstances. She never said, "I love you so much," "I miss you so much," "I can't believe you are not here." But so complete was her reaching out that Magdalena realized, after a few letters, that May was writing on an assumption that they still stood together on a special ground. For May, although she did not demand a response from Magdalena, there was no breach between them, only a separation.

Magdalena purposely made her replies less frequent and coolly affectionate. Whenever she wrote she felt a mixture of emotions that she could not banish—a sense of guilt, a sometimes frantic desire to cut May off so that she need not feel this guilt, and a panic-stricken fear that May might at last give up in despair and write her no more. Her coolness, after a while, did in fact cause May to write less frequently. Some of the life-giving force—yes, Magdalena admitted to herself, there was a quickening in her spirit when she received and read one of May's letters—began to wane. Eventually Magdalena ceased to expect a letter more often than once a month and a chilly feeling settled around her heart when this fact was borne in on her.

Her answer to this turmoil, an emotional struggle with herself which she had never suffered before—was to plunge even more energetically into the social life that her return to the operatic stage had brought about. As the season went on she saw more of Ruddle and, in order to escape from the inevitably increasing intimacy with him, she sought other attachments.

One day, as the end of the operatic season was in sight, Francusi told her about a scheme for an ambitious plan to make a film version of a Mozart opera. It was one of her most famous roles and those who were backing this project wanted her in it. When he spoke to her about it, at a moment of leisure when she was feeling idle and conscious of the fatigue that always set in at the end of a season, she listened with half-awakened interest. It was a new idea still, the projection of an opera as a screen play. It had been done before, abroad, said Francusi. The man whose idea it was had a reputation for success in musical films.

"But grand opera is not musical comedy!" she protested.

No, no, Francusi assured her. It would be nothing like

that. The idea was to make a three-dimensional film, using the new techniques, and as he understood it, the opera itself was to be filmed, not a screenplay based upon it.

Magdalena looked at him, her interest caught. "I cannot be a film star," said Magdalena. "I am a singer with a dramatic instinct, as all opera singers are."

"Oh, yes, he understands that. And of course, it may not succeed. It may prove too expensive, too difficult. All he wants to know is whether you will consider it.

"Who is he?"

"His name is Rodney Winger. He is a young man, young enough to risk everything on a try for something new. But he has already a reputation as a clever producer and director."

In the end she agreed that she might have a try at it. Francusi, she saw, did not really like the idea. He was dubious not only about the popularity of opera with movie audiences. He mistrusted the mechanics of creating a film and imbedding operatic voices into it. As she got more used to the idea she grew more enthusiastic. To become involved in something novel, problematic, would offset the fact that she was not going to sing in London the next season. She had astonished Francusi by refusing to do opera in Covent Garden. Yes, she would sing in Paris, Milan, Vienna, wherever else he wanted, but not there. He was amazed and bewildered by her refusal, for which she would give no reason. The project with the film filled the gap.

She found that Rodney amused her. She was tired of Ruddle's constant presence, afraid that in the end he would win out of sheer persistence. Rodney was a useful foil. He was considerably younger than she, in some ways a callow young man, somewhat awed by her reputation. He was good looking, fair-haired, slim, energetic, exuberant, with the confidence that came from a series of successes achieved as a youthful prodigy. He was young enough also to rebound from failure, ready to pick himself up and go on at once after the lure of another idea. Within a few days he was in amorous pursuit of her, ardent and happy. She was amused that Ruddle, offended by what he saw, left for a trip to Europe.

The developing plans for the opera film added to the excitement, the exhilaration. Francusi watched her with unconcealed concern. Had she forgotten who Magdalena Gibbon was? She tried to reassure him, in too frivolous a mood to give due weight to his complaints. What he did not realize, she knew, was that she felt herself quite uncommitted to anything. This was a lark, a joyride, the final fling of a youth that had already gone and lingered now only in a brief recrudescence.

The gaiety and spontaneity began to fade with the growing difficulties in making the opera film. Francusi's misgivings proved well-founded. There was a fundamental clash between the people whose life was opera and those whose experience lay in the world of motion pictures. At the end of six months the project was bogged down. The slackening in her dalliance with Rodney began at that point. He seemed to become disillusioned with her as the time for the abandonment of the project loomed.

He had wanted, from the very first, to go to bed with her. His eagerness and haste in wanting this struck her first humorously and then annoyed her. For a reason she could not name to herself she rejected the idea. His boyishness, his readiness in leaping the gap in years between them, was charming. But she was sensitive to the gossip she imagined. She was used to playing along with men who pressed their admiration on her, who sought an intimate relationship. She fostered the rumors and speculations growing out of such situations, as part of her public image. But to be seen in the role of aging coquette did not appeal to her.

Also he was bewildered, once they got into the hard

work of preparing for filming, that her first thought was always for her voice, for the role she was to project. He was hardworking himself but it apparently had never occurred to him that an opera diva was also someone who must put the physical effort of creating a role ahead of any less serious concerns. He became resentful, sulky, as if he felt he had been willfully deceived, when she put him off.

Finally the project was abandoned, out of money and in the midst of the disillusionment of those who were backing it. Magdalena was relieved. She could now begin to get ready for the next opera season. Francusi was delighted. He was especially pleased when he heard that Rodney had forsaken his pursuit of Magdalena and had gone back to California. He will make fine films, he said to Magdalena; he will become a great movie maker. Francusi's happiness and optimism rebuilt whatever erosion of her self-confidence had come about because of the failure of the film. She was glad to be back in the opera world, thinking only in terms of music and the dramatic presentation on the opera stage, to an audience visible before her ready to respond to the passions she could evoke with her voice. She was also relieved to be free of Rodney's importunities, which roused in her vague feelings of guilt, as if somehow she was denying him a cherished and deserved reward for his adulation of her.

There was one result of his departure that she did not welcome. Ruddle, as if he had been waiting all the while in the wings, was now at center stage. She treated him as she had treated him before, with impatience and occasional indulgence. In fact, she was often rude to him and cut off his overtures with a brusqueness she was later ashamed of. But now he had one avenue to her attention. He had become her man of business, the manager of her financial affairs.

That had been Francusi's doing. Early in her acquaintance with Ruddle, Francusi had accepted, on her behalf, Ruddle's offer to look after her affairs. She did not altogether welcome the idea, but, in the midst of the more important business of reviving her operatic career, she agreed. She had usually looked after her own investments, her own ventures into the stock market. This was a side of her that many of her friends and admirers knew nothing about—she did not display it to anyone. Only Francusi knew about it. Sometimes she smiled to herself when she thought of how surprised some might be who knew her only as Magdalena Gibbon the opera singer, if they were to learn of the careful success with which she had built up a more than comfortable estate. She supposed she had inherited from her staid ancestors a shrewd sense of what to do with money, a desire to have under her feet a solid financial base. Even as a young woman she had been careful with what she earned. She had been bold when boldness promised a better prize, even with a risk. She was not interested in the accumulation of wealth as an end in itself. She had wanted simply a safeguard for her life as an artist.

Francusi, who lacked her acumen, nevertheless admired it. He also thought that as an artist she should be freed of these preoccupations. He himself detested the need to be careful of outlay. He would rather have the help of others better supplied and more astute. He was surprised when she began to object to Ruddle's function as her financial adviser.

"But, Magdalena, he does everything! He looks after all these worries! Why should you concern yourself with these details? They are for business men. You are an artist, a great artist. Leave these things to these grubbers. He will never steal from you. He is a very able man. Look what he has done for himself. Look at what he is doing for the Opera. Everyone depends on him."

She smiled at him ironically. "I don't think he'd like to hear you call him a grubber. Yes, yes," she said impatiently. "All that is true." They were in the sitting room of her hotel suite, Francusi indulging in a late breakfast of croissants and chocolate. "I know he was very useful a year ago when I was too busy to pay much attention to my affairs. But don't you see, I do not like to be dependent on anyone. I am very well able to look after my own business. Otherwise I would have married, wouldn't I, and had a husband to look after me."

Francusi, holding a fragment of croissant before his mouth, glanced at her shrewdly. "You don't want him?"

"As a husband? Oh, certainly not! Nor as a lover. Don't you see? Because he is taking care of my affairs, I cannot be free to dismiss him, to send him away when I don't want him around."

Francusi put the piece of croissant in his mouth and chewed it. Then he said, "Mia cara, I'm sure you will find it very easy to deal with him. You never had any trouble dealing with men." He smiled at her.

Magdalena laughed. "So you think. I find them a great nuisance sometimes—all except you, mio caro. You know where to stop." It was true, she thought, with a quick inward glance. He had the delicacy of a woman when it came to stopping short of intrusion into her private feelings.

He hunched his shoulders in a deprecatory gesture. But his logic prevailed with her. In spite of her misgivings, too insubstantial to be put into words, she allowed Ruddle to continue as her man of business. Chiefly she realized that Ruddle was financially important to Francusi, and that his connection with her gave Francusi a handle in dealing with people of weight in the world of opera.

She developed a method of dealing with Ruddle— flirtatious on the surface, but capricious, willful, sometimes, when he became too impatient, snappish. He was a man who was not used to being thwarted. He was not discouraged by these moods of hers. In fact, they seemed to fascinate him. Occasionally, watching him out of the corner of her eye, she thought he became angry and wondered if his frustration would keep him away. But within a day or so he was once more at her side.

One afternoon, in the midst of rehearsals for the new opera season, she sat alone in her bedroom all at once aware of something she had not articulated in her own mind. In the eighteen months since she had left England she had found it easy to pass over every sort of invitation that had come her way for erotic pleasure. Rodney had not stirred in her anything but a sense of playfulness, a surface playfulness that would never have led to going to bed with him. He was a boy and she was amused by the earnestness of his infatuation with her. She was certain he was over it by now. No one else had roused the slightest feeling in her—the occasional girl or woman who made it plain that she was desirable, who sought intimacy by any sort of ruse. With a jolt she wondered if this coolness over such a length of time was a sign of age. And thinking about it in this way she realized that in fact desire had been building up in her without her awareness of the fact and without a thought of how it was to be gratified.

She knew she had a well-made body, with a deep bosom and wide pelvis, long, strong legs. She appraised herself without real vanity. Her body, the housing for her voice, was an instrument. She enjoyed the sense of strength and energy that flowed through that body, the feeling of abundant life that filled it. When she was in the throes of an affair she was ever aware of this strength, of the enjoyment of her own sexual vigor. She was not reflective at such times, too absorbed in physical pleasure.

She stirred in her chair and looked across the room to

her writing desk. May's latest letter lay there as she had dropped it after scanning it on arrival. Her eyes were drawn to it as by a magnet. She felt a surge of desire go through her body, so strong that she jumped up and paced about the room. May, May in bed with her, May's slighter body caught in the grip of her thighs, the feel of soft, acquiescent May awakening to the climax of desire under the touch of her hands. There was an extra depth of sensual pleasure with May that left far behind what now seemed to her the superficial, transient excitement of the sex act with anybody else. One reason, she remembered with acute longing, was that May reached out for her, sought to enter into the deepest well of her erotic feeling, as if, to gratify herself, she must plunge thus into Magdalena's.

Pierced by this recollection she stopped in her movement about the room and flung herself down on the bed. For several minutes she was racked by the most enormous surge of sexual feeling she had ever experienced. It came up from the innermost part of her being and wrung her in its grip. In its center May floated. Quieting at last she lay panting, awed by the strength of what she had experienced. As reason once more took over she wondered how this could be, that for weeks and months she had suppressed and, she had thought, gradually banished from her emotional life the memory of May. How she had deceived herself! The smooth surface had covered a smoldering fire that had insulated her from the attraction of anyone else, had made her think that she had outlived that spring of life.

She sat up and looked over again at the letter lying on her desk. She had made a practice lately of glancing hastily at May's letters—they came now at widely spaced intervals—and putting them aside, as if she did not trust herself to read them properly. By doing this she lessened their impact. What was it that this last letter had said? May's father had died. That was it. She should make some immediate response, in ordinary courtesy. This event meant, she supposed, that May was even more firmly bound to her mother. An involuntary shudder went through her and she got up to get dressed and go out in an effort to recover her equilibrium.

The opera season that began that autumn was, in its beginning, as successful as all that preceded it. It was only towards its end that a serious misgiving assailed her. In her last aria, in a performance of Alceste, she had a moment of unsureness. It was fleeting. For a brief moment she seemed to lose command of her voice. Afterwards she put it down to fatigue. It was a demanding role, one which required her to be on stage almost continuously. She watched Francusi anxiously when he came to her dressing room after the last curtain call but she could not detect anything in his manner that showed he had noticed any lapse.

She decided that she had been too assiduously burning the candle at both ends. She must be more careful to save her strength, to turn down the too-frequent social engagements. She took to spending odd hours in her hotel sitting room reading, finding that she had after all a taste for a certain amount of solitude. Even so, as she prepared for a new performance, she felt a hidden strain while she waited for her first cue. The fleeting unsureness was not repeated. The season ended without any untoward happening. She was relieved when the last performance was over. Of course, the critics would have picked up the least faltering in the quality of her singing. After all, she had been for so long the standard against which all other singers had been measured that the slightest lapse would be noticed at once.

But she must not brood. This was the time of year when she had first met May. She tried to convince herself that the event had become remote in her memory, like an episode that had not really happened, a fanciful thing to which her memory had attached a significance that it did not really have. And yet a small inner voice asked if this was really so?

Francusi, aware that something troubled her, had urged her to go abroad for a holiday. She would not listen to him. Instead she responded to an invitation to take part in a summertime musical festival in the New England mountains.

The disaster struck in the first week of the new opera season that following autumn. Again, without warning, she felt the sudden momentary lapse. It was as if a prop had been knocked out from under her. This time it was obvious to others. She saw a look of surprise on the face of the baritone with whom she shared the scene. In her dressing room, out of an irrational fright, she raged at Francusi, who sat bewildered and apprehensive, waiting for the storm to subside. When he had the chance to speak, he said urgently that it was nothing to worry about. It was a moment's weakness, something any singer might experience. Perhaps she had been driving her voice too hard, or herself. She had always been splendidly healthy, except for that breakdown she had had a couple of years ago. But she had fully recovered from that.

She switched around to glare at him. Indeed it was the memory of that breakdown that so frightened her now. It was no consolation for him to remind her of it.

The next morning the lapse was noted by one of the critics in his review. He was not one of those who lay in wait for singers to display imperfections. His tone was meant to be consolatory. After all, he said, Magdalena Gibbon had been above all weakness for so long that no one could wonder that now perhaps there might be some falling short of her usual perfection. Reading this Magdalena thought, He thinks I am getting too old to sing opera, and she flung the paper down in a sudden rage.

The rage was only an expression of the anxiety that now began to gnaw at her. Confident in her power, secure in her feeling of success, she had in the past enjoyed the titillation of nerves that a coming performance gave her. Now there was fear mixed with this. Throughout the performance she waited for another moment when her voice would not respond as she expected it to. Gradually she was aware that, whether or not because of this anxiety, the quality of her singing was not quite what it had always been. The comments of the critics, although veiled in friendly terms, confirmed what she feared.

Francusi said nothing and he did not act as if he noticed anything untoward. But he must, she thought. His ear was very acute. It must be that he did not want to add to the dismay he knew she felt. Or perhaps he too saw in this the first effect of age and accepted it with his usual fatalism. For she knew that his constant optimism was built upon fatalism, the undoubted result of the tragedies in his own life.

In her preoccupation with herself she did not pay much attention to what affected other people. It was February and a flu epidemic swept New York. She still thought of herself as always healthy, immune to the colds and viruses that laid other singers low. The illness that had conquered her in England was an aberration, something not to be repeated. Even that had happened when she was not singing. She had never had to yield her role in an opera, even for one night, to a substitute because she was unable to sing. But one morning she awoke with a fever and a sore throat. The doctor Francusi brought said she must not tax her strength by performing that night. She did not heed him and sang what everyone said was a superlative performance. Sitting up in bed the next morning with the newspapers spread over the coverlet she read such phrases as "The greatest triumph yet," "Finishing the season in a blaze of glory." It had been the final performance of the season. Even the critics who had commented on a certain falling away of the quality of her voice outdid themselves in praising it. A gossip columnist, more outspoken, said that the lack of brilliance in her performances this season must have been caused not by any failure of her voice but by some unhappy episode in her personal life.

And what would that be, she wondered savagely. She was used to having amorous affairs attributed to her, with the most unlikely people. Perhaps she should surprise these gossips sometime by having a public affair with a woman. In disgust she picked up the newspapers and turned over to see if she could sleep and thus ease the tension in her throat.

She could not. Instead she felt again, as if an echo of the past, the depression that had seized her two years before, when the bout of pneumonia had robbed her of her singing voice. Lying there in bed she remembered the cloud of despair that had enveloped her, the dread she had felt of the future. That was it. She had had her future. She could not return to the operatic stage to suffer through another season with the doubt, the fearfulness, the anticipation of failure, that had dogged her through the last few weeks. No one, apparently, had noticed what an effort this last performance had cost her. She remembered the night before only through a haze of fatigue. She had been unaware of anything except the demand she was making on her voice and the response of the audience, which she willed to come forth, this time experienced as a sea, heaving and billowing till it broke at her feet. Suppose her voice had failed at such a crucial moment. She must never risk that possibility again.

It was several days later before she could think clearly and articulate what she thought. She was vaguely aware of nurses and the doctor and that Francusi occasionally stood in the door of her room to greet her softly. When he was allowed to come and sit by her bed she strove to put in words what had been in her mind during the intervening period. He listened carefully.

"You mean, mia cara, that you will not sing opera ever again? This is perhaps hasty. You are weak now. You will get stronger."

She rolled her head on the pillow, impatient with his failure—or refusal—to grasp the finality of her decision. He patted her hand lying on the coverlet. "Another time, another time," he murmured. She was too weak to argue with him.

The next time he came she was sitting propped up by several pillows. He saw that she had been waiting for him.

She said, "I can't go through another season waiting for the moment when my voice will fail. The last few weeks have been torture. Surely you noticed."

He put his head on one side and raised his eyebrows. She knew he was too honest to deny the truth. "You have sung too much, perhaps. You should have more rest. You give too much of yourself. One must learn to conserve one's strength as one grows older."

"Aha! Then you too think I'm getting old!"

He saw the flash of gaiety in her manner. "Magdalena, you'll never be old like other people."

She reached out to take hold of his hand. "You always find excuses for me. Yes, of course I shall get old. Age comes sooner to singers than to other people, as far as their voices are concerned. Yes, of course I can still sing. I suppose I shall croak away till I die. But that is not what I shall do on the opera stage. Do you think I want to go on till I'm a laughingstock, till everybody giggles behind my back? I've seen it happen to other singers. It is better to stop before that."

He protested. "That is not how it is yet! We must make

changes in the roles you sing. We must choose easier—"

Her fragile self-possession cracking, she began to rage at him, until she was gasping for breath. Alarmed he got up from his chair.

"No! No, Magdalena! You must not agitate yourself so! Wait till you've recovered. We'll talk about it then." He looked desperately over his shoulder for the nurse. Magdalena had refused to go to the hospital and her hotel suite had been arranged as a sickroom. She saw his distress and shrank back in the bed. He waited apprehensively, slowly sitting down again as she lay quietly.

She pondered, when he was gone, remembering his words, "That is not how it is yet!" Of course he recognized the fact that she was into her forties and that her voice and physical stamina had lasted remarkably well. He would always save her what humiliation and anxiety he could, for he was the most reliable friend she had. But he would not initiate any change in her life. That she would have to do for herself.

But when she thought of the essence of that change—that her voice was no longer the center of her life—panic overwhelmed her. To stop performing—that would be to be thrust into a kind of limbo. Her misery in brooding over this prospect was such that it interfered with her recovery. She made no effort to rouse herself. She fought against the doctor and the nurses when they tried to get her out of bed and into a new routine of treatment. She hated the world, she hated herself. In only one corner of her consciousness did there seem to be a little ray of light. It held within it an image of May. May seemed a long way off, buried under so much that she must be far beyond reach. When she was alone in the depth of night, even the nurse away, she could not withhold tears. She had lost May and through her own recklessness. She knew that Francusi realized the depth of her despair, though he could not know its source. When he came now he avoided the subject of her retirement from the operatic stage and evaded any reference she tried to make to it.

One morning he came into her room with a special smile on his round face, pink from the cold March air in the street. He sat down by her, reaching into the inner pocket of his coat as he did so. He had not brought her any mail on his other visits, warned by the doctor that he should keep any worries away. But now he brought out a thin airmail letter-sheet, the sort that came from abroad, and held it out to her.

"It is from your little Englishwoman," he said, pleased at being able to offer her something cheering.

For a moment she did not reach for it, astounded at the fact that he knew who May was. He was always observant, more so than many people realized. He must have noted, over the months, that from time to time she had had these letters from England, and how she reacted to them—not as she did when she received other letters from friends abroad. She knew he had a long memory and of all the people she knew in London after she had left the convalescent home, he was the one most likely to have seen that there was someone who absorbed her free time and attention and that that someone was not a man.

Finally she reached out to take the letter from him. She tore it open and then paused to glance at him. He had given her a long look and then had gone away across the room to gaze out of the window.

The letter was brief. Dearest, it said, I must let you know that Mother died a week ago. She was buried last Saturday. I have spent the time since making up my mind about what I should do. I have now decided that I shall sell this house and live altogether in London. You probably do not remember that I have a cousin James who is a solicitor here. He is quite prosperous and he wants to buy the house. So that is settled."

Yes, thought Magdalena, half-angrily. He will pay a pittance for it and you will not give a second thought to the transaction, though you should have a good price since I'm sure this is the only inheritance you will have from your parents.

She went back to the letter. "I shall send you my new address as soon as I am ready to move. That will not be a great thing because I do not wish to take many things from here." Poor darling. At last you have a chance for a new life. Yes, it was typical of May to be unsentimental at such a time. She had done her job. She would now go on to what lay ahead. And I am not in that future. A violent pang of loss went through Magdalena. It was her own fault. She had forfeited what she now knew she most wanted.

She looked back at the letter. There was another line or so. "The opera season is over. Will you be coming abroad this summer?"

She read the question through again. This was the first time that May had made any reference to her returning to London. In fact she had been abroad twice in the two years since they were together, carefully avoiding more than an overnight stay in London and saying nothing in her letters to May of the fact. She admitted to herself that this was a sort of cowardice but what worried her more was the idea that this subterfuge hid a real weakness of character. She had not been able to remove May from her inner consciousness and place her in the anteroom of her emotions as she had done so easily with others who had thought themselves indispensable to her.

Nervously, she glanced up; suddenly returning to the present, looking for Francusi, uneasy at what he might have noticed. But he was no longer there. Taking advantage of her preoccupation he had gone quietly out of the room. She sank back on her pillows and began to cry softly. Eventually she dropped off into an uneasy sleep, the letter still in her hand. She did not know how long she dozed but when she finally roused it was to be aware that she had dreamed of May, of being in bed with May, of feeling May's soft, smooth flesh under her hands, of responding to the delicate yet firm pressure of May's fingers in her most private spot. She roused and lay for a while exhausted with the pleasurable exhaustion of love-making. There had been times during the last months when she had dreamed of May, had wakened to a sense first of ecstasy remembered and then annoyance at the idea that she could not exorcise this desire for May. Now she let it stay with her, unwilling to let the ghost of May elude her. She had never fantasized about anyone else with whom she had gone to bed. She felt something uncomfortable under her body. Reaching for it she found May's letter, crumpled into a ball.

She got out of bed after that, too restless and distraught to lie inertly as she had for the last week or so. There were people who wanted to see her, and the doctor, uncertain whether this sudden change in mood indicated another step in her recovery, said she could have visitors for brief periods. But she refused to see them. There was no question about her returning to the normal life of a singer for some time yet—not rehearsals, not try-outs in new music. The prohibition focussed all her anxiety, all her sense of dread, on the future of her voice. Whenever Francusi came to see her, she raged about this uncertainty. He shook his head compassionately at her.

"Magdalena, you must be reasonable. You must recover from this illness first, before you make decisions. We cannot know for a while, the doctor says, what permanent effect this will have. It is not just your voice. It is your lungs, your body also. You must have patience." He knew this was a useless admonition. She had never had patience for anything except the grueling practice in the use of her voice. There her patience was endless. But in nothing else.

Finally, one morning, when, in spite of her nervous excitement, she seemed obviously stronger, he stopped her in the midst of an outburst by saying, "Magdalena, I think you will be able to sing opera again. But you must know that it will not be as it has been in the past. Cara, you cannot reverse the years. You are marvelous. Even now you are marvelous. You have done what other divas have not been able to do. Nevertheless—"

She stared at him. He could see fury in her eyes and though he kept an imperturbable manner, he quailed inwardly. Then he saw that the fury was changing to despair. He got up and crossed the room to put his arm around her. She was a tall woman and his head was only a little above her shoulder but the strength in his grasp seemed to calm her. This was a rare gesture. They seldom touched one another beyond a light swift kiss on the cheek. Physical endearments had very little to do with the strength of the affection that cemented their friendship. Now, however, Magdalena responded to his gesture of support. She sat down in the nearest chair and burst into tears.

He was silent for a few minutes. He had seldom seen her cry and never with such abandon. It unnerved him. Eventually he patted her shoulder.

"It comes to all of us, mia cara, this moment when we know we cannot call back the past. But we cannot lose courage to go forward on the rest of our journey."

She wiped her eyes and put her hand over his. "I am sorry, old friend. Perhaps you had better go and let me pull myself together." She looked at him with an attempt at lightheartedness. "How many aging divas have you consoled?"

When he had gone she sat for a while mulling over the implications of what he had said. Of course he had noticed the lapses in her singing during the season. Perhaps he had even anticipated them. Beneath his soothing, flattering manner there was a wealth of shrewdness and practicality. She supposed there was little in the world of opera that was new to him. Sing more opera if you must, he said, but don't deceive yourself that you will remain the Magdalena Gibbon you have been in the past.

But she could not be so cold-blooded about it. The panic that had engulfed her since she had begun to recover threatened to come back. She must exorcise it, she must keep it at bay at least. For the next few days she refused to see anyone and even sent away the nurse who was still with her during the day. At first she wallowed in despair but then returning physical strength asserted itself and she realized that she was reaching for some prop, some life preserver in this sea of helplessness.

Throughout this period of disorientation she had held in the back of her mind the memory of May's letter. Several times she had taken it out of the drawer of the nightstand by her bed and reread it. It was a meager little letter. The words and phrases were commonplace, expressing nothing more than the essential news May wished to convey. Beyond that, however, she read what May might have said had they been face to face. There was a life in these ordinary words that was May's impress. The touch of the rumpled paper in her fingers seemed to convey something. The memory of the weeks in London with May surged back into her being as if the intervening years had not happened. Standing by her window looking out at the street below, she was aware for the first time that she saw the bright sunshine, the people walking past, the procession of life.

She was interrupted by a knock on the door of her

sitting room, followed at once by its opening to admit a hotel maid.

The woman said, "Your mail, madam," and deposited several letters on the side table.

Languidly she went over to see what was there. She saw May's handwriting at once. Another letter so soon! She snatched it up and tore it open. My darling, it said, I have just seen in the *Times* a statement that you are recovering from illness. Is it true and is it as it was when you were here and were so long in the convalescent home? I am very much distressed that I have not known about this before. Please do write and tell me that you are really on the mend.

Holding the letter in her hand she went back to look out of the window, as if seeking some answer from the world outside her room. She found herself trembling. What she was looking for was something she could not do without longer. She hurried across the room and sought in a drawer for writing paper. May, she scrawled, you must come to me. Will you come? I need you badly. She sealed the letter in a frenzy and when she had handed it to the maid she had summoned to post it, sat with her head in her hands, unable to control her anxiety. It would be a week before May received the letter. But she could not wire or phone without giving May alarm. Besides—

In the succeeding days her whole being was caught up in the question of whether May would respond. A dialogue went on in her mind between the two voices of herself—the voice that reminded her that this separation from May had been entirely of her own doing, that she had treated May very shabbily, that May's letters lately had showed that at last May herself had begun to accept their separation as final. On the other hand, there was the voice that insisted vehemently that May must come, that May must never have given up, that May would be forgiving, that May had not sought and found any other attachment to take the place of theirs.

In the midst of this inner turmoil she made a great effort to appear calm. She succeeded to the extent that the people she dealt with, the friends she finally saw, thought she was her normal self, though perhaps somewhat depressed. Of course there was gossip, about the fact that her illness might have affected her voice, speculation about her future singing career. She gave no sign that she was aware of these murmurings. In every moment she was alone she was absorbed by her own inner debate. Thousands of times she calculated the days that must elapse before May received her letter. In moments of extreme impatience she thought about a transatlantic phone call but was intimidated by the idea of making her cry of despair on a perhaps unclear telephone, daunted by the possibility that May, taken by surprise, unable to reach a hasty decision, would temporize, say No. She could not face the idea of that answer.

It was she herself who was taken by surprise one morning when the bellhop brought a cable to her door before breakfast. May said, "Am arriving New York, BOAC, Friday," and gave a flight number. For a long moment Magdalena stared at the piece of flimsy paper, benumbed by the swiftness of May's decision, May, who had always hesitated when confronted with a sudden need for action. Gradually she sorted out her own reactions. Of course. May was now a free agent. She was no longer bound by ties to a duty. But all this sober realization faded before the important fact: tomorrow they would be together.

She said nothing to anyone, not even to Francusi, who, she saw, within a few minutes of being with her realized that some magical change had come over her, that she was no longer the brooding, touchy woman he had watched anxiously during the last weeks. This was a different Magdalena, the old Magdalena, a vibrant, eager, exhilarated woman who seemed to have forgotten the unhappiness in which she had been sunk for so long. At a dinner party that evening she had scintillated and when he had escorted her back to her hotel, he saw that she was anxious for him to go. She was looking forward to something else, to someone else. Glancing at him as he said Goodnight, she could imagine him wondering, Is she in love with somebody new, undecided whether to rejoice or to worry—rejoice that something or someone—with Magdalena it must be a person—had brought happiness back to her or worry that she had rushed into some situation that would eventually bring unhappiness.

Friday. An hour before the arrival time of May's flight Magdalena was at the airport. The flight was late—rough weather over the Atlantic delayed it. She paced the open spaces of the terminal. In her mind's eye was the image of May as she had last seen her—a slender woman in a brown tweed suit and a soft hat, indistinguishable on a crowded street until you noticed the direct gaze of the blue eyes. Yes, that was what was remarkable about May, that steady, intelligent gaze, not calculating, not critical, not judging, but weighing the meaning of what it took in. How would she appear to May? All at once she felt abashed, by her own actions and motives in the last couple of years, by the impertinence of her summoning May this way, for her own need. By the time the gate was open and the passengers began to file through to the customs and immigration officials, Magdalena's self-confidence had ebbed to its lowest point. Oh, May! The recollection stabbed through her. May, May. Are you as you used to be? Are you still my May? Shall I be able to reach out to you and touch you as I used?

In her anxiety she almost missed seeing May passing along behind a tall man carrying a raincoat and an attache case. May's attention was fixed on the immigration officer whose hand was outstretched for her passport. Of course this was May's first trip across the Atlantic, probably the first time she had ever flown, though she had at one time or another crossed the Channel to France. The anxiety of a new traveler showed in her face as she handed over her passport and waited for the man to examine it. After that she passed through the line by the table where the luggage lay open while the customs' officer poked into the corners, stirring the garments and toiletries. At last, with a look of relief on her face she closed her bag and turned to look around her.

As they met face to face, Magdalena said lightly, "Did you think they would find contraband of some kind?"

May did not smile but looked at her gravely. When she said nothing, Magdalena took the suitcase away from her and said, "Let's find a cab."

Still silent May followed her through the terminal out to the cab rank. Sitting in the cab Magdalena found herself longing to speak, to say something that would break this pane of clear glass that cut them off from each other. May turned away from her to gaze out of the window, apparently absorbed by the street sights. Her whole attitude seemed to say, I am not ready to talk to you, and Magdalena, disconcerted, said none of the commonplaces that would have filled up this public silence.

When they reached the hotel and while Magdalena told the doorman to pay the cab and take the suitcase to her suite, May gazed about at the street and up at the tall buildings, many times higher than any in London. Still she was wordless. At last they were in the suite, the bellhop dismissed. Magdalena asked tentatively, "May, won't you speak to me?"

May's gaze focussed on her. "Of course. How are you, dear? I am bewildered. I thought perhaps you would be too ill to meet me at the airport. I expected you to send someone else."

The soft unassumingness of her manner, so quintessentially May, broke the barrier. She reached up to take Magdalena's face in her hands. Magdalena seized her in her arms.

"Oh, May! May! What can I say? What can I tell you?" She held May's slighter body against her own, felt the beating of May's heart against her breast. The two years of separation vanished. May, as she had always done, snuggled deeper in her embrace.

After all there was not a great deal of talking, of explaining to be done. May did not ask and Magdalena did not say that she was to stay there with her, that there was ample room for her clothes in the closet, a bed ample for the two of them. It had always been May's way to take things as she held them out to her, without comment, without demur.

When they sat down on the love seat by the window, May said, "But you have been ill, haven't you?" For the first time she was examining Magdalena's appearance, searching her face for changes.

"I've had pneumonia again. It began with the flu, as before. At the end of the season, thank God."

May's eyebrows rose. "Again?" She did not speak the rest of her thought, which Magdalena understood nevertheless. After a moment's silence May added, "I see. That is what made you send for me."

Magdalena said in anguish, "May, you don't hate me, you do forgive me?"

"I could never hate you." She paused for a moment. "I had almost given up. I began to think that you had really cast me out of your life. It did not seem possible to me, after what had happened between us, but I began to think that it could not have meant to you what it did to me."

Magdalena bit her lip. "I tried hard to convince myself that it was just a happy interlude—since you would not abandon your own life and come with me. I tried to think it was just another affair like those I've played with in the past. But it isn't. I'm not proud of myself."

"Nor should you be," said May flatly. She was looking at Magdalena, comparing what she saw with what she remembered. "You talk about affairs. That has nothing to do with you and me. But I do not like to think of your having them."

Compelled to taste the dregs of humiliation Magdalena asked, "You have heard things about me?"

"Yes, of course. You know that your private life is quite public. You were going to make a film of an opera and you were to be married to the man who was producing it."

Magdalena winced. "It was not quite so bald as that. No, I never intended to marry Rodney. And I never went to bed with him, though that is what he wanted. He got tired of the game—or frightened."

"How foolish of him."

Magdalena looked at her in surprise. "Why? What do you mean?"

There was a faint smile on May's face. "Really, my dear, you are quite intimidating."

Nettled, Magdalena said, "Intimidating? Not to you, in any case."

"Of course not to me." May reached over and touched her cheek. Magdalena shivered at the cool, light, intimate touch. May said, "You can never be patient, my darling. You would never be able to wait for anything. So you cannot understand how I could wait and have half a loaf until it was possible to have the whole."

Magdalena sat twisting her hands together, looking

down at the floor. "May, I have really suffered this last week—since I mailed the letter to you asking you to come. It was pretty presumptuous of me, wasn't it? After all, you had an opportunity to make your own life. You might well have found someone else who would not be so foolish as to throw away your love—"

May reached out again and touched her arm. "But you did not, dearest, did you? You thought you were doing that, but you could not. As for me, I could never have thought of anyone but you."

No, thought Magdalena, it was true. Though she did not have May's steadfastness, nevertheless what May said was true for both of them. May always cut through the outward disguise of something to the heart of the matter. But looking at her now she was suddenly aware that May was thin and pale, that in fact, sitting there beside her, May drooped against the back of the seat. The time of their separation had plainly taken a greater toll of May than of herself. And on top of that, the transatlantic flight.

Magdalena stood up abruptly and reached to pull May up also. "May, you are exhausted. We should not be sitting here talking. You must rest. Come into the bedroom."

She led her into the bedroom. May, sitting on the edge of the bed, allowed her to take off her clothes and put her naked between the sheets. With a deep sigh May was almost instantly asleep. Magdalena, looking down at her, felt a wave of love and guilt. She leaned over and passed her hands gently over May's bare body, tracing the too-prominent ribs, thrusting her fingers into the soft fair bush at her pubis. She could not believe that May was here, to be touched, fondled. She did not deserve May yet she rejoiced that it was she who had been fortunate enough to capture May's heart.

May slept soundly into the afternoon. Magdalena was held captive by her presence. She told the hotel telephone operator that she would not take calls. She told the desk clerk that she was not at home to anyone. Everybody else now seemed remote and unimportant in the light of the fact of May's presence. While she slept Magdalena recapitulated her own thoughts and actions in the period of their separation. She looked at her own behavior, the self-concerned impulses, emotions, the excuses, the angry resentments, the self-justifications she had framed, trying to dredge up every unworthy feeling she had called up to bolster her self-esteem. She found that she could remember a great deal—that in itself demonstrated the fact that she had really never convinced herself that her life could go on without May.

This self-examination was in the nature of a confession, she thought—a confession to purge her soul of the shoddy mass of false feeling that weighed on her. It was something that she must somehow put into words to May. May must know the worst about her. What a waste the last two and a half years had been, what an inexcusable, wicked waste of their lives.

As she sat beside the bed draining this cup of bitter self-reproach, May stirred. It was almost four o'clock in the afternoon but she had been unaware of the passage of time. She leaned over as May's eyes opened, seeing first their uncomprehending gaze and then the change to hope and then certainty.

May put her hand up to touch her face as she murmured, "Is it really you, dearest?"

"Of course. You're here, in New York, in my bed. You've been sleeping like the dead. Do you feel better?"

May rolled her head on the pillow. "It is wonderful. I didn't dream it. I'm really here with you."

Magdalena, choked with the self-castigation of the last hours, tried to begin to say what filled her mind and heart. She was unable to find words for it. May watched her as she stumbled through several incoherent sentences. She could see the dreamy contentment in May's eyes turning into alert comprehension.

May said, turning on her side to look at her and pushing the pillow up to raise her head, "I've been asleep too long. You've worked yourself up. Let's not talk about all that. It doesn't matter now, my darling, does it?"

With a great feeling of relief Magdalena took her hands in her own. "May, I cannot let it go as if I hadn't been such a fool—fool enough to separate us this way, to lose the precious moments we might have had if I had done as you wanted—if I had settled for half a loaf, till now."

May contemplated her silently for a while before she said, "Perhaps it would be best if we did let it go. In all the time we were separated I could not believe that we would not be together again, that you were not the person I knew you to be. You see, I was right." She sat up and pushed Magdalena gently away. "Now I simply must go to the bathroom."

When she came back and lay down again in the bed she said, looking up at Magdalena soberly, "I think you have punished yourself enough, without anything I could say. That is what you've been doing, isn't it?"

"I've been taking a close look at what a stupid idiot I have been—more than that—what an utterly selfish egoist. Why do you love me, May?"

May looked at her calmly. "Why, because you are you."

That night, in the warm dark of the bed, they forgot the time of longing. Magdalena lay on her back, luxuriating in the sweet burden of May's body on hers. May laughed, soft, happy laughter as she felt the touch of Magdalenla's hands. By the time they sank into sleep in each other's arms the discord that had stood between them had vanished. They had a whole loaf now, thought Magdalena.

The clear remembrance, the vivid awareness of May, began to fade as fatigue overcame her. But a calmness was settling into her spirit. The fear, the sense of having lost her way, was ebbing away—for the first time in how long? Sitting in the chair in the strange bedroom she sighed. She had crossed over the bridge above the abyss. She was another long step closer to May.

She sank into sleep.

IV

It was Sunday morning and Ailsa had set the breakfast table in the bay of the window that looked out over the river. She and Dina rarely ate breakfast together except on Sunday, when rising late they lingered over the coffee cups and the morning paper.

Today there was a difference. She had set a place for Mary, though Camilla had said that Mary would probably not come out of her room of her own accord. "You're going to have to coax her. She forgets about time. She wants to keep away from people."

Camilla had said that Mary should be given a few days to get used to her new surroundings before she had to endure the interview with Ruddle. Ailsa and Dina had debated whether they should tell him that Mary was with them. Dina had decided against this.

"He's the masterful type," Dina said. "He'll come here demanding to see her at once. I'll tell him that we'll bring her here at an appointed time. He can set the date."

"Won't he ask you where she is in the meantime?"

"I won't tell him. I'll tell him she is under medical care—can't see anybody without a doctor."

Ailsa turned away from gazing out of the window at the midmorning sun glistening on the river. While she had been standing there, Dina had come into the room, yawning and stretching her arms up over her head. The flowing robe she was wearing fell open to show her supple, olive-skinned body.

"You'd better fasten it," said Ailsa, looking at her.

"She's not out here yet," Dina retorted.

Ailsa sighed. "I know. I am going to fetch her. Camilla said she would be passive, would not show any initiative."

She crossed the living room and walked down the short hall to the farthest door and knocked gently. There was no sound from the room. She knocked again, calling softly, "Mary, won't you come and have some breakfast?"

Still there was no response and reluctantly Ailsa opened the door. Her glance went first to the bed. It was empty, the covers turned back. Mary was not a restless sleeper, for the bed and pillow were scarcely rumpled. Ailsa looked toward the window. Mary sat in the armchair in front of it, gazing at her.

"Do come, Mary. Dina and I are waiting for you."

Obediently but silently Mary got up stiffly from her chair and stood still for a moment. She wore a silk dressinggown covered with bright flowers. Camilla must have got her that, thought Ailsa, walking over to take her arm. She was momentarily surprised to find that Mary, standing straight, was so much taller than she. Mary, answering the light pressure of Ailsa's hand, allowed her to lead her down the hall to the breakfast table.

Dina stood near the window, watching them with curiosity.

"Mary," said Ailsa, "this is Dina. We live here together."

Mary looked directly at Dina. God, thought Dina, what a pair of eyes! But Mary looked away almost at once and sat down in the chair Ailsa drew out for her.

It was a strange meal, that breakfast, as Ailsa remembered it later. At first Mary was completely silent, eating the food Ailsa offered her. Dina, for once tongue-tied with embarrassment, kept glancing at her and making absentminded answers to Ailsa's comments. Dina, Ailsa knew, found it difficult to talk to sick people and young children. Obviously her image of Mary had been overlaid by that of Magdalena and the reality sitting here before her rendered her nearly speechless.

Halfway through the meal, while Ailsa was talking about the international news—she was being careful about the topics she chose for conversation and this seemed safe—Mary suddenly raised her head and asked, "What day is it?"

Ailsa stopped in mid-sentence and Dina jumped in, "Why, it's Sunday. That is why we can have breakfast like this."

Mary persisted. "But what is the date? It doesn't seem cold."

Dina, bemused in listening to the depth of tone of her voice, was slow to reply. "It is May 16."

Mary dropped her eyes again and murmured, "May."

Ailsa and Dina exchanged glances.

It was a difficult day for them, seeking ways to communicate with Mary. After breakfast she stayed in the living room, making no effort to return to her bedroom. But though she was physically present she was psychically remote. Dina, unable to endure the strain, found an excuse to go out. Ailsa, torn between anxiety and compassion, tried to read the paper, finding herself reading the same item twice or finishing another without comprehension of what it said. Mary sat quite silent, not even looking out of the window. At last, folding up the paper, Ailsa said, "Would you like to see the paper, Mary?"

At the sound of her voice, Mary turned towards her and seemed to consider. In fact, thought Ailsa, she is trying to grasp what it was I said. Eventually Mary shook her head. She still had made no real response by the time Dina returned. Ailsa and Dina found themselves talking in low tones, as if in a sick room, till Dina impatiently shook off the constraint. She tried to talk to Mary, who at first merely looked at her silently. Dina talked about the theater, about the opera season just past, about summer musical festivals. Ailsa, becoming aware oif her intent, watched apprehensively.

Dina said aggressively, "There is a new singer who is going to sing next season at the Met, in Alceste. That was one of your principal roles, wasn't it, Magdalena?"

Mary slowly turned her head to look at her. "It was a favorite of mine."

Dina sent Ailsa a look of triumph. "You sang it often?"

But the bright gleam that had shone out of the darkness for a moment had fled and Mary simply shook her head. In the hours that followed, Dina, pursuing the idea that challenges would awaken Mary's memory, talked constantly and vigorously about everything to do with music, occasionally throwing in a question meant to surprise an unguarded response. Sometimes Mary answered her with a grave certainty but chiefly she remained wrapped in her own world. Then Ailsa, noticing that she had begun to tire and remembering Camilla's many bits of advice, interrupted and coaxed her to get up and go to her room for a rest.

When Ailsa came back into the living room, Dina said, "There can't be any doubt now, can there, that she is Magdalena?"

Troubled, Ailsa reminded her, "You remember that

Ruddle pointed out that she may be someone under a delusion that she is Magdalena. There are cases of people who adopt someone else's persona, who imagine themselves to be that other person."

"Queen Victoria or Napoleon," said Dina scornfully. "You don't really believe that. Don't you notice the personal details? Don't you remember that she said that she gave up singing Alceste because the strain of being continuously on the stage was too much for her?"

"She could have learned that from reading about Magdalena—or perhaps she might have remembered newspaper accounts. Magdalena was very much in the public eye when she was at her prime. Mary is old enough to remember that sort of thing, especially if she had a fixation on Magdalena. There must have been quite a number of women who fell in love with Magdalena, even if only at a distance. She was that kind of woman."

During the next few days, when her presence became more familiar Mary was less intrusive in their lives. At first, Ailsa, returning to the apartment each afternoon, opened the door with a sense of foreboding. She lingered in the vestibule for a moment listening for some sound that would reassure her. There was never any. Mary was never in the living room. Only when she went to the door of Mary's room and knocked and even then had to open it and glance in, was she sure that Mary was still there. Camilla had said, when Ailsa spoke of her anxiety, that she did not think that Mary would ever run away. "She's afraid of the street now. She won't go back there unless something else frightens her more."

"Something else?"

Camilla had looked at her with her ironic smile. "Like being trapped into some situation she's more afraid of than the street. Look, don't get uptight. She trusts you. I wouldn't have let her go and stay with you if I didn't think she'd stay put. I don't want her back in the street. I'd have to go and find her before she killed herself."

"She is so passive. She responds very little to anything we say."

Camilla shrugged. "She's better than she used to be." She thought for a moment. "You know, she probably has a lot of thinking to do, a lot of sorting out in her own mind, before she can talk to other people. She's been out of it a long time, you know."

"Perhaps you are right," said Ailsa, still in doubt.

* * * * *

She awakened to daylight, aware that she was awakening from sleep, not the semi-consciousness in which she usually was sunk. It was daylight, but the mellowing daylight of late afternoon. She turned her head towards the window. What had awakened her? She turned her head again towards the door. The door opening, of course, slowly, quietly, and in it the brief glimpse of the woman with the pale hair who brought the recollection of May so immediately to her mind, her spirit. The woman did this often—opening the door gently and standing there for a moment and withdrawing again, closing the door softly behind her.

She sighed. She could go back to May now. She must follow this trail of recollection to its bitter end, knowing the anguish she must suffer before she reached it. She could not shirk this, she could not run away from it if she was to recapture May.

The morning after May's arrival she had awakened to find May looking down at her, propped on one elbow.

"You're awake, dearest," May had said.

Magdalena reached up to her. "What a waste of time—sleeping. Oh, May, you're here with me!"

May laughed. "Oof! Don't squeeze me so! Yes, I'm here

and I can feel you and not just imagine," and she sank down into her embrace.

While they breakfasted May explained that she had been able to make so sudden a departure from London because the firm she worked for had leapt at the idea that she should come to the States as their representative. They were anxious to complete an important sale of a recovered painting to a wealthy American who vacillated from day to day.

"He doesn't know anything about painting," she explained. "He is a businessman and he wants to be sure it is a good investment. They thought I might be able to persuade him to make up his mind."

Francusi came to see them that first day. He stared at May for a moment in astonishment and then she could see that a faint memory stirred in his mind, a memory, no doubt, of a glimpse he must have had of her in Magdalena's company in London, at some moment when they were not aware that he had seen them together.

Now he bowed and said, "I am Francusi. I'm an old friend of Magdalena."

How quick he was to seize the essence of a situation! thought Magdalena. She saw that he intended to have May's friendship also.

Others of her friends did not take this change in her life so easily. They were curious about this palely pretty, quiet, unapproachable woman who had suddenly appeared from across the Atlantic to occupy the central place in Magdalena's life. Most of them dissipated their ill feelings in gossip and came to accept the new order quickly. Some of them kept their resentment alive in oblique remarks. Ruddle was the most intransigent. Whenever he could he showed that he did not accept May as an inevitable member of any group in which Magdalena was to be found. He insisted on making engagements with her alone. She saw him whenever she was forced to. When they went out to dinner or out for the evening he obviously brooded over this new threat to the intimacy he had hoped to create with her now that Rodney was no longer on the scene. She ignored his leading remarks.

May said nothing and Magdalena made no explanation to her. She knew May must observe that she was always bad tempered when she must deal with Ruddle. She also realized that her own way of life was changed in a manner and to a degree that she had not foreseen. When at the beginning of their closeness in London she had built her activities around May's weekend visits, it had been a temporary thing, something she was doing to make it possible for them to be together yet something that would presently become unnecessary. Now the situation was quite different. May was the center of her life. She no longer thought and acted as a sole person. There was a dimension to her very identity that was now in May's hands.

She had never thought of this even as a possibility. The reality of what her life might be with May had taken her unawares.

Ruddle served as the catalyst that made this change apparent to her. She had always found him a problem. His importunities in the past had annoyed her. Now he had added a suppressed indignation, a barely contained censure to his manner when he talked to her. Whenever he encountered May he treated her with a contempt that was only thinly disguised by civility. One of these days, thought Magdalena, seething silently, he will forget himself and then I shall let him have it.

The climax came promptly. He had taken her out to dinner and when it was over and she announced that she must go back to her hotel, he exploded in demands that for once she must come to his apartment. There were things he had to say to her and she never allowed him a private time and place in which to say them.

Aware that what he said was true and dimly hopeful that this might be the showdown that would bring his constant pursuit of her to an end, she finally agreed. When they stood in his living room and she had reluctantly let him take her wrap, he began to talk without waiting for her to sit down, as if he could no longer hold back. Didn't she, he demanded, realize what she was doing? Didn't she realize how she was exposing herself to the worst kind of gossip? Even if there was no truth to the gossip—and he knew there could not be—didn't she know that her reputation was being ruined by filthy-minded people who would take delight in dragging her name into the mud? It was not a situation she should tolerate for a moment.

She stood listening to him for a while, unprepared for his attack, more interested at first in his display of angry words whose true meaning he sought to disguise. Looking at him with detachment, she thought how handsome he really was, what power was in his manner, his will, his drive to have his own way. No wonder women were fascinated by him—women, that is, who wanted from a man sexual domination, the social prestige such a man could provide. But gradually it dawned on her that his attack was on her and that the obliqueness of his diatribe was meant to deflect the full impact of what he was saying, that in this way he was allowing her a way in which to escape his censure if she agreed with what he demanded, if she accepted the rightness of his condemnation.

Her temper rising, she cut into the stream of his words. "What are you talking about? You know I don't pay attention to gossip. You can't stop gossip. Anybody in my situation must expect it."

"But you don't have to provide material for it. This is

much worse than anything that's been said about you before this. If you don't put a stop to it, decent people won't have anything to do with you. Why must you act as if there was some truth to this talk? Why don't you send that woman away? What do you want with such an insignificant, meddlesome creature in your life?"

At last he had said it. Her eyes blazed as she looked into his furious ones. "Are you telling me what I am to do? How I should live my life? You may be my lawyer, my financial adviser, but let me tell you, your concern with my affairs stops there!"

The ominous restraint that he heard in her voice put a check on the thrust of his anger. "You are much more to me than a client and you know that. I love you. You are the woman who means more to me than any human being ever has and whom I must have. I've tried for years to get you to accept me, to acknowledge the devotion, the adoration I have given you. I love you, Magdalena. I cannot stand by and see what you are doing."

She stared at him hostilely. "You love yourself. You want me as a part of yourself. I'm not the kind of woman you think you can have to do your bidding. Of course I've never accepted you. I've made it perfectly plain from the beginning that I'll never let you overstep the bounds I set to our friendship. You want what you cannot have because you cannot have it. You don't know what love is."

He walked away from her in a fury and she moved restlessly about, touching the objects that stood on the dark marble-topped table near her. A faint voice in her consciousness said, If I can leave now, this won't go any further. If I don't—She looked at her wrap, thrown over the back of a chair, longing to snatch it up and walk to the door.

But he came back to where she stood. She watched him warily. He said in a voice in which anger was barely under control, "You're doing this to spite me. But this is much worse than that young jackass from California you made a fool of yourself with."

"What is much worse?" She realized fully now what he meant and her own anger was beginning to spill over the dam she had tried to place against it.

"What people say is that you're living with that woman as if she was your paramour. Magdalena, I cannot believe this of you."

Ah, it's out now! she thought, and tried no longer to restrain herself. With a chilling clarity she said, "I am living with her but not as my paramour. She means much more to me than that. It does not matter to me in the slightest what people are saying. I warn you. I will not listen to anything more you have to say."

He was very close to her and when she finished speaking, as if he could not restrain himself, he passed his arm around her shoulder and placed his hand on her bare back, drawing her toward him. His mouth was close to her ear. "That cannot be so. You are the woman for me. This is an aberration, a sick illusion. You have been mesmerized by this woman. You need a man and I intend to be him. I will save you from this madness."

Afterwards she could not remember exactly what happened because his hand on her bare flesh and the closeness of his body lit a counter-fire in her. She could feel the pressure of his erection against her dress. He had never touched her before except for the accidental brushing of his hand as he helped her into her wrap or shepherded her into an automobile. She had carefully avoided even the most casual endearments and he was too rigid a man in his behavior to indulge in any playfulness. Now, before she was fully aware of what she had done she struck him across the face. A ring on her finger caught his cheek and made it bleed. She stared at the bloody mark through a cloud of rage that engulfed her. The blow—she knew she was strong—jerked his head back and stunned him for an instant. When he recovered the fury he had temporarily held back returned. For a moment she thought he would seize hold of her and her muscles tensed to resist him. She stepped back quickly and snatched up her wrap, walking to the door. He said, "I'll not forget this, Magdalena."

"Then I have given you something to remember me by," she replied, speaking through her clenched teeth.

He went with her down in the elevator and waited till the doorman hailed a cab. There was a stony silence between them until with a rigid jaw he wished her goodnight.

She arrived at the hotel suite dimly aware that she had never before been in such a rage. It rendered her speechless, so that when she entered the room where May sat reading she was barely able to respond to her "Oh, there you are!" When she did not cross the room at once to kiss her, May sat silent, watching as she threw off her wrap and went into the bedroom to strip off her evening gown and put on a negligee. She came back and sat down in the chair opposite May and for a while there was no sound in the room.

Slowly the fog of anger cleared. She looked at May for the first time. She said in a stifled voice, "I'm sorry, May, I've had a bad evening."

"You were out with Ruddle," said May, as if this fact was self-explanatory.

"Yes, of course."

"You're always upset when you see him."

"I never want to lay eyes on him again."

May hesitated and at last asked, "Has something happened tonight?"

For a while Magdalena did not answer. "I'll tell you in the morning," she said finally.

When they went to bed she lay for a while consciously

willing herself to be still and not disturb May, who dozed fitfully beside her. At last, unable to withstand the pressure of the desire stirred up in her by the earlier conflict, she rolled over and took May in her arms. She forgot all thought that May might not be ready to respond to her. The only thing that mattered was that she must have May. For the first time she felt May resist her. It was a slight opposition, the result of surprise and anxiety, but the fact that she felt it heightened her desire. When she was spent she buried her face in May's shoulder. May, lying quiet, gently stroked her head.

The next morning, while they sat at the table in their dressinggowns after breakfast, Magdalena said, "At least, I think that has been brought to an end."

May looked across at her. "What has been, dearest?"

"I don't think I'll be troubled by Ruddle now."

"You quarreled with him?"

Magdalena smiled. "It was rather more than a quarrel."

May said, watching her face, "He complained about me."

"Yes. Though I give him his due, he spoke only the truth. He said you've mesmerized me."

May looked annoyed. "I'm sure he said more than that. I've wondered when this would happen. He detests me."

Magdalena got up and walked restlessly to the window. "He had always thought that in time he would wear away my resistance and persuade me to marry him. I've done everything I could to let him see that he would never succeed."

"So he said that it is outrageous for you to live with a woman—that it is unnatural and you should send me away."

Magdalena gave her a one-sided smile. "You might have been there listening to him."

May's face was pale and stern. "That is inevitably what

a man like that would say. How could he accept the idea that a woman would find real contentment with another woman?"

Magdalena said hastily, "Don't be upset, May. I let him know that I would not listen to such rubbish."

"I'm afraid he will not stop with this. He will either try to persuade you further—if he really loves you and wants you, which I think is the case—or he will seek revenge."

"I think he is more likely to want revenge. I hit him."

May stared at her in consternation. "You what?"

Magdalena gave her a savage smile. "I hit him. He drove me beyond patience."

May leaned her head on her hand. When she looked up she asked, "Why?"

"He was beside himself. He tried to embrace me. It was an automatic reflex on my part, because he had made me so angry. I would not have minded so much otherwise. There have been other men, May. But I've never liked him. He has never attracted me physically. There was nothing to hold me back when he spoke of you."

After a moment's silence, May asked, "Why have you always given him so much attention? You always act as if you are forced to see him, forced to deal with him. Why have you always let him have so much to do with your affairs?"

"He is important to Francusi. It was Francusi who got me involved with him in the first place. He is valuable to Francusi and he knows it so he used that power to get Francusi to introduce him to me and then to become my man of affairs. After that I let things ride. He has not annoyed me enough, before this, to make me change the situation."

"Well, what will you do now?"

"He will no longer be in any relationship to me. Francusi will have to make his own peace with him as best he can. In fact, I expect to hear from Ruddle himself that he is no longer my lawyer, my adviser."

They did not discuss the situation any more, though it lay as an anxious cloud in the back of both their minds. Magdalena did not in fact hear directly from Ruddle. It was she who wrote him saying that henceforth she would deal with her own affairs. He replied formally, sending her the necessary documents. She heard from Francusi promptly. He came to see her, obviously upset by an interview with Ruddle.

"Is it true, cara mia, that you have told Mr. Ruddle you do not want him to take care of your affairs any longer?"

They were alone in the sitting room of the suite and she saw from the way he fidgeted, like a cat in a strange place, that he did not know what to expect from her.

"I've given him his walking papers. You know I've never really wanted him to be my adviser, never wanted him to be so important in my affairs. He has become too overbearing. He wants to run my life. No one does that."

Francusi sighed, resigned. In the end, after negotiations through him, she consented to keep Ruddle's law firm as the lawyers that Francusi could depend upon when he needed legal advice about her contracts and other such matters. Ruddle gave no indication that he objected to this arrangement.

"He is still your admirer, Magdalena," Francusi assured her, eager to maintain good relations. "He will always be your friend. He is very honorable."

"We'll see," she retorted briefly.

In fact, she waited warily for a while to see whether Ruddle would use his influence to create trouble about her relationship with May. Time passed and there was nothing that she could attribute to him in this way. Finally she concluded that she did him an injustice. He did have his own code of conduct and seeking revenge for the wound to his dignity by slandering her would not be allowed by that code.

Francusi's alarm subsided as the calm in her dealings with Ruddle prevailed. She never discovered what he had learned from Ruddle nor how much he surmised on his own. He often stopped by to chat with May. She was apt to find him there in the hotel suite happily drinking tea with her in the afternoons.

Curious, one day she asked, after he had gone, "What does he talk about, May?"

"Why, you, of course. You're an inexhaustible subject as far as he is concerned."

Magdalena laughed. "He knows how to win his way with you, doesn't he, May?"

May looked up from the schedule of musical events for the coming season she had been studying. "He is concerned about your return to opera. He says you insist you must return. He thinks your voice is in danger. You must, he says, be careful about the roles you choose."

Magdalena smiled at her. "Even Francusi doesn't have the say about what I shall do."

"But, dearest, you must listen to him. It would be foolish to ignore him. If you retire now, everyone will regret the fact. Everyone will remember you at your prime. Do pay attention to what he says."

"Oh, I am well aware of all that! He should not be concerned. I shall take his advice. However, I need not make the decision just now. When the time comes, I'll decide."

May contemplated her for a moment, weighing in her mind whether to say anything further. Presently she said, "In the meantime, dearest, we must go to London. I must go back and tell them the details of the sales agreement with the American buyer for the painting. They know it is completed, but cable and transatlantic telephone calls—how bad the connection is sometimes!—cannot cover everything. They want me back for a complete accounting."

She gazed at Magdalena, as if waiting to see what she would say. Magdalena looked away, chastened, and said, "Would you like to go by sea?"

Of course she had done what Francusi suggested, had yielded to May's gentle but persistent pressure. They had compromised. She sang several more seasons of opera, in New York and in London. She remembered that. Then she sang on the concert stage. There was that girl who had spoken to her of Rio, who had revived in her mind the memory of those days when May had gone everywhere with her. Yes. She could remember that her singing career had gradually lost its intensity and in the end she and May had withdrawn into a quiet life, free of the great light of publicity that had always shone on her while she was on the operatic stage. They had welcomed this, because now they could be themselves, free from the surveillance of curious and malicious people, free to be a couple, happy chiefly in each other's company. Even in her memory the sweetness of that time—how long had it been? returned to her and soothed her troubled psyche.

But where was May? She drifted into a doze, tired by this long retrieval of the past.

* * * * *

It was Dina who decided that Mary had to be supplied with clothes suitable for Magdalena Gibbon. With a costume designer's eye she chose a long-skirted high-necked gown in brown velvet. She was to look, Dina said, like an opera star who no longer sang in opera. Though Ailsa uneasily demurred, she had to admit that the dress suited Mary, that Mary, in spite of the short, tousled grey hair—"You'll never get her into a beauty parlor," Camilla said—the faded, wrinkled skin, the usually downcast eyes, no longer looked like a homeless old woman abandoned by society. Dina was dissatisfied. The total effect failed to portray the woman she wished they could present to the scrutiny of critical eyes. Ailsa said, "You can't expect it. The inner light is not there. She could look like Magdalena even in rags, if she still felt herself to be Magdalena. There must have been a light that outshone most people. It's out now. I don't think we can ever rekindle it."

The day came when Ruddle was to come to interview Mary. Afternoon, they had agreed, toward the end of the day, when they could find free time. They had had some difficulty persuading Ruddle of this.

"As if he has anything on his hands nowadays," Dina scoffed.

"He has to keep up appearances," said Ailsa. "He doesn't want to be seen as a has-been. I told him that I am in court till four o'clock. It doesn't make any difference to Mary. She's not aware of the time of day. She does not seem to realize that he is coming here to see her. She is quite unconcerned."

When the intercom from the reception desk buzzed softly it was Ailsa who went down the corridor to meet the lawyer.

"Mr. Ruddle," she said, as the tall old man stepped out of the elevator.

He stared at her for a moment, as if he had expected someone else—Dina, perhaps. But he recovered himself and said, "How do you do, Judge Cameron."

So he has remembered, thought Ailsa, that he has met me at bar association dinners. She tried to think of something suitable to say as they walked along the thickly carpeted corridor. He forestalled her by inquiring, "You're still on assignment in the criminal court? That is rough duty. I could never bring myself to practice in criminal matters."

She knew that he had a life-long reputation of never taking cases involving crimes of violence—or, for that matter, divorce. The only criminals he dealt with were those involved in high finance—and she wondered if he had always been unaware of how often the men he represented were as corrupt as any drug peddler. If so, provided that the outward appearance of respectability prevailed, he closed his eyes to what lay beneath the surface. His own reputation for integrity had often been enough to salvage that of his client.

"It is, I think," she said mildly, "a useful lesson in the problems of our contemporary society. I think we should know how the other half lives."

"I daresay." His tone was dry and he glanced at her sideways. "I've often been thankful that my time at the bar has been spent chiefly in a less turbulent age than the present. The younger men will have to deal with that." He glanced at her again. "And the younger women, I should add."

Dina stood at the door of the apartment to greet him. "I'm glad to see you again, Mr. Ruddle. Do come in."

She led him into the living room, to an armchair by the window. They made the usual brief comments about the view. Then Ailsa said, "Mr. Ruddle, I am sure that you must realize that we must deal carefully with this woman. Mary—we call her Mary because she was booked by the police as Mary Brown, since she could not identify herself—"

"Booked by the police!"

"Yes. That is how I first encountered her. She was booked on a vagrancy charge and held as a material witness in the arrest of some drug peddlers. The case was dismissed for reasons I need not go into here and she was taken to Bellevue. She has been under the care of friends since then."

"The care of friends? Who are these friends?"

Conscious of the suspicion in his eyes, Ailsa retorted, "I am one of them. That is why I say you must make allowance for her physical and mental condition. She may not be able to respond satisfactorily to questioning."

Dina, watching him, thought, He looks as if he is being presented with a nest of vipers. He seemed to pull himself together.

He said, "And I must warn you that it is going to be difficult to establish her identity as Magdalena Gibbon, to my satisfaction. Magdalena has been presumed by her real friends, including myself—" He couldn't refrain from saying that, thought Dina "—to have been dead for the last three years. We are merely awaiting the passage of the time required by law to declare her so."

"Yes," said Ailsa, firmly. "I do realize that. I see this present meeting only as a first step in establishing her identity as Magdalena Gibbon. Perhaps you will be able to see enough resemblance to persuade you to cooperate with us. If you do not, we must seek other means."

My, thought Dina, how confident she appears and I know that she isn't. Good for you, Ailsa. She is not going to let him see she has doubts. But he is not used to being challenged like that by a woman.

Ailsa went on, "I think we had better bring her here to meet you." She turned and looked at Dina. Dina nodded and left the room.

Mary was sitting in her own room in her usual posture, her head slightly forward as if she was either dozing or deep in thought. Somewhere between the two, Dina supposed, as she touched her on the shoulder.

"Mary, Mr. Ruddle is here. The lawyer, you know, who may be able to recognize you."

Mary got up from the chair slowly and stiffly and stood for a moment. Her response, Dina saw, was to obey Dina's obvious wish that she get up and go with her. She hasn't really heard what I said and she doesn't care, thought Dina anxiously. They walked slowly to the living room, Mary leaning lightly on Dina's arm. As they came into the room, Ailsa and Ruddle silently watched. Ruddle got to his feet and Dina led Mary to a chair.

Ailsa said, "Mary, this is Mr. Ruddle. Do you remember him?"

Ruddle's voice was harsh as he broke in, "How do you do?" The response was automatic. His mouth closed in a hard line and his eyes were even colder than before.

Mary raised her head to look at him. In her eyes there was a distant look, as if she was seeing not the man standing before her but some other sight that dwelt in her own vision. But she continued to gaze at him for several seconds. Then she moved her head slightly. Ailsa could not tell whether the gesture was an acknowledgement or a denial.

Ruddle, still staring at her coldly, spoke in a harsh voice. "I am told that you believe yourself to be Magdalena Gibbon, the opera singer." He was looking down at her with a hawklike stare. Ailsa, uneasy, moved a step closer. But he stepped back when the woman in the chair continued to gaze at him expressionlessly. He turned to look at Ailsa indignantly.

Ailsa said, "Mr. Ruddle, I warned you that you must be careful in dealing with her."

"Why should I be if she is not Magdalena?" he demanded.

"Then you say she is not?"

He did not answer but turned slightly to glance again at the seated woman. Dina interjected, "You're not sure, are you?"

"She cannot be," he retorted.

Dina challenged him. "And why not?"

Instead of answering her, he stepped back to confront Mary. "Are you aware that I and Magdalena's other friends believe her to be dead—that we have ample reason to believe that she died three years ago?"

The blankness in Mary's eye cleared briefly as she replied, "I did."

Shocked, he demanded, "You did what?"

"I died, three years ago, as you said."

There was a look of horror in his eyes as he turned toward Ailsa, as if for help. Ailsa stepped forward and put her hand on Mary's shoulder. She said, "Mary, do you understand what you said?"

Mary looked up at her and Ailsa saw that this was not the woman she had hitherto dealt with. She asked, "Mary, are you Magdalena Gibbon?"

Mary continued to look at her steadily and said, "I was."

Ailsa glanced at Ruddle. He turned on his heel and stalked across the room toward the window. Ailsa followed him and spoke to his back. "I realize this is upsetting. But do you see any resemblance at all?"

When he finally turned around to face her she saw that he was distraught. "This woman is out of her mind. She doesn't know what she is saying."

"You must make allowance for her condition. But, allowing for the fact that her mind may not be clear, can you say that she is physically what Magdalena might be now? I have only seen photographs of Magdalena, but it seems to me that she is the same build, the same age—"

He was vehement. "It is impossible! This woman cannot be Magdalena Gibbon!"

"You remember her in health and prosperity," Ailsa persisted. "When you saw her last, was she entirely her normal self? I understand that she was under some emotional strain."

He did not answer. Ailsa went on. "I think you told Dina that you were ready to believe that this woman might be under a genuine delusion that she is Magdalena Gibbon. I think it is obvious that she is not an imposter. Either she is Magdalena Gibbon or she is self-deluded."

Anger blazed in his eyes as he looked at her. He spoke in a half-choked voice. "How can you expect me to see in this—derelict the woman I knew as Magdalena? Three years ago she was still the most vital, the most glorious woman—to me, to the world. I can believe that Magdalena killed herself. I can believe that rather than she could be reduced to this wreck!"

He broke off, breathing hard. His old man's wrinkled, chalky cheeks were mottled with red. Ailsa sought for words to quiet him but before she could speak she heard the soft sound of the intercom signal from downstairs. Dina was answering it.

Dina held the instrument in her hand and spoke across the room. "There's a Mr. Francusi downstairs. He says he is here because Mr. Ruddle asked him to come."

Ailsa glanced at Ruddle in surprise. "Is that true, Mr. Ruddle?"

Ruddle said hastily, "Yes. I took the liberty of asking him to join us. It was a last-minute arrangement."

"Then he had better come up," said Ailsa. Her tone was short. "Who is he?" she asked Ruddle as Dina put down the phone.

"He is another friend of Magdalena. He managed her

musical engagements for many years before she retired."

Ailsa was aware that there was an air of reluctance in Ruddle's manner, as if in inviting Francusi to come he had acted against his own inclination. She glanced over at the woman seated in the armchair. Mary seemed sunk in unawareness. The brief clarity of her response to Ruddle had vanished.

It was Dina who went to the elevator to greet Francusi. She looked with curiosity at the short little man who stepped out. Once, she decided, he must have been portly but now with age he had shrunk until his clothes fit loosely. But there was still a sparkle in the dark eyes that looked up into hers as she greeted him. As they walked down the corridor he asked, "Is it true that you have found Magdalena? I could scarcely believe what he told me."

"We don't know if she is Magdalena. Did Mr. Ruddle say that she was?"

"Oh, no! He would never commit himself like that! He is a lawyer, don't you know?" There was a chuckle in his voice. "But does she say she is Magdalena?"

"She seems to believe that she is. That is, she doesn't deny it. It is difficult, Mr. Francusi, to be sure just what she means. She has been homeless, without care, without friends, for quite a long time. She is still ill, really."

He stopped in his tracks and turned to face her. "Magdalena homeless, without friends! That cannot be!"

"That is certainly the situation of this woman. Perhaps she is not Magdalena. Mr. Ruddle seems to think she is not. Why did he ask you to come here? You are an old friend, of course, but was there another reason?"

Francusi stood staring down at the carpet at his feet. At last he replied, "I believe he probably thinks I would be the most likely to be able to recognize her."

"What did he tell you about her?"

"He said that he was being required to see a woman who claimed that she was Magdalena. He had believed her dead—that she killed herself three years ago. To him it seemed the most reasonable explanation for her disappearance. Can someone disappear from the pavement in front of her apartment house and never be seen again, unless she is dead?" He looked at Dina as he asked the question, as if he really wanted her answer.

"There have been such cases, several famous ones. Does this mean that you have not believed that she was dead?"

Again he studied the carpet at his feet. When he looked up he said, "Perhaps you will say that I have not wanted to believe that she is dead. I have kept thinking, perhaps she is somewhere and that sometime she will come back. Mr. Ruddle has pointed out to me that she had no money with her—oh, perhaps, a few pennies in her handbag. How would she live? But alone, homeless, without friends! Dio non voglia!"

"As I said," Dina repeated, "Mr. Ruddle says this woman cannot be Magdalena. He finds her present state too shocking. But he does not say absolutely that she is not."

"Ah, That is interesting. There is something unmistakable about Magdalena. There has always been. Let us see if I am right."

They began walking again towards the apartment door.

Ailsa and Ruddle were standing in the vestibule. Ruddle, towering over Francusi, said, "I think we are on a wild goose chase."

He would have said more, but Francusi put up a soft, beringed hand to stop him. "Let me see for myself." His was a quiet voice but it carried a ring of command. Before stepping past Ruddle he paused in front of Ailsa and bowed. "Judge Cameron," Ruddle said, "Mr. Francusi."

He bowed again and went to stand in the doorway to the living room, looking about its expanse. When his eyes found the woman sitting with her back towards him—he could see only the top of her head—he continued to stand still for a few more moments. He's screwing up his courage, the thought came suddenly to Dina.

After a while he walked across the thick carpet. Dina saw Ruddle's sudden move to follow him and then saw Ailsa put her hand on his arm to restrain him. He gave her an indignant look but he stayed where he was.

Francusi walked around the woman in the chair until he faced her. He stood for a while looking down at her. She did not move. She did not seem aware of his presence. He said something to her that the watchers could not hear. They heard only the murmur of his voice. He stood speaking for several moments. Slowly the attention of the woman in the chair was caught and she raised her head. Francusi stretched out his hand and put it on her shoulder. Ailsa, standing a little closer than the others, heard him say, in a tone of mixed delight and compassion, "Mia cara, it is really you!" and he leaned forward to kiss her on the cheek. When he drew back he fished his handkerchief out of his pocket and dabbed at his eyes.

Ailsa strode across the room to Mary's chair, anxious to see how she was taking his words. She was astonished to see a faint but unmistakable smile on the thin pale face. Mary's attention was still fixed on Francusi. She reached out her hand a little way towards him. He took it and sat down on a nearby chair. She said nothing but he went on talking in a low voice, a mixture of English, Italian, German, the languages, Ailsa supposed, of their habit of communication in the past.

Ruddle had followed Ailsa across the room and said to Francusi, breaking into his monologue, "You realize that we have no proof that this is Magdalena. We must make an investigation into this woman's background." He glared at Mary as he spoke, his mouth working under the stress of emotion. He knows that he has lost, though Ailsa. He is fighting a losing battle.

Francusi got up quickly—he's very spry for his age, thought Dina—and taking hold of Ruddle's arm, tried to move him gently away from Mary's chair. He said, "It is Magdalena. I have no doubt of it. I do recognize her. That is what you sent for me for—to see if I recognized her. I do."

Mary, whose attention was still half-fixed on Francusi, looked away from both men and made a move as if to get up and get away from the discord in the air. Ailsa came forward and took hold of her arm. "Mary," she said, "do you want to go back to your room?"

Mary gave a frightened look around as she got up from the chair. Dina had come over and helped her to her feet. "I'll take her," she said, and they walked slowly out of the room.

Ruddle, resisting the pressure of Francusi's hand on his arm, raged at him. "You think you recognize her! You wish to recognize her. You wish her back alive."

Francusi stared at him. "Don't you?" he demanded.

Ruddle was shocked into silence. Francusi went on, "Do you think I could mistake Magdalena? I tell you I cannot."

As they went on arguing, Ailsa saw that Francusi had noticed that Mary had left, and he nodded approvingly at her. He seemed then to give up the effort to convince Ruddle and stood listening without response to his tirade.

Ruddle turned on Ailsa. "I must make it clear to you that I cannot accept Mr. Francusi's belief as sufficient proof of this woman's identity. As the trustee of Magdalena Gibbon's assets I must require something more certain—some objective evidence."

"Naturally," said Ailsa, in as neutral a voice as she could command. "What do you expect to do now, then?"

"I must have a complete record of the police action concerning her, of the Welfare Department's record of her. I expect you to provide me with that."

"Of course. But you understand, the police can identify her only as a destitute woman who had been living in the street. They cannot supply any connection between her and Magdalena Gibbon—whose disappearance is undoubtedly still on their records as an unsolved case. Of course, they have her fingerprints and the hospital where she spent several days can provide other medical evidence. That can be matched, I suppose, with medical records of Magdalena Gibbon. The only other certain evidence must lie in Mary's own memory, if she can regain enough strength to make a positive statement. In anything she said there would be details you could check from your own personal knowledge."

He shook his head vigorously. "It would have to be a very positive statement indeed. I warn you that I will not accept anything in the least obscure. And now I must leave. I cannot spend another moment on such a hopeless case."

"Then does that mean that you refuse to accept this woman as Magdalena Gibbon, in spite of Mr. Francusi's recognition of her?" Ailsa demanded.

She watched his face working with the conflict of emotions he was struggling with. Finally he said, "I realize that Mr. Francusi's recognition is a matter of serious weight. However, I believe he may be mistaken. I do not see any resemblance in this woman to Magdalena Gibbon."

"Then we must rely on the physical evidence," said Ailsa.

He turned away from her and in a few minutes she saw him to the door and out of the apartment in silence. When she came back into the living room Dina was standing in the window talking to Francusi. They both turned to her without speaking. Ailsa looked inquiringly at Francusi. He shook his head in answer to her unspoken question.

"He knows this is Magdalena. He does not want to acknowledge this to himself. It is a terrible blow to him to see her like this. You must have compassion for him."

Ailsa pondered. "He has always been in love with her?"

Francusi considered her question for a long moment. "He has always been in love with his image of her—the beautiful woman, always unattainable, whom he had never been able to possess and thus has always remained his ideal of perfection. I am afraid he cannot face this reality. He will place every obstacle in the way of proving that she is Magdalena."

"But he sent for you to come here and identify her," Dina objected.

Francusi turned towards her. "He could not accept the burden of denying her without me to protect her, if this was really Magdalena." He turned back to Ailsa with a smile. "We are old men, my dear. We try to keep a few illusions to see us to the grave."

"But you were not deceived by any such self-delusion. You knew her right away."

"Ah, but I have known Magdalena for a long time, a very long time. At the beginning she saved my life. She made it possible for me to escape from Vienna before the Nazis took over. She did her best to save my wife and others of my family. She risked herself, she used her own money. She has that sort of generosity. When I reached London she did everything to help me recover from the abyss of despair I was in and to reestablish me in the musical world, so that I could earn a living. She is the sort of friend who is very rare. She did not care what people said about her because they did not understand what real friendship is. I have been devoted to her since. Ours was never a sentimental or amorous liaison. It is deeper than such things can be, between a man and a woman. I would know Magdalena under any circumstances. There is something unmistakable about her." He turned back to Dina. "Did I not say so?"

Dina nodded, glancing at Ailsa.

Ailsa studied his face for a few moments. He was now staring across the room without seeing, his mind obviously engrossed by memory. When he was silent his mouth worked a bit, as if in response to his thoughts. She finally asked, "Can you tell us about Magdalena's disappearance? What do you know about the circumstances?"

It took him a moment to bring his attention back to her. "She went away because of May."

"May? Her friend?"

"More than a friend. They were close companions for more than thirty years. People called her Magdalena's personal manager, though she had her own profession. She was learned in art attribution. She could identify paintings, tell where they belonged, where they had been stolen from. She was someone Magdalena could trust with all her affairs. She was also much more than that. She looked after Magdalena. She kept her from doing foolish things—something I was never able to accomplish." He paused to give Ailsa a fleeting smile. "She could help me persuade Magdalena to be prudent when she felt reckless. And they were—" He hesitated, glancing at Dina and then at Ailsa.

"They were lovers," said Ailsa coldly.

"Yes," he said, relieved. "True lovers. May was Magdalena's only true lover. Mr. Ruddle realized this and he could never reconcile himself to the fact. At first I think he was even glad when May died. He thought the way would at last be open to him, after so many years of devotion—of spurned devotion. But he was mistaken."

He stopped speaking and was silent until Ailsa prompted him.

"Then he wishes now to revenge himself?"

Francusi considered her question. "Who can tell what

the human heart secretly wishes? He is a cruel man, but he does not know it."

"And what happened when May died?"

"It was a very bad time for Magdalena. I waited to see what would happen. She deceived me without intending to. She was crushed. She was very quiet, not violently grief-stricken as I had expected her to be. I see now that she was stunned. What looked like resignation was something else. I was not as watchful as I should have been. Then one day she went out of her apartment and disappeared, disappeared from the very pavement outside the door." Unconsciously he was clasping and unclasping his hands, ending with a dramatic gesture towards the floor, as if he himself stood on the street in front of the apartment building, illustrating the scene. "I was very uneasy about her, and therefore I used to call her up or drop in to see her several times a day. That day she did not come back. It became night. I called all the people I knew she might visit. I went to all the places I thought she might go to but she was nowhere. I waited a day, because I did not want to expose her to curiosity, impertinence. But then I became frightened. I called Mr. Ruddle. I thought he would protect her from publicity and he was in charge of her legal affairs. It was he who reported to the police that she was missing. They did not act right away. They said after all she might simply have gone away without telling anyone and would come back in a short time. The days went by—and the nights—oh, those nights! I could imagine all sorts of things that might have happened to her. When the police did begin to search there was no trace of her. They could find no one who had seen her after the doorman at the apartment house had said goodbye to her."

"Did they look for her body?" Ailsa asked.

"Yes. It was never found. The police said there were several possible explanations. Perhaps she had committed suicide, somewhere away from here. Or she drowned herself and her body was carried away to sea. Or perhaps she lost her memory and could not find her way home. Or perhaps—" He hesitated again, as if he did not want to speak of what he was thinking "—perhaps she was murdered and her murderers disposed of her body somewhere it was never found. It has been very baffling, very illusive. I have not been able to think of her as being dead. I keep thinking, I will tell this or that to Magdalena when I see her again. And then I realize that the time is going by and probably I won't see her again." He stopped and smiled again at Ailsa. "Like Mr. Ruddle, I have my own problem. He wanted to believe that she killed herself. Since he could not possess her, he wished her to be beyond the reach of another. As for me, I have not been able to think that she was no longer alive, no longer in this world where I still linger. Do you see, dear lady?"

"I see very well. And you think now, after all, you have found her?"

"Oh, yes! This is Magdalena. In time she will tell us what has happened. I feel sure of that."

When he had left, Ailsa said to Dina, "I wish I felt as sure of that as he does."

* * * * *

She was glad to be back in the quiet of the bedroom. She did not want to think of all the things the two men had stirred up. She did not mind Francusi. He had never meant her any harm. He had been May's friend as much as hers.

But Ruddle. Of course she remembered Ruddle. She had always been in conflict with him, wishing him away from her, fending him off. He was like an enemy now. She hoped she was rid of him, since he had disowned her. How strange. He had always clung to her, in spite of his bold, autocratic manner. He wanted something from her that she did not want to give him. But she could not make him believe that.

But he was unimportant now. Everything was unimportant but the journey that lay ahead of her—the end of that journey leading back to May. She had fought her way through the mists in her mind to this point. She shrank from the knowledge of the agony this final passage would entail. She must descend once more into the depths of despair into which she was rapt by the loss of May. Unless she did so, she could not reclaim May. She girded herself for this last bitter stretch down the path of memory.

It began when May first became ill. Her own optimism said that whatever was wrong with May would pass. But Ruddle had wished for the worst at once, as if it would give him a chance, the chance he had been waiting for since she had got rid of Rodney. What a silly idea. She had felt sometimes, when her nerves were especially on edge, that he was willing May to die. That was silly, too. May would never desert her—

Too restless to stay idly indoors, when May slept, with the nurse on duty, she had gone to walk about the streets, wearing off the foreboding she did not acknowledge. It was then that she first began to notice the woman. It was the middle of the morning and she stood for a moment on the pavement in front of the apartment house door, looking restlessly about. The heavier traffic of the early morning was gone and only a few people walked by at a leisurely pace in this mild sunlight. The woman was seated in a small areaway, a couple of steps down from the sidewalk—it at one time had been the entry to a little florist's stand. Now the doorway had been sealed into the wall of the building and only the steps down and the supports for an awning remained. The woman, shapeless in an assortment of shabby, grubby garments, seemed to be sleeping, one hand clutching a large tattered cloth bag overflowing with rags and un-recognizable objects. Magdalena stood and stared at her until the doorman from the apartment house said at her elbow, "She's there every day. I've told the cops about her but they don't do anything. Say she's not creating a nuisance. *I* say she's a nuisance just being there."

Magdalena glanced over her shoulder at him, mildly surprised at the hatred in his voice. "She seems harmless enough."

"I guess she is—but she's an eyesore."

Magdalena did not reply. She walked away, boarded a bus, spent an hour in shops. When she returned to the apartment the woman was still in her shelter but now she was awake, peering up and down the street. On impulse Magdalena stepped close to her and offered her a five dollar bill. The woman's black eyes stared up at her and then at the money, as if considering what strings might be attached to the gift. Eventually she reached out a weathered dirty hand with black nails to take it. She did not speak but began to search among her rags for somewhere to hide it. Magdalena, seeing the fear that showed in her eyes, moved away, watching her from the door of the apartment house. Though she had not thought of the fact that she herself might have been watched, she was glad now that the doorman had not been there. The woman pulled herself up from her seat and began to hobble hastily away, not glancing back at Magdalena. Watching, Magdalena thought, she is my age or perhaps older.

As the days passed the reality of May's illness slowly wore away her optimism. Now when she went out it was to walk about the streets to wear off her despair, to seek for distractions, for sights and sounds that would engage her mind, occupy her thoughts, a search for whatever would prevent her from dwelling on the menace that lay ahead. She still strove to hide from herself what everyone else assumed was inevitable—that May would die. Go out, said the nurse, you can do nothing here and she is asleep.

So while May lay deep in the semi-death of drugs she went out. And each time she did so she saw the woman sitting in her shelter. Magdalena's impulse was each time to give her money, but a sort of prudence restrained her. Partly this was because of the fear she had seen in the woman's eyes—fear, no doubt, that someone else might have seen the money and would set upon her and rob her. And there was the doorman, who seemed to harbor a vindictive anger towards the woman, standing in his own doorway watching. Probably there were other tenants in the apartment house who objected to the sight of this derelict on their doorstep and complained to him, people whose tips were important to him.

But now Magdalena became panicky at the thought that the woman might go away or be driven away. She was aware that this was an irrational feeling. Why should the presence of this poor old wreck mean so much to her? What lay in the existence of this defeated creature that had acquired such a hold on her emotional life? Magdalena realized that she herself had reached such a pitch of desperation that she could not tolerate people, not the people by whom she was normally surrounded, not even those with whom she had the most casual contact. They were an affront to her in their very existence, their presence, their life and vigor, while every day May faded further and further away from her.

All but this derelict old woman, abandoned by society, who now had reached the point where she in her turn spurned society. Vaguely Magdalena's mind dwelt on this but rapidly she was going beyond rationalization. The old woman drew her like a magnet. Each day when she saw her she was aware of the strength of the pull.

She struggled now, sitting in this strange room, to hold to the truth of what had happened. The events she recalled seemed to lose their remembered reality. She could not bring back to her conscious mind the day May died, the sequence and nature of what happened thereafter. She remembered that her whole being rejected the idea that May had gone, that there was a greater loneliness in her life than there had been before and that now it was incurable. For a while she struggled with this sense of complete alienation from herself, from the people who surrounded her, from the material things that framed her life. She lost all sense of time, or place. Everything about her seemed to converge into a vortex. An enormous blackness engulfed her. The earth and the sky was an inky void in which there was nothing, not even herself. She seemed then to be in a tunnel in which there was no sound, no movement and very little light.

That light rested on the figure of the old woman in the street. She remembered dimly going in desperation out of the apartment house, seeking her, remembered following her along the street. At first the old woman had merely hurried along, eager to escape her. She remembered the despair that took possession of her when the old woman succeeded in evading her, the terror-stricken search for her that led into streets and alleyways she had never seen before, the exhaustion that had overtaken her in the day and in the night, the monstrous character that the crowds of people in the street assumed, like people condemned to hell and yet malevolently powerful in menace, in pursuit of her. Then she had once more found the old woman—was it in fact the same sheltered spot where she had first seen her? The old woman had looked out at her, as if afraid she would steal the treasures in her tattered cloth bag. Again she had followed the woman as she hurried along the street, intent on getting away from her. She remembered the old woman shouting frantically at her, bellowing abuse, threatening her in a voice shaking with fear, quavering with the awareness of helplessness.

In the end the old woman gave up and permitted her to come close enough so that they sat together on a bench in the park, the woman muttering a string of questions and threats interspersed with obscenities. She understood none of this, only that in being close to the old woman she felt that she no longer swung wildly through space, that the terror that pursued her was held at bay. After that they toured the streets and alleys together, sharing whatever they could find to eat or drink. But one thing she learned in the very beginning: not to touch the old woman's possessions stored in the bag. The slightest accidental motion towards it roused a fierce attack, even blows. Docilely she accepted this scolding, anxious only to stay near, not to be abandoned.

The seasons changed. In the hot weather they both had food poisoning and were in the hospital and then in a shelter for homeless women. Passive so long as she was not separated from the old woman, Magdalena accepted the circumstances. The old woman grew restless in the shelter, quarreled with the nuns who ran it, found the opportunity to escape out into the streets once more. Magdalena followed her. The old woman had grown so used to her that she no longer heeded her presence, acknowledged her existence only when they shared food or when they came upon other homeless women. These the old woman invariably saw as enemies, as rivals for food scraps, sheltered spots, as potential thieves ready to steal the objects in her bag. Then she seemed to see Magdalena as her ally, someone to guard her back while she confronted these dangers.

Winter came a second time. In the bitter cold it was

difficult to find enough warmth. The old woman sought public places, bus stations, the lobbies of public buildings, places she usually stayed away from, afraid of catching the attention of policemen. They rarely could stay long in such shelters before they were driven away by attendants or policemen who threatened to arrest them. If it gets any worse, the old woman muttered, maybe they'd better get themselves arrested. At least they would not freeze to death in a jail. Then one morning when she stirred from a fitful sleep, roused by the increasing tempo of traffic, Magdalena found the old woman motionless beside her, the bag still clutched in her hands. She did not rouse when passersby spoke to her or occasionally flung a coin in her direction. Magdalena sat lost in despair, nerveless, unable to move or speak, even when the police came and took her and the old woman away. Magdalena was taken to a hospital. The old woman, they said, was dead. They took her body away, leaving the bag of rubbish sitting forlornly on the floor of the hospital reception hall.

Dead. The old woman had escaped her grasp. She felt as though she was being swallowed up in a great void filled with a constant howling wind. She could see nothing and no one around her, except in brilliant flashes, as of lightning, in which the figures of doctors and nurses stood close to her, mouthing words she did not hear. It was the same strange, unknown world from which she had tried to hide in the shadow of the old woman. There was no protection now. She must escape from this place where people came so close to her, with nameless menace. Struggling hard she focused her attention on the hospital ward, keeping back the night that crowded around her, watching for her opportunity. The nurses dressed her in clean, shapeless clothing, forcing her out into the closed-in porch at the end of the corridor with other patients. She waited for a quiet moment, when the old man in the wheelchair opposite had fallen asleep and the drug-addicted young woman beside her sat in a waking trance. Then she crept down the empty corridor to an enclosed stairway and found her way down to the ground floor and out into the street.

The street engulfed her in its noise and movement. For a moment she was panic-stricken and tried to push open the door to go back into the hospital. But the door opened only outwards and she was trapped in the raucous world of fast moving vehicles and people.

Exhausted, her memory lapsed. When she once more awakened to sight and feeling she gazed around her at the unknown room, at the luxurious bed, the thick carpet, the window through which she could see an expanse of sky and the roofs and towers of buildings. Her mind worked slowly to comprehend what she saw, to remember where she was and how she came to be there. When the door opened and the fair-haired woman came into the room she gazed at her silently, her heart skipping a beat. Of course that was not May, but the image roused the memory of May.

May! She sank back in the chair, overwhelmed. May. Had she found May again, in her heart, in her mind, in her soul? May, who had been lost somewhere beyond the fury of madness that had submerged her for so long. May. May was with her once more—May to be remembered, clung to, who would protect her from what the world might hold.

* * * * *

"She does look at you in the strangest way, sometimes," said Ailsa. "It is unnerving."

She stood in the kitchen, a tray in her hands. Dina glanced at the tray and said, "She doesn't eat much."

"No, and less when she is alone. I think she forgets to.

I have the impression that she lives in a dream world of her own."

"She always has, hasn't she, since she's been here, at least."

Ailsa hesitated. "This is a little different. She is much calmer. She doesn't seem to panic the way she did at first. Sometimes I startle her, no matter how careful I am going into her room, but when she sees me she seems to relax. You know, when you coax her back to reality, she gives you very polite attention, as if she was busy thinking about something and you've interrupted. When she has listened to you and answered you, she goes back into her own world again. But she's not nervy. Do you know, I think for some reason she is not so frightened of me any more."

"She shouldn't be by now. You and Camilla have been looking after her like a baby."

Ailsa shot her a quick glance. She never knew when something quite harmless might rouse a flicker of jealousy in Dina. She answered gently, "It's not Camilla and me. It's not us, though she should feel more reassured with us. It is something else, something interior to herself. She has awakened to something, as if she had been having a bad dream and waked to find a more comforting reality."

Dina took the tray out of her hands. "You don't have to stand there holding that thing. You're getting as absent-minded as she is. We've got another problem, you know. Ruddle says he will acknowledge that she is Magdalena Gibbon only if she is examined at the Seabright Clinic. She used to go there for medical check-ups and they have her medical records. Even some of the doctors and nurses might recognize her."

"There are literally dozens of people she knew who can identify her," said Ailsa sharply. "The trouble is exposing her to them. I'm quite sure she won't want what has happened to her in the last three years to be food for gossip among all the people who knew her as the great opera diva."

Dina grimaced. "What a sensation that would make in the news media! You know, for the last twenty years or so she has been out of the public eye, from choice. She evidently did not want publicity about her private life when she retired from the concert stage and lived with her friend May. If she is recovering from her aberrations, she won't want to be faced with that."

Something like a shudder went through Ailsa. "It would be enough to drive her out of her mind again and into the street once more."

"Or to commit suicide. You know, that's probably always been an option with her. She just doesn't have herself together enough yet to."

Ailsa was thoughtful. "I'd say the impulse was there."

"So what are we going to do?"

Ailsa thought for a while. "Physicians have the same responsibility for guarding confidentiality as lawyers—"

"Though you'd hardly guess it from the behavior of a lot of them nowadays," Dina interjected.

Ailsa ignored her. "Therefore, it should be possible to require that the people at the Clinic reveal nothing to anyone not involved in her care. There is only one essential fact that needs to be said—that Magdalena Gibbon has returned to her home. Where she has been and what she has been doing in the meantime is nobody's business."

"That's very easy to say. There will be a lot of curious people."

"Their curiosity need not be satisfied."

"If it is left to you and me, there'd be no problem. But right now we've got to find a way to meet Ruddle's requirement. He won't release her money unless her identity is established by the doctors. And we can't go to law about it. That really would produce the sensation of the year."

Dina thought for a moment. "One thing. She looks much better now than she did. If we dress her properly, no one will guess how far down she's been."

"True enough. But first I must get in touch with Camilla."

Ailsa found it easier to pin Camilla down than usual. It was as if Camilla had been waiting for a call. They met as before in the fast food place, empty now in the middle of the morning. Ailsa, seated in a booth, watched Camilla come in the door and look around. She's not happy, she thought at once, noticing the droop of Camilla's shoulders, the half-sullen expression on her face.

"Is there something wrong, Camilla?" she asked as the young woman sat down opposite.

"No. Why should there be?" Camilla snapped.

"You don't look very happy."

"Do I usually?"

"Don't be so snappish, Camilla. I'm just concerned."

"We're not here to talk about me. What's happened to Mary?"

"Well, we've established the fact that she is Magdalena Gibbon. Beyond a reasonable doubt, I think."

"If she says she is, that's good enough for me. Did she say that?"

Ailsa searched her memory for Mary's exact words. "She did not say, I am Magdalena Gibbon. She seemed to take it for granted—to take for granted that we would know she is." The spell of Mary/Magdalena's presence returned to her. "She said she died three years ago. She startled the lawyer."

"She said what?"

"That she died three years ago. Ruddle told her that her friends had considered her dead after she disappeared. She obviously meant that three years ago she died as Magdalena Gibbon."

Camilla frowned down at the paper cup of coffee before her. "Why would she say that?"

"Because that was when her friend May died and she took off into the streets in despair, I suppose."

"And nobody found her? The police didn't trace her?" There was wonderment in Camilla's voice.

"She must have made an effort to hide so that she could not be traced."

"How could that be, especially if she was out of her mind with grief?"

"I don't know. I thought perhaps you'd have some idea, since you know a lot more about these women who live in the street."

"Why? Am I supposed to be an authority about why these old bags choose to live like animals?"

Ailsa stared at her, shocked. "Camilla! You don't usually talk that way."

Camilla answered her stare with a sulky glance. "I don't talk that way. I don't think that way. That's the sort of thing a lot of people say. How do you know what drives an old woman who hasn't got anything and anybody out into the street to live? Usually she gets thrown out of her place by a landlord that's trying to get rid of his tenants so that he can collect more money from new people. She hasn't anywhere to go and after a bit she's disoriented, wants out of society altogether. People become her enemies. Most of them certainly act as if they were. If she gets taken to a shelter she can't accommodate to living by the rules, putting up with others even if they are in the same fix she is."

Ailsa leaned back in her seat and listened while Camilla's bitterness flowed out in a long tirade. She knew Camilla's fierce rejection of the superficial palliatives that society provided for such deep-seated problems. She knew the excoriating vigor with which Camilla expressed her loyalty to those whose lives were destroyed by a social machine that had no place for them. Her own heart ached sometimes for the pain that so obviously racked Camilla when she dealt with these hapless victims.

When Camilla came to a breathless halt, she said, "But Mary doesn't fit into that pattern. She wasn't destitute and friendless to begin with. She was a well-to-do woman and there were plenty of people to give her emotional support."

"Well, they couldn't. She—she was beyond anybody being able to help her when her friend died." The choked sound of Camilla's voice caught Ailsa's ear. A suspicion stirred in her mind as she watched Camilla covertly. After a while Camilla went on in a more normal voice. "What gets me is how she survived in the beginning—when she first got out into the street. She must have been wearing pretty good clothes. She couldn't have looked like a street woman then. How come she wasn't mugged, raped, murdered? You'd think she'd wind up in the hospital in a few days. Or the morgue. Her friends were looking for her. The police were alerted, you said."

"It was several days after she disappeared that they began to look for her. After a while they gave up. They thought she had committed suicide in some way so that her body was not found."

"Or was murdered."

"They seem to think more of suicide."

In frustration Camilla shrugged. "How she survived is a bigger mystery. She must have had some help from somebody."

"Help? From whom?"

"Maybe some other old woman showed her what to do to protect herself. By the time she was picked up by the police this last time she was pretty savvy when it came to hiding herself from those drug pushers."

"Yes, I suppose so. After all, if she was out on the

street for three years, she must have learned quite a bit about self-preservation. But why did she stay there?"

"Because she'd lost contact with the normal world. It happens all the time."

Ailsa considered this for a while and then said, "Well, in any case, there's a particular reason I wanted to see you, besides telling you how the interview came out."

"I gathered as much."

"Mr. Ruddle—the lawyer—says he has to have some sort of objective evidence beyond her own statement that she is Magdalena Gibbon. We have agreed that he will accept the statements of doctors at the Seabright Clinic, where she used to go and who have her medical records. How are we going to get her to go there?"

"You can get an ambulance and carry her there."

"Don't be smart, Camilla. Yes, of course." Ailsa's voice was full of annoyance. "That's not what I mean and you know it. What I'm talking about is persuading her to go without becoming terrified. Camilla, she does trust you more than anybody. You must come to see her. She's changed a bit. She's much calmer. It would be a pity to undo that."

Camilla sat for a while folding and pleating the paper napkin she had picked up. There was obviously a debate going on in her mind. Finally she said, "She has to be on her own. She was getting too dependent on me. I've got other things to do."

Again the suspicion went through Ailsa's mind. It was on the tip of her tongue to ask about Serafina, but a strong sense of prudence held her back. She said instead, "Perhaps so. But you can't cut her off just yet. She isn't strong enough. I think I understand how you feel. You've got very fond of her. It's amazing. How did you see what she was in all that filthy bundle of rags?"

Camilla gave her a rebuking look. "You can't go by

what people look like. Everybody is worth something, even if they look like trash. You've got to size them up for what they are. But I'll admit, there is something special about Mary. At least, there is to me."

"Well, will you help us then?"

"Oh, all right! I'll come to your place when I have a chance."

She came the next morning, which was a Saturday, and Dina was there alone, still drinking coffee in the kitchen and reading the paper. Dina was dressed in a white, high-collared dressinggown with a skirt that flowed to the ground. "Come and join me, Camilla. This brew is better than the stuff you get at the fast food place."

Camilla nodded and sat down at the small table. It was like Dina, she thought, to leave the front door ajar after she had announced herself downstairs, so that there was no need to get up again to let her in. Suppose somebody had been lurking around in the corridor—

Dina said, "What are you looking so dubious about?"

"You shouldn't leave your door open like that."

"Well, I was expecting you."

"But somebody else might have got here first."

Dina shrugged. It was a spacious kitchen for a town apartment, with shining metal counters and an array of modern appliances. The feeling of luxury reached Camilla and to some extent relaxed the nervousness she always felt in Dina's company.

Dina said, pouring the coffee, "I can't tell you how Magdalena is this morning. She hasn't shown. Ailsa is out. She had special court business this morning." When Camilla did not respond she went on. "What have you been doing with yourself? How's Serafina? I haven't seen her for quite a while."

A sudden frown appeared on Camilla's face. "She's all right, as far as I know."

"As far as you know? Why, isn't she still living with you?"

"Yes. She hasn't taken off yet."

"Taken off? Is she about to?"

Camilla, irritated by Dina's sharp questions, lashed out, "What Fina does is her own business. I've got enough troubles without hers."

Dina contemplated her. "She has troubles? It's never occurred to me that she has troubles or at least that she lets them bother her."

"That's what's the matter."

"Ah, too carefree. Well, Camilla, you must admit that's her nature." Dina added to herself, That's why you're in love with her. She's everything you can't be. Aloud she said, "Let me tell you something. The course of true love never did run smooth. That's from the *Midsummer Night's Dream.*"

"I know it's Shakespeare," Camilla snapped, aware that Dina was needling her. "I don't know anything about true love."

"You only practice it," said Dina in a honeyed voice.

"If you go on talking like this, I'm leaving." Camilla stared at her indignantly.

Dina gazed at her, weighing the angry look on her face as if she did not credit its genuineness. "Now, now, you'll feel better if you really get mad."

Camilla's sudden rage began to dissipate. Yes, it was true. Dina knew how to scatter the resentments that built up in someone. It was not a kindly sympathy like Ailsa's, but it was effective.

As she was silent, Dina went on, "You ought to learn to be a little more easy-going. Have some fun. That's what Serafina wants you to do. You're going to burn out otherwise."

Still Camilla did not reply.

Dina said, "Well, let's get back to Fina. What is she doing with herself? She used to call me up for lunch. She doesn't do that any more."

"She's got a chance for a show. She thinks it might lead to going into films—or TV. That means she'll go to the West Coast."

"Oh, that's the trouble!"

Camilla ignored her. Having started to talk she could not stop. "She acts like she doesn't know which end is up. I tell her she's got to be careful with these showbiz types. She doesn't pay any attention to me. You just wait, Camilla, she says. I'll be a big star and we'll be rich. What's that got to do with me? I ask her." Camilla stopped abruptly, as surprised as Dina that she had burst out with so intimate a memory.

Dina, watching her, thought, And then Fina hugs and kisses her and poor old Camilla melts. She said aloud, "Fina is not very sophisticated in dealing with people of that sort, is she?"

"Fina thinks the whole world is her friend. She just rushes right in, expecting everything to be the way she wants it. The trouble is that most of the time she comes out all right. She's just like that. People get carried away by her enthusiasm, I suppose. Most people don't want to disappoint a child. I'd never get away with it."

"She's young, Camilla, and very pretty and she thinks the world was made just for her."

A new idea seemed to strike Camilla. "You're a theatrical agent, aren't you, Dina? Do you suppose you could check out these people she's dealing with? Maybe you'd recognize them right off."

"Who are they?"

Camilla gave her names and the identities of shows, watching her anxiously.

"They're all right," said Dina. "They're legit. But you

have to be careful dealing with anybody in that line of work. They're mostly operating on a shoestring and half the time they deceive themselves about the prospect for their shows. They'd have to, or they'd get too discouraged before they could get their ideas off the ground. Fina ought to bear in mind that you shouldn't count your chickens till they are hatched. But she is a natural optimist, so she doesn't worry half as much as you do."

A soft sound reached Dina's ear. "That's the front door," she said and sang out, "Ailsa?"

"I'm here," Ailsa appeared in the door of the kitchen. "Why, Camilla! How nice to see you here." She glanced quickly from one to the other, to see how things were between them.

Dina smiled at her, as if to say, We're still friends. Camilla remained preoccupied, until Ailsa asked, "Have you seen her?"

"No," said Camilla, and looked at Dina.

Dina said, "She's still in her room. I didn't know whether to disturb her or not." She glanced at Camilla. "She doesn't come out unless one of us goes and gets her."

Ailsa looked at Camilla. "She's in the room at the end of the hall. Why don't you go and see her, Camilla?"

Camilla got up. She reached automatically for her handbag and then, remembering she was not in a public place, left it on the table and walked toward the door of the kitchen. "Down here?" she asked, and when Ailsa nodded, disappeared through it.

Ailsa sat down in the chair she had left. "What were you talking about?"

"Serafina."

Ailsa gave her an alert glance. "Serafina? Something's wrong there, isn't there?"

"Yes. You noticed something when you talked to her last, didn't you?"

"She was very unhappy. What is it?"

"She's anxious about Serafina. The girl is involved with some people who want to put on a new show. Camilla feels out of her depth and she's worried because she thinks Serafina is naive about such things. She thinks she may get into trouble, walk into a situation she is not prepared to handle and Camilla won't be able to help her."

"What kind of trouble?"

"My guess is financial. I think what's in the back of Camilla's mind is that these people may know that Serafina has wealthy parents and of course they need money, they need an angel. It's the sort of thing that's been done a thousand times. You get a silly young thing who wants to be an entertainer and you give her a chance in return for some financial backing. I'm not saying Serafina hasn't got some talent. I think she has. Maybe she can develop it. But you see what kind of complications that can make for Serafina and Camilla. Camilla is scared to death she's going to lose her, one way or another."

"I see." Ailsa sat silent, listening absentmindedly while Dina went on with further details that occurred to her. Suddenly Dina noticed her preoccupation and asked, "What's on your mind?"

"The thought has occurred to me—I should have thought of it earlier—Serafina is an alien. She came into the country as a student. She has told me so. I wonder if she has reported that she is no longer attending college? If not, she is here illegally. Did Camilla say anything about that?"

"Oh, God, no! What would happen to her if she didn't and they found out?"

"She would be deported. Her parents would certainly find her then. Poor Camilla."

Dina narrowed her eyes as she looked at her. "I'm willing to bet that Serafina did not report. She wouldn't want to take the risk that her people would find out that way where she is. They're surely still looking for her. As you say, poor Camilla. She has a lot to worry about. You'd better talk to her, Ailsa."

Ailsa said slowly, "I don't think talking to Camilla will do much good." She sat for a while, gazing in the direction of the door that led to Mary's room.

* * * * *

Camilla stood in the narrow hall in front of the door to Mary's room. In the turmoil of her own feelings it was hard to bring her mind down to the single thought of Mary. The image of the woman who had claimed her attention so completely at the beginning had faded under the onslaught of Serafina. Now she strove to focus on Mary. She had worried about Mary, leaving her like this in Ailsa's apartment. Of course it seemed necessary and for her own good and Ailsa would look after her. But the bond that had been created between them when she first encountered Mary made her supersensitive to the old woman's feelings. She thought that Mary, in the dimness of her awareness of her surroundings, would be frightened, would suffer from feelings of rejection, abandonment, loss of the protection of the familiar. It was like dealing with a child, except that with these broken, helpless old women you could never tell when a beam of understanding, of remembrance, of a vagrant sense of autonomy, would flood their consciousness, bringing comprehension and resentment with it.

For the first day or so, after she had left Mary with Ailsa, she had half-expected to be called to come and reassure her. She also was aware, whenever she came home to her own apartment, of a blankness, an acute sense of the emptiness of the room where Mary had stayed. When she did not hear from Ailsa this hypersensitivity faded. Serafina claimed her first attention, Serafina coming home bubbling with irrepressible joy at the prospect of becoming a success in a musical show, the winner of a show business award, a superstar on television. Camilla had long since learned that the smallest glimmer of good fortune carried Serafina instantly to the pinnacle of her most extravagant hopes. There were no slow steps in Serafina's imaginary upward path, only leaps. She had had a favorable audition. Now there was nothing in the way of her inevitable triumph.

Camilla, driven by anxiety to throw cold water on this unbounded self-confidence, had said, "But, look, Fina, if you get famous like that, your folks are going to hear about it. Then they'll find out about us."

"Oh, that will be all right! If I'm famous, I don't mind my father knowing about it and about where I am. I will have proved that I can do these things myself, without his help."

"And who's going to pay for all this? Doesn't somebody have to put up some money? Are these people expecting you to do that?"

Serafina brushed aside her suspicions. "How can I give them any money? I can't ask papai for money now. They'll find the money somehow."

"Who are 'they?' Who are these people?"

Serafina told her. The names meant nothing to her. Uneasily she watched Serafina's high spirits, distrustful of their source. Her own spirits flagged under a sense of foreboding, that these developments in Serafina's life meant that she would lose her to the greater attractions that success would bring.

Not wanting to go further down this path of thought, Camilla came down to earth. She was still standing in front of Mary's door. She tapped lightly on it and then opened it. The room she stepped into was large and sunny. Someone must have opened the curtains. Could it have been Mary herself? She looked around the room, at the bed with the covers turned back, at the little table with a tray on it. Someone—it must have been Ailsa—had brought Mary an early cup of tea.

She walked over to the armchair by the window, where the woman sat, and said, "Hi, Mary. How are you?" She waited to see if there was recognition in Mary's face.

The woman in the chair turned her head to look up at her and smiled. "Camilla," she said, reaching out her hand. Camilla seized it, overwhelmed by a feeling that made her for the moment speechless. I must be slipping, she thought. I'm getting soft. It wasn't right to get emotionally involved like this with your clients. It got in the way of your professional responsibilities.

But Mary seemed unaffected by her attempt at retreat. "I am very glad to see you, Camilla. It's been a little while since I saw you."

Overcome by the normality of Mary's response, Camilla stammered, "I—I've been busy. You look fine."

"Sit down, Camilla. Let us talk for a while."

Camilla sat down in the straight chair nearby. She felt awkward dealing with this self-possessed new Mary. There was little in Mary's outward appearance to distinguish her from the woman who had lived in Camilla's apartment. She wore the dressinggown she had bought for her. Her hair, short and more grey than white, was still rough and tousled, as if she had not combed it since getting out of bed. The transformation in her was more subtle. Camilla in spite of herself was abashed at the direct but mild gaze Mary gave her. She took refuge in saying, "You feel a lot better, don't you?"

Mary did not answer right away. She seemed to be pondering the question. She stirred in her chair and finally said, "Yes, that is true."

Making conversation, Camilla said, "You remember Fina? She's got a chance to appear in a musical show."

"Serafina? She has a sweet voice. She is happy about that, I'm sure."

As if she had picked up the trace of anxiety in Camilla's voice, Mary's wandering glance came back to her and stayed. Camilla went on, her anxiety released into speech. "She's so optimistic. You remember that, don't you Mary? She thinks because she has this chance her career is made. She trusts people too much. I'm suspicious about these people she is dealing with. I think they want to get some money out of her. I can't make her see that." With a sense of relief that she could speak out all the thoughts that had stayed pent in her mind, Camilla went on, aware only that Mary's attention remained on her. Occasionally she glanced at Mary, to see a somewhat puzzled expression on her face, a vagueness that nevertheless was full of sympathy. She suddenly realized that it did not matter to her that Mary did not understand all that she was saying. That was it: with Mary she had a home-dwelling feeling, some deeply-rooted affinity, in which criticism and failure of acceptance did not exist. To Camilla this was so rare a feeling that even as she continued to pour out her frustrations she marvelled at herself, at Mary.

"And besides all that," Camilla went on after a pause, "I don't like her going with those people. They don't behave the way I think they should. They go to bed with everybody. I think they take drugs. I know they get drunk pretty regularly. Fina doesn't know how to protect herself. Sometimes she doesn't come home till daylight. She has me fretting that something has happened to her. When I complain about that she laughs at me and says I'm a square, that I belong in the middle ages. That's not the way she used to be."

She fell silent, overcome by the anguish that so often took possession of her. She thought of the nights when she paced the floor, torn between anger at Serafina's callousness and the overriding fear that it was not faithlessness but physical harm that kept Serafina from coming home. And when finally Serafina came bursting into the apartment with her own special exuberance that could survive a night of dissipation, Camilla could not restrain the rage that gave vent to her own inner turmoil. But Serafina knew how to counter that rage. In bed, in the quiet and isolation of their bedroom, Serafina's cooing, coaxing caresses seduced her. Serafina's knowing hands, Serafina's nibbling lips, the pressure of Serafina's vibrant body, instantly touched and roused her own sensual feeling, fanned into flame her desire, which she had tried so hard to bury.

Mary's voice broke into her thoughts. "You are afraid you are going to lose her."

Astonished, Camilla looked up at her. There was no vagueness in Mary's mild eyes now. A slight shiver went through Camilla. How could Mary grasp the wild tumult of her emotions? She said in a chastened voice, "I guess that's right. I guess I don't know what Fina is going to do."

She gazed at the gaunt woman sitting opposite her. Of course there was a great deal in Mary's former life that she knew nothing about. If Mary had been a famous opera star, she was somebody who had lived on her emotions—like Fina, probably. That might make her quicker to understand what other people might be feeling. Camilla heaved a sigh and leaned back in her chair. Mary seemed to have lapsed into her usual preoccupation. What was she thinking about, Camilla wondered. She felt baffled by this withdrawal of Mary's, when she seemed to go to some remote world where she was unreachable. In search of her friend?

Anyhow, Camilla told herself, trying to shake off this pall of introspection, I've got a job to do. I've got to tell her she has to get ready and go and see those doctors.

She said aloud, "Well, anyway, Mary, You know, you've got to go to that Clinic and see the doctors. You remember, they have your medical records and they can say that you're really this opera star. Do you remember those people? Some of them may recognize you."

"Yes, I remember them," said Mary in a firm voice. "They attended May."

Camilla stared at her and then said, "Oh, your friend. Well, are you ready to go there?"

For a moment Mary did not answer. When she did there was a falter in her voice that spoke of a fearfulness that Camilla recognized, "Will you go with me?"

Camilla leaned over and patted her hand. "Sure," she said. "Don't worry."

* * * * *

"You're in a brown study, my sweet," said Dina. "You've been sitting there mourning ever since I got home. It's Magdalena again, isn't it?"

"Yes, it's Magdalena. Camilla came and told me when she had taken her to the Seabright Clinic, as we arranged, and that she thought she'd be all right for the week or so she's supposed to be there. I have been in touch with the Clinic since then. But I can't help worrying about her. Her recovery is still so fragile. They are supposed to have a psychologist examine her and see if she needs to see a psychiatrist. That alarms me."

"You think she'll be scared into another fit of amnesia or whatever it is. Well, we can only hope for the best."

Dina strolled across the living room trailing a cloud of cigarette smoke. She said over her shoulder, "Did Camilla say anything about Serafina?"

"Only that she doesn't see much of her. She has said that before."

"Ah!" Dina turned around to look at her. "Well, I've been seeing something of Serafina in the last few days, and I don't like what I see. You know of course that she is trying to break into the entertainment world. She's been pursuing me. We've had lunch together a couple of times. She comes to that Italian place I like to go to and she waits out everybody else so she can talk to me. She gives me a blow by blow account of her interviews and all about the people she's involved with. She thinks she's on the way to a big success. She's using Camilla, to some extent, anyway. Oh, her emotions are involved. She's not the kind of person who can be really cold-blooded. But when she really does become successful, I'm afraid that she's going to leave Camilla behind. And I don't see Camilla as a hanger-on, even with Serafina. There'll be the devil to pay."

"Dina, I can't believe that! Serafina is a foolish girl but surely she wouldn't treat Camilla that way!"

"She may be foolish—and she is in a lot of ways—but she's out for number one. She's a member of the Me generation."

"I can't really believe that. And I hope you will not say anything like that to Camilla."

"I don't think it is any kindness to her to let her go on living in a fool's paradise."

"Camilla will not thank you for telling her even if it is true. You'll make an enemy of her."

"That's too bad, because I like Camilla. I wouldn't worry about her if I didn't. And there is something else, Ailsa, that you should know. Serafina has not reported the fact to the proper people that she is no longer a student at Hunter. Won't that get her into trouble?"

"She told you this? Yes. The college must make periodic reports about its foreign students. If Hunter reports her absent, she will be in trouble. I've said something to Camilla about this—that she could be deported. And her parents might come and get her and accuse Camilla of corrupting her. But Camilla always finds excuses for her— she's just young, she has to grow up, she's always been treated like a baby. All of which is true, I daresay."

"I don't like to see somebody being deceived like this. I see a lot of it in my business. There are a lot of jealous, ambitious people in the entertainment world. Friendship doesn't count for much. I've told you enough about it for you to realize that, I'm sure. Serafina is all wrapped up in Serafina. She is very good at excuses. She even believes some of these fancy tales she tells, while she is telling them, so it's hard to call them lies. She's always had her way. She thinks she is going to make a grand success and then her daddy can come along and get her out of all the trouble she may cause."

Ailsa sighed. "You won't convince Camilla. She'll tell you Serafina is not cruel, not capricious or fickle. I'm sure the poor girl is having a bad time arguing the matter out with herself. You can't open the eyes of someone who doesn't want to see. I know Serafina is flighty. Camilla knows that, too. But, still, she means everything to her."

"Well, there's somebody who may do the job for us."

"What do you mean?"

"I met Francusi yesterday at a lunch party. He came over to ask me about Magdalena, how she is doing at the Clinic. I told him I didn't know. So then he mentioned Serafina. She has been to see him. She's heard about his connection with Magdalena. I suppose Camilla told her, innocently enough. He's a nice old fellow and quite susceptible to pretty girls. He's amused by her, I gather from what he told me. What she doesn't realize is that he is also very astute. He knows all about aspiring singers. So he played a game with Serafina. He let her tell him all about herself and her ambitions. You know how she rattles along. She is guileless when it comes to talking about herself. By the way, he was in Rio with Magdalena and he has been there on other occasions with other singers and musicians. So of course Serafina chattered about herself and her family."

"He knows she's here on her own and that her parents don't know where she is?"

"I'd say he guessed it, if Serafina hasn't told him in so many words. He's such a mild, sympathetic character that people tell him more than they should. He must have found out, because she reported to me that he told her that some malicious person might give her away—to the immigration authorities."

"Do you think he would do so himself?"

Dina picked a cigarette out of the pack and lit it. "I don't think so. He does not like dealing with governmental authorities. I've learned that from talking to him. He has had some bad experiences in the past."

Dina paused to take a puff on her cigarette. "So?" said Ailsa.

"He really floored me when he said he knows her father—at least, he has met him. Serafina's father is a wealthy businessman who likes to patronize the arts, including music."

"Oh, good heavens! Do you think he will get in touch with him?"

"He did not say he was going to, but why should he tell me this otherwise? You know, he is an old man with some old-fashioned ideas, no matter how tolerant he is of modern ways. He gives a lot of importance to family responsibilities, family loyalty—I suppose, partly because he had lost all of his own. He believes Serafina should not be giving her parents a hard time, leaving them to worry and sorrow over her disappearance. Of course, he said, that is the thoughtlessness of youth. But she will regret what she is doing now when she gets older."

"I see. Camilla doesn't know anything about this, I'm
sure."

"No, unless Serafina has told her that he has been
scolding her. Somehow I don't think Serafina will tell her
about that."

They lapsed into silence, each busy with her own
thoughts. Presently, Ailsa said, "I wonder how Magdalena is
getting along."

"You haven't seen her since she went into the Clinic,
have you?"

"No. The doctors think she shouldn't have any visitors
while she is reorienting herself. But I've had good reports
from the doctors I've talked to."

"Then there's no doubt that she is Magdalena Gibbon."

"Not a shadow of a doubt. Ruddle has capitulated. He
is disbursing money to pay for everything and he has given
the management of her apartment house notice to have her
apartment got ready for occupancy."

"So how much longer is she going to be there?"

"Perhaps another week, I gather. Camilla doesn't like
this at all. She has the darkest suspicions of what they may
be doing to her Mary."

Dina laughed, "I suppose she is her Mary. She wouldn't
be there without her."

* * * * *

Miserable, Camilla sat on a stool in the fast food place,
an untouched cup of coffee on the counter in front of her.
She was doing what she rarely did, taking a mid-afternoon
break.

"Off your feed today?"

Startled she looked up to find that Paula had sat down
next to her. Though they shared the same kind of work,

their paths seldom crossed, a fact that so far as Camilla was concerned was not an accident. There was a certain bond between them. Paula was black, with much the same background as herself. But she was also middle-aged, married, and insatiably curious about other people's business. Especially today Camilla did not want a confidential talk. Her reply was short.

But Paula persisted. She was a pleasant woman and her manner was never intrusive—all the more dangerous, thought Camilla. She said, "I've been watching you, Camilla. You're burning yourself out. What's driving you like this? You know you can't work this way at this kind of a job—not unless you have the hide of an elephant and no nerves. You ought to get away from it for a while every so often."

Holding onto her small fund of patience Camilla retorted, without forethought, "It's not my job," and tried to drink her coffee.

Paula considered her indulgently. "If it isn't your job, it must be your love-life."

Camilla lashed out, "I haven't got any!" and wished she hadn't said it.

"Maybe that's the trouble." There was a gleam in Paula's eyes.

The words, Would you mind your own business, jumped to Camilla's lips but with an effort she stopped them. She had no reason to quarrel with Paula.

After a silence Paula asked, "What became of that old woman you were taking care of? She's not still living with you, is she?"

Now how did she know about Mary? Camilla wondered. The courthouse gossip, she supposed. Seeking desperately for a plausible answer, she said, "Her friends came and fetched her."

"Her friends! She has friends? What kind of friends are they if they let her live like that in the street?"

"They didn't know where she was," said Camilla. She longed to scream at Paula, Why don't you go away and leave me alone? But she knew from experience that Paula would never be put off by her own unfriendliness.

Paula's questions persisted. "How did you find these friends of hers? Did she tell you about them?"

Wildly, Camilla searched for an answer. "She remembered some things and we were able to locate her friends." Camilla got up from the counter as she said this.

"You haven't finished your coffee," said Paula, looking at her cup.

"I shouldn't drink so much of that stuff," said Camilla and walked out of the food shop.

Beside herself with her own misery she walked aimlessly along the street to the next subway entrance. She found herself going down the steps and onto the uptown platform. Presently she reached the stop that was in her mind and automatically got out and walked up onto the street and across the thoroughfare to the park opposite. Sitting down on a bench she stared at the tall building opposite. If she could just see Mary. Never before in her life had she felt this overwhelming need to talk to someone, someone who could have some inkling of the agony through which she was passing. But Mary was over there in that Clinic. She glanced up at the tall building. She might as well be in prison. She looked down again and was lost in another recapitulation of the last forty-eight hours.

She could not believe it was happening when she arrived back home in the evening and found Fina's note propped up on the dresser. Her father had found her, it said, was there with her at that moment, waiting for her to pack up her clothes. She would get in touch with Camilla as soon as she could but it was certain she could not come back to Camilla's place.

For a while Camilla had been too numb to think. When

her mind began to stir she upbraided herself for thinking that this situation could go on forever. Every moment she had feared this would happen. Now the blow had fallen. It had been such a fragile thing, her little episode with Fina, an easily shattered little world, a mere soap bubble in the hard realities of her life. Then the letter had arrived, not from Fina. She had scarcely believed that Fina would write to her. Fina never wrote letters. This was on monogrammed paper, heavy, expensive paper, but handwritten, and it was from Fina's father. He invited her to come and have dinner with him and his family. They wished to express their gratitude to her personally.

She had stared at the letter in bewilderment and incredulity. Of course it was impossible. How could she do such a thing? How could Fina have allowed her father to create such a situation? He surely did not realize what Fina and she were to each other. But how would he know? It wasn't written on their foreheads. Fina could not have told him. And how could she go there—even supposing she could overcome her own extreme shyness in any such a situation—how could she go there under false pretenses, to accept the bland if sincere thanks of a grateful father?

After a night in which her mind had gone round and round seeking a path where there seemed to be none, she knew she had to find someone to talk to, someone who could at least provide a sympathetic ear. She had been drawn to where she was now sitting by an instinct that drew her to Mary. She glanced up again at the tall building. But Mary was inaccessible. Who else could there possibly be? She felt like a small child lost in a wilderness.

Slowly her mind circled around to Ailsa. Instinctively she drew back. The judge. In her mind she always called her the judge. There was a serene, even-tempered quality to the judge's view of things. She had approved of the judge even before she had come to know about her and Dina.

The fact that to herself she always called her the judge was a tacit admission that she maintained a small but vital barrier to full acceptance of her as a friend. Why? She knew the answer: she resisted the idea of giving anyone so much power over her, especially someone who seemed so worthy of it and therefore more dangerous, immune to criticism. Camilla looked into herself at this thought. Humbly she admitted, if she could not accept friendship, she must be condemned to friendlessness. She glanced again up at the tall building opposite. Mary had been able to reach her without effort. That meant she was not unworthy of friendship. And Fina loved her. So why couldn't she go to the judge with her problem. Early in their acquaintance she had bridged her usual initial mistrust of her as a white woman. It was obvious to Camilla from the start that the judge was genuine in her attempt to understand what in their relationship was beyond her own experience.

All at once Camilla came to a decision. There was no point going over and over again in her mind all these counter-arguments. She would go and see the judge. Her decision was so abrupt that she jumped up from the bench with an exclamation, startling the person walking by on the sidewalk. Paula was on the courthouse steps when she got back there. She looked at her in surprise and said, "Why'd you run away like that? Is something the matter?"

Camilla stared at her. She had forgotten about Paula. Paula said, "You look a little wild."

Camilla shook her head. "I just remembered something. I'll see you, Paula." She hurried down the corridor, conscious of Paula's eyes following her. But the judge had gone, she was told. By then the urge to unburden herself was so strong that she did not hesitate at the thought of going to find her in her apartment, the mere suggestion of which would have stopped her at any other time.

The receptionist at the desk glanced at her briefly and

reported her presence on the intercom. It was Ailsa who opened the door at her ring.

"Why, Camilla, this is a surprise! Come in."

"It was too late to get you at the court," said Camilla, conscious that she was breathing fast, as if she had been running.

Without comment Ailsa pointed to the sofa and sat down herself in a nearby chair. Camilla sat down, frowning, bolt upright from tension. They sat in silence until Camilla finally said, "I've got something I want to talk about. You can't tell me what to do, but I've got to talk about it."

Ailsa, recognizing her statement as an expression of an inner debate, said, "Of course. It's Serafina, isn't it?"

Camilla looked at her, unaware of the anguish her face expressed. "Her father found out where she was. Somebody told him—" She stopped, sudden suspicion appearing in her eyes.

Ailsa shook her head.

Camilla sighed in sudden relief and sat a little less rigidly. "I didn't think about you before. But you wouldn't do that."

"No. Neither would Dina."

"He came and took her away from my place when I wasn't there. She left me a note. He says she has to go back to Rio with him."

"He must take her out of the country because otherwise she will be deported. He will have trouble straightening out her situation with the Immigration Service."

"She can come back in, can't she?" Camilla demanded breathlessly.

Ailsa thought for a moment. "She's under age, so I suppose he could bring her back with him sometime."

"Anyway, I can't go and see her and she hasn't tried to get in touch with me."

"He's angry, I suppose, and wants to punish her."

Camilla chewed her lip. Seeing that she was close to tears Ailsa reached out a hand to touch her. "Do you mean he says you can't see her, that she can't come to see you?"

"I don't know. All I've got is a note Fina left me when he came to get her and a letter from him."

"A letter from him! What does he say?"

"He says he wants to see *me*. He's staying at the Regency. He says he wants me to come and have dinner there with him and his wife, tomorrow night."

"May I see the letter? Do you have it with you?"

Camilla rummaged in her big handbag and pulled out the large square white envelope and held it out to Ailsa. Ailsa drew out the double sheet of heavy, monogrammed paper and read the message through to the elaborate, unreadable signature. When she had finished she said, "Of course you're going."

"What the hell do you think I am?" Camilla shouted. "Can you see me going in there looking like some tramp coming for a free meal and a handout? Don't you think I've got any more self-respect than to come running—"

Ailsa said nothing, waiting silently for the tirade to end. When Camilla collapsed into a corner of the sofa she said, "Well, now that that's over, what have you come here to ask me about?"

Camilla wiped her eyes. "I don't know what to do. How can I go and find Fina? How can I explain what she means to me?"

"Of course you can't do that. You'd be in real trouble then." Ailsa looked back at the letter in her hand. "He says he wants to thank you for looking after his daughter. All he knows about you is obviously what Serafina has told him. He doesn't want to humiliate you."

Camilla's rage flared into a new spurt. "Then he's going to pay me off for taking care of his little girl!"

"Well, naturally, that's the way it looks to him. He

couldn't possibly see you as her special friend—unless she tells him that. And then he'd say you seduced her. This letter doesn't show anything like that."

"So what do I do? Turn up at dinner to get a medal?"

Ailsa could not help smiling. "I'd hope the reward was a little more worthwhile than a medal, Camilla. As a matter of fact, yes, that's what you should do. Where's your common sense, Camilla? I always thought you had such a lot for a girl your age. Besides, you'd probably get a chance to talk to Serafina. How else will you get to see her?"

Camilla was silent, sunk in a misery that this ray of hope did not seem to reach. Ailsa got up and sat down beside her on the sofa and put her arm around her. Camilla made no effort to draw away. Ailsa said gently, "Are you in doubt about Serafina herself?"

Camilla said in a choked voice, "I don't know what to think. I haven't seen her much lately. Whenever I've tried to ask her things she talks so much all around about that I don't get any answers."

"You think she may just be glad to be going back to her parents, that she's going to forget you?"

Camilla sat up angrily, "No! She's my girl! She's going to come back to me! Nobody's going to make me think she's just a play girl—"

"Certainly not I," Ailsa interrupted. "I'm just trying to find out what you're afraid of."

Camilla was suddenly quiet. "I don't know what to believe. If I could just see her, talk to her for a few minutes—"

"Then you'll have to go and have dinner with her parents. Perhaps when they see you they'll let you be alone with her for a while."

"But maybe they won't trust me. They're going to take her away. She doesn't have any choice. They don't care about what she wants to do. She's there with them now.

They may be making her believe all kinds of things about me. They probably watch her all the time. She's told me about them."

"Well, there you see. You have only her side of the story. Why should they talk to her about you? They probably don't trust her out of their sight. From the way she has behaved, you can't blame them, can you? Well, in any case, you'd better go to that dinner tomorrow evening. And don't be looking for slights."

* * * * *

Dina reached up and turned off the light at the head of the bed. As she sank down into the warmth next to Ailsa she said, "Did Camilla call you?"

"Yes. She's pretty wrung out over all this, poor girl. Last night's dinner wasn't anything that she thought it would be. She was treated like an honored guest—which she was, of course—and she had a long talk alone with Serafina. I think you do Serafina an injustice, Dina darling. She obviously has been working on her parents to get them to see Camilla as her friend and savior."

Dina slid her hand behind Ailsa's head on the pillow. "Well, what are they going to do?"

"They are taking Serafina home to Rio with them. They even suggested that Camilla go with them, but of course she can't. She pointed out that she has a job. So as soon as possible—as soon as Serafina's father gets the legal problems ironed out—they'll bring Serafina back here. They've agreed that she can go ahead and try to make a career for herself in show business. In fact, her father will help her. But—"

Ailsa broke off and laughed softly. Dina, roused from her preoccupation with Ailsa's breast, asked, "But what?"

"That's the best part of it. They'll allow Serafina to

continue her search for a career here in New York only if Camilla is with her. Serafina's father says Camilla is the only person he can trust to look after her. You know, the poor man has been frightened about something else, which we did not think of. He's always been afraid that somebody might kidnap his daughter. He's wealthy, you know. He says he is too busy to stay here and watch her and he doesn't like to be separated from his wife. So Camilla is to be her watchdog. I asked Camilla what she was going to do. She says she is applying for a leave of absence and she wants my help, which of course I'll give her. She has worked so hard for so long she is entitled to a little special treatment. She wants some time to see how things go. In the meantime—Dina, what are you up to?"

"What do you think?" Dina moved her arm further under Ailsa's body and rolled over against her. "You tend to forget some important things in the midst of all these responsibilities of yours." She was covering Ailsa's cheek and neck with seductive little kisses.

After a while she asked, "What are you going to do about Magdalena? Doesn't she leave the Clinic soon?"

"The day after tomorrow."

"Who is going to look after her? Are you going to take her home? And where is home, come to think of it."

"Her own apartment. It is ready for her. No, I'm not going to fetch her. Camilla will go. She needs something to take her mind off Serafina's absence. Besides, I think she is better able to deal with Mary—Magdalena, that is." She was silent for a moment, during which Dina was aware that her mind had strayed away from the two of them. Then Ailsa said, "You realize, darling, this is going to be a tricky thing—taking her back to her old place—the place she ran away from—reintroducing her to her past."

"What did the doctors say? Did they give their blessing?"

"They're a little baffled by her. She seems perfectly

normal now but very detached. They say she'll just have to go back and see if she can handle it."

"I see." They were quiet then, enjoying the touch of each other's hands, murmuring to each other as if to preserve a privacy that might be invaded from some unknown source, heightening their pleasure by imagining themselves secret and hidden in the delicious feeling of unrestrained sensual play.

When they were drowsy and ready to sink into sleep, Ailsa said, "How terrible it would be to be without you, my darling."

"Now you're thinking of Magdalena again," Dina answered, tightening her grip on Ailsa's body. "Don't ever leave me, Ailsa darling," she muttered and shuddered as she sank back down again in the bed.

V

A brisk breeze from the river blew along the street, flapping the scalloped edging of the marquee that covered the strip of carpet leading to the apartment house door. The doorman, dismissing the cab driver, looked curiously at the little group standing in the middle of the pavement. He had been only a few months in this new job and still did not recognize all the tenants of the building. But he had been warned about the return of this one after a long absence. He studied each of them for future reference.

The tall woman gazed anxiously about, up and down the street. The other two, the young black woman and the old man, seemed to wait for her to make some move.

Magdalena stared at the little areaway beside the entrance to the apartment house. It was scarcely noticeable now. The struts that had held the awning had been taken away. The little space sunk a step below the paving held only a small litter of empty cigarette packets and sandwich wrappings and paper cups, brought there by the wind. A tremendous pain seized her when she glanced that way, a pain compounded of so many things that were forever beyond expression but the memory of which now she could no longer escape. She felt creeping back again the desolation of those days just after May's death, the sense of emptiness that grew until it swallowed everything up, blotted out the sky and the earth, nullified the existence of the people surrounding her. She remembered the blind numbness in which she had gone out of this building, the panic, the terror that swept her at the realization of May's final absence, the unrejectable force that had driven her to seek out the old woman and follow her, the old woman who had sat in that areaway and seemed to beckon.

These feelings, benumbed by the horrors of the last three years, awakened now in a tremendous surge. She saw herself, she felt herself again what she had been in that dreadful moment, adrift from herself, torn loose from May, who had vanished, had dissolved into unreality. As the calm she had achieved threatened to shatter, she sought desperately to feel May's presence, the feeling which had taken possession of her so strongly a few days ago. She had lost May when she had fled out into that unknown world of fury and violence, that jungle of days and nights in the menacing streets. Now she had come full circle, back to May. May was with her again, driving away the terrors, the demons of the black void into which she had been plunged for so long. She reached out her hand to touch May, to cling to her.

Instead it was Camilla's hand which touched her arm. She looked down into Camilla's anxious eyes. Camilla had watched her apprehensively, aware that an emotional crisis had seized her and fearful of its outcome. She had seen Magdalena stand stock still as they waited while Francusi gave the doorman money to pay the cab driver. She had seen her staring, apparently at nothing, perhaps only to orient herself. She was relieved when Magdalena began to walk slowly towards the door of the apartment building. She kept her hand on her arm to guide her. Francusi was saying, "It is all as you left it, mia cara. Nobody has taken anything away. You will be at home."

When they were in the apartment he hurried about, opening curtains, looking to see if there was any disorder, any neglect. Her belongings had been kept intact, by Ruddle's orders, while her fate was unknown. Now, at his orders, the apartment management had cleaned and readied the apartment for her return. Francusi came back from a tour of the other rooms to find Magdalena standing with her back to one of the big windows, gazing about her. Her face was impassive but there was a grief-stricken air to her somewhat stooped erectness. He hurried over to her, anxious to comfort her.

"Come and sit down, mia cara. This is very tiring for you."

But instead she began to walk slowly toward the inner door of the room, as if seeking something she had not found. Camilla looked anxiously at Francusi. He shook his head and said, "She must see the rest of the apartment. The management must have her approval before they will turn the keys over to her. Mr. Ruddle arranged this."

Camilla nodded. Impatiently she waited, counting the minutes by her watch. At last she could wait no longer. Muttering, "I guess I should go and see how she is," she went through the door through which Magdalena had disappeared. The apartment was spacious and she found herself in a center space from which a short passage led to a dining room and the kitchen quarters. There were other doors standing open, down another passage—the bedrooms, she supposed. She went to one of these and saw what was obviously a music room, with a grand piano and bookcases and cabinets of records and tapes. She gazed at the luxury all around her, at the paintings on the walls, the objets d'art, at the mementos of a long career in music. Francusi had said that during the last ten years of her life Magdalena had not lived there but had kept this apartment as a base.

And she just walked away from all this, thought Camilla, as if it was a heap of rubbish. At first she felt a surge of outraged prudence. But quickly another feeling came to her, a feeling of approval and understanding. Of course, to Mary, what did all this matter if the life that gave it value had fled? Methodically Camilla examined the touches of grace in the big bedroom. She looked in the closets and opened the drawers of the bureaus and dressing table, and stared in surprise at their emptiness. The contents must have been placed in storage; perhaps the Barbadian maid had attended to that before she departed, and no one had thought to have them brought back to await Magdalena's return. It was just as well. There would thus be no garment, no toilet articles, no intimate objects to bring back the haunting past. Camilla sighed. How barren, how deadly, to be alone in such a place of memories.

Bemused by what she was seeing, she suddenly realized that she had not found Mary. There was another room, the door of which was opposite that of the music room. It stood open too and she glanced in. It was small and though there were paintings here also, there was an air of simplicity about it, of repose, of privacy. There were several large portfolios of paintings and drawings on the big desk.

Then she saw that Magdalena was standing looking out of the window, her back to her. "Oh, there you are!" said Camilla, her relief obvious in her voice.

The tall woman turned to look at her but said nothing.

"Did you find everything OK?" Camilla heard the worried tone in her own voice. She's off somewhere, she thought, and realized that she would get no answer. She stepped over to Magdalena and put her hand on her arm. "Mary, it's me. Are you all right?"

"Yes, I know you are here with me, Camilla. And, yes, everything is all right. Don't worry, my dear."

At the sound of the sensible words spoken in a calm voice Camilla felt an enormous relief. "Then how about coming back to the living room. Mr. Francusi is waiting for you."

The same calm voice said, "You go on back. I'll be there presently."

Reluctantly Camilla left her and went back to the living room. Francusi was pacing slowly back and forth its length. He stopped when he saw her, a question in his glance.

"If she's going to bolt, this'll be it," Camilla said flatly.

"What do you mean?"

"She's pretty upset, seeing this place, being here again, all these things around her, these photographs—" Camilla pointed to several photographs in cabinet frames, some of them obviously of Magdalena in various operatic roles.

Francusi followed her gestures with his eyes. He said, "These are for public display. There are no photographs here of May, of Magdalena in private."

"But I saw some in the bedroom—"

"Yes, it must be harrowing," he agreed sadly. "But for her to run away again—no, that is impossible—it is unthinkable."

"It wasn't thinkable the first time. She's going to stay here alone?"

He seemed nonplussed. "She is staying here, yes. But there is a person coming, a nurse, to spend the night. I shall stay here for a while. Can you—?"

Camilla shook her head. "I've got to get back to my job." Of course, she thought, the judge would have seen to it that there was some arrangement. Yet she felt uneasy.

They did not hear Magdalena come back into the room, treading on the soft carpeting. Seeing her, Francusi sprang forward. "Ah, Magdalena! Are you satisfied with what you find?"

Magdalena patted his arm and slipped past him to sit down on one of the tall-backed chairs. "Yes. There is an inventory, you know. Especially of the paintings. May made that. Ruddle will probably send somebody to check it." She spoke quietly, as if wanting to reassure him but casually, as if it was after all not a matter of great consequence.

The worried frown cleared from Francusi's face. He cast Camilla a delighted glance and sat down in a chair near Magdalena, talking happily.

Camilla, still uncertain, watched them for a while. He was right to be cheered and relieved. Mary seemed completely in control of herself. In fact, Camilla became aware that she was intimidating in the thoroughness with which she had taken command of her re-entry into her former life—at least, from the evidence of these few minutes since they had entered the apartment.

In a sudden recollection of practical matters Camilla said, "If you're going to stay here, do you want me to bring your things from my place?" She thought, a cheap dressinggown, some department store lingerie. There was nothing to match the luxury of these surroundings. Of course, there were the things the judge had provided.

Magdalena turned a quiet gaze on her. "I'm going to need something, aren't I, Camilla?"

"Yes, you will. I'll bring the things you have at my place around this evening. What about the things you had at the Clinic?"

"Perhaps the nurse will bring them when she comes," said Magdalena calmly.

When Camilla finally left, Francusi was on the telephone,

ordering tea to be sent by a caterer. When she arrived back at the apartment that evening twilight was deepening into night. She was surprised when a maid opened the door but then realized that the judge would have made arrangements for that, too. The big living room was softly lit. Magdalena sat at the farther end. A small table had been set with two places. Camilla walked across to her, still carrying the parcel she had brought. She had purposely not given it to the maid. No need for her to unwrap and examine these modest garments, she thought. And even as she thought of this, she realized that to Magdalena the maid's opinion of the clothes would mean nothing. Face it, Camilla, she said to herself; it's your own pride that's concerned.

Magdalena broke into her thoughts. "Camilla? Come and sit down."

"I thought it was a nurse you were going to have."

"She is coming later. Do come here."

"Just a minute," said Camilla, walking towards the door that led to the bedroom. "I've brought your things. I'll put them in your room."

When she returned the maid was arranging glasses and decanters on the coffee table. Magdalena said, "You'll stay and have dinner with me, won't you, Camilla?"

It was a very quiet meal, to Camilla almost dreamlike. Magdalena said little. That had always been the case. Mary had been silent. Camilla knew herself not to be talkative and the muted luxury of her surroundings made her aware of her own fatigue. Serafina had been gone from her for a week now, from the country for three days. Her absence drove Camilla to seek more activity in the evenings, to take on responsibilities she did not need to. So that she was grateful for this respite with this quiet partner whose sympathy she could take for granted. She was startled when Magdalena said suddenly, "How is Serafina? Will she come to see me?"

Touched on the quick Camilla blurted out, "She can't do that. Her father came and took her away to Rio."

Magdalena leaned back in her chair, her dessert untouched—she doesn't eat well even now, thought Camilla, automatically noting the fact. Magdalena said, "Is this final?"

"No. He says she can come back to New York and go on trying to be a singer. But she got in trouble with the Immigration Service. She didn't report to them when she was supposed to. He has to straighten that out."

"I see. So when do you expect her back?"

"I don't know. I hope it's soon. They wanted me to go with them to Rio but I've got my job—" The dam of her reserve broken, the pent-up flood of longing, fear and anxiety poured out, while Magdalena listened. Finally she fell silent and after a few moments Magdalena said, "There are things I want to talk to you about, Camilla, but not today. Today has been very tiring."

You bet it has, Camilla thought, with sudden realization of the time. It was well past nine o'clock. "You'd better go to bed. Is that nurse here?"

Magdalena nodded. "I did not invite her to join us because I wanted a tete-a-tete."

My, what a sweet smile she's got, thought Camilla.

When Camilla stepped out of the apartment building the night was fine and clear. She paused for a moment on the paving and looked absently about. She remembered the sight of Magdalena standing here, looking about with a troubled face. This was the spot from which she had vanished three years before. What had overwhelmed her at that moment? In her heart she understood. It was despair, despair at having been so finally abandoned, robbed by death, of her darling. That Camilla understood, with a pang for her own bereavement—temporary, please God, she breathed.

But where had Mary gone and what had she done that made her invisible, untraceable by the police, by the private detectives her friends had hired? Several days had passed between the afternoon when she had vanished and when the search had begun. In some way she had become unrecognizable in that short time. Or was it that the searchers were not searching for the right sort of woman? That was it. In that short time she had ceased to be the woman they sought.

Camilla became aware that the doorman standing in the doorway was watching her with disapproval. Of course, I'm black, she thought, at once, and I'm not dressed up like the people who live in this place. The thought fled as quickly as it had come and she returned to her preoccupation, walking off down the street towards the subway entrance.

After that, each morning she found a few minutes to take the subway and go up and pay Magdalena a visit. She was always met with a reassuring normality. Magdalena was always up and dressed—as she must have been dressed in the days before she had become Mary, thought Camilla. Noticing Camilla's up and down glance she smiled and said that Dina had gone on a shopping expedition for her. The nurse had not stayed beyond the first day or so. There seemed no need. She managed very well with just the maid during the day.

But what about the nights, Camilla wondered. The worry came to her mind every so often in the midst of her daily routine, until finally she decided to call on the judge.

Ailsa was surprised, as she straightened her desk and gathered up her belongings, to see her office door open and Camilla's head appear around it.

Camilla said, "Have you got a minute?"

"Of course. Come in."

"It's about Mary."

"Mary? Oh, Magdalena. You have to get used to calling

her Magdalena now, Camilla."

"She'll always be Mary to me," said Camilla firmly.

Ailsa looked at her. "Yes, I suppose she will be. In any case, has something happened? I saw her yesterday."

"No, nothing's happened—at least, not since I saw her last, which was yesterday evening."

"Well, good heavens, Camilla! Are you expecting something to happen?"

Camilla shrugged. "I don't know whether I do or not."

"That's not a very satisfactory frame of mind. What are you worried about?"

"She's alone in that place at night. The maid is only there during the day."

"I know. She wants it that way. I hired the maid. I told Magdalena I could find a live-in maid if she wanted one."

Camilla put her head on one side. "You think it's a good idea for her to be there alone all night?"

"I see. That is what you're worried about." Ailsa was thoughtful for a moment and then murmured, "Black-winged Night, when Chaos reigns."

Camilla gave her a sharp glance. "Put it any way you like. That place is full of—" she hesitated.

"Of May," Ailsa finished for her. "Does she talk to you about her?"

"She doesn't have to. She's all over the place."

"I've seen only one photograph—in the music room. It must have been taken when they first met, when they were younger. It is charming."

"There's another one, in the bedroom. It's a snapshot, somewhere abroad, when they were old. But that's not what I mean. There's something in the air."

"You don't believe in ghosts, do you, Camilla?"

"Depends on what you mean. I don't believe in them the way Fina does—come gibbering at you, or messing with your affairs. But May is always in Mary's mind."

"That is probably true. I go to see her quite a bit. She seems to like me to be there. She looks more directly at me than she used to. She sometimes mentions May but only incidentally, when she is telling an anecdote about some past event."

"It's all that light hair you've got," said Camilla, staring at Ailsa. "It reminds her of May."

"How do you know that?"

"Just something she said once."

"Well," said Ailsa, busying herself with some papers on her desk. "Are you worried enough that you think we ought to do something about it?"

Camilla shook her head. "I just wanted to let you know how I feel. I don't like having all this on my mind by myself."

"I see. Well, there are two reasons I don't want to disturb the present arrangement. One is that I think I understand why she wants to be alone—it means being alone with May. Don't you see?"

Camilla answered slowly, "I guess I do."

"The other thing is that she is determined to stay there. She was talking about that yesterday. She is determined to stay there and she insists on taking back the control of her affairs, including her financial affairs. Ruddle is upset about that. He called to talk to me about it. He can't stop her unless he gets the court to declare her incompetent."

"Can he do that?"

"He could make a good case for it, on the evidence of her actions during the last three years and the condition she was in when she was found. In fact, I'll tell you privately, I think it is a little too early to say whether she is able to look after herself. But I wouldn't let Ruddle know that."

Camilla spoke with sudden heat. "It would be criminal

to do that to her now. You wouldn't let him, would you?"

"I'd do what I could. You'd have to help."

"Any court is going to believe you before me."

"I think we'll just have to convince Ruddle he shouldn't do it. Francusi will help. I'll point out to Ruddle that he can always move to have her declared incompetent later, if she really proves to be so."

Camilla sat frowning down at the floor. "She's getting better every day. That's why I leave her there by herself so much. She wouldn't mind if I moved in. But I think she's doing better by herself. It's just that I worry whether I ought to do that, whether I'm right, whether it's just wishful thinking. I think there is something going on inside her, I mean. Remember, she began to change when she was at your place."

"I admit she is not at all like the woman I first saw. She's changed a good deal. Of course, that means she is recovering, she's becoming the woman she used to be. But there is always this business about May. I notice that, while she is so rational now and so amenable, she can be very remote, very far away, somewhere where she doesn't want anybody to follow her."

"She's right there when you ask her a practical question," Camilla objected defensively. "She just doesn't have any use left for the world. She's just putting up with it."

They looked at one another, aware that this was the crux of their interchange. Ailsa asked, hesitating, "Do you think it is all right for her to be alone so much? She would not try to—?"

Camilla answered vigorously, "She's not going to commit suicide. She's not going to run away into the street again, which would amount to the same thing. She's going to stick it out, just waiting."

Ailsa nodded and closed her briefcase. They walked out of the office together.

But Ailsa was still preoccupied when she reached home and found Dina ahead of her.

Dina, kissing her, looked at her critically. "What is it this time?"

"Camilla stopped in to talk to me."

"So, it's Magdalena."

"She is worried about whether it is right to leave her alone so much."

"Doesn't she have people who come to see her? Everybody has heard that she's back now."

"Well, yes. Though she doesn't encourage visitors. I think she shrinks from having to satisfy curiosity about her absence—where she was and what she was doing. Francusi says she has given most people the impression that she lost her memory. I suppose that's true in a way."

"I can see that she wouldn't want to talk about it. How much do you think she does remember about those three years, anyway?"

"There's no way of knowing. She will never say."

Dina walked across the room, trailing a cloud of cigarette smoke, to pick up an ashtray. "I've only seen her a few times. She makes me uneasy."

"Why?" Ailsa sat down in a chair near the window, watching the beginning of evening in the sky.

Dina stood holding her elbow with her cigaretteless hand. "She seems so much more than a human woman. When we touch it is as if I was touching something that reaches beyond—"

"Beyond what?"

"The normal boundaries of the senses."

"Dina, what nonsense! You did not feel this when she was here."

"She was just poor old Mary then. That's when she first came here. She was different when she left."

"Of course she was. She had come to realize who she

really was. Dina, you're being primitive, as irrational as Serafina."

Dina shrugged and moved away. "Does she talk about her friend—May?"

"Not very much. Sometimes she mentions her when she is talking about something else—for instance, the paintings. They are quite valuable. May was an art historian, an expert in identifying old paintings. She made the selection of paintings Magdalena has on the walls there. Magdalena always speaks as if May is alive."

"See!" said Dina, triumphantly.

"See what?" Ailsa's tone was annoyed. "Of course May is alive to her. Oh, I don't mean that she thinks she is still here in the flesh. But she is alive to Magdalena."

"Don't you see? That is what I mean. She goes beyond what is here and now. You touch her and you feel something more than an ordinary woman." Dina moved her shoulders as if feeling a cool draught.

"Of course she isn't an ordinary woman. She never was. Dina, are you afraid of her?"

Dina said slowly, "No, not afraid."

Ailsa said sternly, "You think she's wandering on the shore at the entrance to Tartarus with the poor souls who have no coin to give Charon to row them across the Styx."

Dina said petulantly, "Oh, you and your classical education."

* * * * *

In these night hours, in the quiet dark, May was there with her. She felt her close, answering her every move, her every thought. May was there to remind her of the blissful years.

It was always May who kept her on the right path. When they had come back from her last opera season in London, flushed with its triumph, the applause still ringing in her ears, she had wavered in her announced intention of making the coming season the last in New York.

"But don't you see, May dear, singing opera was what I was born for. It is my life blood. It is not just using my voice. It is performing—there is joy in that beyond everything except music itself. It has always been like that. I love the drama. It thrills me to be able to stir up in the audience the emotions I've taught my voice to project. Most people cannot really say what they feel, in moments of deep emotion. It is much easier to sing it—and for many someone else must sing for them—"

She stood over May, seated in the comfortable chair by the bed, willing her to accept the force of her protest. May, looking up at her with characteristic patient calm, said, "Of course, dearest. I've known this since I first met you. You were devastated then—don't you remember, there in the garden that lovely June day?—because you thought you might not be able to sing opera again. But you cannot make time stand still. Your voice is as lovely as ever. You're as beautiful as ever you were. But there is a worm i' the bud, hidden still, but soon it will be seen—or heard, rather." May had smirked up at her, saying this, with a mischievous glint in her eye, aware that what she was saying was vexing and nevertheless determined that Magdalena should accept the truth. "This should be your last season anywhere. Don't say you can't do it. You have a precedent. Rosa Ponselle did it—retired at the height of her powers, when you were young and just starting. And then she was the age you are now. It is not only possible, but you must do it."

And of course she had done it, with a dreadful pang of

regret the night of her last performance at the Metropolitan, standing in the footlights with her arms full of flowers, while the audience thundered and the theater blazed with light in her honor.

The first anguish past, she recognized the fact that she had left the operatic stage at the right moment, thankful when the time came round when she would otherwise have had to consume herself in the drudgery of rehearsals. The concert stage, she was told, would be less strenuous. She doubted this, because perfection never came with reduced effort. She made a practice of giving advice to young singers, but she had no wish nor need to be a voice coach. The main thing was that her new career did not demand as much time and what she saved she could spend more fully with May.

It was then that she realized how adroit May had always been in fitting her own professional requirements into hers—just as, in fact, she fitted her body into the contours of Magdalena's. May seldom spoke about the work she did, the dealers she contended with, the patrons whose wishes were ever vacillating. When she did talk about all this it was in an anecdotal vein, to embellish a moment of leisure.

She was suddenly made aware of all this when one day she came upon May absorbed in the examination of an oil painting, and asked, "What are you doing?"

"Ah," said May, suddenly aware of her attention, "if I could only make up my mind!"

Magdalena glanced at the painting, an Italian seventeenth century painting depicting, she supposed, an episode from the Old Testament. It portrayed a young woman of great beauty but it was the expression on her face, great determination, courage, intelligence, that took Magdalena's eye.

Her attention lingering on the painting, she asked, "About what?"

"Whether this is by the painter to whom it is attributed."

Magdalena glanced back at the painting. "Is it so important? If it is something one would want, does it matter? What difference does it make? I should want this one because of that girl—" she pointed to the figure.

May laughed. "Darling! Of course you know the answer. The price. The dealer who wants to sell this and the man who wants to buy it have agreed to accept my attribution." She paused to gaze at the painting, smiling. "The thing is that I think this is by a woman. It is undoubtedly a masterpiece, so of course it is not attributed to a woman, but to her father, who is a well-known artist of that time. I say it is not his. I have reproductions of some of his that I can show you and you will see the difference. And I have seen other paintings by her, attributed to her father, of course. Of course you know that many of these old painters had studios where they were helped by their sons and their apprentices—and their daughters. But this is more than that. This painter is a master in her own right. Her women are beautiful but they are also strong, with bones under their fine skin—not dolls made for caressing."

Magdalena looked at her, noting with pleasure the flush in May's face. "So what will you do?"

"I have made up my mind—right now. I shall attribute it to the daughter. One day I may be able to demonstrate the truth of my supposition. And if the buyer does not want it, I will buy it myself and you shall help me pay for it."

She had stood up and now came closer to Magdalena. Magdalena, reaching out for her warmth, her softness, the response of her body, found only the bland smoothness of the sheets on the bed. For a while she suffered again the exquisite sense of loss, the pain of separation. Then she lapsed into a doze which after a while merged once more into a waking dream. It was a dream filled with happiness, contentment.

Francusi had been right. Withdrawing from opera now with her voice intact, her reputation unaffected, she was in demand for the concert stage. They traveled everywhere. May, she was now aware, was always intent, whenever time allowed beyond the requirements of the concert tour, to look for paintings and other objects of art. That was the reason that they had agreed to acquire this apartment in the heart of Manhattan, as a base for their belongings, since sometimes May found things that she said they should have. Magdalena, in earlier years, had taken museums and art galleries for granted, something one did in rainy weather. She learned now to follow May about them, with a far greater attention, marveling sometimes at the erudition May unselfconsciously displayed. She learned also that there were people who knew and admired May who had heard of herself only in a distant and casual manner. A very useful lesson in humility, she thought.

She also found it now unnecessary and distasteful to fill her life with the sort of social whirl she had cultivated before—and had, she realized, imposed upon May. That, she saw now, had come about in the beginning because the world she inhabited professionally was a gregarious, competitive one and she had used the conviviality as a means of bolstering her self-esteem and to guard against loneliness. Now with May nothing of this was any longer valid.

The time came, after a number of years of concertizing, when they began to think of extending the quieter part of their lives. She would retire altogether from professional singing. She was into her fifties and her voice, remarkably durable, nevertheless was showing the signs of age. She noticed, too, that the life of constant traveling, which concert tours required, was taking a toll of May, who often grew tired but said nothing. For a few more years she could record and give an occasional recital. And then they could be entirely free of the world, no longer objects of worldly speculation.

She remembered the occasion when they finally made their decision. They had been to the Edinburgh Festival and afterward had gone to the wilder part of northern Scotland for a holiday. They stayed in a tall red brick house trimmed in white stone, built in Queen Victoria's time by a wealthy man on a high ridge above a deep glen. Even in the midst of summer it was not warm and Magdalena remembered the chilly bedroom as she stood in her dressinggown by one of the tall windows. In the early morning the loch below, emerging from the mist, was a silver sheet bordered by steep banks covered with dark evergreens. As the day wore on the brief pale beams of sunlight ceased to break through the clouds, while the fine rain turned to a downpour that sent rivers of water streaming down the window panes.

May, still in bed, the London papers strewn around her on the coverlet, raised her head to say, "No climbing through the bracken today, my darling. Much better to stay here and read your mystery story."

Magdalena came to sit beside her. "At any rate, Salzburg, where we go for the Mozart, will be drier."

"And then it's Paris and London, for the opening of the season, and then it's back to the States and—how many cities is it?—all the way to the West Coast and back to New York."

Magdalena looked down at her as she lay on her back, her head sunk into the soft pillow. "You're a little weary of it, aren't you, May?"

May looked past her at the ceiling. "I like your concerts. I like hearing you sing so full out, soaring above even a big orchestra. It is not quite the same when you sing at home or in a private recital. I expect that comes of your opera years. It gives you a little of that back, doesn't it? I should miss that, if you were to stop."

"But it is true that I choose the easier things now to sing. I don't depend on my voice as I used to. You know that."

May was silent for a moment. "If it wasn't for the flying and the hotels and worrying about the luggage and the time schedules—" May did not finish her sentence.

They watched the rain flowing down the window panes. May's spirits, she knew, were never affected by dark days and stormy weather. She seemed to accept them for what they were, natural phenomena to be compensated for in other ways. Right now she seemed to be enjoying this opportunity for an unforeseen moment of leisure and snuggled down luxuriously into the bedclothes. Magdalena leaned over her.

"I can remember a different day, in a garden, and I plucked a rose," she said.

May reached up to take her head in her hands. "My darling, how fortunate for me that you did not hesitate to pluck. I could never have reached for you as you did for me. And I would have mourned ever after."

"I could not possibly have left you there, to be a pretty memory. But now you don't want to traipse after me any more."

May's gaze was serious. "I did not say that. I do get tired when we are on tour. But, dearest, so do you. And I think—"

She paused and Magdalena said, taking off her dressing-gown, "What do you think?"

"I think perhaps you should not go on demanding so much of your voice, of your body."

"It takes discipline," said Magdalena, sliding under the

covers beside her. "So why don't I tell Francusi that there will be no more tours after this one? I am tired of discipline."

"I think he will be delighted. He thinks you are ruining your voice—"

"What is left of it."

"And overtaxing your strength."

"I'm still as strong as an ox."

"Hm, perhaps not. But, after all, you must decide for yourself."

Magdalena's laugh was muffled by the bedclothes as she drew May's body against her own. "You've just made the decision for us," she said.

They forgot for a while the stormy weather beyond their high nest, except when an occasional heavy gust of wind flung the rain against the window pane with a crash. They knew now, with the experience of twenty years, exactly how to please each other, how to seek and achieve delight for them both, bask in the pleasure they could each produce for the other. It was an extra boon, thought Magdalena, that would only be the result of the sort of one-ness that had been theirs over the years, that could not be predicated solely on the sexual pleasure of their comings-together in bed.

May fell asleep after they had eaten the lunch that was sent to their room. Magdalena sat in the chintz-covered armchair by the window, watching the mist blown before the wind, the clearing patches of sky, mountain and water. Occasionally she caught a glimpse of the loch, which emerged for a moment like a scene from another world. The paperback book in her hand did not hold her attention and she began to wonder what really it would have been like to reach this stage of her life without May—what the steady slipping away of the years would have meant to her, what toll the natural fading of her career would have taken of her spirit in such a case. She regretted the need to acknowledge the physical decay that time wrought. No one could regret it more, for her voice, her physical powers had always been of prime importance to her. But the presence of May, the reality of May, become her second self, seemed to deflect the full impact of this universal tragedy upon her spirit.

She got up and went to the window for a better look at the view outside. As the afternoon waned the storm had abated. Long trailing clouds streamed away toward the farther end of the loch and the grounds of the guesthouse, the footpath down to the small dock where the loch-ferry tied up, a few sheep trotting demurely down the hillside, a glimpse of the distant shore were visible in the pearly light from the patch of brightening sky. Yes, she thought, it was time to call an end to her public life. She wanted more time with May.

She felt May's arms circling her waist. May had awakened with the increasing light in the room and had come over to join her. They stood together watching the scene. "Look," said May, finishing a yawn. "There is a patch of blue sky. At least, it was blue once, I suppose, before the rain washed it out."

"Wouldn't you be washed out, if you'd been in that downpour for twelve hours?" Magdalena demanded, drawing her close, and May laughed into her shoulder.

They had stuck to this resolution. From time to time they came to New York so that Magdalena could hear the young singers she encouraged and who were now Francusi's proteges. They came to this apartment, to this bed. May did not like the city and its crowds, but she accepted the necessity with her usual even temper. She even laughed a little at Francusi, who became more and more absorbed in the new techniques of making television films of live opera.

Times had changed, said Magdalena, since the days when they had tried to make a movie of a Mozart opera.

These last years had been for them alone. There was no history to record of them. She began to drift again into forgetfulness. May's soft little laugh was in her ears as she sank into a deeper sleep.

* * * * *

"Why do you suppose Magdalena is giving a dinner party for us?" Dina asked, standing in the shower.

"Well, finally, after all this time, Serafina is back. It took a while but she is back, with her father and mother. They came to call on Magdalena yesterday when I was there. He says he heard Magdalena sing in Rio years ago when he was a very young man. He's quite charming and it's obvious that Serafina gets her looks from her mother. It is also obvious that Serafina is the apple of their eyes."

"Are they going to be at the dinner?"

"Good heavens, no! This is to be—what is the opposite of a stag party—a hen party?" Smiling to herself Ailsa waited for an explosion from Dina.

It came. "Ailsa, how disgusting! How can you use those terrible old sexist labels?"

"Because I am not a graduate of consciousness-raising sessions, like you. I've always raised my own. And I live in the bad old world where people still talk like that."

"Not with me you don't!"

Ailsa stepped into the shower and laughed when Dina seized her around the waist. "Don't get fresh. I'm only here because I can't hear what you say above the noise of the water."

"Oh, I do believe you, I do!" said Dina, hugging her tighter.

"How can I wash if you don't let go?"

"Do you really need to?"

Some minutes later, when Ailsa was sitting on a three-legged stool drying her feet, Dina said, "Do you think Serafina's father has any inkling of how it is between her and Camilla?"

"If he does, he doesn't give any indication of it. Perhaps he thinks it prudent to shut his eyes. He seems to believe that Camilla is the answer to prayer."

"So this is a dinner party for Serafina."

"For Camilla really. You know, because I've told you, that we have won against Ruddle. He's thrown in the sponge. Magdalena has control of her own affairs. I'm a little sorry for the poor man. He goes to see her quite often. She has no more to say to him than she does to anyone else. He sits and stares at her as if he is baffled by the whole thing."

"Perhaps he's afraid of her, like some of us."

"If so, I should say that it is the first time in his life that he was ever afraid of anyone," said Ailsa crisply. She watched as Dina walked naked across the bedroom to find her cigarettes. She always felt great pleasure in seeing the lithe, vigorous movement of Dina's long legs. Dina had an athlete's body. When she walked along the street it was with a swift, impetuous step as she dodged through the crowd with practiced ease.

Ailsa got up from the stool and stepped into the bedroom. "I've been waiting for him to threaten action against what Magdalena wants to do with her money. But he has surprised me. He has accepted her decision meekly."

"And what is it that she wants to do? You haven't told me."

"She wants to establish a foundation to look after destitute women, to do something about preventing so many from becoming homeless and friendless. She wants

Camilla to run it. She says she would not trust anyone else to do it right."

"Whew! She's going to keep enough to live on, I hope."

"Oh, she's practical enough. She has no intention of becoming dependent on anyone again. But she wants to disperse her possessions—be free of such burdens, she says. The paintings are to go to an art museum, in May's name. You know that they are very valuable, don't you? They've been in a bank vault while Magdalena was missing."

"Where is she going to live?"

"She has not said but I expect it will be abroad. For the last ten years of her life with May, after she retired from the concert stage, they lived in retirement, away from publicity, somewhere in England. I think she wants to return to that life, to wait it out."

"To wait it out!" Dina stared at her in doubt and then said, "Oh, I see!" She took a pair of dangling earrings out of a drawer and put them in her ears. "So this is a party for Camilla, not Serafina."

"For both of them, really," said Ailsa, clasping a necklace around her neck.

* * * * *

Magdalena sat in a large armchair that almost hid her from the sight of anyone coming into the big living room. She was aware of this and rather liked it, felt it something of a shield. A shield from what? Even now that she had left behind the abyss from which she had been snatched, she shrank from the thrust of a too-aggressive world. She looked at her hands, to remind herself of her deliverance from the darkness into which May's death had plunged her. Her hands showed the disfigurements of age but they were now clean and well-cared-for, not the shriveled claws with blackened, ragged fingernails they had been. She was recovering her natural capacities, as much as she ever could without May, for without May she knew herself to be a hollow person. She steeled herself daily to deal with the people who came about her. There was pain even in dealing with those few whom she knew to be most truly sympathetic to her. There was always the barrier of what had happened to her, which she could never explain to anyone but May. She could never explain because she could never describe to anyone what there had been between May and herself. These friends—they see me, she thought, as alone, abandoned, the subject of their care. I am recovered now more wholly than they think, because I have recovered May. How can I tell them of those thirty years when for me the world was emptied of everything but May and yet for the same reason overflowed with life and joy? How can I tell them how I lost you, May, and now have found you again? How tell them that in my mind and heart I live with you in a land where there is no parting, no pain of any sort? How solitude—what they see as solitude—is not, nor the night dark, because you are with me? How tell them any of this? They would think me mad—more deranged than they once thought me.

The soft sound of voices came from the direction of the vestibule. The maid must be ushering someone in. Magdalena glanced over her shoulder. She saw Ailsa come into the room. She wore a low-necked dress of a pale color and the light from the tall lamp by the door shone into her blonde hair. Magdalena felt a catch at her heart. For the moment it might have been May who stood there. As Ailsa came across to her she saw the lamplight flash on Dina's black cap of hair. She smiled. She recognized something in Dina—that rebellious, impatient spirit.

"Do sit down," said Magdalena, and signalled to the maid to bring drinks. "Camilla and Serafina will be here presently. You know Serafina's father has brought her back. But of course you know. You were here when he came to call."

Dina, standing with a glass in her hand, gazed at the big portrait of an eighteenth-century lady that hung on the wall over an antique side table. But her attention was on Magdalena and Ailsa. Ailsa seemed entirely at ease, but of course she saw Magdalena nearly every day. They were talking about Serafina, about her father, about Francusi. Yes, it was Francusi who had told her parents where they could find Serafina. "He has an enormous acquaintance," said Magdalena, "everywhere. I do not know how he can remember them all."

After a short while there was a soft buzz and the maid went to open the door. Serafina's voice preceded her into the room. She was wearing a tight-fitting silver lame dress with very little top and a pair of silver slippers. She ran across the room to Magdalena, calling her Titia and babbling in the mixture of Portuguese and English she used whenever she wanted to dramatize her actions. The little clown, thought Dina. She speaks English perfectly well. I suppose she doesn't want to get out of practice in this role of the foreign ingenue. Dina watched with amusement how Magdalena received this homage. Magdalena smiled and stroked Serafina's head when she leaned down to kiss her. After all it was Serafina who had first struck a chord in Magdalena's memory, resulting in her being brought back from the dead—yes, from the dead was not an exaggeration. Dina studied Magdalena's face more carefully and unconsciously shook her head. It was impossible to fathom from it the depths in that strange woman.

Ailsa looked at Camilla coming more slowly across the room, giving Serafina time to finish before she greeted Magdalena herself. Camilla grinned as she caught Ailsa's eyes looking her up and down, surprised by the white silk Turkish trousers and sleeveless, low-necked blouse that showed off the satin smoothness of her dark-brown skin.

But Camilla's attention went back at once to Serafina. Ailsa saw that she was smiling, the almost fatuous smile of an indulgent mother. Camilla nodded to Ailsa and at Dina, who glanced round over her shoulder to say Hello. Only when she had gone over to pat Magdalena's shoulder and ask her how she was did she come out of her preoccupation with Serafina.

When she straightened up, Ailsa said, "You look stunning tonight."

Camilla focused on her and then looked down at herself.

"This monkey suit is Fina's idea," she said.

"She looks happy," said Ailsa, glancing across the room.

"She ought to be. She's got everything the way she wants it now. Including me."

"And how about you?"

Camilla grimaced. "I'm her nursemaid and bodyguard. It's a new career for me."

"Aren't you happy about it? Don't you think you can handle it?"

"Oh, I can fight off the burglars all right. I can see that she doesn't get kidnapped or hooked on drugs. She'd better not try that." Camilla paused before adding, "Her father is counting on me to keep her out of trouble in this big wicked place."

"Well, don't look so glum, Camilla. It's what you wanted. But how about Magdalena?"

"You mean, her idea for me to run her foundation. That's the real serious business for the future. Mary says there's no rush. She knows I've got to get myself and Fina sorted out first. Mary says she can wait. But I know she is hankering to get rid of this place and all these things." Camilla gazed about at the furnishings and paintings. She took the glass of gingerale on the tray the maid offered and looked down into it as if seeking a divination.

You're worried about something, Camilla."

"It's Fina. I feel as if I was in a goldfish bowl. I know everybody over there at the courthouse thinks I'm funny, always have. They don't understand about my private life but they've got their suspicions. Paula especially. She knows how I react when men try to hassle me. I don't stand for anything like that."

"But they don't know about Serafina, do they?"

"No, and they won't, if I can help it. But I've always been careful about how I behave, at least in public. Now here's Fina, acting as if she wants to advertise what we are. I've told her she shouldn't go kissing and hugging me in public. But she pays no mind."

"I wouldn't worry about that. Serafina acts like that about everybody. And in her background there's a lot more show of affection than with us." Ailsa patted her arm, smiling. "Camilla, you've got some things to learn now and I think Fina is teaching them to you."

A little shriek from the other end of the room broke into their talk. Serafina, watched by Dina, had continued to coo and fuss over Magdalena, who sat quietly, only half attentive to her. Serafina, pirouetting away from her, returned to touch her once more, patting her cheek, coaxing her to smile, saying, "Titia, querida, aren't you glad to see me? I've been away so long." Magdalena, with a surprisingly swift movement, caught her hand and held it for a moment.

She said, "Of course, dear child. I am very glad to see you." Serafina, under the gaze of her wide open eyes, their expression half indulgent, half satirical, shrank back from her like a bird that tries to break its thrall. Magdalena loosened her hold almost at once. Serafina's chatter was still for a while and she stayed a little away from her, with uneasy glances in her direction.

After that it was a lively dinner party, the gaiety fueled by the interchange between Dina's sharp wit and Serafina's effervescence, Magdalena sat chiefly silent. But, Ailsa noticed, she hasn't gone away from us as she used. Occasionally she smiled. Once or twice, looking up, Ailsa met Magdalena's eyes as they lingered on her, but she could not fathom what lay in that brooding gaze.

Afterwards, when they had left the dinner-table and had gone back to the living room, Ailsa wandered about looking at the paintings and the photographs, her spirit held in a mist that was half contentment and half melancholy. There, she saw, was Magdalena in the Rosencavalier, as the Queen Thessaly. Yes, she thought, it was easy to see how such a place, in the magnificence of its furnishings and mementos, would become a mausoleum. That would not be what Magdalena would want, would not be the setting in which she would seek the memory of May. She paused for a while in the small room that had been May's study, fingering with curiosity the portfolios on the desk. There was the photograph of May as a young woman. She examined it closely. It was such a reserved face and yet it held the key to so much. When that photograph was taken there was a lifetime to come for her, for Magdalena—a lifetime filled with a whole compound of riches—not merely the sensual wealth of bodies in harmony but also the intermingling of feelings, understanding, shared defeats and triumphs. What a severing death must bring to such a vibrantly lived community of their spirits!

A soft sound made her aware that Dina was in the music room opposite. She felt suddenly an overpowering desire to be with Dina. She stepped across the narrow passage. Dina glanced at her as she came into the room but went on busying herself with the devices for playing music. Ailsa looked about. The big piano was closed. Obviously it was never used, for a couple of large photographs were placed on its shining lid—one of Magdalena in satin knee breeches, laughing, audacious as Cherubino in Mozart's *Marriage of Figaro*. She must have been young then, thought Ailsa. The other—Ailsa's eyes were fixed on it—she was Orpheus, Gluck's androgynous musician, leading Eurydice forth from Hades.

Dina's voice said softly, "This is it," and she held up a record. Seeing what it was Ailsa said, alarmed, "Should you?"

Dina answered her only with a movement of her head. In a moment the great voice, caught in its prime, filled the apartment with Orpheus' lament to Eurydice, What is life to me without thee?

Spellbound for a moment Ailsa listened, the music piercing her heart with its dramatic truth. Then, her alarm returning, she stepped to the doorway, where she could see Magdalena, seated again in the high-backed chair, Camilla standing beside her. Her hand, outstretched, stroking Serafina's glossy curls as the girl sat on a hassock at her feet, paused in its motion.

For Magdalena was listening and what she heard stilled her hand, entered her heart. That music was May. Gluck's music spoke of May—grave, sweet, leading one's spirit into limitless space, where boundless happiness and unfathomable melancholy mingled. She remembered how it had been whenever she had sung Orpheus—how she had been filled with the physical joy of singing, how she had felt her whole body to be an instrument to bring forth from the dry page of the written score the immense feeling in that haunting music. Yes, it was May's music. Hearing it now, it was May's voice, calling her to leave this place to go wherever she wanted. She must follow May—patient, undemanding May, who nevertheless would never leave the path upon which her feet were set. It did not matter where she went now, for May would always dwell within her, in her heart, in her spirit, dispelling sorrow, dread.

Ailsa stepped back into the music room. She answered Dina's questioning glance with a shake of her head.

"She seems all right," she murmured, and noticed Dina's sigh of relief. How like Dina, she thought, to put something so important to the test like that. As Magdalena's voice reached the end of the aria, she leaned over and put her arms around Dina.

"My darling,"she said, and thought, How marvelous to feel the answering strength of Dina's body.

AUTHOR'S NOTE

Some will hear in this novel a lesbian echo of the ancient Greek myth of Orpheus, the first and greatest of musicians, and the nymph Eurydice, his love. It will be remembered that Orpheus followed Eurydice down into Hades in an attempt to bring her back to earth. His attempt failed.

After Orpheus had lost Eurydice, the Maenads (according to Aristophanes and Ovid, says Robert Graves), at the instigation of the jealous god Dionysus, tore him limb from limb and threw his head into the river Hebrus. It floated, still singing, down to the sea and fetched up on the island of Lesbos, where it continued to sing for a while longer. Orpheus' lyre also drifted to Lesbos and eventually, at the behest of the Muses (Orpheus was the son of one of them, Calliope), was hung in the heavens as a constellation.

The librettist of Gluck's opera provided it with a happy ending: The god Amor, seeing Orpheus about to kill himself with his sword and touched by his love and constancy, revived Eurydice. But then Eurydice was young when she died of a snakebite.

The three principal roles of Gluck's opera—Orpheus, Eurydice and Amor—are sung by women.

A few of the publications of
THE NAIAD PRESS, INC.
P.O. Box 10543 ● Tallahassee, Florida 32302
Phone (904) 539-9322
Mail orders welcome. Please include 15% postage.

THE PEARLS by Shelley Smith. 176 pp. Passion and fun in the Caribbean sun. ISBN 0-930044-93-2 $7.95

MAGDALENA by Sarah Aldridge. 352 pp. Epic Lesbian novel set on three continents. ISBN 0-930044-99-1 $8.95

THE BLACK AND WHITE OF IT by Ann Allen Shockley. 144 pp. Short stories. ISBN 0-930044-96-7 $7.95

SAY JESUS AND COME TO ME by Ann Allen Shockley. 288 pp. Contemporary romance. ISBN 0-930044-98-3   8.95

LOVING HER by Ann Allen Shockley. 192 pp. Romantic love story. ISBN 0-930044-97-5   7.95

MURDER AT THE NIGHTWOOD BAR by Katherine V. Forrest. 240 pp. A Kate Delafield mystery. Second in a series. ISBN 0-930044-92-4   8.95

ZOE'S BOOK by Gail Pass. 224 pp. Passionate, obsessive love story. ISBN 0-930044-95-9   7.95

WINGED DANCER by Camarin Grae. 228 pp. Erotic Lesbian adventure story. ISBN 0-930044-88-6   8.95

PAZ by Camarin Grae. 336 pp. Romantic Lesbian adventurer with the power to change the world. ISBN 0-930044-89-4   8.95

SOUL SNATCHER by Camarin Grae. 224 pp. A puzzle, an adventure, a mystery—Lesbian romance. ISBN 0-930044-90-8   8.95

THE LOVE OF GOOD WOMEN by Isabel Miller. 224 pp. Long-awaited new novel by the author of the beloved *Patience and Sarah*. ISBN 0-930044-81-9   8.95

THE HOUSE AT PELHAM FALLS by Brenda Weathers. 240 pp. Suspenseful Lesbian ghost story. ISBN 0-930044-79-7   7.95

HOME IN YOUR HANDS by Lee Lynch. 240 pp. More stories from the author of *Old Dyke Tales*. ISBN 0-930044-80-0   7.95

EACH HAND A MAP by Anita Skeen. 112 pp. Real-life poems that touch us all. ISBN 0-930044-82-7   6.95

SURPLUS by Sylvia Stevenson. 342 pp. A classic early Lesbian novel. ISBN 0-930044-78-9   7.95

PEMBROKE PARK by Michelle Martin. 256 pp. Derring-do and daring romance in Regency England. ISBN 0-930044-77-0   7.95

THE LONG TRAIL by Penny Hayes. 248 pp. Vivid adventures of two women in love in the old west. ISBN 0-930044-76-2   8.95

HORIZON OF THE HEART by Shelley Smith. 192 pp. Hot romance in summertime New England. ISBN 0-930044-75-4   7.95

LOVERS IN THE PRESENT AFTERNOON by Kathleen
Fleming. 288 pp. A novel about recovery and growth.
ISBN 0-930044-46-0   8.50

TOOTHPICK HOUSE by Lee Lynch. 264 pp. Love between
two Lesbians of different classes.   ISBN 0-930044-45-2   7.95

MADAME AURORA by Sarah Aldridge. 256 pp. Historical
novel featuring a charismatic "seer."   ISBN 0-930044-44-4   7.95

CURIOUS WINE by Katherine V. Forrest. 176 pp. Passionate
Lesbian love story, a best-seller.   ISBN 0-930044-43-6   7.95

BLACK LESBIAN IN WHITE AMERICA by Anita Cornwell.
141 pp. Stories, essays, autobiography.   ISBN 0-930044-41-X   7.50

CONTRACT WITH THE WORLD by Jane Rule. 340 pp.
Powerful, panoramic novel of gay life.   ISBN 0-930044-28-2   7.95

YANTRAS OF WOMANLOVE by Tee A. Corinne. 64 pp.
Photos by noted Lesbian photographer.   ISBN 0-930044-30-4   6.95

MRS. PORTER'S LETTER by Vicki P. McConnell. 224 pp.
The first Nyla Wade mystery.   ISBN 0-930044-29-0   7.95

TO THE CLEVELAND STATION by Carol Anne Douglas.
192 pp. Interracial Lesbian love story.   ISBN 0-930044-27-4   6.95

THE NESTING PLACE by Sarah Aldridge. 224 pp. Historical
novel, a three-woman triangle.   ISBN 0-930044-26-6   7.95

THIS IS NOT FOR YOU by Jane Rule. 284 pp. A letter to a
beloved is also an intricate novel.   ISBN 0-930044-25-8   7.95

FAULTLINE by Sheila Ortiz Taylor. 140 pp. Warm, funny,
literate story of a startling family.   ISBN 0-930044-24-X   6.95

THE LESBIAN IN LITERATURE by Barbara Grier. 3d ed.
Foreword by Maida Tilchen. 240 pp. Comprehensive bibliography. Literary ratings; rare photos.   ISBN 0-930044-23-1   7.95

ANNA'S COUNTRY by Elizabeth Lang. 208 pp. A woman
finds her Lesbian identity.   ISBN 0-930044-19-3   6.95

PRISM by Valerie Taylor. 158 pp. A love affair between two
women in their sixties.   ISBN 0-930044-18-5   6.95

BLACK LESBIANS: AN ANNOTATED BIBLIOGRAPHY
compiled by J.R. Roberts. Foreword by Barbara Smith. 112
pp. Award winning bibliography.   ISBN 0-930044-21-5   5.95

THE MARQUISE AND THE NOVICE by Victoria Ramstetter.
108 pp. A Lesbian Gothic novel.   ISBN 0-930044-16-9   4.95

OUTLANDER by Jane Rule. 207 pp. Short stories and essays
by one of our finest writers.   ISBN 0-930044-17-7   6.95

SAPPHISTRY: THE BOOK OF LESBIAN SEXUALITY by
Pat Califia. 2d edition, revised. 195 pp.   ISBN 0-930044-47-9   7.95

ALL TRUE LOVERS by Sarah Aldridge. 292 pp. Romantic
novel set in the 1930s and 1940s.   ISBN 0-930044-10-X   7.95

A WOMAN APPEARED TO ME by Renee Vivien. 65 pp. A
classic; translated by Jeannette H. Foster. ISBN 0-930044-06-1   5.00

CYTHEREA'S BREATH by Sarah Aldridge. 240 pp. Women
first enter medicine and the law: a novel. ISBN 0-930044-02-9   6.95

TOTTIE by Sarah Aldridge. 181 pp. Lesbian romance in the
turmoil of the sixties.   ISBN 0-930044-01-0   6.95

THE LATECOMER by Sarah Aldridge. 107 pp. A delicate love
story set in days gone by.   ISBN 0-930044-00-2   5.00

ODD GIRL OUT by Ann Bannon   ISBN 0-930044-83-5   5.95
I AM A WOMAN by Ann Bannon.   ISBN 0-930044-84-3   5.95
WOMEN IN THE SHADOWS by Ann Bannon.
                                  ISBN 0-930044-85-1   5.95
JOURNEY TO A WOMAN by Ann Bannon.
                                  ISBN 0-930044-86-X   5.95
BEEBO BRINKER by Ann Bannon   ISBN 0-930044-87-8   5.95
          Legendary novels written in the fifties and sixties,
               set in the gay mecca of Greenwich Village.

VOLUTE BOOKS

JOURNEY TO FULFILLMENT   Early classics by Valerie   3.95
A WORLD WITHOUT MEN   Taylor: The Erika Frohmann   3.95
RETURN TO LESBOS   series.   3.95

These are just a few of the many Naiad Press titles—we are the oldest
and largest lesbian/feminist publishing company in the world. Please
request a complete catalog. We offer personal service; we encourage and
welcome direct mail orders from individuals who have limited access to
bookstores carrying our publications.